Totally Bound Publishing books by C.J. Burright

Music, Love and Other Miseries
Every Kiss
Every Minute

I0646175

Music, Love and Other Miseries

EVERY MINUTE

C.J. BURRIGHT

Every Minute
ISBN # 978-1-83943-829-5
©Copyright C.J. Burright 2019
Cover Art by Erin Dameron-Hill ©Copyright December 2019
Interior text design by Claire Siemaszkiewicz
Totally Bound Publishing

This is a work of fiction. All characters, places and events are from the author's imagination and should not be confused with fact. Any resemblance to persons, living or dead, events or places is purely coincidental.

All rights reserved. No part of this publication may be reproduced in any material form, whether by printing, photocopying, scanning or otherwise without the written permission of the publisher, Totally Bound Publishing.

Applications should be addressed in the first instance, in writing, to Totally Bound Publishing. Unauthorised or restricted acts in relation to this publication may result in civil proceedings and/or criminal prosecution.

The author and illustrator have asserted their respective rights under the Copyright Designs and Patents Acts 1988 (as amended) to be identified as the author of this book and illustrator of the artwork.

Published in 2019 by Totally Bound Publishing, United Kingdom.

No part of this book may be reproduced, scanned, or distributed in any printed or electronic form without permission. Please do not participate in or encourage piracy of copyrighted materials in violation of the authors' rights. Purchase only authorised copies.

Totally Bound Publishing is an imprint of Totally Entwined Group Limited.

If you purchased this book without a cover you should be aware that this book is stolen property. It was reported as "unsold and destroyed" to the publisher and neither the author nor the publisher has received any payment for this "stripped book".

EVERY MINUTE

Dedication

To Tatum, for irrevocably stealing a piece of my heart when, at the tender age of six, you stomped in and screeched, "Get the hell out of my kitchen."

Chapter One

Adara never should've made any deathbed promises to her brother. Pebbles cracked like bones beneath her heels as she trudged between the boxwood hedging the country club's parking lot. If she hadn't made a sacred vow to accept all social invites from Gia, her brother's wildly still-alive girlfriend, she wouldn't be facing the torture of another Hamilton & Associates Belated Yule Celebration...in February. Apparently with prestige and power came the ability to reschedule Christmas.

She slipped between two cars too expensive to breathe on, the glowing mansion lights guiding her. While only a few miles out of town, the country club felt another universe away, especially tonight. Over a year had screamed by in a blur, and it felt like no time had passed since she'd walked this same path—same shoes, same black dress.

Different Adara.

She bit her lip. *Nope, not going there.* Especially not tonight when she had to cope in public.

The rolling pebbles gave way to smooth courtyard pavestones. Gia waited beside the gurgling center fountain with one hip cocked, cute as always in an eye-burning red sequin-and-chiffon number.

"Halloween was two months ago." Gia arched one perfectly shaped blonde eyebrow. "What happened to classic winter white?"

Adara slogged the last few steps between them. *No slinking away now.* Gia would send out the SWAT team to track her and was more than willing to take her down at gunpoint. "Black is appropriate for every occasion. Besides, it encompasses all colors."

"So does a black hole." Gia batted her spiked lashes, not at all innocent.

"You're right." Adara spun back toward her car. "I'll go home and change."

"Not even." Gia lunged and latched onto her arm, bringing a breeze of spicy perfume. "I anticipated your usual wardrobe tragedy and came prepared." With her free hand, she dug in her clutch and whipped out a strip of shiny material. "Hold still or I'll smack you."

Adara reluctantly obeyed while Gia wrapped a festive green and red plaid sash around her waist and cinched it tight, Christmas resurrected two months too late. She resisted cringing when Gia's scrutiny lifted from the ribbon to her zero-makeup face.

That blonde eyebrow went up again. Faster than any sharp-shooter, Gia popped open a tube of scarlet lipstick and held it to Adara's mouth like a weapon. "Resistance is futile. Clown or glam, Dar. Your choice."

Resistance was tempting. A circus look might keep people back. Then again, looking deranged would give people even more reason to talk. Some secrets didn't need to be shared. She glared as a matter of principle.

"I knew you could be rational." The makeup session was over in three seconds. Gia smiled, triumphant. "There. You're perfect."

"Perfect for what?" Adara didn't bother hiding the snarl in her voice.

"To be out in the world of the living." The words were teasing but Gia's tone was gentle, understanding.

A single pang pierced her heart, sharp as any arrow, so fierce it threatened to steal her breath. It was an improvement, though. A year ago, the pain had been nonstop, debilitating. She managed a hoarse whisper. "I never should've made that promise to him."

"As if you had a choice." Gia snorted, thankfully ignoring her emotional slip. "Joey could've persuaded a nun to strip—and she'd be the one paying him. He knew you'd stay in your one-person bubble forever unless he coerced your immortal oath to truly live after he"—her throat worked and her smile wobbled for a second—"after he left."

Adara focused on the mansion's pillared entrance. She wanted to think about her brother's death almost as much as she wanted to be at this party. She cleared her throat and the shadow of sorrow with it. "Truly living equals soirées with stuffed suits using liquid cheer as an excuse for lewd behavior? Dance moves my mind can't possibly unsee? Dodging covertly placed mistletoe and any awaiting tongues?"

"Tonight it does." Gia looped her arm through Adara's and tugged her up the brick stairs. "Show me you still know how to smile."

She bared her teeth.

Gia shuddered. "Forget it. Just look pretty and focus on your goal."

"I have a goal?" She thought merely showing up was a victory.

"Yep. Be nice."

"I'm nice."

"To plants and children, not so much to adult humans."

Plants and children were easy. They didn't expect deep conversation or emotional displays. Adara dragged her feet, the mansion close enough to spill hints of the party happening inside. Red and green lights blinked through the windows onto the stone sidewalk, and buzzing chatter filtered free with the occasional laugh. No music yet. Once the band started, she might fake an excuse to leave. Not even General Gia was heartless enough to make her stay and suffer if particular music started playing.

"Cheer up, Dar." Gia squeezed her arm as she opened the great iron door, freeing a wave of warm air. "Ian will be here."

Adara almost growled. Ian, the lawyer with the supersonic smile who'd taken advantage of Gia's grief at last year's party... *Scum-sucking dirtbag shark.* "Perfect. I can castrate him for Christmas. It's never too late for gifts."

Gia paused in the foyer and stared at her. "Honestly, don't smile. I like my job. If you give Mr. Hamilton a heart attack, I'll have to be your teacher's aide, and you know I'm allergic to chalk and children."

Closing the door behind them, Adara drew a long breath laced with pine and cinnamon. "Let the fun begin."

* * * *

Garret dumped his leather jacket over his violin case and straightened his white button-down shirt. He hadn't even changed after the plane had landed, instead loading his luggage and instruments into a rental, confirming Ian's obnoxious email invite a second time and heading here, Millionaire Estates. Ian probably thought he'd flake — and maybe he should — but it had been years since they'd met up, years since he'd been home, and performing a few numbers at a postponed holiday work party was the recharge kickoff he needed.

Hushed laughter drifted into the coat room, the intimate sound easing the last travel tension from his shoulders, whispering he'd made the right choice in returning. Not that he doubted his decision... The second he'd stepped onto pavement, energy had buzzed through his boots like lightning. Three years on the overseas concert circuit and its large audience disconnect had stolen a piece of him.

He was home to take it back — with interest.

Tucking his violin and bow beneath one arm, Garret entered the candlelit hallway draped in clove-laced garlands and followed the soft pulse of '60s music. It had been too long since he'd celebrated Christmas with family or friends, and he didn't mind rewinding a couple of months, another catch-up on things he'd missed while on tour. This particular bash had been going on for at least an hour, long enough for pleasantly toasted guests to miss any latecomers sliding in for the festivities but not so much that the old-timers had taken off.

He wandered through the double-door entrance and the holiday aura washed through him. People were gathered in talking packs, either standing or sitting, most with a bottle or glass in hand. More danced to the Beach Boys song blasting from unseen speakers. Even with Garret's height advantage, Ian would be hard to spot. A medley of glitter and glass dazzled from every direction, dominated by a giant tree with twinkling tinsel and obnoxious ornaments, its pine scent a reminder of Christmases past.

Attention on the crowd, searching for a hint of Ian, Garret eased past chatting people and around tables decorated with cinnamon-scented pinecones. He bumped into something and caught his balance just as a giant plastic reindeer nosedived. Tail in the air, it fell at the feet of a woman leaning against the wall, paying homage from the tip of its blinking red nose. For a brief, searing moment, her gaze met his.

The festival of chaos and colors faded into the background, leaving room for only her. She blended with the shadows, as if hoping to vanish with the night. Sorrow haunted her eyes, a thousand notes trapped.

Garret blinked and the moment passed. *Ben-zonna.* His favorite foreign curse fit the occasion. *A thousand notes trapped?* That was remarkably sappy, even for him.

No smile, no words, she picked up the glittering Rudolph monstrosity and settled all four twinkling hooves solidly on the floor. Without looking at him again, she resumed watching the other people like they were on a carousel revolving around her, moving too fast to touch.

Anyone who could make his world stand still for even a heartbeat demanded at least an introduction. Keeping his violin protectively close, he eased past the reindeer decoration and mimicked her wallflower pose, barely a foot separating them.

She didn't acknowledge him, her laser-point focus set on something or someone in the crowd.

Garret followed her gaze and hid a groan. Of course it had to be Ian. His childhood friend mingled with a cluster of women wearing Santa hats and short skirts.

All smiles and hands, Ian played his part. Interestingly enough, his glances kept straying to the petite blonde in the red dress another conversation group away.

He leaned slightly in the woman's direction. "So is it Ian or the blonde in red?"

The barely-there pursing of her generous crimson lips promised she'd heard, and the following silence went on long enough to mark a protest. She sighed softly, not sparing him a glance. "What?"

No matter the impatience threading her tone, her husky voice held a song all its own, low and heady, hitting him straight in the gut. "I was wondering whether you're plotting to murder Ian or the blonde." He shrugged. "From the fire and brimstone look you're sending that way, one of them is going down."

"Ian's the only one deserving of a pitchfork stab in sensitive places." She uncrossed her arms and dropped them to her sides, still not making eye contact. "I'm just watching Gia's back. And in case you were also wondering, I don't need a drink, I'm not lonely and I loathe dancing. Any mistletoe I find on your person will be promptly stuffed up your nose."

He gave a startled laugh. "Duly noted. For the record, I rarely drink, I don't mind solitude and I keep my dance moves private to prevent public panic. Mistletoe gives me hives, so I'm relatively safe from your anti-vegetation assault."

Her mouth twitched, a mere tremble and nothing close to a smile, but it was a start.

Before he could turn that tic into a true smile or ask her name, the beach music choked and a snow-haired man in a designer suit climbed the stairs to a stage across the room, presumably the esteemed Mr. Hamilton.

The mystery woman beside him straightened and shifted toward the stage. Apparently, the only way to get her to look at him would be if he was there, on display. He tightened his grip on the violin. Becoming the center of attention was one of his super skills.

Mr. Hamilton launched into a speech about success and the justice system, and Garret tuned him out, riveted on the woman so close. Her hair gleamed like obsidian in the twinkling lights, stopping bluntly at the slender line of her neck. She wasn't wearing glitter, eyeliner or powder like the other women, which made her crimson lips all the more sinful.

Polite clapping erupted, the only reason he knew the speech had ended. Old man Hamilton departed the stage and Ian stepped aside, the prince waiting to ascend once his king cleared the way.

Some opportunities couldn't be resisted. Garret tucked his violin beneath his chin and readied the bow. As Ian's polished shoe hit the first step, Darth Vader's theme song marched up from his instrument and into the vaulted ceiling, shaking the crowd into a momentary silence. A few brave souls snickered, and he didn't miss how the woman beside him stiffened. Faces turned his way, but Ian's response was the one he watched for.

The flip of emotions on his friend's face was everything he'd hoped for, annoyance to realization to amusement. It took Ian less than a millisecond to target Garret in the shadows. He grabbed the microphone and said in a heavy-breather voice, "If only you knew the power of the dark side."

Laughter rippled over the crowd, and Garret grinned. Ian hadn't lost his sense of humor over the last three years, a good sign. Lawyering could strangle happiness until only bitterness and jaded opinions remained.

"I came up here to spread cheer through overpriced and frivolous gifts, but that will have to wait a little while longer." Ignoring the good-hearted groans, Ian straightened his slouchy elf hat. "Patience, people."

Garret sawed out a measure of the *Jeopardy* game show theme. He'd perfected musical harassment decades ago, as his older sister London could attest. It was his best self-defense tactic besides quick reflexes.

Ian pointed threateningly at Garret and flashed one of his trademark smiles, white and brilliant with a bite. "If you're going to play, get on stage and do it right."

When he'd accepted Ian's invitation to the party, he knew companionship and conversation weren't all that Ian would expect. Ian liked to impress, and with stodgy lawyers who appreciated fine music in their midst, he probably hoped for an edge when it came to earning the coveted partner title. Being friends with an accomplished musician might be the one—Garret drummed his fingers once on his jeans, right at the frayed hole near his pocket—or not. Not everyone at this particular party would appreciate his rendition of *Thunderstruck*. He didn't possess the concert musician vibe and his tastes weren't always geared to Bach and Mozart, as Ian well knew. He'd never quite fit into the classical musician stereotype, not even in the long years he'd focused on the classics. He straightened from the wall. Classical preferences or not, he could make everyone happy.

His intriguing companion folded her arms and shifted at an even sharper angle toward the stage. She still hadn't looked at him again, as if determined to burn Ian alive with her stare while keeping all intruders—including him, insultingly—outside her personal bubble.

Hooking his thumb in his pocket, Garret strolled into her direct line of vision, resisting the urge to look over his shoulder and capture her gaze. Breaking bubbles was another one of his super skills.

Chapter Two

Her heart beating fast, Adara focused on the stage as her chatty interloper found a more suitable victim in Ian. He stepped right in front of her, his broad back filling her sight. The consequences of ignoring people were the little details she missed, such as the random violins they might hold.

A violin. An icy shudder tripped through her. It *had* to be a violin, didn't it?

She planted her clammy hands on the wall. When the strings had erupted right beside her ear, time had stopped and splintered into a thousand shrieking seconds. She'd flashbacked to when Joey still lived, when his music had floated through their house—a reminder that no matter the space separating them, she had never been alone. Just as fast, reality crashed back into her, demolishing the memory and whispering the truth.

Joey was gone.

She was alone.

"Having fun yet?" Gia slipped beside her, knowing enough not to ask if she was okay. She jerked her chin at the man heading toward the stage. "Making new friends?"

Adara sucked in a quick breath and followed Gia's gaze. Longish blond hair pulled back in Thor-style, jeans and untucked shirt, combat boots, shiny black violin. Joey would've approved.

"Typical grownup band geek." Gia leaned near, her breath tinged with citrus and tequila. "Still trying to claw out of the box to coolness."

Grateful for the distraction, she snorted softly in agreement.

"He'd probably rather gouge out an eye than play Beethoven." Gia twirled her margarita glass, her blue eyes sparkling. "Bet you lunch tomorrow at Antoine's he goes with *Kashmir* or *Wherever I May Roam*—you know, some real man tune."

"Not taking that bet, because you're probably right." The fist around her heart eased. Gia had nailed it. No way would someone who looked like a part-time pirate play anything that could penetrate her shields.

"Karen from accounting gave me the scoop on him," Gia continued, her focus on the stage, where the violinist joined Ian in the spotlight. "Guess he's well-known overseas. Grew up with Ian, and he's taking a break to mentor grade-school kids." She elbowed her in the ribs. "At Graywood."

Mentor. Grade school. Crap. Adara briefly closed her eyes. Weeks ago, Principal Austin had warned staff about the possibility of a part-time music mentor, but he'd been sparse on the details. She'd thought the idea had fallen through the cracks since that was the last she'd heard about it. And since dinky Graywood—population everyone-knew-practically-everyone—had only one grade school, the odds of seeing him around rocketed up. *To infinity and beyond.*

"Perfect. William Kidd reincarnated as a musician." She settled back into her leave-me-alone position. "The world is now complete."

Gia flashed a wicked grin and returned her attention to the stage.

Gazing upon Mr. Gabby from afar wasn't a punishment. He had a ready smile, a five o'clock shadow-beard going on — presumably to go with the pirate vibe — and carried himself with the confidence of a man who didn't question his identity. He wouldn't have any trouble finding one of Santa's helpers to keep him company.

Silver rings glinted on his fingers as he settled the violin against his shoulder. Adara rolled her eyes and resisted humming *He's a Pirate*. He must have forgotten his bandana. For a moment, he looked in her direction, as if singling her out in the shadows and crowd. Then, he closed his eyes and set the bow to strings.

Slow, plaintive notes flowed from the violin, and Adara instantly relaxed at the familiar melody. Queen's *Somebody to Love* — nothing classical, nothing that could reach into her soul. She was safe for the next few minutes.

After the short, slow introduction, the violinist stomped his foot for a stand-in drum rhythm, and it took the crowd less than two seconds to clap along, taking up the beat themselves. By the chorus, people were singing along — a happy, bouncing holiday mob.

Adara kept her arms crossed and let Gia clap loud enough for the both of them. She'd tolerated the party for nearly two hours, longer than she'd planned, but it had been forever since she'd seen Gia having fun without wearing the smiling mask to hide her loss.

She knew all about the necessity of masks.

Seamlessly, the musician blended notes into another song, and while the clapping and swaying continued, the singing died out.

She bit her lip, almost tempted to smile for the second time that night. *Teddy Bear*, a decent Elvis Presley choice. Near the stage, Mr. Hamilton bobbed his head, clearly a fan of the King. Everyone else, not so much. The remaining tension in her shoulders drained away. She wouldn't have to reinforce her shields, not for this guy's melodic selection, but she had to admit he was good. Really good. He involved the crowd, clearly comfortable with attention. He hit every note with smooth, expert precision, the love affair with his instrument apparent in every plucked string and pull of the bow. The dreamy smile he wore spoke of secrets shared only between a master musician and the melody he spun. She'd seen the same expression on Joey's face.

The void in her soul echoed with the memory. He was everything Joey could have been. Should have been.

Without a miss in beat, the violinist again blended one song into another, switching genres, subtle and unexpected. Sweet notes wrapped around her and slid a slow, sharp needle into her heart. The clapping died into an awed hush, and the violin moaned, filling all the hollow spaces, alone again, more alive and terrifying in its seclusion.

She choked on the giant sob building up from deep within. *Think of Me.* Instead of the thousand other songs that couldn't touch her, he'd unsuspectingly chosen one that demolished her defenses. *The Phantom of the Opera* was the first musical Joey had dragged her to, the first time she'd cried in public, the first step in convincing her to join him in his love for music.

Stitch by stitch, the music ripped her open. Emptiness clawed up her throat like a demon toward the surface, an emptiness she couldn't face — not here, not now. No matter how she pretended, how she tried to deal, she wasn't fine.

Before she fell apart completely for everyone to see, Adara brushed past Gia and hurried from the banquet room, out of the mansion into the cool night. She didn't slow until the pavestones beneath her heels changed to the clink of gravel and stopped only when the mansion lights made a dull reflection on the parked cars.

Tears scalded her eyes and her heart stabbed her chest with each beat, a relentless knife digging for the ashes of her soul. She'd abandoned Gia and broken her promise to Joey.

The night and silence surrounded her, a familiar crutch slowly soothing, calling her back to its embrace. She sucked in a shaky breath of crisp air and lifted her face to the dark, endless sky. She'd stuff everything back into place and patch herself up, lock tonight away with all the other memories. Tomorrow, she'd return to her version of normal.

* * * *

The morning after his hometown debut, Garret plopped his boots on Ian's gleaming cherrywood desk and inhaled the scent of leather, paperwork and wealth stained by conflict. "I met someone at the party last night, but I didn't get her name." He hid a grin at the annoyed twitch of Ian's manscaped eyebrow. "You know everyone who wears a skirt, so I figured you could help."

"True." Ian leaned across his desk and shoved Garret's boots off. He straightened his blood-red tie.

"My skills are up to the task, despite the countless groupies who succumbed to your musical seduction last night. Was it the leggy legal assistant with the red hair that makes you wonder if — ?"

"No."

Garret sat back into the pompous leather chair and sipped his peppermint mocha.

"The little blonde in the black mini with those curves to — ?"

"Nope."

Ian narrowed his eyes, the blue sparkling with what had to be his typical lewd and lascivious thoughts. Some people never emerged from high-school sexual mentality. When it came to relationships with women, his oldest friend happily hovered in that emotionally safe chasm. He snapped his fingers. "That mocha-skinned intern who kept bringing you chocolate-covered cherries. Don't tell me you didn't hit that."

Garret pinched his nose and exhaled loudly. "The girl I'm looking for is the reason I jumped off the stage mid-song. She ditched while I was still playing. I tried to catch up with her, but she was already gone."

Ian folded his arms over his buttoned-up blazer and cocked his head, his chair creaking. "I need details. What did she look like?"

"A bit taller than average." He lifted a hand to his collarbone. "Her head came about here. Brunette. Hard to tell how dark with the lighting, but sleek, not curly — one of those chin-length cuts. And her mouth, *chara*." His pulse kicked in memory. "It was made to be kissed."

"Speak English." Ian scratched his clean-shaven jaw, apparently going for the boy-next-door impression today. Anyone who knew him at all wouldn't be fooled. "You've been hanging around your Israeli guitarist too long, and I'm a few espresso shots short this morning to endure you waxing poetic over a random woman whose name you forgot to ask for."

"Not random. Magnetic, and I didn't forget. My music doesn't usually drive women away. It threw me off. The only makeup she wore was red lipstick on that delectable mouth, so forgive me for being captivated. I don't think she wanted to be there, and she passionately didn't like you anywhere near her friend."

"Women are always jealous of each other." Ian tapped his chin with a pen. "Which friend?"

"The cute blonde in a red dress that you watched all night but didn't touch or even talk to." Garret didn't miss Ian's flashfire grimace, out of place considering the topic involved — women, his favorite subject. "Which I find interesting, considering you're you."

Ian's eyes widened and he jumped to his feet so fast his chair spun behind him in a crazy, squeaky circle. "Not the Stark princess."

"Stark princess?"

"Appropriate title, trust me on this one. She's cold as winter." He swiped his fingers through his short, dark hair. "Listen to me, my friend. Forget her. She's so far out of anyone's reach that you couldn't get through her armor with the Death Star on steroids. Let me set you up with Karen from accounting instead. She's accessible, easy in the hands and totally pliable after two beers and a pizza."

Every nerve caught on challenging fire at the picture Ian painted, and it had nothing to do with pizza and beer. *Cold, inaccessible, in need of inspiration.* He could work with that.

Ian stared at him in silence, some learned lawyer tactic that had no effect on him. Finally, he slouched and set his jaw. "You aren't going to follow my sage advice, are you? You're going for what you can't have. Again."

"I'm not fourteen anymore." Garret grinned. "And I'm not into pliable. You know that. Inspiration is everything."

"You're an idjit. That's an irrefutable fact."

"Objection. That's a cynical lawyer's opinion with no bearing on the truth. Are you going to help me or not?" He already knew the answer. Ian may not approve of his choice, but he'd never pass a quest to win a woman. The main difference between them was that Ian was more of a one-night conqueror—a weekend at most. Garret shot for longer, and once he found the right girl, he'd hold on for life.

Ian sank into the empty leather chair beside him, offering a whiff of his cologne, sharp and rich. He propped an ankle on his knee and looked Garret straight in the eye. "You sure about this? Idjitdom aside, you're still my friend—far too optimistic and your romantic ideologies are outdated, not to mention impractical. You search for the best in people, and I can tell you right now, dude, that people suck. They'll pretend to care while carving away everything you are and leave you bleeding in the ditch without once dropping their sweet and innocent smile."

"Says the lawyer." He cocked an eyebrow.

"The thing about the justice system is you see the worst, the reality, the true darkness inside—the stuff that's only in the spotlight because they got caught or can't manipulate, coerce or buy their way into whatever they're trying to get. That's who most people really are behind their disguises." He fidgeted with his shoelace, keeping his focus there. "You're not like everybody else, Garret." He sharpened his voice to a knife's edge. "You've somehow held on to your ideals without letting the world stain you, and I don't want to play any part in changing that."

"Aww, he cares." Garret clutched his heart and leered to lessen the sting of the surprising confession. "I love you too. Want a hug?"

"Shut up." Ian curled his lip into a snarl. "Keep your pansy musician paws off my bod. Ladies only."

"Now that our mutual affection is settled" — he plowed through Ian's curse — "let's focus on my dilemma. What's her name?"

Ian laid his head back on the chair and closed his eyes, as if revealing any detail pained him. "Adara Dumont. Rabid introvert. Resistant to all charm. A teacher, I think. That's all I know."

Adara. "Hang on… Did you say *teacher*? Any chance a teacher at the grade school?"

A groan rose from Ian and lines furrowed his brow, but he kept his eyes squeezed shut. "It's not too late to cancel your latest whim. Forget mentoring kids. Hot, lonely women in pubs and pool halls need mentoring too."

An attempt at distraction was the same as a confirmation when it came from Ian. So, he'd be working with her. *Adara.* He couldn't contain his smile. "Serendipitous."

"No…unfortunate."

"What else do you know about her?" Garret pressed, bracing his forearms on his thighs.

"Isn't that enough?" Ian's voice verged on a whip-snap, a last stand.

"What about her friend, the cute blonde with the Ian-force-field up last night?"

Ian cracked an eye. "What about her?"

"She'd know more, something useful to my cause. Is she a lawyer too?"

25

"No."

The cutthroat reply prodded awake Garret's curiosity. There was a mystery surrounding his friend and this woman, and he wanted to know what it was. Clearly, Ian wouldn't surrender any details voluntarily. He'd have to be subtle, discover the answer piece by piece without alerting Ian.

"But she does work here, doesn't she?" He set his coffee cup on the desk and strolled to the wall of windows overlooking a city park. A few bundled-up kids ran and played, their laughter silenced by glass. A shame. The music in laughter could infect the coldest space.

A pause, followed by an exhale. "Yes."

"Can you use your prestigious law school powers of persuasion to subtly glean some details or not?"

Another pause, longer this time. Leather squeaked, and clothes rustled as Ian stood. "I'll be back."

The door clicked shut and Garret remained at his post by the window. In the grass below, a man threw a tennis ball for his yellow Lab, his breath making temporal white clouds in the air. The slate-gray sky promised snow soon, an empty canvas for sled tracks, snow angels and footprint trails. The last time he'd paused in performing to enjoy the pleasure of a snowball fight had been winter vacation three years ago with Tatum and Bryan, his niece and nephew. *They're what now? Eight and ten?* He'd been away too long. Emails and the occasional Skype session didn't cut it.

The door opened again and Garret pivoted.

The blonde from last night entered, without Ian, a file in her grip. Her gaze landed on him, and her eyebrows shot up. "You're the musician from last night."

He performed a mini bow. "Garret Ambrose. And you are?"

"Gia Hellman." She glanced at the door and back at him, gnawing on her bottom lip. "Sorry to interrupt. I was supposed to deliver this file to Ian." A faint flush crept into her cheeks and she straightened her skirt. "Mr. O'Connor, I mean."

Garret kept his expression bland, filing away every detail. *First name basis. A blush. Interesting.* "No need to apologize. I was simply waiting for Ian."

She stepped forward and laid the file on Ian's glossy desk, her stilettos silent on the Persian rug. "Everyone is still talking about your performance last night. Your rendition of *Think of Me* was brilliant, by the way. How long have you played?"

"Since I could hold a bow in my chubby fingers — and thank you." He leaned against the windowsill. "You're a *Phantom* fan?"

She laughed a little and shook her head, one blonde curl slipping free of her loose bun. "Crap, no. I'm a rocker all the way, despite many fruitless attempts to broaden my horizons."

A spark of hope flared. Did that mean Adara was more of a music connoisseur than her friend and might appreciate his dedication? Not that there was anything wrong with rock music in all its forms, but if he had an angle to work with, he'd grab it. "And your friend who left the party last night without saying goodbye? She's into rock too?"

Gia's smile faltered for an instant before firming back in place, no longer real. "Don't take it personally. She's not much of a party animal." She turned for the door. "Nice meeting you, Mr. Ambrose."

"Call me Garret. And before you go, I have one question."

She paused, her eyes bright.

"What are the odds that she'd have coffee with me?"

Facing him fully, she folded her arms over her pink sweater, the kind that invited touch. She swept him with a long, assessing look, from the tips of his combat boots to his faded jeans, his over-loved Sean's Pub T-shirt to the platinum cross necklace. She spent twice as long on his face, enough to make him squirm. He hadn't been self-conscious for years, but ten seconds under Gia's scrutiny and he time-warped back into middle school, when he had zero confidence, extra padding in all the wrong places and being a band geek was not fashionable in any social circles beyond other band geeks.

"First, tell Ian I don't appreciate being manipulated."

He winced at the ice in her tone. "He didn't —"

"Save it." She held up a palm, the universal female sign for silence. "Second, the mere fact that you're a musician puts you in the no-date zone for Adara — not that she dates anyone, but still."

"Care to explain?" Despite a potential aversion to musicians, he couldn't deny a slow warmth. If she didn't date, he'd have her full attention — all the better to unlock her secrets.

"Not particularly." Her expression softened a smidge as she grabbed the doorknob. "You have your pick of women. That much was obvious last night. Adara doesn't play hard-to-get and she doesn't need to be chased." She pulled the door open, still looking over her shoulder at Garret and thereby having no clue Ian stood at the doorway. "Especially by a friend of Ian's."

Ian made a most unprofessional and unlawyerlike growl.

She gasped and faced him.

He anchored the doorframe with his hands, blocking her way, his expression thunderous. "First, Ms. Hellman, I did *not* manipulate you. I needed the Jackson file." He advanced on her and she backed up, keeping perfect time with his slow steps. "Second, Garret is the finest man I know, dimensions above the ilk of me, and if he feels some insane notion that Adara is a princess in need of being broken out of her northern castle, then I will do everything in my power to assist him. If Adara deems him unworthy of sharing coffee, that will be her choice and, quite frankly, I hope she rejects him so he won't waste his time or get his heart bruised. But again, that is *his* choice—not mine, not yours. Understood?"

Gia's butt hit the desk, and she gripped the edge with both hands, as if she might topple otherwise. "Yes, sir."

Ian smiled, and it was the wolfish grin of a lawyer who knew he'd won the case.

The two-step dance between the couple was strangely fascinating. Gia was breathless, her face flushed, as if she'd just aced a difficult performance. Ian loomed over her, his nose inches from hers, but what should have been a threatening pose radiated something else—something caged, hungry and craving release. Suddenly, Garret itched to be someplace—anyplace—else, and since he couldn't simply stroll past them without adding to the awkwardness, he cleared his throat.

Ian immediately straightened and tugged his jacket smooth, giving Gia space to breathe. "Very well." All business now, his friend circled the desk. "Take a seat, Ms. Hellman. Your deposition is about to begin."

Chapter Three

Thursday afternoon, Adara blinked at Principal Austin and strained not to leap up and release her inner lunatic. "What do you mean my job will probably be cut in June? Even if voters don't pass the new bond, the students can't afford to lose another teacher. Surely there are other expenses that can be cut or reduced."

"None that equal a salary." Austin spun his squeaky chair in a half-circle, grabbed a huge three-ring binder off the overloaded bookcase and tossed it onto the desk between them. It *thunked* like a corpse hitting the ground. "Trust me, Miss Dumont. I've rearranged the budget a dozen times, always with the same result — a position has to go. And since you were the last one hired, you're it." He spread his hands in a helpless gesture.

Adara gripped the edges of her plastic chair, anchoring herself in place. *Worst case all around.* A small town meant limited opportunities, and losing her job would require either hours of commuting or relocation, and that was only if she were lucky enough to land another rarely open teaching job. And if she lost her one outlet, the one activity that still held some meaning for her, she'd combust. "But that's a worst-case scenario. The school bond —"

"Looks grim." Austin pushed up his wire-rim glasses. "People are having enough trouble keeping their own floundering households afloat, let alone the school system. Belts are already tight. We have better odds of finding oil under the monkey bars than taxpayers approving additional funds, which leaves me to figure out how to give students the education they need with the money we already don't have."

"Let me look at the budget." Adara swallowed the knot in her throat. "I minored in accounting. Maybe I'll see something you didn't."

He barked a laugh and pushed the binder closer to her. "Great weekend reading with a box of wine. Be my guest, but don't get your hopes up. I majored in accounting then decided teaching was the profession of nobles." He patted his slight paunch. "Look at me now."

She dragged the notebook from the desk and nearly dropped it. It was even heavier than it looked.

"Carry that thing around and you can skip your daily run." Austin smirked and snatched the half-eaten doughnut propped against his monster-sized stapler. "Both sound equally fun."

"Or I can stuff it in a backpack and run with the extra weight while you fill your face with heart-clogging poisons." She stood and hefted it onto her hip like a toddler. "How many trees died for this monster? What happened to the electronic information age?"

Austin swallowed his mouthful of doughnut and brushed crumbs from his mustache. "Don't go just yet. There's more...some good news. As I'm sure you commit all my announcements to memory like the important gems they are, you'll recall the music mentor program I mentioned a few weeks back."

No. No, no, no.

He ignored her frantic mental message and kept going. "Your class was selected. He starts next week."

"What? Why? Why *my* class?"

The principal raised his eyebrows. "I thought you'd be happy that your students get this opportunity, and whatever publicity he generates may sway a few bond votes our way. Mr. Ambrose is a gifted musician and he's generously donating his time and skills. Can't go wrong with free."

That depends on perspective. He was right in that she should be happy for her students, but it involved music and a particular verbose violinist who'd invaded her space too much already. She pasted on a serene expression. "I meant, how did we get so lucky?"

Austin gave her a weasel smile, made oilier by his mustache. She hadn't tricked him at all. "I felt your class would benefit the most, and while this is an elective program, I expect a combined weekly progress report from you and Mr. Ambrose. I need documentation that the students are learning something." The phone rang before she could make another ineffectual protest and he sighed. "No rest for the Wicked Principal of the West."

Adara turned away as he answered the call. She really wanted to be miffed at him for both suggesting her job would be cut and assigning the musical mishap to her, but as far as principals went, he was fair, practical and truly had the kids' best interests at heart. Not all schools were so fortunate.

"Hold on," Austin said into the receiver. "One last item, Dumont. Mrs. Johnson brought to my attention that we're short a few volunteers for the school carnival tomorrow. She also noted you forgot to sign up."

She cringed. 'Forgot' was a nice way of saying 'neglected while stuck in a state of apathy'. Mrs. Johnson, president of the volunteer committee, kept a chart on all school activities and each teacher's volunteer ratio, the perfect scoreboard to detect anyone who slid under the carnival radar, intentionally or not. She smoothed out her expression before facing him again. "Let me guess. Only clean-up is left."

Austin's eyes gleamed behind his glasses, a sure sign he was either refraining from smirking or was giving her a pitying look. "Even better. Buckle up. You're on for final patrol duty."

So much for baking cookies in solitude and dropping them off, no contact required. She'd be stuck there until closing, enforcing boundaries, stalling sibling fights and restraining parents from killing their precious flesh and blood, all while keeping her glued pieces together. *This week is getting brighter by the day.*

Leaving Mr. Austin to his call, she slipped into the empty hall and her phone buzzed. Adara juggled the budget notebook and dug her phone from her blazer pocket. Gia's number flashed. She didn't want to talk about her breakdown the previous night, but she'd also killed her promise. Gia at least deserved an explanation. Leaning against a carnival poster, she faced the inevitable.

"You're skipping your evening run." Gia didn't give her a second to say hello, speaking fast and loud. "We have plans."

Her chest squeezed. As much as she didn't want to go anywhere tonight, violating her Joey vow again wasn't happening. *Wait a second.* Gia hadn't even mentioned her sudden departure the previous night. *Very suspicious.* "What plans?"

"Dinner. Antoine's. Six sharp."

She pushed off the wall and continued toward the exit, the notebook a dead weight in her other arm. The extra poundage made her pumps echo louder than normal. "I'm not required to be present when you decide you're hungry for Italian. Joey specified social events. Dinner at Antoine's isn't a social event."

"We need to talk."

"Please tell me this has nothing to do with any trouble you got into after I left last night."

"Kinda. Sort of. Maybe."

Adara groaned. "How many margaritas did you down?"

"Only two." Gia huffed. "It's not *that* kind of trouble, not like last year." She hesitated. "You ditched me."

She closed her eyes. "Sorry."

"Meet me at Antoine's." A pleading entered Gia's tone. "We'll eat too much bread and pasta, and dessert will erase the score of any and all betrayals."

"Can't." Shifting the notebook, she resumed the trek to the door. "Austin just told me that if the bond proposal doesn't pass, I'm fired, so I'm studying the numbers tonight to see if I can save my job."

"Dang." Gia sucked in a breath. "Okay, I'll do this without garlic bread to soften you up. Don't freak out."

Adara jerked to a stop. Something bad was coming. Any combination of Gia and the word 'freak' equaled catastrophe. "Should I destroy you now or after lasagna?"

Gia's laugh was too shrill to be believable. "Nobody needs maiming, torturing or quartering. Besides, this isn't about me. It's about you."

"Me?"

"I get that life without Joey sucks for you and you're doing your best because you promised him you would." Her voice dropped to a whisper, and the unusual gravity shot a chill through Adara. "I made promises to him too. It's been over a year, and instead of snapping out of it, every day you sink deeper into indifference. Dar, you're the closest thing I have to him and I can't—I won't—watch you fade away too."

That chill deepened, draining into her bones. She didn't have the energy to deal with unwanted sympathy and good intentions. "How I deal is no one's business but my own."

"True." Gia sounded wistful. "Moving on is a decision only you can make. The thing is, this morning I stumbled on to an interesting theory. I was skeptical at first, not going to lie, but after a thorough"—she hesitated—"investigation, I'm convinced this deserves a shot. All I ask is that you give it a *real* shot, not just Gia lip service."

Perfect. An Adara intervention and her arm was getting tired. She set the notebook down and planted her butt on it. If she admitted she hadn't moved on at all, Gia would never quit. She'd be plagued with frivolous social invites until she puked. Then again, humbly acquiescing would raise all sorts of suspicion. Her reaction had to be somewhere in between to make it believable.

"Don't you trust me?" Gia's wounded tone could complement an abused animal ad.

"Not even a little bit." She slouched and pushed her hair behind her ear. "I need a few details." *Is it a therapy dog?* Or maybe a counseling session where she'd pretend to have it all together long enough to appease everyone, whatever it took to keep Gia happy and off her case.

"One word—Garret Ambrose. I know that's technically two words, but one name."

Ambrose. Why does that name sound familiar? Ambrose. Warning bells clanged in her head. *Ambrose...*the same name Principal Austin had invoked. Her voice shook, echoing the building heat in her gut. "What did you do, G?"

"He asked about you, and I was persuaded to spill a few details."

"So it's settled. You're dead *before* pasta." Traitors didn't deserve dessert.

"I wouldn't have if I wasn't convinced he's a good guy," Gia rushed on. "At the very least, have coffee with him—or forget the coffee and just jump on him. I bet he could cure any blues."

Keeping her voice icy casual, Adara stood. "I'm going for my run. Period."

She shut off her phone, cutting out whatever Gia said in response. The notebook back in her arms, she sped past lockers and drinking fountains, needing the open air. Her hands trembled, and her heart pummeled her ribs as if she'd already run. Of all the things she expected Gia to slam her with, it wasn't a date...with *him*. Man therapy might be Gia's go-to drug, but it wasn't hers. *Please.* As if a guy could replace the lost connection with her brother. No one had ever understood her like Joey, and no matter how much she missed her brother, loneliness was preferable to dealing with the pain again.

After a push through the school doors, she paused, gulping a deep breath of lung-freezing air. Cold skittered over her nose and cheeks. She blinked a snowflake from her eyelashes and lifted her gaze to a sky dark with clouds. Snow, earlier than the weatherman had predicted. With any luck, the white stuff would stick and last long enough to keep some of the more cautious carnival enthusiasts home.

For the first time that week, she almost smiled.

Chapter Four

The power-eating, whiteout, carnival-canceling blizzard Adara had hoped for left only a worthless dusting, nothing to slow a crowd. She joined the mob of bobbing and weaving children with stained hands, big eyes and even bigger voices and navigated to the sidelines, where the fifth-grade teacher and current security overseer, Olivia, argued with a parent.

"I don't make the rules, Mr. Vergara." Olivia's jowls wobbled with each word and she looked ready to stab Mr. Vergara with the crochet needles she always kept handy. "Billy violated rule twelve—"

Mr. Vergara stormed away, muttering words in Spanish that definitely violated school language policy, a wailing Billy in tow.

"You're two minutes late," Olivia crowed above the surround-sound cacophony, the buzz of too many people stuffed in one place. "Two eternal, torturous minutes." She struggled out of the neon-green security vest and shoved the eye-burning garment into Adara's arms. "The monsters are all yours, and I'm not talking about the kids. If I have to tell one more Mr. or Mrs. I'm Better Than You that they need to control their perfect child, my inner ninja will come out—and nobody wants that."

Imagining the rotund woman cartwheeling in her gingham dress and flinging crochet needles like shrunken stars into the prim and proper behinds of a few football dads and their trophy wives inspired a small grin. "Great idea for our next fundraiser."

Olivia laid a heavy hand on her shoulder and leaned near, close enough for Adara to count the ready-to-retire wrinkles around her eyes. "Honey, some things I don't do for free, and the school couldn't afford me." She straightened and her eyes flared, usually a sign of gossip to be spilled. "I stumbled into your new music mentor in Austin's office after school."

Adara ground her molars.

"If you don't have babies with him—"

"Not happening. Not with him or anyone else." She added a growl to her tone and let her glare fly free. "I like being alone, and that's never going to change. *Ever.* End of discussion." Adara didn't need nudges added to the knowing glances she already got in the breakroom. What was it with everyone trying to hook her up with Mr. Musicality?

"Just saying." Olivia shrugged, clearly unfazed by her lingering Mr. T glower. "Good luck tonight. I have a date with my needles and a new spool of red for the sweater I'm making you. I'm tired of seeing you in black." She bulldozed through the crowd toward the door.

"I like black," Adara said to her retreating back. "It's my happy color."

Olivia waggled her fingers in farewell.

Adara took in the carnival layout. *What a nightmare.* Unchaperoned kids ran in all directions, chittering and screaming with handfuls of plastic prizes and balloons. It was a wonder there hadn't been any bloodshed yet. Paint changed faces into clowns, tigers and demented fairies. Temporary hair dye added neon rainbows to tiny heads. Some of the more dutiful parents trailed their children or held hands while others huddled in their invitation-only cliques, dismissing the rules and letting their spawn run free.

Interactive games circled the gym and the stuffy air was choked with a junk food blend of buttered popcorn, hotdogs and grease. It was enough to clog her pores by simply breathing. In one corner, the ever-popular bouncy house shivered and huffed, as if possessed. Joey used to love climbing into the bouncy house with the kids. He'd refuse to come out until Gia threatened him.

She cast the memory away, refocusing on the here and now. What a way to spend her Friday night. She'd rather be studying the budget and figuring out how to keep her job.

Unwadding the security vest, Adara pulled the pink note stuck crookedly on the back of the mesh material. It read in rough, penciled handwriting 'I want to marry Principal Austin'. Whichever brave kid had stuck this on Olivia's back was lucky she hadn't noticed. She shrugged into the garment, leaving the Velcro straps free. That made it easier to take it off and check for stray notes on her back.

"Miss Dumont!" Tatum, her best student despite the girl's love for shenanigans aimed at whatever boy she happened to be crushing on, skidded to a stop. Purple replaced her golden hair, clashing with the green snake painted from her forehead to her chin. Its red tongue flickered between her eyebrows. No typical girly hearts or flowers for Tatum. "Look what I won!"

Adara accepted the stick of cotton candy from Tatum's pink, sticky hands. "Aren't you supposed to stay close to your parents?"

"I'm not with my parents." She swiped the candy back, tore off a piece and stuffed it in her mouth. "Dad's volunteering at the Potty Toss. Mom stayed home with baby G, so my uncle's chap'roning."

"Total chaperone fail." She tweaked Tatum's nose. "Tell your uncle to step it up."

"It's not really his fault. I waited until he helped Bryan with a game so I could chase Zachary."

Zachary. Current Tatum crush. Third-grade romance was so simple—catch and release. "Did you snag him?"

"I cornered him at the cakewalk but he got away. He runs really, really fast. I'll get him next time." She grinned, a little scary with all those teeth and a snake coiled around half her face. Zachary was smart to run.

"No running in the gym, remember?"

Tatum shuffled her feet, pasting on an appropriate guilty look.

"Let's track your uncle down before he gets into trouble for losing you." She took the girl's small, gluey hand. "Shall we?"

"We shall, Mr. Collins," Tatum replied in a lofty tone, nose in the air and her cotton candy hand on her hip.

Adara pressed her lips together until the urge to smile passed. "You didn't learn that in my class. Who teaches you these things?"

"Mom. We have *Pride and Prejudice* nights," she said in a sing-song voice, "No boys allowed."

"That's...awesome." She hadn't been old enough to appreciate *P and P* with her mom before the car accident had taken both her parents, but she vaguely remembered snuggle sessions on the couch. She could imagine gushing with her mom over a bowl of popcorn, watching Mr. Darcy win Elizabeth over and over—the television version, not the movie.

Shaking off the if-only, she joined in the third-grade fantasy. *"But I protest. I will not stand to be named Mr. Collins. He is a dolt, madam."*

Tatum giggled as they waited for some boys horsing around with balloons to get out of the way. "How about Kitty?"

"Kitty?" She snorted. "Please. She's a follower, and don't even suggest Mrs. Bennet or Lydia."

Tatum twisted her mouth to one side. "What about Lady de Bourgh?"

Adara gasped, only partly pretending. Did Tatum really think she was as old and pompous as Lady Catherine? "How dare you?"

"All right." Tatum added a skip to her step. "You're Jane. You can't be Lizzy, 'cause that's me. But if you're Jane," Tatum said, her eyes narrowed, "you need a Mr. Bingley."

"Indeed, I do not."

The little girl jerked on her hand, surprisingly hard, towing her in a determined path. She cut off other kids and pushed through a knot of parents without slowing down.

Adara barely avoided colliding with a dad holding a giant stuffed neon-pink dinosaur under his other arm. She should hand her security vest over to Tatum. The girl had some serious authority going on. "Slow down, Tatum. We need to find your—"

"Uncle Garret!"

Garret.

The name clicked before Adara's eyes could signal a warning to her brain, and there he was, the captain without his ship, Tatum's brother Bryan at his side. He'd ditched his instrument, but his appearance hadn't changed much—blond hair pulled neatly back, two-day stubble giving him the ruffian look, jeans with a few strategically placed holes, same black rocker boots and a more casual flannel over an abstract T-shirt. Today, he looked less like a pirate and closer to a panicked uncle who'd lost his niece in wild-child chaos. The relief on his face almost made her feel sorry for him. *Almost.*

His gaze flicked from her to Tatum and back to her. "I almost didn't recognize you in direct light without a monstrous reindeer bowing at your feet."

Adara tried to subtly pry free of Tatum's hold and escape, without success. How did she not know he was Tatum's uncle? Maybe she should've paid more attention to her surroundings instead of blocking the Graywood small-town snoopiness whenever possible. After three years living here, she still hadn't adjusted to it.

"Garret Ambrose, Tatum's favorite uncle." He held out his hand. If he thought his smile would soften her, he was sadly mistaken.

She hid a sigh, facing the inevitable. As of Monday, they'd be working together, and Austin had undoubtedly already told him her name. She couldn't escape, but she didn't have to play nice. "Adara Dumont." She took his introduction in a quick shake and release, ignoring how his big hand swallowed hers. "Teacher extraordinaire."

Tatum tugged on Garret's shirt with her other hand, smearing pink cotton candy on the sleeve. "Miss Dumont's Jane and I'm Lizzy."

"Hey there, Lizzy." He scratched his cheek and looked at Adara. "Jane?"

"You're not family. You can't use her first name." Tatum performed a halfway decent curtsy. "Call her Miss Bennet, good sir."

Bryan groaned and rolled his eyes. "Stupid *Pride and Prejudice*. How can anyone like that show? Except for the version with zombies. That one's cool." He held up a fist for Garret to bump.

Completely ignoring her brother, Tatum looked up at Garret, her blue eyes innocent and pleading. "Zachary's my Mr. Darcy, but Jane needs her Mr. Bingley."

No. Adara saw the train wreck coming at her but couldn't move fast enough to get out of the way.

"Will you be Mr. Bingley, Uncle Garret? Puh-lease?"

"Sure." Garret's smile made a flashlight look dim.

"This particular Jane is on carnival security duty." She met his gaze head-on. "She doesn't want or need a Mr. Bingley."

"Oh, come now, Miss Bennet. Every Jane needs her Charles," Garret said.

Blast. He was familiar with *Pride and Prejudice*. Not helpful in her quest to dislike him.

Tatum's persuasion tactics turned on her, those blue eyes huge in her elfin face, hopeful and pleading.

Adara stood firm beneath the assault. "On second thought, I choose Mary. With Mr. Collins married to Charlotte, no one else could meet her very particular standards." She arched an eyebrow at Garret, which had no effect at all on his smile. "She preferred to be alone."

"With her music," he added.

"With her books."

"Who cares?" Bryan gave Garret a look of betrayal. "You're as bad as the girls."

"I grew up with your mother. It twisted me." He ruffled Bryan's sandy hair. "But this matter must be settled." He straightened to his full height and lifted his chin, imperious. "Miss Bennet, I propose a contest."

"I accept!" Tatum jumped up and down, her cotton candy dangerously close to falling off its stick.

"My apologies, Miss Lizzy." Garret planted his palm on Tatum's head, holding her still. "I was challenging the other Miss Bennet." Before Tatum's crestfallen expression turned to tears, he added, "But, of course, you may join us. If I win, I shall be Mr. Bingley. If I lose, Miss Bennet shall remain unattached."

Bryan groaned again and slouched. "Can I go get a hot dog?"

"Meet us at your dad's game." Garret forked out some cash and the boy dashed away.

"No running!" Adara dutifully called after him.

"I don't believe he heard you." He kept his tone smooth, but his mouth twitched in a poor attempt not to smile. He held out his arm. "Shall we?"

She eyed his arm, hoping she looked hostile. "I haven't agreed to your challenge, and I'm ninety-nine percent sure the games are for the kids."

Garret exchanged glances with Tatum, and as if they'd choreographed the move, Tatum broke into a chicken dance, flapping her wings, while Garret made loud clucking noises. Clearly, the entire family was mentally unstable and craved attention, no matter how it came about. Kids and adults alike paused to watch them. *And I have to work with this insufferable man?* As carnival security, Adara had the duty to escort disruptive attendees out, and as much as she'd love to kick Garret out of the door, Tatum and Bryan would have to go with him. She couldn't do that to the kids.

"Fine," she snapped. "Which game are you losing at?"

Tatum gave Garret a high-five. *Jerks.*

"The Potty Toss." Garret gave her a sly look, so like Tatum's it was uncanny. "Unless you prefer a more ladylike competition, such as the sumo wrestling ring."

Fighting her way into one of those blow-up suits wasn't happening, and rolling around with Garret Ambrose? Definitely not. She curled her lip. "The Potty Toss works."

He offered his arm again, which she ignored again, and they weaved through the crowd toward the Potty Toss.

"Have you heard the good news?" Garret lifted his eyebrows at her. "I'm the new third-grade school music mentor. We'll be working together."

"I hoped if I ignored that nasty rumor, it would go away." She forced her gaze on the Bozo contorting balloons into animals and the kids clamoring around him. Creepy clowns were preferable to musicians posing as pirates.

"I don't go away that easily," he said close to her ear.

"In her tell-all, Gia must have forgot to mention I have zero interest in the habits of music mentors." She bared her teeth at him.

Garret had the grace to wince. "None of the blame belongs to Gia. Ian has a gift for persuasion...or coercion." He cleared his throat. "His intentions were good."

"Good intentions? Ian?" She snorted. "Right."

He shrugged. "It happens more often than you'd think."

Tatum's father, Bob, manned the Potty Toss, a set-up of several toilet seats hanging from the ceiling at varying distances. The point was to throw rolls of toilet paper through the holes — the higher the seat, the higher the score. She had no idea who had thought up these twisted games.

"Step right up, ladies and gentlemen, and test your skills with the amazing Potty Toss!" As far as she knew, the carnival didn't have a particular theme or costume requirement, but Bob went all out with a medieval faire vibe. Donning a multicolored tunic any gypsy would envy, high leather boots and what looked to be suede breeches, he topped it off with a hat spotlighting a long peacock feather.

"Tickets please, little miss," he said to Tatum, his blue eyes sparkling, hand outstretched.

"Miss Bennet," she corrected him in a snooty lady tone. "Although, I suppose you may call me Lizzy since you're family."

"Indeed. Even so, Miss Lizzy, I need a ticket before allowing you to play the great Potty Toss, where only skill and stamina will earn you a prize."

Without looking back, Tatum snapped her fingers over her shoulder. "Mr. Bingley, three tickets."

Bob's smile switched to a disapproving frown. "Manners, Miss Lizzy."

Tatum sighed. "Mr. Bingley, three tickets. *Please.*"

"Better," Bob said as Garret fished three tickets from his pocket, grinning over the top of Tatum's head. "Next time, no oppressed peasant sigh."

"Yes, Daddy." She huffed. "Can we play now?"

"First, we must name the stakes." Garret handed a toilet paper roll to Tatum then Adara.

"You're playing too, Miss Dumont?" Bob's eyebrows climbed toward his hairline.

Interaction Girl hadn't been her MO since Joey. Last year, she hadn't attended the carnival and no one had pushed her to volunteer, but she'd played tons of games the year before. Maybe everybody else had forgotten who she used to be too.

"Oh yeah, she's playing." Garret tossed his roll in the air.

"Not Miss Dumont, Daddy. Jane Bennet." Tatum gave her father a serious look. "Uncle Garret's trying to win so he can be her Mr. Bingley."

Bob looked from Garret to Adara and back to Garret, his brow wrinkled in his 'concerned father' look.

Adara squeezed the soft tissue. *Right.* No one wanted their brother-in-law to be interested in the emotionally unavailable teacher. She got it, even agreed, but still... She hadn't asked for any of this. "Don't worry, Mr. Sullivan. He's going to lose."

"Fighting words, Miss Bennet." Garret bumped her shoulder with his, almost making her stumble. "Want me to go first so you understand how truly overconfident you are?"

"Go ahead. Just don't let the cheap toilet paper hurt those fragile violin fingers."

His quick-fire grin appeared and the underlying dare awakened a mild echo of her sibling rivalry with Joey, although theirs had been much fiercer. It was her elbow that had broken Joey's nose in a sheet music scuffle, not that he'd complained much afterward. All the girls seemed to love the permanent bump. She crushed the tissue, strangling the memory.

"Prepare to be courted Bingley-style." Challenge glowing in his eyes, he lifted his gaze to the toilet seats hanging behind Bob. He bounced on the balls of his feet a few times and lobbed his roll at the highest ring. It missed.

Adara shook her head. *Typical man... He didn't even try for the lower one.*

"I've got two more." His tone was cool, confident.

"Can I try one first?" Tatum held her paper above her head and spun. Bob rescued the cotton candy as it flipped from her hand, catching it before it hit the gym floor. *Score one for practiced dads everywhere.*

"Go ahead, sweetheart." Garret stepped beside Adara and tucked his hands behind his back as Tatum took her turn. "Missing once means nothing. It was a practice shot."

"Whatever you say, Ambrose." Adara shifted away from him, away from his heat and the faint nip of his citrusy cologne. Sadly, he didn't smell like a pirate. "Not everyone has more than one skill."

Tatum bent her knees and heaved the roll into the air, shot-put style. It bounced off a higher seat and ricocheted into a lower ring. "Ten points for me!" She jumped up and down like a pogo stick. "I'm beating Uncle Garret!"

He looked sideways at Adara. A few strands of his too-long blond hair had slipped free of the band at his nape and framed his jaw, adding to his bohemian vibe. "So you admit you like my music?"

"I wasn't implying your singular talent has anything to do with music." Adara gripped her tissue roll and heaved it neatly through the thirty-pointer. She cocked a hip and tilted her chin, going for bored.

Garret caught the second roll Bob chucked at him. "You just met me, have spoken to me only through polite necessity, yet you magically know the talents I possess?" He leaned closer, close enough his breath brushed her cheek, warm and intimate. "Do tell."

"Talent. Singular."

"If it's not my music — which wounds me gravely, by the way — and it's clearly not heaving TP through porcelain crowns, what do you believe it is?"

"Harassing the innocent, obviously."

"I presume you speak of your innocent person."

"Indeed."

He focused on the fifty-point shot, set up and missed again. His smile dimmed to a sixty-watt. "And they expect kids to score on this?"

"Bummer." Adara pressed her lips together. "All I have to do is make another shot and Mr. Bingley goes solo."

"Mr. Bingley *never* surrenders. Your last throw was pure luck."

Tatum hurled her second roll, and it flew between two seats. She stomped a foot and glared at her dad. "You made the ropes shorter when I wasn't looking, didn't you?"

"All is honorable, fair and just at Bob's Potty Toss." Bob twirled a roll on one finger, his mouth set to stern-father mode. "And poor sportsmanship will end your turn right now, young lady."

She mumbled an apology, which was enough to earn her last paper roll.

Adara squared off with the targets, aimed and swished it. She couldn't hold back a little smirk. "Buh-bye, Mr. Bingley."

Tatum planted her fists on her hips. "Nice going, Uncle Garret. I thought you were a basketb—"

Garret muffled the rest of her sentence with one large hand. "Let's not bore Miss Dumont with my illustrious past."

"Let me guess, benchwarmer of the middle school B-string?" Adara hooked a finger in the vest strap. It wasn't hard to picture him participating in sports. She'd guess his height at six foot plus a few, and with those long limbs and lean form, he probably had some natural athleticism going on with his music. But apparently not enough to keep his shooting skills sharp.

"My life revolved around music." He winked, and she pretended she hadn't been sizing him up. With any luck, her face didn't look as warm as it felt. "I didn't have time for other activities."

Sounds familiar. Tearing Joey away from his violin took force, trickery or a coconut cake—sometimes all three. Her throat tightened and she turned away.

"Double or nothing," Bob blurted, drawing everyone's attention. "That was either a fluke or beginner's luck, both bad and good. Besides, no one else is in line." He gathered an armload of toilet paper rolls. "Up the ante. If Garret wins, he holds the honorary carnival-night-only title of Mr. Bingley, and…?" He looked pointedly at Garret.

Garret's smile returned. "And Adara agrees to have dinner with me."

Chapter Five

Dinner with Garret Ambrose wasn't happening. Adara slipped her hands in her jeans' pockets. "Nope. Gotta go wrangle up a balloon weiner dog. Top-secret carnival security stuff."

"Good." Garret took toilet paper rolls in each hand and looked at her, his eyes sparkling. "I expected you'd accept and make your stakes that I never harass your innocent person outside of work. Graywood is a small town. We'll be running into each other" — he flashed all his teeth — "often."

He'd made a valid point. Sharing her classroom with him would be bad enough. It would be even worse having to deal with him in the feminine products aisle of the grocery aisle. She snatched one roll from his hand. "Done, with the understanding that you won't say a word to me outside of work."

Had she thought he'd displayed all his teeth earlier? Nope, he had more, and they all beamed back at her, white and straight. If nothing else, he had a really nice smile. It was infectious. Dangerous. "Beginner's luck, my sweet a—"

Tatum watched her, alert to every word.

"Aunt Mary's apple pie." As a grade school teacher, she'd had lots of practice with creative cursing. She usually didn't get preoccupied enough to slip. *Annoying musician wannabe pirate and his contagious smile.*

"Nice save," Garret murmured, scratching his ear and gazing up at the gymnasium ceiling.

"Shut up," she said under her breath and focused on the toilet seats. If she made the fifty-pointer, that would almost guarantee a win, and since having dinner with him wasn't an option, going for it seemed the thing to do. If she missed, she still had two more shots to beat him. *Piece of pie.* Aunt Mary's apple, to be exact.

Releasing a breath, Adara pitched the paper at the target. It bounced off the rim and dropped to the ground, trailing white.

"Close." Bob tsked, his disappointment not at all convincing.

"Victory is so sweet. I already taste it." Garret flexed his fingers and rolled his neck. He jumped a few times, shaking out his arms like a boxer readying for the ring.

"Miss Dumont, it's not polite to roll your eyes. That will cost you a sticker." Tatum stuck out a hand, waiting for the price of rolling one's eyes while on Miss Dumont's time.

Practicing what she preached in the classroom wasn't easy around Garret Ambrose. "You're right. That was rude, and I apologize."

The little hand didn't budge, expectant.

"I don't have any stickers with me… Oh, wait." She dug the pink note she'd earlier found stuck to the vest out of her pocket. "Here you go. It's all I've got."

Tatum read the note and her face scrunched up. "Ew. You want to marry Principal Austin?"

Garret's warmup moves stopped cold, and even Bob paused.

"Yeah, sure." She performed a dreamy sigh. "Everyone wants to marry Principal Austin. He's like a current-day Mr. Darcy."

Tatum looked so horrified that it took everything Adara had not to smile. Holding the note as if it contained a disease, she flicked it back to her. "I don't want a sticker."

"Fine." She slapped it on the vest, showing off the penciled letters scrawled by a juvenile hand. "I'll keep it for myself."

Garret scanned the note, and the relief in his dark eyes stirred a small, fragile fluttering right behind her breastbone in the place her heart had once resided. He honestly wanted to win this bet, to spend more time with her. It made zero sense. She knew some men found her attractive, despite the fact she never bothered with makeup, always wore threatening black and discouraged romantic advances without mercy. Maybe he just liked the thrill of the chase. She lifted her chin. *This particular prey won't be caught.*

Apparently through with his prep moves, he spun and launched his roll at the forty-point ring. It sailed through, a perfect shot.

"Forty points for the gentleman," Bob helpfully announced while Tatum bounced up and down, clapping.

"Traitor." Adara narrowed her eyes at her favorite student. "I thought you were on my side."

"I am—*uh.*" Tatum drew out the word in the whiny way children loved to do when protesting. "I want you to be Jane—not Mary—and Jane needs a Mr. Bingley." She fluttered her eyelashes. "Uncle Garret will be a perfect Mr. Bingley."

"Thank you, Miss Bennet." He executed a fancy bow so expertly that it had to be a move he practiced often. "Your confidence in me warms my heart."

"Misplaced though it is in this circumstance." Adara swiped her second roll from Bob. "Plus, as far as I recall, in no version of *P and P* did Mr. Bingley have a pirate predilection."

Bob chuckled. "Thank you, Miss Dumont. I've been saying that for years, and no one else claims to see his ill-concealed longing to be Blackbeard."

"I do not have any desire to be a pirate." A deadly edge entered Garret's voice, and he gave his brother-in-law a glare worthy of any scallywag. "The skull ring was a gift from your wife and offspring, as you well know. What sort of ingrate would I be if I didn't wear it?"

"No judgment." Bob held up his hands, his eyes sparkling. "Bet you'll love the eye patch they're getting for your birthday."

The snicker stuck in Adara's throat slipped free.

"I see how it is. Disrespect and disloyalty on all sides." Garret folded his arms and his biceps bunched beneath the sleeves of his thermal shirt—arms that would make most men envious. *Must be all the violin holding.* He loomed over Bob. "There better be a cutlass with that eye patch, scurvy dog."

Adara smiled, unintentional and genuine. She killed the expression quick, her heart kicking hard. She could see herself in the mix of this family, connecting, getting closer, sharing laughs, being vulnerable…allowing an avenue to that debilitating pain wasn't happening again.

She ripped her gaze from Garret and settled on the toilet seats. *Fifty points.* Losing wasn't a choice. Forcing her hands steady, she heaved her roll. It nicked the rim, bounced and went through. Not pretty, but it had worked.

"Dam—" Garret caught Tatum's wide-eyed look just in time. "—mmmage." He tossed his second paper roll from hand to hand and surveyed the targets, his expression serious. "Go big or go home, right?" He threw the missile at the fifty…and missed.

"Step it up, Uncle Garret!" Tatum screeched, scowling up at the man she'd looked at so adoringly three seconds ago.

The knot in Adara's neck eased a degree. They were back on almost-even ground. All she needed was another fifty and she'd be free of any commitments, free of the pesky violinist outside of work, free to stay in her safe cocoon.

She met Garret's gaze. "Want to take your last shot now? Your miss will save me the effort."

He studied her for a lingering moment. Without his smile going on, his intent focus solely on her, she could understand why he excelled at his music. The determination there suggested that once his mind was set, he never gave up, no matter the difficulty or challenge. Conquer or die. He slowly shook his head.

Adara shrugged and adjusted her grip on the final roll. Fifty points would secure the win, but forty would be an easier shot and make it a tie if Garret got lucky. No way could he beat her in a tie-breaker. She aimed for the forty.

The roll repeated Tatum's earlier score, bouncing off the forty's rim. It flipped as it fell and ricocheted into the thirty. *Blast and bullocks.* He could still beat her. She never should've let Tatum drag her into this mess. Yeah, third-graders made great scapegoats.

Garret resumed studying her, absently rolling the toilet paper between his palms — that same, serious concentration making her feel like he could see every vulnerable sliver of her soul. "Fifty to win, Adara."

Almost as mesmerizing as being under his scrutiny, his low, sensuous tone curled around her. She coughed to break the spell. He'd missed the fifty every time. No way he'd hit it now. "Forty to tie."

His smile returned, and it was nothing like the friendly shot of joy he'd worn before. This one was a wolf's toothy grin, confident and hungry. "I don't like to share."

He pivoted, aimed and sank the toilet paper into the fifty.

Adara blinked. *Crap.*

Both Tatum and Bob whooped in triumph.

Garret wisely kept his celebration to the tiniest smirk, a smart move. A victory dance would've sparked violence. "For the record, my only basketball trophy is the plastic dollar-store award won on the family driveway court. It passed between my sister London and me while we grew up, sometimes on a daily basis. I won our final match, so I claimed its final resting place." He stretched leisurely, as if releasing the tension of an exciting victory. His dimple reappeared. "I didn't play you, honest. It was a lucky shot."

Adara's stomach twisted. She had to have dinner with this man who affected her even without his violin, alone, no children to distract her. Enduring it without consequences might take some new tricks.

A tap on her shoulder scattered her thoughts. A girl with a lollipop hanging in her long, blonde hair slumped. "I have a problem."

Thank God. Something to focus on that didn't involve lost bets, future food or musicians. "Let's go to my classroom. I keep an emergency jar of peanut butter handy." She set a hand on the girl's shoulder and propelled her forward. If she didn't look back and she pretended the last fifteen minutes hadn't transpired, maybe she could chalk it up to another nightmare.

"I'll call on you, Miss Bennet." Garret's voice followed her, full of knowing humor, as if he knew exactly what she'd thought. "Charles Bingley always keeps his word."

The girl looked sidelong at Adara, her eyebrows high.

"You don't want to know. Trust me." She shook her head. "I wish *I* could forget."

* * * *

Garret rested a hip against the Potty Toss counter while Adara headed into the crowd with the lollipop-assaulted girl. She didn't look back once, even though he'd waited for it, hoped for it. Her slender form disappeared behind a tangle of teenage boys. The neon security vest flashed through once then she was gone, a raven swallowed by the colorful carnival sea.

He didn't bother holding back a smile. *Chara*, her dry humor killed him, an unashamed sincerity he'd missed overseas. No matter that she meant to drive him away, her responses revealed how observant she truly was, and if she wasn't a little interested, she wouldn't be paying attention.

The more minutes he spent with her, the more he wanted to know. He'd cracked her surface tonight and what slipped free had awakened every sense. Her laughter was enough to inspire angel choirs, but she was more skittish than a woodland creature. Earning her trust would take patience. Luckily, patience was another one of his super skills. He'd use a jewel hammer to chink away her armor until nothing remained between them.

"What's the deal, Bob?" He turned to his brother-in-law and folded his arms. "Double or nothing? I'm not sure if you were trying to help me or sink me."

"It's been a long time since I've seen Adara even remotely enjoy herself." Pity dimmed the open friendliness in Bob's expression. "Keeping the game going a while longer seemed the thing to do."

Garret hated that grief fogged her in, isolating. "So it had nothing to do with helping me out." He tapped the counter, releasing the beat pulsing in his head. "What if I'd lost? I doubt even a double-dog dare would've kept her going."

Bob's eyes crinkled, erasing any concern. "London's complained enough about that ridiculous plastic basketball trophy. She hates that you still have it. I had faith in you."

"Have you never watched us play? We both stink." Garret grabbed another roll and threw it, missing. "But only a natural disaster would've stopped me. You probably saved me months of making a fool of myself. And that would be to finagle one measly date."

"You're staying around that long?" The surprise in Bob's voice wasn't offensive. Since gaining his adult freedom, he rarely planned his next move, letting his heart lead him. He hadn't plotted a timeline beyond his temporary music mentor gig, courtesy of Tatum's pleading and strings Bob had pulled with the principal. His manager had relayed a couple offers when — if — he decided to return. Those offers wouldn't stay open forever.

"Nothing's set in stone. Maybe I'll see how things go with music mentoring" — he cleared the strange scratch in his throat — "and Miss Dumont."

"Just be careful. You can't inspire everyone."

Garret squared his shoulders and lifted his chin. "Watch me."

"Good lord, you're as stubborn as London." Bob held out his fist and waited for Garret to bump it with his own. "You're welcome."

"Come on, Uncle Garret." Tatum tugged on his sleeve and left another set of sticky pink fingerprints, apparently done with enduring adult-talk and forgetting all about pretending to be Elizabeth Bennet. "You promised I could go in the bouncy house, and Bryan isn't back yet, so I bet he's already there. Let's go- uh."

As Tatum dragged him by the arm, Bob called after him. "Heads up, Garret. Once London hears about tonight, she'll demand a rematch. She wants that trophy back."

He lifted his hand to signal he'd heard then grinned at nobody in particular.

It's good to be home.

Chapter Six

Saturday morning came too soon and not soon enough. Adara stretched her quadriceps as the sun slowly revealed itself, winking gray through the mixed evergreens and bare-limbed trees in her backyard. Ever since Joey had gotten sick, sleep had been an unpredictable beast, and she'd learned not to fight it. Pills didn't always work, and better a naturally groggy grouch than a chemical zombie.

Warmed up and stretched, she pulled on her jacket and slipped the fleece headband from her neck to her ears. While black made the main staple in her wardrobe, she made exceptions for running in dim light and went with red gloves, ear warmer and jacket. Sticking to solitude didn't mean she had a death wish.

Cold air stung her face as she opened the door. Adara pulled on her gloves and carefully descended the steps, testing for slippery spots. Snow glittered in the barely-there light, and leafless tree branches held an inch or so of white fluff. No one else occupied the sidewalk. Only psychos, idiots and the unhinged were out this early on a winter Saturday morning. Her type of crowd.

It took the typical half-hour to jog from her house to the park, enough to get the blood pumping hot and her rhythm in sync. The hush at dawn, when life was on the cusp of awakening, always held a hint of magic, as if she ran fast enough that she could slip into a different world. The snow crunched a steady beat beneath her shoes, and the air whipped her hair, fresh and crisp, a call to temporary freedom from her past, her pain, her thoughts. She picked up the pace, leaving everything behind except the blood roaring in her veins, the pounding of her feet and the burn in her legs.

If only everything could be left behind so easily.

Swerving into the parking lot leading to all the running trails, she didn't slow. The most difficult path called to her, but it was longer than the others and the gunmetal-gray clouds and dropping temperature promised more snow soon. Or worse — ice. Besides, she needed the extra time to figure out the budget this weekend, to come up with a solution and present it to Austin, give him time to study it for himself. Whatever the plan, she had to make it good and compelling enough to save her job.

She loved her job. Pre-Joey, she knew she'd been the fun teacher, the one kids liked and parents hoped their child got. Post-Joey, she'd shifted into strictness, and she didn't know if she could go back to before, but she had no idea what she'd do if she wasn't a teacher, how she'd start over somewhere else. Alone. Her breath clouded the air, a temporal phantom gone in a blink. She *had* to keep her job.

The terrain changed from pavement to soil, squishing beneath her shoes enough that she slowed. Color flashed in the trees ahead, around a bend in the path. *Dang.* Another early bird. She'd wanted the trails all to herself.

Each slushy step brought her closer to the other jogger. Broad shoulders, narrow hips, definitely a man, and he was struggling. He gasped in rhythm with his slow jog and his bright pink-and-orange beanie bounced on his head, slowly slipping. *Good for him, working to get in shape.*

The beanie slid another inch and fell to the ground, exposing the runner's hair, golden in the muted light, pulled back in a messy man-bun. He stopped and turned for his hat.

Garret.

You've got to be kidding. Whether she spun and ran the other direction or sprinted ahead, she couldn't avoid being noticed. He was less than ten yards away.

Garret stopped and braced his hands on his thighs, wheezing. At least he wasn't throwing up. He plucked his hat from the snow, a hat that looked a lot like the scraggly tea cozy Tatum had crocheted for her as a Christmas present.

Something unsettling sprouted behind her breastbone. He could have chosen any hat, and he went with a colorful monstrosity crocheted by his niece's inept third-grade fingers. She shook her head, kicking the thought out of her head and her heart. *Any decent uncle would do the same.*

His shoulders heaving, he stuffed the beanie back on his head and attempted to smile. It looked more like the grimace of someone about to toss his cookies. "Great morning" — he gulped in a quick breath — "for a run."

Sighing, she stopped beside him. "I'm not sure what you're doing could be called running. You look a little...doughy."

"Doughy?" He gasped, lifting his eyebrows. "Like that little baker boy" —huff—"made of dough"— puff—"who giggles when you poke him in the stomach?"

She poked his belly, and heat invaded her face. *What am I doing? Touching someone I hardly even know, let alone poking him like an undercooked pastry?*

To his credit, he tried to roll with it and giggle, but it came out more as a dying Wookie gurgle.

Adara wiped her brow to hide an almost-smile. His pallor might look doughy, but his stomach hadn't felt mushy. *At all.* She jogged ahead before she did anything else stupid. "Okay, then. Happy hobbling."

"I could use a running mentor," he called after her, "for inspiration." His voice grew more distant as she put space between them. "Or resuscitation!"

Since he couldn't see her, she surrendered to a smile. A small one. If he was well enough to joke, he'd make it without her and hopefully be gone by the time she made her second round.

The cold kept tempo with the heat building from her run, and the sky slowly darkened to a foreboding blue-black. Adara ran faster, pushing her legs and lungs with her luck. Her breath left lingering clouds in the air. The snow didn't worry her, but if the heavens decided to pelt ice, it would be slow and sketchy getting home on foot.

Three-quarters of the way through her second round, she found Garret, limping. She slouched. If a snowstorm struck and he froze to death because he couldn't shamble home in time, his death might weigh on her conscience. Then again, if he happened to have a granola bar on hand and shared it with her, it could totally count as fulfilling their dinner bet. Dinner was open to interpretation. Sometimes it was popcorn, when she remembered to eat.

She slowed to match his gimp. "Hurt your ankle?"

His smile erupted like sunshine from behind a cloud. "I knew you cared."

She snorted and adjusted her ear warmer, her blood thrumming hot and fast. Freezing to death wouldn't be a worry for at least a few more minutes. "You're overestimating your charm."

"Adara, you don't need to pretend, not with me. Simply admit you couldn't wait until our dinner date to bask in my presence." His dark eyes gleamed. "I'm not offended...truly."

She managed not to roll her eyes. "Do you have a granola bar handy?"

The sudden subject change must have thrown him off. His smile stumbled, and he patted his jacket, as if searching for a snack. "Sorry, no."

So much for her plan to avoid dinner with him. She slid her hands into her pockets and steadied her breath. "With your Igor shuffle going on, you'll probably finish the trail in an hour or so. I'm sure you'll make it before the storm hits." As if even the weather plotted against her, a dusting of snow chose that moment to drift from the sky. Leaving him to become an icicle was too unfeeling, even for her. She could at least make sure he made it out of the park. If he collapsed on the streets, someone was bound to find him sooner or later. "When I see Tatum on Monday, I'll ask her if you showed up. If not, I'll know where to send the search party."

"You'll see me before Monday. You're not getting out of our bet, Miss Dumont."

"We didn't set a particular day or time. Who's to say it can't happen a year from now? Or better still, ten years? If you had a granola bar, it could happen right now."

"You sly vixen." His expression was equal parts accusation and approval. "Were you trying to avoid our date?"

"It's not a date. It's a dinner so you can gloat over an extremely lucky win."

He laid a hand on his heart. "I do *not* gloat. I celebrate."

"Semantics. Why are you running so early this morning? Here, of all places?" Gia was so dead for divulging her running routine.

The fast subject change didn't seem to faze him. "This park borders my back yard, I was already up, and I've been neglecting exercise. I'm not ready to be chubby again."

She looked him up and down as they walked, unable to picture him other than tall, lean and strong.

"It's true," he continued, with no prodding from her. "Pudgy duckling to sexy swan." He ignored her exaggerated gag. "My life was violin, school and sleep. Violin practice before school, violin at school, private lessons after school, violin, violin, violin. Plus, I loved food." He shot her a grin. "I still love food."

Adara didn't want to know about his past, didn't want to spend extra time with him, didn't want to keep walking companionably beside him as if they were a couple out for their usual early morning run, because it felt that way. It felt like it would be so simple to fall into step with him and hold that rhythm for days, months, years. She picked up her pace. "So you grew out of your pudginess and your violin lessons paid off. End of story."

"Yes and no." He dropped his gaze to the path, frowning slightly. "I sometimes fantasized about quitting for something cool, like football or basketball, but my moment of clarity came when I asked the girl I liked to the eighth-grade dance. The biggest deal of middle school, right? She laughed at me and said she'd never go anywhere with a fat band geek."

"Bummer." Adara kept her voice toneless. She didn't care, but ouch. That was rough.

"Devastating." He didn't look particularly bothered by the memory. "I decided then I'd never let someone else marginalize me. I took stock of what I did and didn't like about myself, what I could change and what I wouldn't. Violin is an essential part of who I am, a fact I understood even then. I like my food, and that wasn't about to change. My extra padding, however, was a source of woe."

Adara hid another smile. Barely. "A source of woe?"

He nodded, solemn. "I started getting my chunky butt out of bed early and worked out before my morning violin practice. I cut back on the doughnuts, chips and candy and learned to like vegetables, which was harder than playing Bach, by the way. But I don't believe in surrender."

No matter his determination factor, when it came to pursuing her, he'd quit. She'd make sure of that. "Is that what made you long to be a pirate? To escape all those mean girls by sailing the seven seas and playing your violin while swabbing the deck? I can't believe you left your boots and silver rings behind on your run—and no gold tooth? Total fail."

He stared at her a moment then threw his head back and laughed, a rich, rolling sound that seemed to fill the park and expand into the sky.

For a second, her breath hitched, and no matter how much she wanted to, she couldn't turn away. He was joy personified, pure and unselfish, utterly captivating.

His laughter faded but his smile didn't. He straightened his hat and sighed. "Ah, you remind me what it's like to be back in the real world."

She forced her gaze away. "As opposed to Never Never Land?"

"Never Never Land's an accurate description of my last three years. Days blurred by until I couldn't remember the last time I'd personally seen my family. The last song I composed was before I went on tour." He looked down at his shoes, his eyes crinkling as his smile dimmed. "In the string of anonymous audiences and empty parties with emptier people, I had a moment of clarity. If I didn't get off the carousel, at least for a while, I'd burn out. I was fulfilling my dream but not really living." He lifted his head and met her gaze. "Sometimes, you have to step back from the crowd and focus on the individual. So I came home — and here I am."

That fluttering aberration in her heart stirred weakly again and she countered it with a cold stare into his dark eyes. *Is this the therapy session Gia wanted for me with Dr. Violinist? So not happening.* "Whatever Gia told you, I'm not anyone's project. I don't need to be fixed."

"I wouldn't fix you for anything," he said softly, all humor gone. "It's our brokenness that makes us who we are. Without the shattered pieces, our lights would never filter through to the rest of the world."

The fluttering in her chest rose, out of reach. She clenched her hands into fists, to anchor herself to the ground where she belonged, where it was safe.

"Which reminds me," he said, "what time is sunset?"

Weird change of subject, but if it veered away from broken things and life stories, she'd go with it. "I'm guessing five-forty-five-ish."

He nodded. "Will five-forty-five work?"

"For another run?" She glanced at her watch, pretending he wasn't talking about their evening food bet. She refused to call it a date. "Sure."

"You like being difficult, don't you?"

"Difficult keeps my personal space clear, the way I like it." She arched an eyebrow at his smirk. "Usually."

"Must take a lot of energy, keeping people out."

"Tons."

"You'd better stock up on the carbs, girl." He bumped her with his shoulder, sending her a step to the side. "You're going to need them."

Adara regained her balance and focused on the familiar fir trees lining the path, a sign the parking lot was near. *Thank God.* For reasons beyond her comprehension, Garret refused to be shut down. She liked other people fine, but connecting beyond casual was rare, and only Joey had dogged her into abandoning her solitude. With Garret, it felt like accidentally alighting on land after floating on the wind, and whatever that meant, she couldn't go back to being part of someone else. It hurt too much when the most important piece went missing.

The trees opened into the empty parking lot. The sky loomed low, clouds twisting in ominous forms shaped by the hand of a raking wind and the darkness shadowed the snow, stealing its brightness. It was time to get home, as fast as her feet could carry her — as far away from Garret Ambrose as possible.

"Come Monday, we'll be working together." His tone was all reason and logic. "We should get to know each other first."

"I know enough." She sloshed through the snow faster. She'd waited with him longer than necessary. He could get home on his own.

He gave her puppy-dog eyes, his limp seeming to improve. *Insufferable man.*

But getting it over with was better than giving him another reason to harass her. "Fine. Five-forty-five. Dinner. That's it."

"To be clear, five-forty-five p.m. *tonight*. Dinner. The beginning...." He used the same snap she had, with the exception of the last two words, which were soft and alluring.

She huffed, her breath clouding in the air. "And you say *I'm* difficult?"

"Persistent," he said smoothly, digging in his jacket pocket. "Completely different." He pulled out a pen and scrap of paper and scribbled something.

"You take pen and paper when you run?" Weirdo.

"Of course. When inspiration strikes, you have to be prepared." With nimble fingers, he folded the paper into a tiny origami boat and shoved it into her hand.

"I don't need your phone number."

"It's not my phone number." Even though she hardly knew him, she knew a devious smile when she saw one.

She unfolded the note. 'GAA' was embossed at the bottom in silver and small, neat numbers took up the center. Forty-seven. It didn't make any sense. "What's this?"

"Something for you to figure out." He moved ahead toward the sidewalk, looking smug. "I heard you like puzzles."

She clenched her teeth. She loathed puzzles with a passion, mainly because she sucked at them and was too proud to admit it. Somehow, some way Gia would get major payback for spilling unauthorized personal details. Good intentions meant nothing.

"Don't worry, Adara. If you get stuck, I'll give you a hint." He spun to face her, walking backward a few steps, long enough to wiggle his eyebrows. "Although, it might cost you."

Adara crinkled the number in her fist and shoved it in her pocket. She surged into a run and left him and his laughter behind. If only he'd challenged her to a race. Then she wouldn't be stuck with him tonight. She lifted her face to the ice chips falling from the dark sky. Then again, convincing him to set his sights elsewhere over dinner would be a more satisfying challenge.

And that was one challenge she wouldn't lose.

Chapter Seven

After a brain-numbing day of crunching numbers, Adara squinted in the bathroom mirror at her eyes, bloodshot from staring at scratched out equations, a price she'd pay again for the progress she'd made. It wasn't ideal, but she had a plan to save her job if the budget failed.

Now to get through dinner with Garret Ambrose — persistent violinist, gloater and slowest jogger *ever*.

She smirked at her reflection. She had a plan set in motion for that hurdle too. Her best 'go away' vibe — worn-out jeans and an old university sweatshirt, sass and snark. No man would last long, no matter how much he smiled and let stuff roll off him. She'd be home by eight and would never have to bother with him again, beyond the classroom. Three months and he'd be gone from there too.

Despite the lingering annoyance at the intervention attempt, Adara had forced herself to text Gia, to find out what information she'd leaked. As it turned out, not enough to hold a grudge. Joey's death was common knowledge, as was her occupation. Gia swore that the remainder of her discussion with Garret had revolved around him. He'd assured Gia his intentions were nothing but honorable.

Pshaw. He was friends with Ian. Enough said.

And when Gia had suggested again that jumping on Garret Ambrose would end her funk, she had quit the conversation with a final few sentences on preposterous theories, the joy of solitude and how to best prepare for silent treatment of an indeterminable length of time. Friends were overrated.

She scrunched her nose, practicing her disgusted look. *Perfection.* She had only a few more minutes to prepare for Operation Shutdown. Garret had, sadly, been provided a staff directory, and had, most vexingly, located her number and address. He'd texted her not long after their unfortunate meeting on her sacred running trails, which she was still trying to forget, and she'd agreed to let him pick her up. That way, she'd be forced to deal with him and set him straight. She had a feeling that was the only way Garret Ambrose would understand she wasn't relationship material—or even one-night material.

Leaning over the sink, she gazed at her reflection for a closer inspection, the first time she'd really studied herself in months. No wonder people whispered. The shadows beneath her eyes added five years to her twenty-five. Her pale skin could rival any vampire's and with her smooth black hair, she'd fit right into the Addams family. Lines that hadn't been there pre-Joey bracketed her mouth.

She twitched her lips into an almost-smile, softening those lines. Joey had always teased her about having a

Steve Tyler mouth, that it was the one thing that saved her face from being severe. An ache ricocheted in her heart. He probably wouldn't say that now. She ran a comb through her already-perfect hair one last time. Making a public appearance in purposely shabby clothes wasn't a problem. Her hair was a different story.

Beethoven's *Fifth* gonged, vibrating through the walls, impossible to miss. One of Joey's first implementations after they'd bought the house was to personalize the boring doorbell. Garret was here. *Showtime.*

She clicked off the bathroom light and strolled into the blank hallway, her boot heels a sharp, sure echo in the silence. Tonight, she'd sever this strange and unwanted connection between them. Whatever intentions he had, she'd kill them. She grabbed her coat off the hook in the foyer and shoved it on. A quick pat of her pockets confirmed keys and phone were still there. Choking back a sigh, she opened the door.

Garret stood on the porch, his hands in his jean pockets, his shoulders hunched. His smile was almost shy. He wasn't dressed like she'd expected, not the smooth presentation of a guy bent on charming a reluctant date. His jeans were grungier than hers. He'd hidden his too-long hair beneath a slouchy black beanie. He wore an obscure graphic T over a thermal long-sleeved shirt, and if he'd brought a coat, he must've left it in his — she blinked — vehicular *beast*.

Black. Sleek. The kind of automobile that screamed too much money. *So that's why he doesn't feel the need to dress up.* He let his wheels do all the work, a mistake on his part. Material possessions didn't impress her.

"You have snow tires on that thing?" She shook her head and buttoned her coat, sealing out the chill. "I'm not sure I trust your driving skills, unless you drive like you run."

"The tires are fine, jokester." He straightened. "And I've yet to get a traffic citation or be in an accident, not even a fender-bender."

"Easy to say when you've been driven around by a tour bus and limousines for three years."

"Doesn't change the facts." He offered his arm. "Ready?"

"Not even." She ignored his arm and plodded down the stairs, inhaling a long breath of icy air. "Let's get this over with."

Garret smirked at Adara's slender back as she headed for his Maserati, two steps ahead of him, as if determined to leave him in the dust. No matter what she said or did, her back-off attitude was a ruse. Any idiot who took two seconds to truly look at her could see that. She was waiting to be found, not left behind.

His heart made an odd jump-squeeze. The jump correlated to an evening alone with Adara. The squeeze was for everything locked beneath her surface, clawing to get out. Pushing her in that area would get nowhere, which was okay. Sometimes inspiration took sudden intervals, broken sparks, long minutes to connect the dots and take flight, and while he intended to be the trigger, she controlled the absorption and reaction. He checked his watch. The timer clicked away, starting exactly at sunset.

He broke into a trot and beat her to the car door, thankfully without slipping on the snow crusting the sidewalk. Making a fool of himself wasn't how he hoped to inspire his date. And no matter how much she protested, bet or no, this *was* a date. *Our first.*

"I can handle my own door." She kicked a snow tuft at him as he hit the lock button and opened the door for her.

"Of course you can." He performed his best standing ovation bow. "Allow me the indulgence of pretending to be a gentleman."

Hand on the door frame, she paused and met his gaze. "This isn't a date."

The challenging flash in her eyes reignited his smile. "Standing around in the cold doesn't count toward your obligation, Adara."

Her mouth tightened, but she settled into the passenger seat and jerked the door out of his hands, slamming it shut. The entire car rattled.

Garret pressed his lips together to keep a laugh inside. She was in rare form tonight, which meant he was getting to her. It was only a matter of minutes before she cracked and let him in.

He slid into the driver seat and shut out the winter bite. Adara stared straight ahead through the windshield, her hands fisted on her thighs.

"Why are you so tense?" He added a tease to his tone. "I thought you said this wasn't a date, and Tatum made me promise to be nice to her favorite teacher. Nothing to worry about."

"I'm not worried." She relaxed her fingers and slouched in the seat, squeaking against the leather. He wasn't sure she meant to look at him, but she angled her face his way. "Tatum said I was her favorite teacher?"

"Among other things." With a turn of the key, the motor purred to life, and he pulled away from the curb.

"Among other things?" She looked straight at him, her brow wrinkled. "What's that supposed to mean?"

He shrugged, the gesture far more casual than the words he considered. The night had barely begun and he didn't want to start out with the heavy stuff, yet he doubted Adara would ever bring it up. Better to take the opening than miss it altogether. "She told me you were her teacher last year too, that when the principal bumped you up to third grade, you asked her to be a student guide."

"Which I regret at times." The words were softened by the affection in her tone. "She's supposed to be an example to my more challenging students, not their ringleader."

"She also said you were a lot more fun last year."

Her throat worked and she refocused out the windshield.

Garret loosened his grip on the steering wheel. Adara hadn't wigged out at the implication that she was a different person since her brother's death, a promising sign. *Baby steps.* He softened the impact by returning the blame to Tatum. "I think she's tired of getting in trouble."

"There are consequences for going into drama-queen mode."

"Odd. I've never seen her do drama queen." He smiled at her incredulous look. "At least not more than four times a day."

"I wouldn't expect my star student to neglect tormenting people outside the classroom too." She laid her head back. "She's too smart for her own good, and she either has a natural ability to manipulate people or someone with uncanny expertise taught her." Her narrowed gaze aimed at him, accusing.

"Not me." He laid a hand on his heart. "My influence is nothing but good, pure and kind. She also mentioned the Peppermint Patties you keep in your bottom drawer."

Her mouth opened. "The little stinker. I keep that drawer locked."

"She's a natural Ambrose. Locks don't keep us out long, no matter the type." He didn't bother telling her that the deadbolt she kept on her heart wouldn't keep him out. She'd discover that soon enough.

"Where are you taking me?" She peered out the window into the darkness. The streetlamps had dwindled until only the headlights broke the night. "I'm happy to stuff my face and fulfill this obligation with a corn dog from the convenience store we passed a mile ago."

"You'd regret that corn dog on your morning run." He nodded, happy to share wisdom gained through personal experience. "Trust me on that one."

Her lips twitched into the tiniest of smirks.

Maybe the expression was meant as condescending or malicious, but he took it as an encouragement. Anything even close to a smile from her he'd hold close to his heart. "I won the bet, so the location is my choice."

She rolled her eyes but the tenseness didn't return.

A few minutes longer brought them to their destination, and Garret parked in the first row of the science center lot, close to the front door.

As the motor settled into silence, Adara leaned forward, nearly pressing her face to the glass. "I'm pretty sure the science center café is closed for the night. Good. We can go back for the corn dog."

He jangled a key and wriggled his eyebrows. "Everything's closed, except to us."

She actually looked impressed. "You stole the key to university property? Learning things from Tatum?"

"Not stole...manipulated. Big difference." He got out of the car and hurried for her door, too slow. His leg muscles still burned from his frozen hell morning jog attempt. She'd already closed the door and leaned a hip on the car by the time he reached her, her gaze on the dark science center. Without the stir of students or faculty, the place held an eerie graveyard quiet.

"If you're a serial murderer hiding behind a musician's mask who bets women at carnival games hoping to win so you can drag them to deserted science centers at night for the perfect kill spot, just be honest and say so."

"An honest murderer? Sounds legit." He gestured for her to follow him on the cement path leading around the back, shoveled mostly clear of snow.

After a marked hesitation, she did, her steps a ballad tempo behind him.

The pinch in his shoulders eased. He'd hate to have to drag her with him and corroborate her theory. "What if I'm a musician who simply commits petty crimes?"

"Like harassment?" Her eyes sparked, undercutting her serious expression.

"More like jaywalking, speeding and the occasional skinny dipping." While he'd crossed a few lines simply to get her here, he hadn't earned stalker-harassment status. Stalking nudged the edge of selfish obsession, a place he'd never go. But if Adara decided to stalk him, he'd be a willing victim.

"Skinny dipping?" She glanced at him, long enough to give the impression she was picturing him in the water. Naked.

Good.

"You haven't truly lived until you've iced your testicles in Lake Lucerne in the spring." He shuddered. "That was one bet I lost."

"Aw, dang. Guess I'll never truly live." Her lovely mouth, a mouth he hadn't stopped thinking about, twisted. "Since I don't have testicles."

"Hilarious."

They stopped at the solid metal door leading into the planetarium. Garret hit the alarm code, waited for the beep and unlocked the door with the key he'd traded for a future violin performance. It had taken more friendly negotiation than manipulation with the director—the bond between fellow middle school band geeks was eternal—but Adara didn't need to know that. Besides, he would've stooped to manipulation, if necessary. He didn't mind bending a few minor moral codes for a good cause.

He waved her inside, waiting until she'd passed before sliding in behind her. The door snicked shut, swallowing them in utter darkness.

"I should've asked your MO." Her husky voice threaded through the black. "Do you use a knife, gun or ax? Should I expect a torture session with body parts cut off every minute?" The snap of fingers followed. "That's why you gave me that note with a number on it, isn't it? That's how many times you're going to stab me."

Blind, he eased toward her voice, and his arm brushed against her solid warmth. He hadn't realized she was so close but he wasn't about to move away. He leaned down where he thought her ear might be. Her smooth hair tickled his chin. "Tatum's right," he murmured. "You have a sick mind, Adara. Truly morbid. But if you must know, I prefer a nail file. I whittle my victims down, slowly and relentlessly, until they beg for surrender."

She huffed, a noise dangerously close to a laugh. "Tatum told you I have a sick mind?"

"When threatened with death by nail file, that's what you want to know?" He surrendered to the urge to graze her hair, a brief touch. Maybe she'd pretend not to notice in the dark or dismiss it as nothing more than him bumping into her. It was silk, soft and sleek against his fingertips. Tingles pulsed down his spine, a heady rush. He wished he could feel her hair on his mouth too.

"It takes a sick mind to know one." Her voice lowered, velvet in the void, speeding up the electricity pumping in his veins. "I'm beginning to think it runs in the Ambrose bloodline."

"Huh. And all this time I thought I was a prodigy, not a mad genius."

"Wow. Full of yourself much?"

"Honest. There's a difference." He flicked on the light switch.

The planetarium had been set up exactly as he'd instructed. Glowing lamps circled the entire dome floor, just enough light to see what lay ahead. A small table was set up in the center of the auditorium, its vanilla-scented candles a delicate tinge in the air, but Adara didn't even seem to notice those details. Her gaze immediately lifted, and her gasp of wonder made every second of prep time worthwhile. If he hadn't known what to expect, he would've gasped too. The heavens spread above them, a clear night sky showcasing uncountable stars, swirling clouds tinged in pink and purple, accented by a midnight backdrop. It was space brought to Earth, just for her. In that second, all her masks fell away, leaving only a girl awestruck by nature, the shadows of her grief forgotten.

His chest tightened, the planetarium's wonders gone beneath the marvel of Adara. *Ben-zonna*, he wanted to see her like this all the time—happy, entranced and free. Pity she wouldn't let him use his music to put that same expression on her face. *Someday.* Someday, wonder would be only one of the expressions he'd inspire in her. The setting would have been pure magic with music, but he didn't want to test Adara in that area yet. For her, he'd nixed the *Star Wars* soundtrack the director had suggested and settled for silence. As it was, not too shabby.

"I don't want to know what you did to pull this off." She still faced the stars, all lines in her face gone. "It's almost worth losing the Potty Toss."

He grinned. "Almost?"

"I confess," she whispered. "Totally worth it."

His body tightened in uncomfortable places. He'd trade his violin to hear her talk about him in that sexy, breathless voice. "There's food too." He itched to hold her hand, make some type of physical contact. Instead, he stuffed his hands in his pockets. "Better than stale, cold corn dogs."

"With this for scenery, I don't care if it's haggis and rocky mountain oysters." Her voice was still low, awed.

"That's just wrong." Maybe he should've saved the stars for later, when she seemed antsy to go, something to lure her to stay. As it was, he wasn't sure how he'd redirect her attention to him. "Let's eat. You can watch the stars all night, if that's what you want."

"I want." She used that same, breathy voice.

He squirmed as imagination took him to another place, where she said that about him, in that voice. He wanted too, and the stars weren't part of it. Although, they could be. Further down the relationship road, a night in the planetarium alone with Adara would be astronomical — the stars overhead, her in his arms, skin on skin. He scratched his jaw. Since Adara had yet to look at him again, he had some work ahead before making that happen.

Gently, he guided her forward with a hand on the small of her back. His splayed fingers encompassed its entirety. She needed more food and less running. He caught her elbow as she stumbled into one of the stargazing recliners scattered around the auditorium. "The stars aren't going anywhere, Adara. If you trip and get hurt, I'll have to take you to the hospital. Then it'll be no stars and only me for a lot longer than dinner."

"Good point. That would be terrible." The fact her voice was still velvet and breathy softened any intended insult. She circumnavigated the couch, breaking from his light contact.

Reaching the table, she suddenly spun and faced him. Only inches away, her scent skated along his senses, sweet and tropical. *Maybe coconut.* "Why are you doing this? I'm not interested in a relationship, and if I were going to date, I'd never choose a musician." She pointed an elegant finger in the air, as if a brilliant idea just came to mind. "You should ask Gia out. You'd be perfect together. She's into musicians."

"Gia's not my type." While Gia might have been attracted to musicians, he suspected her preferences had shifted to suits, ties and courtrooms, not that he planned to bring up that particular topic. He wanted to focus on Adara, not the Ian and Gia plane crash on the horizon. "You don't have to be afraid of me, and running away from your fears won't fix them. Trust me, I know. Most people don't realize I used to get stage fright. My hands used to shake so badly I could barely hold the violin, let alone play, until my teacher, a ninety-year-old Jewish lady who could barely speak English, gave me this tip." Dropping his voice, he leaned in closer. "Name your fear. Own it, and it won't own you." He winked. "*Yutzi.*"

Her eyes sparkled and her mouth twitched. "Idiot. Your teacher knew what she was talking about. You, on the other hand, don't have a clue. Me afraid of you?" She lifted her chin. "I don't think so."

"No?" He slid nearer, forcing her to tip her chin to hold his gaze. "Then let me play violin for you."

"I don't really like music." She said it too casually to be believed.

He arched an eyebrow. "Everyone likes music of some type. It fills the whole world in one form or another. Birds, the wind in the trees, the sea against the shore, insects, rain... It's everywhere, inescapable. Trying to avoid it is like trying to stop your heart from beating. It's part of you, even when you deny it."

"Have you heard a rooster crow at one in the morning?" She flicked her fingers, dismissive, impatient. "I wouldn't call that music."

"The hens might disagree." He rubbed his bottom lip, his pulse quickening. He was losing her. Food wouldn't tempt her, and not even the stars would hold her here if he made the wrong move. "What if I promise to play only songs that hold no personal meaning? What if we create new emotional ties, you, music and me?" He snapped his fingers. "*Name That Tune.*"

She looked at him as if he'd lost his mind. "What?"

"I'm challenging you to a match of *Name That Tune*. If you can name the twenty-five songs I play on my violin by the end of the chorus, I'll take you home, bet fulfilled. Three strikes and you're out. The faster you name them, the less you have to endure."

"You brought your violin?" Her voice trembled on the last word, only enough that someone paying attention would notice.

He nodded, ready to chase her if she ran.

"Confident of you." The tense set of her shoulders didn't ease.

"Hopeful." Garret casually stuck his hands in his back pockets. "Big difference."

After a moment, her eyes flared in challenge and he relaxed. Such a contradiction, Adara. If solitude was her ultimate goal, she wouldn't have risked it by taking the carnival bet in the first place. She wouldn't have accompanied him as he gimped along the running trail. She wouldn't have answered when he'd rung the doorbell tonight.

It seemed challenges eclipsed solitude in Adara Dumont's playlist.

"Counter-offer." She fiddled with her coat buttons and narrowed her gaze. "Ten songs, but they must have been released to the public and played on the radio at some point or another, no songs composed by you or some other obsolete artist. They must have words…no classical."

"Obsolete artist? You wound me." He hid his triumphant smile behind a calm mask. For at least tonight, she was his. She just didn't know it yet—and he wasn't going to ruin it by telling her—but there was no possible way she knew more music than he did. "I'm big in Belgium—Google me if you dare—and I agree to your terms, but ten is too few. Twenty."

"Eleven."

He folded his arms. "I went down five, and you add one? What kind of bargainer are you?"

"The not-desperate kind."

"Determined isn't the same as desperate. Nineteen."

She rolled her eyes. "Fine. Fifteen."

Fifteen, twenty, the number didn't really matter. This was a bet he couldn't lose. Garret dropped his chin and slowly grinned. "Done."

Her smile was wide, beautiful and just a little on the sly side, as if she were the one suckering him. Heat unfolded in his chest, filling every corner. Even if he'd made a mistake with this wager, he couldn't regret it. She'd smiled, and for now, that was all that mattered.

Chapter Eight

Perched on the edge of one round stargazing couch, Adara chewed the last bite of delectable roasted chicken, savoring every second. The food alone was almost worth wasting her night. She couldn't even remember the last time she'd eaten real food. As Garret tuned his violin from the cushion opposite hers, she kept her expression blank. He wore a small, confident smile. Clearly, he thought he'd crush her in the *Name That Tune* competition because he was a musician.

She sipped raspberry-flavored sparkling water — her favorite, another small Gia betrayal — to hide a smirk. Music might not be her passion but it had been Joey's. *So yeah...* Ambrose the aspiring pirate was about to get demolished and he had no idea. The anticipation was exhilarating.

"There have to be contest parameters." She set her glass on the floor, swiped the last baby carrot from her plate and pointed it at him. "Tunes spanning centuries are too broad." She chomped the carrot in half and hoped her crunching annoyed him.

The strings plinked cheerfully beneath his long fingers at his experimental strum, and he looked up from his instrument. "For you, I'll take a handicap." Starlight sparked silver in his dark eyes. "Your proposal?"

She wrinkled her nose at him. "We already established no classical and no *Phantom of the Opera*. Eighties and nineties only."

"An unduly harsh and narrow musical window." His smile faltered before snapping back into place. "Done. No whining when you lose." Garret picked up the bow on the seat beside him. "And no questioning my honor with accusations of cheating."

"Stop stalling. I have an appointment with a crossword puzzle at eight."

"Cancel it." He tucked the violin beneath his chin. "This night's just beginning." *Cocky man.* Setting the bow to strings, he wriggled his eyebrows. "Your music memory pop quiz begins now, Miss Dumont."

Adara crossed her legs and clasped her hands primly over her knee. She was the pop quiz queen. A long, high note flowed from the violin and rose to the celestial sky. Even without the help of a full band or beat, she wasn't worried—

Her heart throbbed once, hard and awful.

With or Without You, she croaked, thanks to her tight throat. The bow immediately stopped and she blew out a silent breath. Joey had held an undying affection for U2. She should've added the band to the no-play list.

"One point for you." Whether he sympathized with her or hoped to take advantage of her weakness, he didn't give her recovery time. A slower song spilled from the instrument, lilting and undeniably Irish.

Red Is the Rose. She subtly wiped her clammy palms on her jeans and launched into her hard-core teacher tone. "No more Celtic."

He lowered the violin, his eyebrows tented. "You can't just change the rules along the way."

"No Celtic," she repeated, her jaw tight. She wasn't sure she could take another unwitting hit from Garret. He seemed to have a knack for choosing Joey's favorite songs.

Studying her with his soul-searching look, he tilted his head. "For an X in your column, I'll agree."

"Done." She relaxed slightly. It was a fair trade. No way, no how did she want to review all the Irish songs Joey loved, reminding her of the trip to Ireland they'd planned before he'd gotten sick.

Garret grinned, as if it were a win on his part, and slipped his instrument back into place. He sawed out a slow, country tune, one she let him play all the way through the chorus. There was nothing better than a false sense of hope to break an opponent's confidence, and he so needed to be brought down a peg or two.

He finished and pointed the bow at her, his dimple on display. "*Name That Tune*, if you can."

She tapped her chin and gazed up at the ceiling of stars, drawing it out. The hardest part was controlling her smirk.

"Three second warning." Anticipation laced his voice, as if he couldn't wait to celebrate...aka gloat.

"Country isn't my thing." She toyed with her sweatshirt's fraying hem, going for meek. "Wild guess. *Misguided Angel?*"

He dropped his chin and his smile. His eyes narrowed. "Are you playing me?"

She huffed, but her mouth betrayed her, twitching.

"Challenge heartily accepted, Miss Dumont." Intensity shadowed his features, the same intensity he'd used to win at the carnival. He set his jaw and replaced the violin on his shoulder, his fiery gaze never leaving hers.

A delicious thrill slid through her and gathered low in her belly, warm and tingling. She chalked it up to annoyance — definitely not desire or any of its counterparts — but maybe duping him had been a mistake. Garret, looking at her as if she was the prize he'd do anything to win, almost made her forget tonight's goal. Adara straightened and clenched her hands together, focusing. She had to finish this, finish with him.

After a quick-fire round of mixed genres, from hard rock to indie to pop, Adara leaned back on her hands, enjoying the starry universe above and the fine flavor of victory. "No shame in concession, violin boy. I'll only remind you Monday through Friday."

"That word isn't in my vocabulary." Steel lay at the core of his voice. No man liked to lose, and some people didn't know when to yield.

"What? Shame?" She bared her teeth.

"Name this one." Bittersweet notes spun a fanciful tune to match the stars. Garret slowly circled her couch, his expression relaxing with each slide of the bow. His shoulder blades subtly shifted beneath his shirt layers as he played, and she had the unnerving urge to touch his broad back, to feel him move beneath her fingers. He was so easy to watch, so mesmerizing, that she didn't stop him right away. *But please.* Every grade-school teacher knew her animated movie theme songs. The last note rippled across the darkness and faded into silence. He looked at her expectantly, wearing a hopeful expression.

She almost felt sorry for him. *Beauty and the Beast.*

Instead of frowning, he went into a slow, sensual bass rhythm, watching her the whole time. Seductive, the music crept into her blood, heating every molecule along the way, reminding her how long it had been since she'd even thought about being touched. Kissed. Held. She crossed her legs and pretended to be bored, pretended she wasn't tempted to take the violin's place in Garret's hands and let him play her instead. She was the first to break eye contact.

This was *not* a date.

By chorus' end, she still didn't know the song. But she kind of wanted to, a secret she'd never reveal. He dropped his chin, waiting for her answer.

Ignoring the dancing prickles in her bloodstream, she shook her head.

His smile was brighter than the moon hanging in the amphitheater sky behind him. "Not a Dave Matthews Band fan?"

"Obviously. And you can't play more of their songs to win." Later tonight, though, she'd familiarize herself with that particular song — another thing he didn't need to know.

"I don't have to rely on Dave to prevail." He propped the violin on his cocked hip and scratched his stubbly jaw with the bow, his tone arrogant. "You only have one strike left."

"And you only have four songs left."

"No problem." He went into a quick, bright tune, one any skilled violinist or fiddler knew, not to mention the general masses.

"Please." She rolled her eyes. "*Devil Went Down to Georgia*, and I didn't sign up for a hoedown."

His smile widened. Still playing, he jumped into a weird step and hop that might be considered some version of dance, if chickens pirouetted free-form—most definitely a move that could cause public panic.

When he reached the devil's portion of the song, she flung herself back on the couch and gazed at the stars, mostly so she'd stop being tempted to smile. Joey had hated country, and she'd taken every opportunity possible to sing with a hayseed twang. Annoying her brother was a sisterly duty, one she took very seriously.

Garret blended songs without pausing, exactly as he had at the party, sliding seamlessly from country to slow and sweet. Wearing that dreamy smile, he gave up his dancing and sat beside her, as if to make sure she knew he played this song for her. It didn't help that his citrus and honey cologne invaded her space, making it impossible to disregard him. *Dang.* She couldn't deny he was smooth with the violin—but not smooth enough to distract her from the game.

Still flat on her back, she arched an eyebrow until he finished. "*World Stand Still*, and that costs you a song because it's from the twenty-first century."

"Worth it." Too fast and unexpected for her to move, he brushed a callused fingertip down her cheek and slid out of reach.

The line where his finger had been remained defiantly warm. With the stars spread over her, the soothing darkness close and the way Garret comfortably hooked her in his space, her need to win dulled beneath a strange tug in her chest. She couldn't remember the last time she'd felt normal with someone else.

"Crunch time, Ambrose." The words came out more of a whisper than she'd planned.

He sucked in a breath and released it, assuming his serious, refuse-to-lose look. Without a word, his burning gaze still on her, he played his last song.

Notes washed over her and her heart flipped with the beat keeping time in her head. *I Knew I Loved You.* Without warning, a rush of longing broke free, so sharp and poignant that she went utterly still. She'd forgotten the song, forgotten how once upon a time she'd dreamed of finding the one person created precisely for her, the sort of love that was inexorable. Irresistible. Deep and destined. The dream, she could handle. It was the pain in reality that sucked.

The violin lapsed into an aching quiet. Garret sank onto the couch across from hers and gently laid his instrument across his knees. Absently toying with a hole in his jeans, he studied her with dark, liquid eyes, his usual smile absent.

If she named the tune, he'd stay true to his word and take her home, back to her safe haven. She didn't doubt that for a second. Yet returning to a crossword puzzle, ghosts and silence had lost its appeal somewhere between the stars and the unfailing dare in Garret's every move. She wanted to stay. Staying didn't mean anything. Even introverted monks wanted company once in a while. Tomorrow, she could return to life as usual, no damage done.

She shook her head, and lied. "Don't know it."

"Shame." The in-your-face victory dance she expected didn't come. Instead, he placed the violin back in its case and switched seats to sit beside her, close enough that their knees touched. "Perhaps you should expand your music selection to Top Forty. *I Knew I Loved You*. Popular song."

He knew, knew she'd fibbed. Her face heated. She couldn't go back and admit she'd lied, but she had to do something. No way would she confess she'd lost just to stay in his magic a few minutes longer. That would ruin everything. "Are you sure that song's in the correct timeframe?" She pulled out her phone before he could object. "I'm checking."

He sat still and mute while she researched, his gaze on her never wavering.

"It hit number one in January, 2000." Sure, the release was in late 1999, but maybe he wouldn't know. "2000, Ambrose."

He rubbed his bottom lip, his dark eyes probing. "If you want to get technical, we'll have to agree to a tie."

A tie. She could roll with that. She sighed to throw him off. "I guess."

"Sometimes a tie is as good as a win," he said in a low, serious voice and lifted his attention to the stars.

Fully processing his meaning wasn't something she cared to do. His abnormal quietness chafed her nerves. The auditorium darkness felt too vast, too aware. The void needed to be filled. She guessed she had to dust off her rusty conversation skills. She cleared her throat. "Musicians hardly have trouble finding willing company. Middle school band geeks excluded, of course. Why harass me instead?"

He laughed softly, his focus still on the sky. "I came home to recharge, to find my inspiration in the more personal connection of smaller venues. I'd missed that in the last three years."

That was so not an answer to her question, but she let it slide since she'd only asked the question to get him talking again.

"I love music because it inspires," he continued, as if sensing her discomfort. "It evokes emotion, unites people, creates memories. I needed mine to be revived." His voice dropped to a murmur. "You're doing that for me."

Adara blinked. No way had she heard him right. The most her safe, silent world could ever awaken was a yawn. But his expression was serene, matter-of-fact. "Are you messing with me?"

"By no means."

"That makes zero sense." Unless…Gia must've told him something else, more than what she'd confessed. She twisted to face him. "What, exactly, did Gia tell you about me?"

He kept his focus on the stars, but his mouth ticked into a small smile. "Not much. I didn't want to learn about you secondhand." At last, he met her gaze. "I want to discover you myself."

"So let me get this straight. You find a reserved, anti-music third-grade teacher who will only go out with you by losing a bet inspiring?"

He shifted, his knee bumping hers. "What I find inspiring is a woman who uses her pain as a shield and yet, despite her best efforts, can't keep her light hidden behind all her cracked pieces."

Her breath bottled up. Was he some sort of violinist guru who could see inside souls, read the truth in people's eyes? She had to break free of him before he searched deeper, learned more and she split completely, letting him in. Letting in more pain. "That woman is petitioning the school board to cut the music program if the budget fails."

His eyebrows shot up and his smile vanished. "Cut the music program?"

"It's either that or lose a teaching position." She refused to tell him it was *her* job in particular or that she also planned to propose a hefty personal pay cut to make up any difference left after the music ended. Sympathy wasn't what she was looking for. "Only the fourth- and fifth-graders participate in the music program anyway, taught by the high school band teacher two cities away. He'll still have a job. Besides, music is a luxury. People can get by without it, unlike reading and writing."

"*I* can't get by without it." He studied her as if truly seeing her for the first time, brokenness and all.

Her strike had finally hit home. It was what she'd aimed for. She hadn't expected the success to cause the emptiness in her heart to throb.

"Adara, music is a memory book of life, written with emotions words can't hope to relay." He stood and paced, ripping off his beanie and wringing it. Metallic sparks from the fabricated starlight gleamed in his golden hair, a welcome distraction. She'd always thought guys with long hair looked scraggly. Somehow, Garret made a man-bun sexy.

"It's communication of the soul." He circled around, his rant increasing in volume and strength, his boots a quick cadence with his voice. "Timeless, priceless, a bond connecting people to each other in an incomparable way." Each word he uttered was punctuated with passion, joined by sharp hand gestures in the air. "Cutting music is like chopping off a finger or carving out half the heart."

"I see where Tatum gets her drama tendency." She forced her tone to be calm, hiding the fast tempo of her heart. *What is wrong with me?* Crushing his interest had to happen. She clasped her hands together to keep them steady. "If kids really want to learn music, they'll find a way."

He spun on his heel and faced her. "Would you steal that opportunity from your brother, knowing the joy it gave him?"

No, I wouldn't. "Moot point. Joey isn't here."

"So no one else matters?"

She ground her teeth.

He crossed the distance he'd put between them and sat beside her, bracing his forearms on his thighs. "I don't believe you think that. I don't believe you'd want to deprive anyone of happiness or deny someone their life purpose."

She refused the powerful urge to look away, to surrender any ground. "You don't know me very well."

"I know enough."

"Look… I understand most people like music more than math." She had to say something or start squirming beneath his scrutiny. "Joey sucked at school."

"With the exception of music?" Darkness glittered in his eyes, a challenge to deny it.

"My point is he could've functioned in society without learning music."

"Functioning isn't the same as living, Adara." His tone was deliberate, as if he saw right through her façade and wanted her to know it.

"Can you truly live without functioning first?" She folded her arms and crossed her legs. *Suck on that bit of rationale, musician.*

His mouth turned down in a considering expression then softened into reluctant humor. "I suppose that might be difficult."

"We can't all be lucky enough to spend our days on arts-and-crafts time."

"You're right. I'm fortunate that my passion pays for groceries."

"And swanky cars."

"My violin cost more than the car, Miss Dumont." He squared his shoulders, his eyes hooded. "It's not a crime to possess a luxury."

"Never said it was. Guilty conscience?"

He grinned, and just like that, the tension vanished. "Very well, in case the music program is indeed cut, I'll make my time with the kids count. I'll pack the most I can into our hours together and make the recital something they'll never forget." A dozen new ideas sparkled in his eyes. "It'll be a grade-school musical masterpiece."

Adara planted her palms on the couch, suddenly lightheaded. The weapons in her arsenal seemed only to scratch. It was a battle utterly lost. He refused to let her drive him away. She'd intended to destroy pieces of his passion, and he instead found a way to twist it into something positive. This was bad. Forced to fight his smile every day would wind up with casualties...hers.

He bumped her shoulder with his, and while it was a friendly gesture, not romantic, it sent warmth skidding through her. "Are you running tomorrow?"

"Probably." *Blast.* The subject change and disturbance combo threw her off, enough she answered before thinking it through.

"Good. I'll go with you. It'll be a trade-off for getting ice cream tonight, the consequences of our tie. We can go look at some real stars." He held out a hand to her. "You in?"

She hesitated. Slipping her fingers into his would be a huge mistake, give him the wrong idea and reveal that he'd won. Instead, she held out her fist and waited until he bumped her knuckles with his. "Just this once."

Chapter Nine

Garret locked the science center door and reset the alarm. So he'd got an Adara fist bump instead of the privilege of holding her hand. The fact that she'd offered any contact at all was a victory.

Stuffing the keys into his pocket, he pivoted toward the parking lot and paused. Adara strolled along the sidewalk, her face tipped to the sky, already on her stargazing mission without him. The snow-crusted lawn on either side glittered in the glow from the streetlight near his car, a winter wonderland created to contrast the night, to highlight Adara's ethereal beauty. She could hide beneath old jeans and ratty sweatshirts all she wanted. Nothing could diminish her, not even the cage she kept securely sealed around herself.

His chest ached — a quick, hard spasm. She'd heard *I Knew I Loved You* before — the light in her eyes had revealed that much — yet she'd denied it, denied her win, given up her chance to go home. He wasn't sure why, and he certainly wasn't going to press her.

Whatever the reason, he'd make the most of their time together.

On a whim, he crouched and gathered a handful of snow, carefully packing it, watching Adara to make sure she didn't turn around and see what he was up to. He stood and lobbed the snowball at her. It smacked her in the butt instead of between her shoulder blades. His aim needed some work. He winced as she spun, her glare on high.

"Practicing at fitting in with the third-graders, Ambrose?" Adara swiped at her jeans, dislodging snow and ice. She leaned over and scraped snow into her hand. "I have no qualms with putting temporary music mentors in a time-out."

He didn't bother trying to shut down his smile. "Do you have a naughty chair, Miss Dumont? I might make a point to misbehave if I get to sit there with you —"

Adara's missile exploded in his face, shooting white into his mouth and eyes. Her aim needed no practice. *None. Guh.* Was there a rock mixed with the snow? He shook his head, wiped the wet from his eyes, and met her gaze. "Challenge accepted."

"That was a reprisal, not a dare." She stared him down as he bent to arm himself. "Don't go there, violin boy."

"Or what?" He scooped more snow and wriggled his eyebrows. "Afraid you'll lose yet again?"

Her full, lovely mouth thinned, exactly the same way it had a second before she'd accepted his carnival game challenge. She was so easy to read, and if all it took to stay in her life was presenting her with an endless line of contests? *Done.*

In the next breath, she had another fistful of snow and fired it at his head. He ducked and the ice bomb hissed by his ear, barely missing. Once Adara started playing, she went for the kill, but the fire in her eyes was worth any potential pain. And he planned to entice her to play often.

Since she was paying attention, he flung his next snowball with more force. It hit her square in the chest—a fine, wet splatter right down the neck of her sweatshirt.

She stiffened and gasped. "You're *so* dead." Her gray eyes flashed like storm clouds, and she grabbed a fistful of snow, ice and rocks. Drawing her arm back, readying to destroy him, her boot slipped. She landed flat on her back with an *oof*...and didn't move.

"Adara!" Garret rushed to where she sprawled on the sidewalk, staring up at the sky as if she'd merely resumed her stargazing. He dropped to his knees beside her, not caring that snow seeped into his jeans, cold and wet. "Talk to me. Are you okay?"

She shook her head, the movement so small, so weak, that his heart squeezed. He was entirely to blame. If he'd just walked her to the car instead of goofing off, she wouldn't be hurt. "I'm so sorry—"

Grabbing his shirt, she jerked him down and shoved what she'd hidden in her other hand down his collar. While he wheezed, she ground the snow against his chest with the heel of her hand, her grip on his shirt unrelenting.

"There." She released him and sat up. "I feel one hundred percent better now."

He leaped up and shook the loose snow from his shirt, an icy rivulet or two trailing his stomach, into his jeans. "Vicious woman."

"Don't forget it." Adara tried to stand then sat back down, wincing. The wince almost immediately morphed into an accusing glare. "My ankle is messed up."

"Um, yeah." Garret shook his head. "Not falling for that one again."

"I'm not screwing around, Ambrose." She shoved up one pant leg, not that it revealed anything but her boot. "I twisted my ankle."

He inched closer, keeping an eye on her hands and any hidden fistfuls of snow, but she truly seemed to be in pain, grimacing as she worked at her boot laces. He crouched by her foot. "Let me."

Adara sighed with an edge of annoyance but gave in. Laces undone, he attempted to remove the boot and she yelped.

He gently set her foot down and sat back on his heels. "I'm taking you to the ER."

"No, you're not." Her gaze was steady but a betraying sheen of sweat glistened on her brow. "It's just a mild sprain. Take me home. I'll deal."

He straightened. Any other day he'd gladly help her deal with anything at her home. But he'd caused this, she was injured and he wasn't about to leave her to her own devices. He scooped her off the ground.

"Hey!" Even as she scowled, she hooked an arm around his neck. "It's only a few yards to the car. I prefer hopping on one foot over being manhandled. Put me down. I'll be fine."

"Sure you will." He grinned at her, liking the press of her against him, close enough to feel her warmth, smell her sweet shampoo. *Definitely coconut.* "You'd slip again, and since I feel responsible, I'd have to push you around in a wheelchair, feed you grapes and cater to your every need. No matter what you believe, I do have other life matters to attend to."

She rolled her eyes then hissed as he strode toward the car. Her arm around his neck tightened. If the slight jostling from simply walking hurt, that wheelchair he'd joked about might be a reality. He got her into the car, seatbelt snicked and began their drive across town.

Fifteen minutes later, Garret carried a pale-faced and increasingly snappish Adara through the emergency room doors. She adamantly refused to let him accompany her to the exam, so he waited with expired nature magazines and watered-down coffee. An hour later, the doctor finally appeared.

"The swelling and bruising make it look uglier than it is." He handed Garret what was left of Adara's boot. One side was sliced open, ruined. He guessed he owed her a pair of boots too. Next, a handful of paperwork crackled in his grip. "She needs to stay off the foot for at least two weeks, so crutches are in order." The exam room door swished open and a nurse wheeled Adara near. "I gave her a shot for the pain. Don't expect any deep conversation tonight."

Chara. If he wasn't previously on her kill list, he was now. He shook the doctor's hand. "Thanks. I'll make sure she avoids anymore snowball fights."

Garret barely noticed the doctor's departure or the nurse as she parked the wheelchair before him and left too. He crouched before Adara. Her usually straight, sleek hair looked as if she'd forgot to comb it after a restless night, and one leg of her over-loved jeans had been cut to allow room for the bulky medical boot strapped to her injured foot. The lines of pain in her face had vanished, leaving her skin smooth, her expression utterly relaxed.

She blinked slowly at him, her gray eyes dove soft. "There you are."

"Here I am," he agreed. She sounded happy to find him waiting for her. He could get used to that. "Feeling better?"

"Oh." Her generous lips stretched into a dreamy smile. "Yeah."

He sighed. "Of course. You have to be drugged up to smile at me like that."

Her brow furrowed. "How else would I smile at you?"

"I've experienced the Dumont sneer, an occasional smirk when you think I'm not looking, a twitch of those gorgeous lips that I've pegged as the Adara Absolute Refusal, but not once have you genuinely smiled for me."

Still frowning, she dragged his beanie off his head and patted him. He might as well be a dog. "You have pretty hair."

"Thank you?"

"You're welcome." Her smile switched to brilliant.

He sucked in a breath. *Ben-zonna*. He'd do everything in his power to earn another of those smiles — a true one, not influenced by narcotics. "I like this version of Adara. Can I keep you?"

"Yeah-uh." She stuck his hat on her head at a lopsided angle and leaned forward. Her gaze locked on his, her expression suddenly serious. "I can't run with you tomorrow. The doctor said. You shouldn't go alone." She petted his face — first his nose, then his jaw, then his forehead. "You might die."

He closed his eyes and laughed, even as he struggled not to take her hand between his and kiss her palm. Letting her freely stroke him like her favorite cat gave him ideas — none that he could explore with her tonight — and whether or not she was aware of what she'd said, he'd chalk it up to a reflection of the inner sweetness that she kept leashed tight and hidden, particularly from him.

"I need to get you home before I lose all pride, curl up on your lap and purr." He stood, and she dragged her fingertips down his shirt and hooked at his belt, shooting sparks through his veins. Gently, he removed her grip and, despite his earlier resolve, pressed his lips to her knuckles.

She cocked her head, her eyes wide and considering. "You purr?"

His laugh was a little on the strained side. "For you, *neshama*, I'd do more than purr, but we'll have to save that for another day."

"Tomorrow." She said the word like a promise, hushed and solemn.

Garret slipped behind the wheelchair and started pushing her toward the exit before he made any more promises, promises that, when she came to her senses tomorrow, she probably wouldn't want him to keep.

Adara fell asleep before he'd buckled his seatbelt and she didn't move the entire drive back to her house. The sedatives prevented any protest to his music selection, but he'd prefer to listen to her husky voice articulating non-answers to his snoopy questions. She didn't stir, even when he unbuckled the seatbelt and drew her close again.

Luckily, she kept her keys in her coat pocket. He fumbled one-handed with the lock. It opened easily, already unlocked. He'd have to talk to her about that. Small towns did not mean safe.

He pushed the door shut with his heel, thankful the foyer light was on. Besides a glimpse from the porch, he hadn't seen the layout of her house and groping around in the dark would probably end up with bumping Adara's foot and shooting him higher on her black list, if he didn't already hold the number one spot.

Moving deeper into the house, he shivered as his chin brushed her sleek hair, still coconut-sweet after everything. No matter how much she denied it — and she would — tonight he'd made progress. She'd cracked her heart door, compromised when she could have won their contest. She could blame the stars all she wanted, but sedated, she was as sweet as a kitten, all pretenses and guardrails gone.

He peeked into the closest room, the darkness not hiding the lines of light-colored living room furniture, and kept going. Cozying her up on a couch wasn't good enough. He passed the kitchen entrance and paused in the hallway, the line of closed doors offering no clue as to which one was Adara's bedroom. With her head nestled in the crook of his neck, her steady breath warm on his collarbone, he hated to wake her up. He'd go with trial and error.

The first door led to the bathroom. As he opened the next door, a cold draft slipped free, smelling of dust and disuse. He flicked the light switch on and froze. A baby grand slept in the corner, its lid down, a layer of gray dulling the maple finish. Various-sized instrument cases leaned against the piano, boxed in by stacks of music books, paper and a broken guitar. The bed, neatly made, held a definite masculine air, from the navy-blue comforter to the mahogany furniture.

Joey's room.

His heart lodged in his throat, a sharp, jagged rock, and he slowly backed out and shut the door without a sound. She'd kept her brother's belongings, and from the coat of grime, probably hadn't disturbed his room since his death. She held on to his possessions as tightly as she did her grief. He gently squeezed her tighter and rested his cheek on her hair, as if he could shield her from the memories, the pain. But there was no shield that could prevent the pain life brought, and the only way to get through the hard moments was to embrace them, sieve them through the soul and let them go. Not that he wouldn't shield her if he could... Garret kissed her cool brow.

Adara's room was the last door. The second he stepped inside, he knew it was hers, no light required. The coconut lacing the air gave it away. He hit the light switch and paused. Shelves lined one wall, with books and knickknacks arranged in an almost-artistic pattern. Someday, he'd return to investigate what books she kept, what little things she'd arranged so carefully among the books and what they meant to her. White walls, black shelves, white down comforter on the queen bed, black nightstand. The only splash of color came from the plants tucked on the windowsill, subtle proof that life persisted.

He eased her onto the bed and wrangled her jacket free, thankful his muttered curse didn't wake her. She rolled onto her side and curled up with a sigh. He slipped off her remaining boot, pulled the comforter over her and crouched beside the bed, drinking her in.

Chara, she was so beautiful and lost, the lamplight a soft glow on her moon-pale skin, her sleek hair framing her delicate face. All the careful emotions she clung to while awake had softened into only peace.

That tiny part inside him that was always loose and restless shifted, winding around his heart and settling in place. He wanted to climb into her bed and wrap around her until she believed that, someday, everything would be okay — until she believed that the good parts of life were worth living.

Garret wiped a hand over his face. In only a few days, she'd completely enchanted him. One minute at a time, he'd convince her not to push him away.

He stood and pulled off the last page of the doctor's instructions containing the usual warnings of medical side effects and checked his watch. Eleven-thirty-nine p.m. While the conclusion wasn't what he'd hoped, the night was longer than he'd expected. He carefully wrote a number at the center of the paper, folded it into an origami boat and set it on her nightstand.

"Sweet dreams, *neshama*." He killed the light and left her to her dreams.

Chapter Ten

The smell of bacon cooking dragged Adara awake. Morning sunlight leaked through her window and dazzled off the white walls. She'd been dreaming of a snowman conducting an orchestra in space, which had zero connection to the mouth-watering sizzle of frying meat. She rolled over and smacked her bare toes on the clunky contraption strapped to her other ankle.

Pain radiated through her booted foot and everything rushed back to her—the *Name That Tune* contest, the stars, the snowball tussle and subsequent slip.

Garret frickin' Ambrose.

She sat up fast and the room spun. Planting her hands on the mattress, she squeezed her eyes shut and waited for the dizziness to pass. Somehow, someway, the aroma of food wafted nearer.

"Good morning, my dark ray of starshine." Garret's voice joined the carousel in her head. He stood in the doorway, a plate in one hand, a cup of steaming coffee in the other, his smile bright.

Adara squinted at him, ignoring how her stomach growled. Her annoyance burned too hot to allow for any surprise. "You."

"Me," he agreed smoothly. "With a breakfast peace offering."

"Not hungry."

"Don't be grumpy." He set the food and mug on her nightstand and lifted the pair of crutches she hadn't noticed leaning against the wall. "For travel." He tapped the prescription bottle beside the plate. "For pain."

"What about that?" She pointed at the origami boat on the nightstand corner.

"Homework." He crouched beside the bed, bringing a draft of sunshine and citrus-scented air. His hair was shower-damp and his clothes were a few steps up from the ones from the previous night, jeans minus holes and a button-down shirt. His smile faded and his dark eyes searched her face. "I feel terrible."

"If the shoe fits."

"Adara—"

"It's a sprained ankle, not a death wound." She jerked free of her down comforter, swung her legs over the bed and grabbed the closest crutch. "You've done your part. See ya. Door's around the corner."

He stood and handed her the other crutch. "Speaking of, you need to lock your door. Crime happens in small towns too, and under your doormat is the worst possible hiding spot for a spare key. I found it in two seconds. It has a new spot, under the pavestone next to the azalea."

"Thanks for the home-improvement tip." She swiped the crutch from his hand and glared. "With you slinking around, I'll be sure to deadbolt too."

His mouth twitched, not the sullen expression she'd hoped for at all. He was clearly trying not to smile, the uncooperative jerk.

"Ambrose, you have two seconds to get out of my house before I pummel you with the pointy end of this crutch."

Shoving his hands in his pockets, he made a show of examining the crutch. "I don't see any pointy parts."

"It'll be pointy after I crack it in half over your head." She added a snarl to her tone.

He danced out of reach and had the nerve to laugh. "Fine. I can take a hint."

She snorted.

"I have someplace to be, anyway. Text me if you need anything." He talked over her growl. "Or if you fall and can't get up." He ducked into the hallway, out of sight as she chucked one crutch at him. "Looking forward to Monday!" His footsteps tapped away and the door snapped shut, leaving her in silence.

She groaned and collapsed on the bed, her ankle throbbing. Monday, the first of her three-month torture term with the music mentor and he was already slithering beneath her skin after a few days, her shield useless. *Insufferable man.*

The bacon lured her with its irresistible aroma and her stomach gurgled again. She snagged a crispy bacon strip, ripped off a bite and moaned. The last time her kitchen had been used beyond the microwave was toast a week ago. A musician and a culinary artist... So unfair. *How did he win the skills jackpot?*

She chewed slowly, savoring. This was intolerable — invading her kitchen, whipping up delectable grub and violating her personal space with noise and homey happenings. Settling the plate on her lap, she grabbed the fork and dug into the eggs. Garret wouldn't know whether or not she ate his peace offering. Besides, she'd need the strength for Monday and dismantling his infuriatingly unstoppable smile.

* * * *

Monday morning passed by in the usual routine. Tatum chased Zachary and got a trip to the Chair of Consequences. What she'd silently dubbed the Triple Terror — a girl-clique of Ava, Dalaynee and Haley — had two boys crying ten minutes after recess, and one kid had thrown up on the classroom pet plant. And now she had to deal with Garret.

She stared at his too-long hair in its neat ponytail to prevent a forbidden classroom eye roll as he paced in front of her desk, boring students with an introduction lecture. She could tell him to drop the words and go with the hands-on goods, but she was merely here to observe, not to help him.

Maybe finally figuring out that the class was getting antsy, he hefted the gigantic duffel bag he'd dropped beside her desk earlier. "Since we're starting out, today will only be about fun," he said, unzipping the bag. "Come on up and pick out an instrument."

She hid a snort and kept her teacher mask on tight while kids mobbed him. Rookie mistake, asking kids to pick something out. There'd be at least five scuffles guaranteed, an opportunity she couldn't resist.

"Looks like you've got things under control, Mr. Ambrose." She twisted in her chair and nabbed her crutches leaning against the chalkboard. "I'll be in the breakroom." He may or may not have heard her over the litany of 'I want the bell' and 'Is there a pink one?' *Not my problem.* A cheap coffee was calling her name.

She hobbled out of the classroom and into the hallway. The second the door clicked shut behind her, she let her evil smirk fly free. So far, she'd managed to match his sunshine with icy professionalism and rebuff his apologies with cool disdain. He'd turn his attention on someone else soon enough, find another inspiration.

As it should be.

The breakroom was an easy jaunt away, with or without crutches, and despite the fact it wasn't break time for most of the staff, voices floated to her.

"I hate to say it, but maybe it's for the best." Carl, the PE teacher, his deep voice unmistakable. "Kids pick up on everything, and if a teacher loses their spark" — the snap of fingers followed — "the effects show up in the students. I'd prefer the larger class sizes."

Adara's stomach twisted but she didn't slow down or turn around. She had a good idea which teacher he referred to.

"Stick to pushups and running and leave psychology behind." Olivia's backup loosened the knot in her stomach. She could just imagine the older woman pointing her crochet needle at Carl. "Anyone with one eye can see her switch is ready to flip. She won't stay in the dark much longer. Mark me."

Approaching the breakroom door, she sighed and lifted her chin. Time for another awkward conversation interruption.

"And if you ask me," Olivia continued, her crochet needles creating a smooth, steady beat, "that music mentor will do more than flip her switch."

"It's funny how voices carry when students are tucked away in their classrooms." Adara paused in the doorway and leveled both teachers with a cool stare. "I could've sworn you two were discussing lightbulbs."

"Yep, those gym lightbulbs. Always burning out." Carl nodded, too jerky to be believable.

Olivia snorted and resumed crocheting the hat she worked on. She was always crocheting something for cancer patients, the homeless or people who preferred to wear black. "We were talking about you."

That was new. Usually, no one acknowledged she was the topic of conversation, let alone owned up to it. Adara lurched into the chair beside Olivia and propped her crutches against the counter behind her, within easy reach of the coffee pot. "Do tell."

She never stopped crocheting, the needles tapping together. "Carl thinks the kids would be better off without you." She ignored Carl's splutter. "I disagree. I know you've had a rough year, but winter always ends."

"Metaphor much?" Adara twisted in her chair and poured some coffee into a disposable cup. Adding enough creamer to disguise the bitterness of cheap grounds, she swung back to face her coworkers. "And thanks for the vote of confidence, Carl. Appreciate it."

"And my point is proven." Olivia kept her gaze on the orange lines forming into a hat, click by click. "Just last week, your best response would have been an uncaring shrug." She lowered her crochet and leaned forward. "Your switch is simply waiting for the right fingers to flip it."

Adara sipped her coffee before answering, the warmth steadying her. If she showed too much emotion, it would merely set Olivia off. If she didn't respond at all, Carl would go back to believing she wasn't teacher material. She might not be fit for most things, but teaching kids was one of them.

"Let me get this straight." She set her cup down and gave Olivia her best find-another-hobby stare. "You think my switch only responds to violin fingers."

Olivia grinned and went back to her project. "That's one way of saying it."

"I thought I made it clear that I have no interest in my switch being touched — by anyone. That includes music mentors."

Carl leaned back and crossed his arms, a funny look on his face.

Adara glared at him. "You have something to add?"

He shook his head and scooted his chair back, scraping the tile loud enough to rattle eardrums. "Gotta go. Dodgeball today." And he was gone.

"See what I mean?" Olivia pursed her lips, the needles tick-ticking a slow torture rhythm. "Even Carl recognizes it."

"Seriously. I don't care if you talk about my teaching methods or my spark or lack thereof, but leave Garret out of it. Please. I don't need the drama."

The needles stopped, and Olivia arched one thin eyebrow. "Garret?"

Adara gritted her teeth. "Mr. Ambrose."

"Oh, *him*." Olivia packed the needles and hat in her flowery yarn bag and stood. "Babies. Think about it."

"I already have twenty-five babies waiting in my classroom, thank you."

"And if I'm not mistaken," Olivia said, shuffling from the breakroom and wisely out of reach, "they're all with Garret, aren't they? Ta-ta."

The second Olivia was out of sight, Adara slouched. With Garret around, school was no longer a safe haven.

Three months. All she had to do was ride it out, then things would return to her version of normal.

She chugged the last of the poor excuse for coffee and limped into the hallway. An odd sound drifted from farther down, completely out of place during instruction hours. Musical clangs or squeaks would've been expected, but this? This was a muffled roar.

Hurrying, she swung-hopped to her classroom and flung open the door. Cacophony was a better description of the utter chaos taking over her once systematic classroom. The noise was deafening, caused by screaming, running, laughing children and the instruments they carried. Garret scrambled after Ava, who held a recorder out like a baton, which was nabbed by Dalaynee. When Garret closed in, Dalaynee threw it to Haley. The girl shrieked like a bird of prey and dove beneath a desk.

Adara blew out a slow breath. The Triple Terror played keep away from Garret while the rest of the kids did whatever they wanted. *Zero control.* Clearly, leaving him to his own devices had been a mistake, which meant that when he was here, she'd have to be here too. *This day gets better and better.* She limped farther into the room and stood by her desk, still as an ice sculpture.

Zachary was the first to lock gazes with her. The boy paled and dropped the two erasers he'd been using to chalk Tatum. He scurried to his seat and the chain reaction began. Mid-chase, Tatum noticed her and followed Zachary's lead. The Triple Terror were the last ones to surrender their fun. Haley tossed the recorder at Garret and scrambled to her desk. In less than thirty seconds, all her students sat silently, stiffly, fearfully in their seats. Garret stood dead center, huffing, his hair escaping the queue at his nape, his collar askew. He looked a little scared himself.

"Starting with Ava and going down the row," she said in a clear, crisp disappointed teacher voice, "you will stand up, walk to Mr. Ambrose, shake his hand and apologize for being disrespectful."

One by one, the students slouched to Garret and muttered their apologies while he looked utterly uncomfortable, obviously wanting to but deciding not to defy her. *Smart man.*

At last, the apologies were over. She swept them all with a death stare. "In complete silence, you will replace every rubber band, pencil and paper to their proper place. If I hear a single word from anyone, the rest of the day will be spent on math problems. No recess. Understood?"

Every head bobbed, even Garret's.

As the students trudged to their tasks in sullen quiet, Adara fixed her narrowed gaze on him. "Mr. Ambrose, a minute in the hall?"

A deeper hush fell across the room and eyes widened. Everyone knew hall-time was Big Trouble. Except, apparently, for Garret. He wore a relieved smile.

Adara kept the door ajar, unwilling to give the kids an edge, and she glared up at him. "What was that?"

His smile widened. "They're really excited about music."

"And exploiting weakness." She shook her head. "Haven't you ever dealt with kids?"

"Of course." He lifted his chin, a look of offense. "I babysat Tatum and Bryan once or twice before going on tour. We got along great."

She closed her eyes and slumped on her crutches. She'd envisioned her days with him in separate rooms, her as far away as possible, checking in every so often. *Plans, meet flames.* "You can't let them walk all over you, Garret. They'll eat you alive."

He tucked his hands behind his back and rocked on his heels, his smile returning. "They won't if I have you as backup, and it warms my heart, truly, that you care."

"That care extends to my kids, not you."

He continued smiling like an imbecile.

"Vocabulary lesson of the day, Ambrose." She leaned slightly forward. "Inept. Look it up."

"Out of the box, Miss Dumont. Big difference." His black eyes glittered, and she had the odd impression he'd just won a contest she didn't know about. He stuffed his hands in his pockets and strolled back into the room, humming.

She had no idea if he was some kind of mad genius or seriously disillusioned. Either way, it looked like she was stuck with him. Three months of hell. She'd better sharpen her pitchfork.

Chapter Eleven

Friday afternoon Garret slipped into Adara's classroom a few minutes early. He offered her a quick smile, not letting her disinterested expression affect him, and tiptoed to the back of the room while she finished up her lesson on American presidents. Again.

He made a quick survey of the crowd. The slack faces and glazed eyes made him want to yawn. A black-haired boy in the back corner—Sam, maybe—doodled on his paper rather than take notes next to the president pictures. And the knobby-kneed girl two seats ahead who had yet to meet his gaze blinked slowly, ready for an afternoon nap. He might not have the inhuman control over kids that Adara possessed, but he could inspire any president lesson with music.

"Quiz on Monday," Adara announced, shutting her book with a purposeful thud. "I expect studying on your own this weekend." Amid a chorus of groans, she met Garret's gaze and handed a stack of study guides to Tatum to pass out. "Sorry, but with music, we don't have as much in-class time to study."

Garret widened his smile, not missing the miffed flash in her gray eyes. *Ben-zonna*, he loved it when she reacted to him.

"Get a drink, then Mr. Ambrose is up." Adara grabbed a pen as the students scrambled from their seats and thundered to the water cooler in a pack, giving Garret a chance to get close. He leaned near her chair.

"I have an idea," he said beside her ear, drawing a coconut-laced breath. He'd never see macaroons the same way.

"Scary thought." She made a show of studying his navy-blue V-neck sweater. "Feeling okay? Sweater, jeans with no rips, tennis shoes? I didn't know you could do Average Joe."

He had no intention of disclosing he'd worn his tennis shoes to break them in more. Adara on crutches for weeks was an advantage he'd jumped on. Next time she found him on the running trails, he wouldn't represent creampuffs everywhere. "It's not nice to stereotype, Miss Dumont."

"Never mind." She returned her attention to the neat stack of papers on her desk. "The ungodly number of silver rings ruined your disguise."

"So glad you noticed, and your plaid skirt is ravishing. The black checks match your black sweater and your black hair." He resisted asking if her underwear was black too. The mere thought made him twitch in awkward places. Truth be told, black complimented her pale beauty, but if she wore red? He might develop control issues.

"You're here to harass kids, not me." She scribbled a word in the margin and flipped the paper to the bottom of the stack.

"I completely underestimated the fun I'd have as a music mentor." He lowered his voice. "Bantering with the adorable teacher is an unexpected benefit."

"Wrong answer." She sniffed and jotted an angry red slash on some unlucky kid's homework. "Annoyed, not adorable."

"Both. But I'm working on undermining the former."

"Good luck with that."

"Thank you." He bowed. "Be warned, Miss Dumont. Once I make a decision, I don't surrender."

"Some battles can't be won."

"A motto for the defeated." He turned his attention to the kids trickling back to their seats. "Grab an instrument from the bin. I don't care which one." As boys and girls raced for the container stashed at the back of the room, he quickly added, "And no pushing or elbowing!"

"A glimmer of hope for the music mentor." Adara shifted her booted foot and her mouth tightened.

"Ankle getting better?" he asked, killing any sign of humor. When it came to the fact she couldn't run to burn off steam, she was downright cranky, especially since she obviously still blamed him.

She shrugged, the friendliest response he'd received since offering her breakfast Sunday morning. *A glimmer of hope, indeed.*

He faced the class. "Whatever instrument you're holding, find the others who have the same instrument and stand together, so I know who has what." He wasn't surprised at all to find Tatum had nabbed a kazoo, the same as Zachary. The trio of girls who'd in a few years run a terrorist group had all chosen recorders. The black-haired boy held tight to a bongo and the shy girl studied the triangle in her hands, which had probably been the last instrument in the tub. She seemed willing to take whatever was left over.

"Since music is invading learning time, I figure we can do both." A few students exchanged skeptical glances but he strolled to the girls with the recorders. "Who is America's first president?"

Tatum huffed and cocked her hip. "Washington, duh."

"Mr. Ambrose isn't your uncle in my classroom, Tatum," Adara said from her desk, without bite. "Show him proper respect."

"Sorry." Tatum slouched, her expression grumpy.

If only Adara extended that courtesy rule beyond the school walls… Then again, it might not be as fun. "I bet you didn't know that Washington loved dogs." Some eyes brightened at that. "And while we don't have any dog whistles in our orchestra, the recorders are the closest we have. Give me a note, girls. Any note."

The screech of three different notes pierced the classroom. He refused to wince. "Good." The notes kept going. "You can stop now." No luck. "Girls!"

As if they'd choreographed it, the girls dropped their recorders at the same time, grinning like imps.

"So we have our Washington dog whistlers. Next president?"

"Adams!" Zachary bounced up and down beside Tatum, waving his kazoo.

"Adams created the United States Marine Band, America's oldest band." Garret crouched beside the boy with the bongo. "What's your name again?"

"Sammy." He came very close to an eye roll, not that Garret would've turned him in.

"And since percussion is the oldest instrument, you're Adams' drum. Can you handle that?"

Sammy thumped the drum a few times, looking defiant.

"So Washington." Garret pointed at the recorder girls, and got a triple eardrum shattering squeak. "And Adams." It only took a look for Sammy to pound the drum in an uneven beat.

"Next president?"

"Jefferson!" several kids sang out.

"Jefferson fun fact— He kept pet mockingbirds." He stopped beside a Shirley Temple-like redheaded girl holding an Irish whistle.

She smiled. "I'm Riley."

He smiled back. "Riley, I want you to blow on the whistle, and while you're blowing, cover the first two holes with your first and second fingers." He helped her with the finger arrangement. The note was clear and high, smoother than the recorders. The girl had promise. "Good, now take your second finger off while blowing. And we've got our Jefferson mockingbird."

"Washington recorders." He didn't even have to point this time. Hearty squeaks ricocheted off the walls. "Adams drum." A crooked rhythm set in. "Jefferson mockingbird." The whistle rang loud and clear.

He didn't bother looking at Adara. He'd felt her stare weighing on him since mentioning Washington. She might not be his fan—yet—but as a teacher, she'd appreciate unique teaching methods, not that he expected her to admit it.

By recess, they'd made it through Tyler's Texas triangle. Close to a quarter of the musical presidents wasn't bad. As the kids stashed their instruments and rushed off to recess, he meandered to Adara's desk.

"Since it's Friday and we're supposed to compile a weekly report for Principal Austin, what time do you want to meet?" He planted his hands on her desk and leaned toward her. "Dinner tonight?"

She jerked a stray paper edge from beneath his palm. "Not even."

"After school?"

"I've got a doctor's appointment." Setting her pen down, she gave him her icy stare.

He freed his smile. "Great. Then it's Saturday."

"Can't." She folded her arms. "I'm finalizing my cut-the-music program presentation for the board meeting on Wednesday."

Ouch. Keeping his smile on full force, he nabbed her pen and a sticky note. "That's okay. I'm free Sunday."

She sighed heavily. "Fine, but I can only do it at six" — she paused — "a.m."

"No problem." *Cheeky girl.* He scribbled his number for the week on the sticky note and carefully folded it into a tiny boat. *Thank you, London, for forcing me into girly crafts in between violin lessons.* "Your place?"

"Not happening."

"Perfect. My place." He set the origami boat and pen on her desk.

If they hadn't been in her classroom, he had no doubt she'd have rolled her eyes. "Twelfth Street coffee shop. I'll meet you there."

"Can't wait." He stuffed his hands in his pockets and strolled out of the classroom. He didn't have to look to know she watched him go. Her glare was hot on his back, but he couldn't hold back his smile. An extra day to erode Adara's walls.

Score.

Chapter Twelve

Warm and cozy in her flannel sheep pajamas, Adara sat on her bed, laptop resting on her thighs, the perfectionist in her demanding a final review of the budget proposal she'd already memorized. The moon peeked through her window, silhouetting her room in silver. Computer work in the dark killed her eyes, but since they already felt like sandpaper, a little longer wouldn't hurt. She swigged another mouthful of raspberry-infused water.

An incoming email pinged in the screen corner.

For future encounters. GAA.

She studied the message until it faded and vanished altogether, her jaw clenched. Garret knew the cryptic message would intrigue her, the jerk. Grumbling at her weakness, she opened it. Only a glowing blue link was included. *Blast.* She couldn't just not open it, but if it led her to some computer-killing virus, at least she'd have a valid reason to destroy him.

The link led her to a playlist containing all the songs of their *Name That Tune* contest, and her mouth twitched. Did he really have nothing better to do on a Saturday night than harass her from afar? Unintentionally, she pictured him with his violin, the stars in his hair, the supple roll of his muscles as he wielded the bow. Her breath came faster. If she hadn't hurt her ankle that night, if she'd stayed with him, she might have done something stupid—maybe touched his jaw to feel the scrape of stubble or tangled her fingers in that overlong hair that looked so soft, maybe kissed the smile right off him.

The computer screen went black, and she sat in the dark, her pulse too loud. *'Google me, if you dare.'* His challenge from the planetarium tapped at her brain, a woodpecker that wouldn't leave. Watching him use music to teach her kids American presidents had done unmentionable things to her heart. She couldn't afford to go wimp in only a week. She needed reinforcement.

She rested her fingers on the keyboard, waiting for the next move. She had no idea how much or what the Internet would reveal about him, if it would fuel her fascination or dilute it, but she had to start somewhere. If she could find something negative, something unlikeable, she could cling to it whenever his presence crippled her resolve. She blew out a breath.

"I'm doing this. My first venture into Internet stalking." She tapped a key. The screen lit up and she squinted, readjusting to its brightness. A few clicks, and Garret Ambrose popped up. He had his own webpage, Facebook, Twitter and YouTube channel, but she skipped all those. It wasn't like she'd find anything adverse on his personal promotional sites. She clicked a random link farther down the page, *Belgian Beauty*

Unedited, some foreign site listing Garret's name. What she needed was juicy gossip, if there was any. Not that she expected to find much. It wasn't like he was...a...celebrity...

She whistled, long and low. He hadn't been lying about Belgium, and he'd left out the love in Switzerland, France and the Netherlands. She ticked the website photo tab. Candid pictures splashed the screen, all of him, everywhere, eating at a restaurant, walking, grocery shopping, even a distant hotel room balcony invasion of privacy. There were also photos of him with a woman...a beautiful woman. And selfies with Garret in the background. Lots and lots of selfies taken by this woman, the owner of the site.

Her stomach knotted tight and she snapped the laptop shut, cloaking herself in darkness and moonlight again. *Perfect.* She'd cement that image in her mind, bring it out whenever he smiled her way. He had a beautiful fan-girlfriend-lover-whatever tucked away in Belgium. It was exactly what she needed.

She set the laptop aside and slid beneath the covers. *Mission accomplished.*

If only she felt like celebrating.

Hours later, a ruthless knock at the front door pulled Adara out of sleep. She blinked at the light streaming past the curtains. *Morning. Sun.* She'd slept the whole night. Weird. Even weirder, her mouth felt cotton dry and her head pounded, as if she'd slammed shots last night instead of bottled water.

The knocking started up again, and she stumbled out of bed and thumped into the hallway without her crutches. Whoever had woken her up should prepare to die. She grabbed an umbrella from the wall hooks, brandishing it like a weapon, pointy-end first. Without looking through the peephole, she flung open the door.

Garret stood on the porch, a coffee cup in his hand, the steam curling in the misty air. "Since you didn't show for our meeting, I assumed your doctor gave you bad news." His gaze drifted down to her still-there boot. "Diagnosed a permanent limp? I feel terrible."

She dropped the umbrella, and it clattered to the tile, the echo throbbing in her head. Offering her best zombie groan, she shuffled away, not bothering to shut the door. Garret's footsteps trailed her and she didn't have the energy to care. She'd slept twice as much as she usually did and only wanted to curl beneath the covers and stay there. Getting sick right now would be the worst timing ever, especially with the upcoming budget presentation.

"Are you going back to bed?" he asked.

The husky hitch in his voice shot straight to her gut, and an image of climbing into bed with Garret wormed through her haze. *Nope, not going there.* She pivoted.

Looking equally befuddled, fascinated and all kinds of morning-air sexy, he lurked in the foyer, coffee still in hand. He wore jogging pants, a hoodie and the same neon-green running shoes he'd worn on Friday. *Did he go running first and wants to rub it in? Jerk.* She lurched forward and swiped the coffee from his fingers. Without a word, she limped away.

"Cute pajamas."

She spun and marched back to him as well as she could with a boot on, stopping only when her toes brushed his tennis shoes, all the better to threaten his personal space. "My pajamas are none of your business." She took a swig of the coffee and moaned before she thought better of it. Peppermint mocha. *Delicious.*

His gaze dropped to her mouth and stayed there.

So not the reaction she was going for. She gripped the cup with both hands to deny the urge to lean into him, lay her head on his chest and let him pet her head — which wasn't happening with a guy who kept a beautiful bimbo flame on the side. "I understand now why you're friends with Ian." She took another sip and her eyes slipped closed briefly, but she resisted another moan. "And don't bring me coffee ever again."

He stuffed his hands in his hoodie pockets. "Who said I brought the coffee for you?"

She shrugged and took another drink.

"What is this new revelation you've had concerning my friendship with Ian?"

She hadn't planned to tell him anything, but he'd woken her up. She hadn't had time to put on any masks. "Two words. Belgian Beauty."

His forehead wrinkled. "Still lost."

"Google it."

One corner of his mouth curled up. "You looked me up?"

"Don't flatter yourself. I don't trust Austin's background check." She took another sip, keeping her glare on him. "'*Hottest Violinist Ever.*' Belgian Beauty's words, not mine. How much did you pay her?"

He leaned one shoulder against the wall, his dark eyes twinkling. "Compliments are free, darling."

"Not your darling."

"*Ben-zonna*, you're adorably irascible in the morning."

"Go away." She gave his chest a weak push, ignoring — completely — the firm muscles there, and she lumbered off while she still had enough energy to drag herself back to bed. "Close the door on your way out."

"I'm not going anywhere until you adequately explain what your secret insight is into my long-term Ian bromance, why you stood me up and why you stole my coffee."

"Ungh. It's way too early to think about Ian." She threw her head back and continued down the hall in her uneven zombie shuffle. "Not that there's any good time to waste brain cells on that dirtbag."

The door thudded shut behind her and she was absolutely not disappointed that he'd left—no fight, no argument. *Nope.* The fact that he didn't deny knowledge of foreign fan sites or any connection to beautiful Belgian women was exactly what she'd hoped for. She swallowed the lump in her throat.

Making it to her bedroom, she sluffed to her bed, set the coffee on the end table and crawled under the covers with a sigh.

"Still waiting for your answer."

She squeaked and sat up at Garret's voice so close. He lingered in her bedroom doorway, scanning the room as if taking in every little detail and committing it to memory. "I thought you'd left."

"You must've missed it when I said I'm not going anywhere." He traced the blank space on her wall where the family collages once hung, his finger following the line of slightly darker paint marking where each frame used to be. "I dragged myself out of my warm, cozy bed at dawn and shivered in the cold, alone, waiting for you. You must have forgotten the coffee shop on Twelfth isn't open on Sundays."

Adara summoned enough energy to smirk.

He turned away from the erased memorial and strolled toward her, his expression almost menacing. "And here I find you lazing about in your warm" —he stepped closer—"cozy"—another step closer—"bed." He leaned over her, bringing a hint of his citrusy cologne. "Without me."

Her heart jumped into a presto beat. She pulled her comforter up to her chin, the best shield available. "Don't you have somewhere to go? Someone else to torment?"

"Church is at nine, so yes." He sat on the edge of the bed and his eyes sparkled, the same way Tatum's did when she plotted mischief. "And you're the only one I want to torment."

"You go to *church*?" She wasn't especially shocked. In Graywood, church was another opportunity for small-town socializing, potluck after the service. The whole town went. *Almost.*

He cocked his head. "You don't?"

Not since Joey's funeral, information she had no need to share, especially with a man who wriggled through her defenses effortlessly—a man who had a beauty waiting for him in Belgium. "Better hurry. You wouldn't want to miss the music."

"I'm not going anywhere until you explain why you stood me up." He planted a hand beside her drawn-up feet and leaned closer, his voice low. "Don't pretend you didn't."

"Forgot to set my alarm." She held his gaze. If she didn't, he'd sense her weakness and increase his attack. Music mentors weren't that different from third-graders.

"So you merely overslept? You didn't intend to ditch me?" He dropped his chin, shadowing his features.

"Yes."

He studied her with those dark, knowing eyes. "You had fun last week. Admit it."

"My fun meter is also none of your business. Besides, I discovered...things about you."

"It's not fair to judge me on things you refuse to share. How am I supposed to prepare a defense?"

"That's your problem."

"Adara" — he said her name like a caress, and she hid a shiver at the hot spark in her belly — "at least give me the courtesy of disclosing the crimes I'm being charged with."

The niggling need to hear his explanation combatted rationality. This was a chance to get rid of him, to barricade him from her life. She could withstand the weeks between now and when he left, but if she didn't hear the truth, she might wonder — and wondering would keep her mind on him. She had to kill her growing respect for him, the best anti-aphrodisiac ever. And if he had a beau on the side, that would do the trick.

"Fine. If you insist." She pushed the blankets off and nabbed her laptop. The screen beeped to life, and she navigated to the telling website. "*Belgian Beauty Unedited.* Very educational." She handed the computer to him.

He settled farther back on the bed and set the laptop on his knees. In all of three seconds, his jaw bunched and his shoulders tensed. Foreign words underscored his breath, and while she didn't understand the language, she had a feeling none of them were nice. It was probably a good thing he was headed to church.

"Look familiar?" She kept her tone innocent.

Groaning, he set the laptop aside and collapsed backward on the bed, making the mattress shudder. "I thought I'd escaped Bella." He gazed up at the ceiling, as if praying for aid. "I thought she'd given up her obsession."

Obsession. She couldn't really blame the girl. Garret was crush material, and she had a feeling it wouldn't take much to turn that crush into a demolition. Another reason to keep her distance. "Former flame?"

"Not really." His smile was sickly.

She waited for more, but he simply stared at the ceiling. "Fan?"

"Oh yeah."

It was refreshing to see him being the one who didn't want to share his secrets for once, and it made her want them. She rested her chin on her knee, all the better to stare him into submission. "Stalker?"

He turned his head and met her gaze, all humor long gone. "She's a small part of the reason I came home. Not the deciding factor, but she helped finalize the decision. An ocean-wide barrier seemed like a good idea, at least until things settled down."

A chill crept down her neck. "What happened?"

He rolled to his side and faced her, propping his head one hand. "We went out. Once. It wasn't even dinner, just a late interview lunch for her blog, which used to be called *Isabella Unlimited*. It wasn't my best judgment call." He grimaced. "Or giving her my cell number. I try very hard not to hurt other people, but nice isn't strong enough for someone who doesn't have 'no' in her vocabulary. I was hopeful the protection order had gotten through to her."

"Dang. What'd she do to earn a protective order?"

He tightened his mouth and sat up. "It's in the past, unimportant."

Adara straightened, all the better to watch him squirm. "Did she leave your cat in a pot on the stove? Bug your violin?"

"Not funny." He grabbed the coffee from the end table and took a sip.

"You shouldn't drink this now." She stole the coffee back. "I think I'm getting a cold." And she wasn't about to let this subject go. "Did she send you creepy letters demanding private concerts by candlelight?"

"She's an unbalanced individual in desperate need of help. I hope she finds it." He twisted to face her so suddenly that she jerked. "I never took you for the jealous type." A slow smile stretched his mouth, brimming with triumph. "From you, I think I like it."

"You're so off-base it's ridiculous."

His smile didn't fade. "Sorry you stood me up?"

"Nope. You better get to church and ask forgiveness for your potty mouth."

"Curses don't count in a different language. That's a rule." He stood, but instead of leaving, he wandered to her shelves and ran his fingers along the book spines. He paused and tapped one. "*Frankenstein*?"

The intimacy of the moment hit her. He was in her bedroom, perusing through her personal possessions, digging deeper into Adara Dumont the person, not the teacher. "I'll write up a report to give Austin and email it to you. You can add what you want." She ignored the tightrope strain in her voice. "Now go away."

He tucked his hands in his pockets and faced her. "What are you doing this afternoon?"

"Researching how to get my own protective order." She sipped the coffee, and heat slipped down her throat, making her feel more like herself. But her head still throbbed. "Think I might subscribe to *Belgian Beauty*, see if I can discover what she did to shut you down."

"No one shuts me down, darling." He meandered to the doorway and paused at the threshold. "Just so you know, I did bring that coffee for you. Stay in bed. Get well. I'll be back for lunch with chicken soup." He winked and ducked out.

"I don't want you to bring me—"

The front door slammed shut.

"Anything." She threw a pillow across the room. None of her efforts were going as planned, and she had the sinking feeling that when it came to Garret Ambrose, planning was pointless.

Chapter Thirteen

Wednesday night Adara softly shut the door, leaving the school board to discuss the remainder of their agenda items. Suddenly surrounded by silence in the empty hallway, she slouched, mentally exhausted. They'd bought into her plan to cut the music program instead of her job...with a condition. She had to gather signatures from seventy percent of the parents agreeing to eliminate it. Signatures had to be turned in by the next meeting.

Luckily, she didn't have any weekend plans. *Ever.*

Voices drifted from around the corner, and she straightened just as an unlikely threesome came into view. Ashton, the shiest student in her class, with her older brother...and Garret. His expression flashed from surprised, to guilty, to delighted. It was fascinating to watch.

"What are you doing here?" She aimed the question at Garret but turned her focus on Ashton.

The little girl held a green felt case stitched with ladybugs and skipped along beside her brother, positively beaming. Ashton never beamed. She gave Adara a small smile in passing.

"Special project." Garret, unfortunately, stopped as the kids continued on. He stuffed his hands in his faded jeans pockets and rocked on his heels. His shirt was too clingy, hinting at all the muscles underneath, the last thing she needed to think about. "Serendipitous to find you here."

"Nope, coincidence." She limped toward the exit, her vexing ankle boot preventing a quick escape. "School board presentation tonight."

"And?" he pressed, strolling easily beside her. His intoxicating cologne invaded her senses, impossible to ignore.

"Nailed it." He didn't need to know more than that.

"I never doubted you." He pushed the door open and held it for her. "Lose your Sunday cold?"

"I think I got a bad batch of bottled water." She slipped by him, her sleeve brushing his, completely and annoyingly aware how he moved in synch with her out of the door.

"Glad you're feeling better. What are you doing now?"

"Hobbling to my car." The air fingered through her hair, abnormally cold for March. Summer and the end of her Garret sentence felt a lifetime away.

"We should celebrate your victory."

She stopped and stared him down. "Violin boy wants to celebrate the death of music in school?"

"Of course not, but you worked hard on this project, and the idea of you going home and having no one to share in your victory saddens me." He looked completely serious.

She rolled her eyes.

"Besides, I owe you ice cream." He bumped her shoulder with his.

"And pain and suffering for a sprained ankle. Why were you here with Ashton?"

He grinned, looking sly. "You want to share my free time too, darling? I'm okay with that."

"Monday through Friday afternoons are enough, thank you very much. And don't call me 'darling'." She resumed lurching to her car, which, regrettably, had a sleek, black Maserati parked right beside it. "I don't even want to contemplate what you do in your free time. You probably take selfies with bimbos and post them on foreign websites."

"That's mean-spirited of you." He didn't sound troubled at all, immune to her attempts at deflection. "I gave up bimbos two years ago and switched to smart-mouthed, third-grade teachers."

"Ungh, you're incorrigible." She opened her car door and plopped into the seat.

"Honest. There's a difference." He leaned on her door, preventing her from shutting it. "Technically, you still owe me a stargazing trip, Miss Dumont." He looked up at the clear sky. "Full moon's tonight. Ice cream, stars and moonlight. What do you say?"

An image flashed in her mind of his mouth on hers, tasting of ice cream, her hands in his hair, all beneath the silver starlight. She shook her head, dislodging the thought but not the tingling in her blood. Adding the night and ice cream to their inexplicable connection would be nothing short of explosive. "Your ice cream fail cancels out stargazing. We're even. No IOUs."

"Have you figured out the puzzle yet?" His dark eyes gleamed in the moonlight, reflecting the truth. He knew she hadn't figured out his weird origami numbers.

She pulled on her door handle, and he held on tight. "Yep. You're deranged. Easiest mystery ever."

He laughed and she wanted to kick something, mainly herself for making him laugh. Apparently, offending him was impossible. "Can I have that napkin on your seat?"

"Deranged," she repeated, but handed him the napkin.

He pulled a pen from his jacket pocket, scribbled something—undoubtedly another abstract number—and she had yet another flimsy origami boat to add to her collection. She wasn't about to tell him that she'd kept every one.

"Awesome. I needed my trash to be more presentable when I dumped it in the garbage can."

"Anything for you, *neshama*." The purr in his voice coiled through her and pooled low in her stomach, adding to the bomb inside. Defusing it seemed more and more hopeless. It was only a matter of time before she detonated. "Tomorrow, then. Don't forget to put on your seatbelt." He shut her door before she could respond.

On principle, she didn't fasten her seatbelt until she'd pulled out of the parking lot and was out of his sight.

* * * *

Adara flicked the mismatched fleet of origami boats off her coffee table one by one, waiting for the soft plunk of paper on carpet before sinking the next. Saturday night and she was studying stupid numbers

140

when she should be soaking her throbbing foot. An entire day of limping around neighborhoods and coaxing signatures for her petition had taken its toll, and she hadn't made much headway. More parents than she expected seemed to be of Garret Ambrose's opinion that music mattered...a lot.

Her cell phone buzzed from the couch beside her. Garret. Her pulse quickened. Maybe by thinking his name she'd somehow summoned him.

Help!

She hesitated. He couldn't be in serious trouble. It was easier to dial nine-one-one than her phone number. He'd probably texted her by accident.

Think you butt dialed me. This is Adara.

Finger dialed. Butt's busy. I need your help.

She drummed her fingers on her jeans. This had to be some kind of Ambrose trap.

Why are you asking me and not Ian?

Children aren't one of his superpowers. I have a baby who won't stop screaming, a boy who refuses to come out of his room and a girl whose idea of a good time is putting Vaseline on all the doorknobs. Bob and London are out on their first real date in three years. I can't ruin their evening. I'm begging. Have mercy on my soul. I've got ice cream.

Garret holding a wailing baby while Tatum ran around the house trailing toilet paper and tormenting Bryan? *Beautiful.* Her laugh echoed in the silence, and she paused. How long had it been since anyone had laughed in this house? Probably before Joey got sick, when everything was right and normal and sane.

His text blinked, waiting for her answer. The house's emptiness surrounded her, graveyard-quiet again. Maybe watching someone else's chaos would remind her why she preferred the solitude and silence.

Are you at Tatum's?

Yes. Hurry!

Fifteen minutes later, Adara trotted up the steps to Casa Sullivan. An infant's lasting shriek filtered through walls, roof and door, as did an older voice screeching. She wasn't sure if the screeching belonged to Garret, Bryan or Tatum. She knocked and hunkered into her wool jacket.

A deep yell harmonized the screech, and the baby's squeal, after a brief intercession, went on to round two. She turned the doorknob. Locked. She pulled her cell from her pocket and texted him.

I'm at the door.

What sounded awfully close to 'hallelujah' replaced the yelling, and a second later, the door opened, spilling chaos.

Garret filled the doorway, his hair a golden curtain in his eyes, a red-faced one-year-old tucked under one arm like a football. Tatum hung on Garret's silver-studded belt, cackling, something red smeared all over her mouth. White powder — maybe flour — spotted his short-sleeved T-shirt and face, and the sour odor of spit-up wafted from the dribbles on his shoulder. The gleam in his eyes was a combo of terror and giddy relief.

"Help me," he croaked.

"Miss Dumont!" Tatum dropped from Garret's belt to the floor and wrapped her arms around his ankles, almost toppling him.

"Give me that." Adara nabbed the shrieking baby and closed the door with her boot heel. She nestled the kid on her hip and met the tear-filled eyes. "I know," she said in her best tantrum-soothing voice. "It sucks to be consigned to a novice, doesn't it?"

The howl ended on a shaky sob, and the child nestled on her shoulder, exhausted.

Garret narrowed his eyes at her. "Who are you? Some kind of sorceress? Is that why you're a teacher, to slowly steal the souls of children?"

"It seems you've discovered all my secrets." She rubbed the kid's back in circles. "Now I have to kill you too."

"You don't steal souls, Miss Dumont." Still hanging onto Garret's legs, Tatum leaned back and looked at her upside down. "You warp minds."

"Also true." Adara did the magic rocking motion and smiled as the baby slowly slumped into a limp ball. "What's the kid's name? I need a name to collect a soul."

Tatum's laugh was close to a possessed cackle, and Adara turned to Garret. "What did you feed her?"

He held on to his belt as Tatum jerked on his shredded jeans, trying to climb him. "The usual kid fare—mac and cheese, green beans and some of those cartoon-character-shaped chicken nuggets."

"You forgot the marshmallows, Uncle Garret." Tatum made it up to his arm and clung there like a demented monkey.

"Two marshmallows." He pushed loose hair from his face and flipped Tatum upside down by her ankles, inspiring a shriek. "That's not a sugar overload."

"You left the bag on the counter." The girl swayed in the air, using his grip on her ankles for a full-body swing. "I had two plus two plus two." She flipped her fingers out one by one, counting until she ran out of digits. Her smile was wicked. "Twenty-two marshmallows."

Garret groaned. "*Ben-zonna.* You were so much easier to babysit three years ago."

"I'm not a baby!" Tatum reached around and pinched his calf.

"No, you're a demon-child." His pleading gaze lifted to Adara. "What should I do with her?"

Was it wrong to find him adorable while at a loss and looking like a frazzled housewife? "Play *Simon Says.* Use lots of jumping jacks." The baby's soft breath on her neck indicated that he? she?—slept. The white pajamas with yellow ducks offered no gender clue. "What's this one's name?"

"Baby G." Tatum laughed as Garret bonked her head gently on the floor.

"Technically, his name is Garron." He released his niece into a giggling heap and held her down with his boot on her ribs. "London thought it was cute to meld our names."

Her heart squeezed. *Yeah.* If she ever had a kid, she'd definitely honor her brother that way, although blending Adara and Joey might take some creativity. *Jodara? Adarey?* Not that she planned to have kids.

Beyond wanting to keep her job and zero emotional ties, she hadn't considered the future. Plans could be ripped apart too easily.

"He's sleeping." Garret's broad shoulders hunched as he hooked his thumbs in his belt. "I don't care if you're a soul-stealing sorceress. You're my hero."

"No mask or cape required?" Adara pressed her cheek to the fuzz on Garron's head.

He paused, his bemused gaze lingering on her and the baby. As if realizing he stared, he smiled again. "Stay tuned." He glanced down at the eight-year-old girl, pretending to be a steamroller by squashing his toes. "More challenges await."

"Where should I put this thing?" Adara gently jiggled Garron.

"Upstairs, third door on the left—*ouch*!" He danced out of Tatum's reach. "You used to be sweet. What happened?"

"I'm sweet." Tatum sat on her haunches and panted like a dog. "I just ate twenty-two marshmallows."

"I sense an upcoming need for reinforcement, Adara." He backed up as Tatum advanced on him. "Hurry. I don't know how long I can survive." He spun and raced down the hall, out of sight, Tatum following on hands and feet like a disjointed dog.

A few minutes later, Baby G safely in his crib and baby monitor on, she followed the muffled voices to the basement. The walls of the brightly lit stairwell leading down were filled with framed photographs, family moments captured in time. She used to have collages like this hanging all over the house, but once Joey was gone, she'd taken them down. Looking at his face every day, considering all the moments he'd never have, weighed too heavy, hurt too much.

Laughter floated up, and she paused, each foot on a different step, her pulse a sledgehammer at her throat. Being here was a mistake. She pivoted to go back upstairs.

"Miss Dumont!" Tatum's voice stopped her cold. "You'll be on the girl team."

Pasting on her polite smile, she turned around. "I should go home."

Tatum stuck out her bottom lip. "You just got here."

"No pouting." It was so much easier to stay detached when playing the part of teacher.

"If you don't stay, I'll be the only girl." Tears filled Tatum's blue eyes and her lip wobbled. "Please don't go."

And there it was. She could steel herself against Garret's charms and any whiny protest, but a child's honest tears sawed straight through her defensive walls. Not abandoning a little girl overruled personal pain. She released the breath she'd been holding. "I guess I can stay for a couple of games."

"Hooray!" Tatum whirled and rolled down the steps without breaking anything. *The girl should be an acrobat.* "Hurry up or we'll miss the coin toss to see who goes first."

Adara slouched in Tatum's wake. This was bound to come back to bite her. She clipped the corner and paused in the doorway. The basement had been molded into a playroom. A big-screen TV took up one wall and a sectional formed a semi-circle, perfectly placed to either watch the tube or play games in the center of the room. Garret sprawled smack-dab in the middle, watching Bryan fiddle with a gadget on the coffee table. The other part of the baby monitor sat on the end table. At least he could handle that part of babysitting.

His gaze met hers, and that smile she was becoming too familiar with lit up. He patted the spot beside him in invitation. "You were right. A hundred jumping jacks cut the sugar buzz."

"A hundred and two jumping jacks." Tatum bounced onto the couch. "And ten pushups."

"What are you, a family of athletes?" Ignoring Garret's offer, Adara leaned a hip on the couch arm rest.

Garret snorted and folded his arms behind his head. Those biceps definitely didn't represent a typical band geek. "London inherited all the agility genes. I got music."

"Mommy used to be a gymnast." Tatum cartwheeled off the couch, did some sort of flip off the coffee table and disrupted Bryan and his electronics. She landed in front of the TV with a low bow.

"Knock it off, Tatum." Bryan lunged for her.

For professing to have no athleticism, Garret moved fast. He grabbed Bryan by the belt loop and hauled him back. "No more fighting or gymnastics tonight." He actually sounded stern. "Do you want to do this competition or not?"

Competition? She'd had enough competitions with Garret already. Every win included a loss on her part. "It looks like you're handling things now." She hooked a thumb at the stairs. "Maybe I should…" The look in Tatum's big blue eyes nailed her coffin shut. Hiding a sigh, she shrugged out of her coat. "What did I sign up for?"

Both Bryan and Tatum crowed in unison, "Karaoke competition!"

Music. Of course it had to be music.

"Not your everyday, wannabe lounge-singer karaoke competition." Garret leaned over the side of the couch, lifted his violin case and wriggled his eyebrows.

"Karaoke Ambrosified." Clapping, Tatum jumped on the couch, jostling Garret.

"I have no idea what that means." Adara rubbed her forearms through her sweater, needing something solid to hold onto. Karaoke couldn't be hard to handle. There wouldn't be any classical pieces to drag her deep into Joey memories.

"Bryan inherited the Ambrose music, along with Bob's techie skills." Garret smiled proudly at the boy hunched over the coffee table with his gadget. "He figured out how to manipulate the karaoke machine to project only the bass line and harmony. The melody is up to the competitor" — he unhooked the clasps on the case and gingerly lifted his instrument — "and me."

Watching him handle the violin with such care, those large hands gentle and deft, did something strange to her blood, made it run faster, hotter. She refocused on Tatum. "So it's girls against boys?"

"Yup." Tatum spun, her blonde hair flying. "Usually it's me and Mommy against Bryan and Daddy. Uncle Garret's gonna have to sing this time."

Garret chuckled as he adjusted the violin strings. "The boys might as well concede now."

"Speak for yourself, Uncle G." Bryan snapped something in place and sat back on his heels.

"What's the prize?" Adara asked.

Garret's gaze lifted from the violin to her, dark and glittering, and his voice was inappropriately low and sexy, considering the minors in the room. "What do you want it to be, *neshama*?"

Warm tendrils unfurled everywhere, weakening her knees, and she was glad to be sitting. Falling on her face might tip him off. *Neshama.* He kept calling her that, and she definitely needed to look up the definition, but when he used that tone, she didn't care what he called her. She gave herself a mental shake. She had to focus on him going down.

Going down.

An image of him moving slowly down her body, caressing, kissing, licking skipped through her brain. Her face heated, and she bit the inside of her cheek. Where were these thoughts coming from? 'Going down', as in losing. That's what she meant. She had to look at him more as a eunuch than a man.

Perfect. A eunuch. No manly bits, no sexual lure—just a person who happened to be in the same room...a person who still watched her with enough heat to sear her nerve endings.

Oh yeah...the prize. "How can there be a winner without a judge?"

"We're all honest and impartial judges." Garret relaxed into the couch cushions, the violin resting across his knees, bow hanging loosely in one hand. If he sensed her on the verge of combustion, he didn't show it. "And since you haven't named a prize, I will. Losers have to make the winners sundaes."

"Boom. All ready." Bryan flipped on the TV. The karaoke instructions rolled across the screen. "So you can prepare, Miss Dumont, I like extra chocolate." He smiled, and it was so much like Garret's that Adara blinked twice. The boy might be a techie geek, but he wouldn't have any trouble finding girls to go to the eighth-grade dance.

"And I like extra cherries." Tatum lifted her chin, taking the challenge.

"You're giving her more sugar?" Adara whispered to Garret.

"By the time the sugar buzz kicks back into high gear, I'll be long gone." He smiled, slow and sly. "The benefits of being an uncle."

She pressed her lips together to stop a grin. It was so easy to joke with him, to forget she needed to stay aloof. To forget everything.

Bryan won the coin toss and stuck out his tongue at Tatum. "I choose *Wanted Dead or Alive*."

Adara's shoulders relaxed. Bon Jovi tunes wouldn't stir up any memories. "Is there a master song list? I need to prepare."

Tucking the violin beneath his chin, Garret looked at her from beneath lowered lashes. "Worried, Adara? I like lots of whipped cream on my sundae." His smile turned wicked. "Lots and lots of whipped cream."

She pictured whipped cream — lots and lots — but it definitely wasn't on ice cream. *Eunuch. He's a eunuch.* She cleared her throat. "That's great" — she crossed her legs and primly settled her hands in her lap — "fatty."

He gasped and paused, bow set on the strings. "I reveal my deepest, darkest adolescent wound to you and this is how you respond? With hurtful name-calling?"

"Just testing your mettle. All's fair in karaoke competition." She shrugged. "If you can't take the heat —"

Garret lunged, taking her completely by surprise. He grabbed her uninjured ankle and dragged her fully onto the couch. "Tickle attack!"

Tatum and Bryan dove in, tickling her with fierce, little fingers while Garret held her ankles gently but firmly hostage. Adara's stern pretense lasted all of two seconds. The itch to squirm and laugh burst free, uncontrollable. She kicked for freedom, flailed at the relentless hands in her ribs. The tickling didn't stop until her laughter was closer to breathless snorts.

"Cease, minions." Laughing, Garret released her legs. After a final tickle in her armpit, Tatum backed off, giggling, her blue eyes bright.

"Monsters," Adara wheezed. "All of you." She sprawled helplessly in the skewed cushions, her chest heaving, ribs aching. Her feet were still in Garret's lap but she didn't have the energy to care. She was completely out of shape when it came to laughing.

Garret squeezed her calf, the warmth from his hand seeping through denim, lingering on her skin. "All's fair in karaoke."

She kicked him lightly in the thigh with her free foot and rolled enough to find Tatum. "You're supposed to be on my team, traitor."

"No teams in tickling," she said, completely unapologetic.

Adara narrowed her eyes. "Just remember, payback comes when you least expect it." She turned her glare on Bryan, then Garret. "I shall have my vengeance."

"Promises." Garret wriggled his eyebrows, recovered his violin from its safe spot beside the couch in the corner. "Ready or not, *neshama*, here I come."

Chapter Fourteen

Adara snatched the song list Bryan tossed to her and rolled to a sit, crossing her legs pretzel-style on the couch. She flipped through the booklet. Nothing in the list could chip at her fragile composure, even if a violin was involved, and she knew exactly what song she'd sing.

Garret tapped her knee with his fist, the contact lingering with his words. "Pay attention. We're the judges this round."

She lifted her gaze to his and her pulse stuttered. No more than a few inches separated them. How had she not noticed she'd scooched so close? Heat rolled off his big body. One of the ceiling lamps was aimed straight on his face, showcasing the color range in his dark eyes. Upon first inspection, his irises appeared black, but spotlighted as they were, the striated shades varied from coffee to chocolate to sepia. She could get lost there.

"Paying attention?" He used that same low, husky voice that shot straight through her, leaving a fiery trail in all the right places.

She chanced an eye roll. Even if Tatum caught the forbidden move, it would be worth a few stickers if the ploy threw Garret off. She seriously needed to pay attention, more to herself than the competition. "What's taking you so long to start?"

His smile widened and he set the bow to strings once more. He glanced at Bryan and Tatum, who'd positioned themselves center stage, one microphone each. "Ready?"

"Ready," they said in unison, their voices amplified and fuzzed by the microphones. Bryan smacked a button on his revamped karaoke machine, and the music and words appeared on the television screen. A soft, barely discernible beat began.

Garret looked once at the TV and closed his eyes. After a handful of breaths, he joined the beat at exactly the right moment...with his eyes shut.

Her moments-old vow to pay attention only to herself drifted away. He was magic. It was the best, most applicable word in her vocabulary. As he had the night they met, he seemed to exude the music. His dreamy smile belonged to someone who was completely happy, blissfully unaware of anything beyond the quick, sweet notes pouring from his instrument. It didn't matter that he played an '80s hair-band ballad instead of Tchaikovsky. He was a creature of irresistible beauty, the Pied Piper in the flesh, replacing a pipe with a violin.

Bryan's voice started in with the lyrics, cracking her daze. She gulped air. Since when did she forget to breathe? Adara forced herself to turn from Garret and face the kids. It took all her willpower. Despite the hazard to her health, she didn't want to stop watching him.

The chorus came and Bryan belted it out, not bad at all. Then, it was Tatum's turn.

Adara forced her hands to remain on her lap instead of covering her ears as instinct demanded. As Tatum sang, watching her with big, earnest eyes, she did her best not to wince or shudder. Whatever family musical genes Bryan inherited had left a negative balance for his sister. She couldn't match a note.

Tatum screamed into the chorus, and not even the professional violin could help. The final duet was an auditory bloodbath. Tatum screeched an impromptu finale and the song finally ended. An unnatural twist of sweet violin and shriek echoed in the sudden silence.

"Dear God," Adara whispered and slumped into the couch, her eardrums aching.

Garret leaned close and his warm breath stirred her hair. "Told you I needed help."

"You didn't want to suffer alone." She turned her head enough to meet his gaze, only inches away. "Not the same thing."

"True. But I won't apologize, since it got you here." His quick-fire grin stole her breath, causing her lips tingle. A small shift by either one of them could breach that distance, make contact, mouth to soft mouth.

"Well?" Tatum asked.

Garret suddenly straightened and applauded with gusto. His gentle elbow nudge reminded Adara to join in. Bryan bowed and Tatum performed a cross between a curtsy and a twirl, all smiles.

He rubbed his chin, his expression grave. His gaze cut to Adara, amusement sparkling like fireworks. "Perhaps our guest judge should comment first."

"Coward," she muttered, ignoring his chuckle. She struggled free of the couch and perched on the cushion edge. "You both clearly gave one hundred percent effort. Well done. Tatum, your enthusiasm was reflected in every note." The little girl's toothy smile inspired the warm and fuzzies. "Bryan, you'd make a great Jon Bon Jovi impersonator." The boy's smile was even bigger than his sister's. "But, since I'm forced to choose a winner, my vote goes to" — she steeled herself for the tantrum — "Bryan."

"Aw, man." Tatum stomped a foot and crossed her arms, but her sharp gaze had already dismissed Adara and gone straight to Garret's jugular. If she was going down in flames, it would be because her favorite uncle allowed it.

"Sorry, sweetie." Garret made a sad face. "Bryan got you on this one. Keep practicing. You'll get him next time."

While Bryan fist-pumped the air, Tatum blazed a glare at them all. Adara bit her cheek to hide a smile. One of the things that made Tatum her favorite student was her passion. Win or lose, she always made it clear how she felt, and surprisingly, Garret's gentle encouragement seemed to bank any tantrum.

"Is that what your violin mentor told you? Keep practicing?" She refused to retreat when he rested his forearms on his thighs, his elbow brushing her knee.

His expression softened, full of memories. "She'd smack me on the back of the head with her bow and say, '*Why you not practice? Lazy American. Ten more times you play, then go home and play ten more. I watch you with my third eye.'"*

"Third eye?" That wasn't at all creepy.

He laughed. "She haunted my nightmares. Scary woman, but a great violinist."

"Your turn, Miss Dumont." Bryan handed her his microphone while Tatum held onto hers, keeping her performance spot. "Just choose the song number on the karaoke machine. The beat will start and the words will come up on the screen."

"Wait, I have to compete with Tatum? I thought we were a team."

"You're both on the girl team, but after losing once, each person gets one more shot. Lose twice and you're out. Whoever's standing last wins for the team. Family game rules."

She joined Tatum at center stage. "So either way, we win this round, right?"

"Right." Tatum lifted her hand for a high-five, and they smacked palms. "And since you're the guest, you get to pick the song."

Adara leaned down and whispered, "The boys are *so* losing."

Tatum's grin brightened her whole being, and Adara returned her smile. Funny, she couldn't remember the last time she'd shared a smile with her favorite student. But she didn't stop.

"Prepare for three minutes of mush." Bryan flopped onto the couch, stretched out his legs, and crossed his ankles on Garret's thigh. "Girls always choose love songs or bubble-gum pop."

Garret lifted his eyebrows and cocked his head, openly studying Adara. "Not sure I agree with you, Bry. Miss Dumont's a contradiction. She seems reserved, but check out her black sweater and black boots—and I don't mean her sprained ankle boot. That could mark a secret Goth vibe, possibly an indication she's into indie rock or grunge."

Bryan glanced at her normal boot, looking dubious. "She looks like a teacher."

"That's her disguise, and she's conditioned you to see it because you're a student." Garret nodded, his eyes gleaming. "You have to take a step back and look deeper."

Adara crossed her arms and glared. How did he know about her love for Goth?

"Check out her hair. Sleek and straight, every strand in place." Garret's eyes narrowed, assessing. "What does that tell you?"

"That she uses a comb?" Bryan's voice hissed with exasperation.

"No, get with it, bro." He lightly backhanded his nephew's foot. "The art of observation is useful in all aspects of life, so start learning. Her hair contradicts her choice in attire and reveals to the careful observer that, despite her best efforts not to care, deep down, she does. And the style she's chosen, a sleek bob, indicates she prefers to stay in control."

His accuracy was unnerving. Adara punched the song selection in the karaoke machine. "Let's just wrap this up, shall we? I have a hearts and flowers meeting in an hour."

Garret's teeth flashed. "Sassy when riled. Good thing to remember too, Bry, especially if your study subject is a woman."

"Specimen has wriggled off the slide," she said into the mic and pushed the Start button.

"Whatever." Bryan slipped his hands behind his head and closed his eyes. "Wake me up when it's over."

The song started, a light beat of nothing but crash cymbal, and since the music was technically supposed to start with the beat, Garret was already behind. He scrambled to set up, straightening and bracing the violin. He caught the rhythm with the next note and closed his eyes, that same, dreamy smile revived.

Bryan perked up, and she suspected it had something to do with her music selection. Garret had pegged her correctly in that area too, not that she'd admit anything. Unless she was in a particularly melancholy mood, she avoided love songs. And she'd always loved a hard beat and rough-voiced lead singer, dark lyrics not quite tipping completely into metal.

Enter Sandman by Metallica was perfect.

Since the lyrics came after a fair stretch of music and drums, she had time and reason to ogle Garret without fear of being caught. He must have lots of karaoke time with the kids because he seemed to know her song choice by heart, which only added to her begrudging respect. Not every violinist would memorize Metallica.

He opened his eyes and smiled straight at her, pulling her into his magic.

That fluttering abnormality between her ribs awakened, and she didn't have time to force it back down. The lyrics came up, and she had to sing.

Funny thing about family genes... In the Dumont family, Joey had scored. He'd inherited magnetism, good looks, an outgoing nature and musical skills up the ying-yang. The arts category hadn't touched her, but Joey had charmed her into singing while he played, so she wasn't Tatum-terrible. She added some head-banging to mess up her hair, just to prove Garret wrong.

The violin scratched off-tune and missed a single beat before smoothly falling back into rhythm.

Tatum's turn came and Adara straightened before she fell over. Head-banging took more skills than she had. She was clearly not born to be a musician. Even with hair hanging in her eyes, she didn't miss Garret's wide smile, his full attention on her. She gripped the microphone harder as warmth joined the butterflies inside. The perfect violinist had messed up because of her. Maybe it was wrong to feel smug about that.

But it felt…right.

Three more songs, a final win over Bryan and a victory sundae later, Adara quietly set her half-eaten ice cream in the sink while Garret and Bryan argued the eternal question—guitar or violin? Joey had always sworn that whatever a guitar could do, a violin could do better, not that she'd back up Garret by mentioning it.

"See you Monday, Tatum." Adara high-fived her karaoke partner's sticky hand, and Tatum went back to her sundae, her face smeared with chocolate. Poor Bob and London were going to have a long night, and she preferred to be far away before they returned.

"I'll walk you out." Garret licked his spoon and dropped it in the sink with a clatter.

"Not necessary." She headed for the door.

"Mandatory." He jogged around the kitchen island, following her. "What sort of peasant lets the hero depart without an appropriate display of appreciation?"

Adara snorted. "I prefer to be appreciated from afar."

"Appreciation cannot be appropriately administered from a distance." Laughter thrummed in his voice. "Sorry."

She grabbed the doorknob and twisted, but the deadbolt blocked her quick escape. Garret planted a palm on the door above her head.

"Thanks for saving me, *neshama*." The solid wall of his body was a heat lamp at her back. His voice dropped to that low, sexy rumble that made her thighs clench. "Truly, I would've been lost tonight without you."

"Doubtful." Steeling herself, she pivoted to face him. His closeness kicked her heart into overdrive, made it hard to breathe. "Is *neshama* another word for 'sucker'?"

"No," he murmured, leaning into her. His breath fanned her cheek, sending shivers down her back. She expected his trademark smile to show up. Instead, his expression intensified to serious, almost longing. His gaze drifted to her mouth.

The fluttering went wild, and she swallowed, pressing harder into the solid door. She wasn't ready to be kissed by him, wasn't ready to let someone else into her life, didn't know if she'd ever be ready. Finding the deadbolt by feel alone, she turned it.

The click seemed to snap his somber moment, and he straightened, removing his hand from the door.

She rushed into the cold night without looking back.

Chapter Fifteen

Another two weeks watching Garret woo her kids with his music while denying his persistent, invasive charm drove Adara to the edge. She needed to run, to burn off the various frustrations, all converging into the perfect storm. Cursing her sore ankle, she limped from the kitchen to the living room to her bedroom and back again. For some reason she couldn't name, she hesitated outside Joey's room. She hadn't gone in since after the funeral, when she'd stashed everything of his, every picture, memento, instrument and stray rosin container inside, set a bouquet of white roses on his dresser and shut the door, sealing it like a tomb.

It *was* a tomb, everything Joey decomposing inside.

Her hand trembling, she touched the cool doorknob. She missed him so much, but opening the tomb, remembering, would crack all her pieces. She wasn't sure she could put them back together again.

A hushed scrape, no louder than a mouse bumping an empty box, came from within.

The hair on her nape lifted. Considering that she hadn't cleaned Joey's room for over a year, a rodent infestation wasn't beyond the realm of possibility. There hadn't been any signs, no poop pellets or nibbled packages. Goosebumps prickled down her arms. What if it was something else, like spiders? Cockroaches?

Joey's restless spirit come back to haunt her?

The doorbell boomed Beethoven's *Fifth*, and she jumped with a gasp. One hand pressed to her hammering heart, she gimped for the door. Maybe there was such a thing as too much alone time.

She opened the door and her stomach somersaulted. Garret stood on her porch, his hair neatly pulled back, the blazer, white button-down and jeans combo an upgrade. His beast was parked in her driveway, still rumbling. It was so unexpected, finding him there on her porch as if her discontent had conjured him, that her mind freeze-framed.

His eyebrows bunched. "You didn't just open the door without checking who waited on the other side, did you?"

She tried to look innocent.

"Adara" — he said her name like a reprimand — "you need to be more careful. A small town isn't a protection. Always, *always* look before you open the door. And for God's sake, keep it locked."

Maybe she should be annoyed, but his concern was kind of...nice. "You're right." Tucking her hands behind her back, she made sure her tone was sweet. "Next time I see it's you on the other side of the door, I won't answer. For the record, there hasn't been a murder in Graywood since at least 1902, but statistics show harassment by traveling musicians is on the rise. Speaking of, why are you here?"

"I agreed to play at the college tonight for students and their guests." He straightened and dropped his chin, the seductive look sparking heat all the way to her toes. If he had any idea how much that look affected her, he'd use it more. "Will you go with me?"

"Nope."

He exhaled, long and slow. "I need someone there for support."

"So take London or your BFF Ian."

"Ian wouldn't last past the first song before pissing someone off. London canceled five minutes ago. Bob and the kids are all sick with the flu." He gave her puppy-dog eyes. "Please?"

"You play professionally but need a posse for support?" She planted a hand on her hip and gave him a hard stare. "You're the most confident person I've met. Not buying it, not going."

"Okay. Fine. I'll reveal another deep, dark secret if that's what it takes to convince you." He swiped a hand down his face, his fingers trembling slightly. "My mother demanded that London and I excel at our natural gifts. For London, it was gymnastics, and me? Well..." His mouth twisted. "She laid the violin in my hands and pushed me to perfection. Relentlessly. We weren't allowed to even think the word 'quit', and second place was a curse word at the Ambrose residence."

If Garret had smiled at all while he spoke, she might have questioned the believability of so stringent an upbringing. But he hadn't, and with each word, her heart wrenched tighter.

"I fought for her approval, of course, but in her role of pushing, I think she forgot the art of encouragement. She'd criticize, never compliment. Once she pointed out my mistakes, she made me practice until I could perform the song flawlessly — for hours, until my arms shook."

"Mother drill sergeant?" She tried for humor, an out he didn't take.

His throat worked. "I often questioned whether she actually loved me or London, let alone liked us. But that's not the point I'm trying to make. I continued with my lessons and applied to Curtis Institute. I wanted her to be there for my audition, not only for encouragement in a time when I really needed it, but also so I could show her that I'm worthy of her approval." His voice snagged and stumbled on. "She refused. She informed me that Juilliard was the only acceptable school for an Ambrose."

Adara swallowed hard. Joey had wanted to study at Curtis, and she'd accompanied him to the audition. Despite rocking his performance, he hadn't gotten in. The rejection had hit him hard, made him question his talent and path in life. It had taken him almost a year to bounce back, then he'd got sick.

"I was accepted into Curtis," he continued in a soft tone, "but I'll never forget the empty chair in the front row. It was her silent censure, a sign that, no matter my accomplishments, I'd never meet her expectations. She died suddenly of a heart attack a week later. I know it's not true, but I sometimes still feel it was her final refusal to give me her blessing."

She smoothed her sweater, fighting a losing urge to give him a hug. How could anyone, let alone his mother, watch Garret play the violin and not be awed?

"I know it's irrational. I'm a grown man, a successful musician, and I'm confident in who I am. I don't need anyone's approval, yet sometimes I can't push her words or that empty chair from my head." He stooped and looked her full in the face, his eyes shadowed with memories. "Tonight, if you don't come, there will be four empty chairs—no family, no faces I can use to buffer that image. Adara, I need you. Please."

Crap. She understood the emptiness when someone you expected to be there was suddenly gone, the lasting effects of that absence. Despite the potential consequences, she couldn't let him go alone. Still wearing her teacher clothes, she fingered her pencil skirt. Calf-length flat boots hid the prescribed ankle brace and a sweater made up her ensemble, good enough to wear to a community college concert. She met his gaze. "How long is it supposed to last and how many classical songs will I have to endure?"

His smile came to life, brilliant and just for her. He threw his arms around her and squeezed a squeak from her. "No longer than an hour," he murmured against her temple. "Thank you."

Standing stiff in his arms, Adara tried to ignore his warm, solid strength and how good it felt to be held, held by him. The consequences were starting already.

"Grab your coat, Miss Dumont. It's cold." His breath brushed the rim of her ear, hot and intimate. "And don't forget to lock your door."

Screw the door. It was the iron bars protecting her heart she needed to worry about.

* * * *

Fifteen minutes later, Adara perched on a hard, plastic chair in the college auditorium. Three empty chairs lined up beside her, tagged with 'reserved' signs, and she considered taking them down. Then again, if she did that, other people would sit close to her, want to talk, make her pretend to be sociable. She could handle only so much at one time, and dealing with an hour of classical music and a barrage of Joey memories were enough.

The audience behind her hummed, their excitement an infection. Apparently, Garret had a reputation in other places this side of the pond. The chairs, music stands and a drum set looked deceptively small and innocent on the stage. He'd mentioned that he'd hand-selected the students who were playing with him tonight, which she supposed only added to the community interaction. The smaller venue he wanted for inspiration.

She clasped her trembling hands in her lap. The cello, viola and violin crouched beside the chairs, shadowed assassins ready to strike. Part of her normal life when Joey was alive had included lounging around on the couch reading while he whirled around the house with his violin, unable to sit still. Tears burned her eyes and she blinked them away before they pooled. The music hadn't even started and her seams threatened to split.

Staring at the velvet maroon curtain hiding other horrors behind the stage, she focused on everything Garret had told her. The fact that he'd continued with his violin in light of his mother's influence only showed what sort of person he was. He could have focused on the bitter journey that brought him to this point, rejected his natural talent and taken a different road. Instead, he embraced both the positive and negative moments and used his pain and triumphs to bring joy to the world. He stayed true to what he loved. He cared about others. Whatever he committed to, he was all in, devoted all the way.

Blasted man. Annoying, persistent, bane of her life. He was impossible to dislike.

The curtain stirred, and the crowd quieted as the sections parted. The selected students filed in one by one, Garret coming in last to a rippling applause. He paused and bowed, wearing one of his pure sunshine smiles.

Dang, he's breathtaking. He was made for the spotlight and owned it unapologetically. Had he chosen a different instrument to master or picked an alternate career, it wouldn't have mattered. He'd be front and center, completely involved, no matter what he did. And since he was on the stage and she was part of the audience, it was her obligation to admire him from afar. Or twentyish feet, the space between the front row and the stage. She could handle that.

He launched into an introduction speech, and maybe she should've listened but she needed to prepare for the musical onslaught, and Garret made that challenge a little easier. The long hair, jeans and Gothic jewelry gave the proper blazer and button-down shirt a dangerous edge, reminders that he might rock your socks off as easily as play a lullaby. He didn't let anyone leash him into any category.

She liked that about him too.

Even more, she liked how natural it was with him, how easy. He didn't remind her that she wasn't normal. He didn't give her those sad, knowing looks that everyone else did, as if she couldn't see them. He didn't try to fix her. Instead, he let her just be. Only Joey had ever done that.

Garret stopped talking and lifted his violin.

The already-sizzling tension in Adara's body wrenched tight. The cello thrummed to life, a deep heartbeat, the viola quickly threading in, and a tremor ripped at her defenses. Garret and the other musicians faded into the background. She didn't need to hear more than a measure to recognize Vivaldi's *Winter*. Joey had adored the *Four Seasons*. *Summer* was his favorite, *Winter* second best. The smooth violin took over the melody, but the past morphed the music, stealing Garret's particular, sleek flavor and replacing it with one more familiar, more painful — an open wound on her soul.

Visions of Joey sawing on his violin filled her head, the way he'd perch on the back of the couch swaying in time to the music, his fingers flying, his eyes closed. His smile had always been vicious when he played Vivaldi, as if he himself was the seasons released on the world to do as he wished.

Adara sucked in air through her closed throat, released it. Two sucked in, two out. *Winter* didn't last more than four minutes. *Four minutes. Two hundred and forty breaths.* As much as she wanted to run, the music paralyzed her, holding her prisoner. She was vaguely aware of clamping the chair edge to stay upright. The hairline fracture in her shell lengthened with each beat, seconds away from cracking completely, leaving her defenseless. Time passed in sharp, endless movie clips.

Joey in his ratty U2 T-shirt, spinning, spinning.

Don't crack.

Joey jumping on her bed while she read, doing his best to annoy her.

Breathe.

Her, breaking Joey's bow in a tussle. He hadn't talked to her for a week.

Focus.

Joey and Gia cackling at some tasteless joke, Joey on stage at Curtis in his Converse and suit, his heart in every note, Joey dragging her to the piano, Joey wearing his brave face, Joey so pale, crushing her hand.

Joey dying.

The last note rang, a canyon echo from far off, and Garret's voice replaced the music, his words indecipherable through the buzzing in her head. The stage and auditorium blackened with nightmare shadows, desperately surreal.

Bass started up with cymbal, then drum, and the viola kicked in with the next beat. Note by note, she was hauled free from the mire of the past. Not classical at all. Not music usually played for professors and music snobs. Hard, in your face rock, and not any random song.

Enter Sandman.

Adara sucked in a deep breath, her relieved sob drowned by the drum. She lifted her gaze. Blurred by her tears, Garret stood on the stage directly across from her, as if simply waiting patiently for her to confirm she was with him before moving on. He winked once, and the music again swept him away.

'What if we create new emotional ties, you, music and me?'

Only a few weeks ago he'd asked that, beneath the planetarium stars, crafting a memory she could cling to, as if he'd known all along that this moment would come, that he'd need to drag her back to the present. Numb, she watched him coax a smile from the serious viola player. He did this for her, disrupted custom, risked his local reputation to rescue her from herself.

Something inside her snapped, whether into place or breaking free, she wasn't sure. All along, she'd thought he was lost in the music, but she was wrong. He *was* the music, a harmony that inexplicably tethered her, there for as long as his focus remained on her.

The terror in that realization didn't come.

Chapter Sixteen

As the last college stragglers filtered out, Adara slumped beside a colorful corkboard offering student services. She ripped a paper strip off a poster titled "Going Solo? Take a Wookie." Single or not, everyone could always use a Chewbacca sidekick.

Since Garret was her ride, she had no choice but to wait around for him, not that she minded much. She needed some transition time. Returning to the echoing silence while music still rang in her soul would be too much.

She proffered an appropriately polite smile to a passing couple and let it slip away when they turned the corner, their voices fading in the distance. More than an hour of music, misery and memories and she'd survived—not because she'd been tough enough, though. Over and over, Garret had flung her a musical lifeline. To top it off, the undeniably snooty classical music audience had given him a standing ovation. She had too, once she'd gotten her legs working again.

He'd seduced another sliver of her, and she didn't know how to get it back — or if she even wanted to. She was too emotionally drained to determine if she was stronger without it or more brittle.

"There you are." His violin case strapped to his back, Garret strode down the hallway toward her. "I thought you might have ditched me."

"It's too far to limp back." She surrendered to another few seconds of admiring him from afar. It would help her resistance if he resembled Shrek instead of Apollo, but even if he did, she had a sinking feeling she'd still be here, leaning against the wall, unable to look away as he drew ever closer. He was magnetic.

Soon enough, he stood right in front of her, too close to openly ogle without being awkward. "You could have called a cab," he said softly, "or Gia."

She shrugged one shoulder, still relying on the wall for support.

He cocked his head, studying her with those dark eyes that seemed to see everything. "I'm not sorry that you came with me instead of my family."

"That's cold. I'm sure each time they barfed, they were thinking about you."

"Not what I mean." His grin was hardly more than a twitch. "I realized something tonight. As I looked out into the crowd, it was your face I searched for first and last, your approval I wanted."

She straightened, her pulse picking up speed. He was tiptoeing close to forbidden ground, prepping to talk about emotions and uncomfortable stuff. She could feel it. "Didn't you see me clapping along with everyone else? Kick-butt moral support, empty chair-filler extraordinaire."

"It wasn't about moral support or memories or battling ghosts. I wanted, more than anything, to find you there every time I looked." He paused, as if making sure she listened. "Only you."

Dealing with more feelings tonight was beyond her capacity. She turned for the hallway and the safety of the door around the corner.

He stopped her escape with a gentle grasp on her coat sleeve. "It's okay to be affected, Adara."

Not really. Not when her pieces, if broken again, might never fit back together. "I'm sure your fan club membership shot up tonight. Ready to go?"

"Are you honestly claiming you felt nothing tonight?" A hint of defiance invaded his expression. "Not even for a minute? Not for the music?" His voice dropped to a husky murmur. "Not for me?"

Wildly beating wings erupted inside, and it took all her teacher discipline to hold his unblinking gaze and keep her mask on. "Your version of *Enter Sandman* was decent."

The performance must have erased his sense of humor. Deadly intensity replaced his trademark smile. He stepped forward, forcing her to backtrack. It was either that or stand toe-to-toe with him. Already, his heat licked her skin. Any closer and she might combust.

"So, to clarify," he said in a low, dangerous tone that made her stomach clench, "you feel nothing for me." He eased even closer.

Adara retreated and her butt hit the wall. Electricity charged the air between them. She couldn't move, couldn't breathe. Cold fury set his features in stone and his eyes sparked, fierce and relentless. An always-smiling Garret was tempting enough, but this menacing man here now, who refused to let her escape, scrambled all her senses.

"Correct." She somehow managed to keep her voice calm, to hide the storm rising inside.

Leaning in slowly, he planted a hand on each side of her head, holding both her gaze and body captive. His breath mingled with hers. "I don't believe you."

"Sounds like a personal problem." *Blast.* She could barely get the words out.

His full, generous mouth was too close to hers, making her traitorous lips tingle. The stubble on his lean jaw called to her fingers, and she fisted her hands to keep them under control. She'd never wanted to touch something so badly. Not *something* — him. Garret. But giving in would unlace the cocoon she'd kept so carefully constructed since Joey.

Without warning, he tucked her hair behind her ear. His callused fingertips trailed her jaw and her mouth went dry. Gently, he cupped her chin. "You feel nothing now?"

"Nothing." Her voice surrendered to him first, nothing more than a breathless whisper. He had to feel her thundering heart vibrate through his fingers.

His eyes flashed, dark and daring. She should duck under his arm and run like snarling hell hounds were chasing her, but her willpower snuffed out. As if sensing her incapacity, he pressed his lips beneath her ear. Her uncooperative eyelids fluttered, the next defense to fail. His stubble scraped her cheek, and that simple hint of rough on smooth shot flames into every cold spot. His breath brushed her ear. "Now?"

His low voice nibbled along every nerve. She couldn't answer. She wanted to slide her fingers over his jaw then tangle them in his too-long hair, to press against him and fit her body into his until all her broken pieces were forged in his heat and remade. She wanted his arms around her, his mouth on hers and nothing between them but skin.

He eased back and held her gaze. "Nothing?"

The overload of sensations, the longing and hiding and defending all blended into an Adara bomb. If she didn't do something, she'd erupt. With trembling fingers, she caressed his jaw. The sensation was everything she'd hoped for, bristly and rough, unexpectedly intimate.

Garret sucked in a breath and closed his eyes. When his lashes lifted, his eyes gleamed like obsidian fire. Then his mouth was on hers. He pressed his hard, strong body into hers, trapping her fully against the wall.

She slipped her fingers into his hair, unable to resist. It was even silkier than she'd imagined. In the next breath, his mouth claimed her full attention. The man knew how to kiss, with the perfect combination of lips and tongue, just enough to make her want more. Hints of coffee and mint laced his breath, and his cologne, citrus and honey and summer, infused her senses, another link in the chain connecting her to him.

He cupped her face with both hands, and she wrapped her fingers around his forearms, needing the extra stability to prevent a knee-buckling slump to the floor. She hadn't realized how hungry she was for contact, her need verging on ravenous. Her need for *him*.

A need her heart couldn't allow.

Adara tensed, and as suddenly as Garret had kissed her, she pushed him back a step and ducked past him. She limped away as fast as she could, around the corner, out the door, into the cold night air, her mouth still warm and tingling. She shouldn't have gone with him tonight, shouldn't have let his sob story melt her defenses or stayed past the first song.

She should've had the foresight to drive herself.

The parking lot was all but empty with the exception of Garret's car. Her options were either catch a ride home with him or call a cab and wait, and he'd undoubtedly feel obligated to keep her company until the cab arrived. It was a lose-lose situation. Jaw clenched, she lurched off the sidewalk and onto the blacktop, her ankle throbbing as she reached his car.

"Adara, wait." Again, he was too close, right behind her. He planted a hand on the door, caging her on one side. His heat at her back sank through her coat and his breath brushed her ear.

She didn't turn, her weakness for him too close to the surface. If she faced him, she'd crumble again, no question.

"Come home with me," he said, his voice shadow-soft.

Adara blinked. Did he honestly think, after one kiss, she'd turn into one of his overzealous fans and join the ranks of violinist-crazed bimbos? Maybe his ego was bigger than she'd originally thought. She spun around and he backpedaled, wisely giving her room.

"You're clearly overestimating your charm, Ambrose." She pointed a finger in his face. "Just because I lost my head for a second doesn't mean I'm jumping into bed with you."

"Slow down, darling. I wasn't suggesting anything sordid or sexual." He tilted his head, and the barest hint of a smile returned. "Not that I can't be persuaded otherwise."

"I'm not your 'darling'." She barred her arms over her coat and blasted him with her coldest stare, the one that made most people slink away. As usual, he seemed immune.

"You haven't been to my house yet." A vulnerability she'd never heard before laced his tone, erasing her original assumption. It was too real, too compelling to be a play. "I want to show you who I am, pieces of my life that I don't share with most people."

"I already know who you are." Her heart was thundering again, a hard vibration against her collar. And as much as she wanted to deny it, the offer to know more was tempting. Yet, he'd expect reciprocation and she wasn't ready for that, didn't know if she'd ever be ready.

"I'm more than Tatum's uncle, more than that wheezing wannabe runner, more than a musician." He swiped a hand over his face. "This is all about me showing you who I am, nothing else. I don't expect anything more than what you're willing to freely offer." Dropping his chin, he said in a coaxing sing-song, "I've got rocky road ice cream."

Adara focused on the cross hanging right below his powerful throat, a throat she could spend a lot of time nibbling, nuzzling. *Not helpful.* She dropped her gaze to his black boots. Every minute spent with him eroded her failing willpower, opening the potential for pain, but her self-control seemed to have melted with his music, his kiss the final strike. "Fine. Only because you owe me ice cream."

Chapter Seventeen

Garret kept his mouth shut the entire drive back to his house. He'd pushed Adara farther than he'd meant to, and while she was still with him, he sensed it wouldn't take more than a wrong word or move to send her running.

He gripped the steering wheel and kept his expression cool, even though he wanted to smile, big and goofy. She'd responded to his past with compassion, attended his performance even knowing the potential personal consequences, stayed long enough to let him prove she could trust him — that he'd catch her before she fell, that he'd be there for her when she needed him.

At least, that's what he hoped she got from tonight, an open window to the other side, to show she could survive the pain and still find joy. Maybe not today, but eventually.

And absolutely with him.

He stole a glance, unable to stop himself. She gazed out of the side window into the night, her fingers tight in her lap, revealing how close she was to snapping. *Ben-zonna*, she was beautiful, broken and brave. If it took gallons of rocky road ice cream to convince her she didn't need to pretend with him, he'd buy the factory.

He turned onto his street. Only one elderly couple lived on the corner of the dead-end lane, and his long, paved driveway increased the neighborly space to reclusive. His home--away-from-motel-room home sat bullseye in a ten-acre woodland lot. He hadn't spent much time here, but he liked the impression of country quiet, such a welcome contradiction to his last three years, cities, noise and people.

He pulled in and parked. "Here we are." With the motor turned off, the silence thrummed. "What do you think?"

Adara leaned closer to the windshield and studied his house.

He joined her, trying to view it through her eyes. He'd bought the acreage the second he'd scraped enough money together for a down payment, after paying off his violin. A few years had passed before his finances settled into security, and by then, his vision was ready for blueprints and construction. A year later, he had his house. The property manager had spent more time inside than he had.

"It's...big." She quirked an eyebrow at him. "Gothic mansion much?"

The backdrop of night accentuated the eaves and steep gables, adding to the impression — and the fact that she'd pegged it correctly stirred a secret warmth. Even while she resisted the tension between them, she discerned his hidden trappings. He released the smile he'd been reining in. "Maybe."

"Do you conduct experiments in the attic?" She resumed studying the architecture, but she'd unfastened her seatbelt, a good sign. "I bet that weathervane on the roof is to harness lightning."

"You have the best imagination, *neshama*. But my lab is only open on Tuesdays and Fridays, and I ran out of phosphate and frog eyes last week, so you're safe."

As fast as he could, he opened the door and hurried to her side, too slow. She climbed out first, quashing his attempt to be pamper her. He instead retrieved his violin from the trunk — at least one lady appreciated his attention — and returned to Adara's side. She still examined the house, her expression shuttered in the floodlight. He hated that look on her, the look that said she'd sunk deeper into herself, putting distance between them.

"I designed it myself," he said softly, watching her face, alert to any hint he might be losing her before even getting her inside.

Her gaze flicked to his, glittering with curiosity. That warmth inside him spread. "Really?"

"A boy has to have something else to do and dream about besides violin." He offered his arm. "The rocky road is inside."

She eyed his arm and the seconds ticked away, each one a battle between withdrawal and advance. The war ended on an almost soundless sigh, the verdict yet unannounced. "That's not creepy at all, kind of like a guy handing out candy to little girls in his white, windowless van."

He leaned nearer and whispered, "I might have candy too."

The corners of her lovely mouth lifted, not much, but enough. "You're reprehensible."

"But honest."

"I bet most liars don't announce their dishonesty." She took another look at his house, as if giving herself one last chance to retreat. Then, she slipped her fingers in the crook of his arm.

Willing contact.

His heart expanded, pounding a triumphant beat. He wanted to pull her closer, tight against his side, but the fact Adara had chosen to take his arm rather than reject it? Huge. Gigantic. Monumental. Especially after he'd kissed her. But to be fair, they'd been equal partners in the kiss. *Chara,* her mouth was as delectable as he'd fantasized – soft, supple and enough to drive a man to do almost anything for a shot at another kiss.

"Don't judge my housekeeping skills." He waited for the alarm system to beep before opening the door wide and flicking on the foyer light. "I haven't quite settled in."

Her attention might have been on the house, but his was all on her, gauging her reaction. Her lips were parted. All traces of tension vanished in the bright sparkle of her eyes. Their steps tapped hollowly on the wood floor, a victory call rising to the vaulted ceiling.

"Want a tour?" He set his violin case down and shrugged out of his coat.

Just as with the planetarium stars, she'd lost all interest in him. She tilted her head back, studying the coffered ceiling. "Is there a basement?"

He smirked. He knew her well enough to predict where her question headed. "Only an attic for ghosties, goblins and human experiments. I'm relatively certain no people of any culture have been buried on the property, no questionable rituals have occurred in the near proximity and no ravens were harmed while building."

"I was only wondering if you have a wine cellar, psycho." The words held zero bite.

"Of course you were. Hand over your jacket." He didn't miss the twitch of her mouth as she unbuttoned her wool pea coat and handed it to him. Her chilled fingers brushed his and he resisted the need to take them in his. He wanted to wrap her in his warmth until every bit of cold eked away, but acting on that desire would send her backpedaling out of the door. He wasn't ready to let her go just yet.

"You designed everything?" Adara faced the curving stairway sweeping upstairs, one of his favorite pieces of the house. Iron spokes in an abstract design formed the balustrade, and the ceiling purposefully created an oval portal above the stairwell, small enough to leave everything above obscured in mystery.

"I had the ideas and hired an architect. He taught me the meaning of 'fenestration' and other words I'll never use again and didn't hesitate to point out when my ideas were impractical"—he grinned and headed up the stairs—"or ostentatious."

"You? Ostentatious?" Following him, she clasped her hands behind her back, clearly going for an innocent look. "I can't imagine."

"I blame it on my repressed childhood and all the moments I stole back from violin practice, usually late at night when everyone else slept."

"It's not hard to picture you as one of those kids who climbed out of the window and tormented the neighbors." Adara trailed the iron railing with one finger, the touch almost a caress. Maybe if he wore iron, she'd touch *him* that way.

He paused at the landing. "No windows for me. I'd turn the television down to almost inaudible, sit close to the screen and watch horror — all those old, cheesy Gothic movies with the dark shadows and monsters. I promised myself I'd live in a castle one day. Never outgrew that one." He lovingly admired his creation, from the Circassian walnut walls to the detailed cornices he'd spent a ridiculous number of hours hunting down. "While this isn't quite a castle, it's close enough to make me happy."

Examining him as if he were a glitch in the human species, she stopped beside him. "You're never what I expect."

"Is that a bad thing?"

She hesitated, then a tiny smile curled her mouth. "Jury's out."

That smile was enough of a verdict for him. He returned her smile tenfold and continued their stroll down the hall. "I haven't furnished anything up here yet. I basically occupy one-eighth of my house — the kitchen, one bathroom and the temporary music slash living room."

"All this space." Adara's voice echoed, filling the emptiness. "Do you plan to adopt a cat herd to keep you company?"

"Would you visit me again if I did?"

She made a show of considering it, her mouth twisted, her gaze heavenward, and he couldn't help but hold his breath, waiting for her answer. "Odds of visitation might go up."

Felines and an ice cream factory, a small price to pay to lure her back. "Then tomorrow I'm going to the pet shelter. Will you join me?"

"Can't." She didn't look at him. "I have plans."

A chill pierced his chest, followed by an ungodly heat. She had plans...with someone else, someone who wasn't him. He managed to keep his tone calm and his steps easy as they moved to his as-of-yet vacant bedroom. He clicked on the light. "Anything exciting?"

Adara stalled in the threshold, her eyes wide. "This room..." The words were barely a murmur. She glided inside and made a slow circle, her gaze roaming from the mahogany wainscoting to the matching parquet floor to the picture windows. "It's...awesome."

Her contagious wonder temporarily overshadowed the fact she had plans without him. He joined her in admiring the oversized iron ceiling medallion. "This is the master bedroom...or will be, eventually."

"What's wrong with you?" She gave him a bewildered look. "Why waste moments downstairs when you could be here?"

Her words made his imagination spin, of a giant bed right where they stood, pillows, silk sheets and her. *Ben-zonna.* He wiped a hand over his face, which did nothing to ease the steel cords suddenly strung taut through his entire body. She belonged here, with him. She just hadn't recognized it. It was just as well he hadn't ordered a bed and set it up. Otherwise, he'd be sorely tempted to take her down with a few tickles then kiss her until she admitted she didn't want to leave. Taking the necessary baby steps to win her over was slowly killing him. He blew out a silent breath, willing certain stiff parts of his body to relax before she noticed.

That would send her running, no matter how much rocky road inhabited his freezer.

"Yes, well"—he cleared his throat—"you haven't seen the downstairs yet."

"Lead on." She followed him out, but not before one final, longing glance back.

"So what pressing activity do you have on a Friday night that is more important than helping me select my future feline companions?" He stuffed his hands in his pockets and went for casual.

"I have a board-approved, cut-the-music-program strategy to implement. The only caveat is collecting enough parent signatures." She kept her gaze on her feet, as if she might stumble down the stairs. The dark fall of her hair hid half her face. "That's what I'm doing all weekend. Canvassing. Collecting signatures. I can't do it on school time, and interrupting weekday evening dinners and family time won't win me any points, so weekends are it."

His throat tightened. Tatum didn't have a musical bone in her body, but no matter what the school program provided, he made certain both she and Bryan were exposed to its glory. Most kids didn't have an Uncle Garret, might never be introduced to Bach, Beethoven, Mozart or experience the joy only an instrument produced. It killed him that Adara would play a part in assassinating music.

"You're sure that's the right path? To eliminate the music program?" Reaching the bottom of the staircase, he pivoted to face her. "There's no other alternative?"

"Absolutely…and no." She stopped on the last step and finally met his gaze. "Music is a luxury. Teachers aren't. Most kids will rely on skills other than music to succeed in life."

He couldn't argue with that, but it felt like leeching color from the world, leaving it gray.

Her expression softened. "I understand you think it's a tragedy."

"I *know* it's a tragedy."

"I can't lose my job." Her voice was equal amounts softness and steel. "I can't." She bit her bottom lip and looked away.

He blinked, stunned. It wasn't any random budget cut that drove her to eliminate music. It was her job. A tightness in his chest, one he hadn't realized was there until now, eased. Adara wasn't out to destroy music. She simply wanted to keep her job. Even if he didn't approve of her methods, he couldn't blame her for that. Before he could rethink his no-push game plan, he leaned in and cupped her chin. "I also know losing you as a teacher would devastate Tatum."

"Right. For about five minutes." She rolled her eyes. "Once she has a new teacher to torment, she'll forget all about me." She took the last step down, putting space between them. "What other rooms do you have down here?"

He went along with the swift change in subject, letting her take the lead. Tonight, he wanted her to stay and he had no intention of expanding her boundaries more. But if she wanted to kiss him again, he wouldn't resist. "Besides the torture chamber and the kitchen?" He shrugged and strolled away from the staircase, not giving her a chance to head for the door instead. "Not much."

She fell into step beside him and the lines around her mouth relaxed. He'd make sure that he wasn't the reason for them coming back.

"Just so we're clear, Adara, you're wrong about Tatum." He leaned close to her ear, close enough to breathe in her coconut shampoo. "You're unforgettable."

Chapter Eighteen

'You're unforgettable.'

A dozen different snarky responses came to mind, but Garret opened the next door and slithered inside before Adara could choose which one to use. *Sly man.*

Sly man with a fabulous house he'd designed. Everything about it was perfection, from the parquet flooring to the carved wood ceilings. It was as if he'd strolled into her dreams, picked out the best parts and created a place specifically for her.

Her heart contracted...a warning. If his kiss hadn't stolen all common sense, she'd forget the ice cream excuse and demand to go home, but tonight felt disoriented, surreal, out of her control. He pulled her strings like a puppeteer and she couldn't find enough strength to cut the tethers.

She followed him into the room and froze, catching her gasp before it escaped. *He has a library.* Garret stopped a few steps from the entrance, and even though his intensity weighed on her, she couldn't bring herself to care. *He has a frickin' library.* She wandered inside the fairy-tale room. Built-in shelves rose at least ten feet high, along with an old-fashioned rolling ladder. True, all the shelves were empty, but it didn't take a lot to picture them full. Windows made up one entire wall, looking out into the utter blackness of night. Without close neighbors, there weren't any lights to ruin the night-sky view. Sunlight would spill inside during the day, making it perfect for morning reading...or afternoon reading...or evening.

"You have a frickin' library." She ignored the breathlessness in the words.

"Technically." He joined her in looking out of the window, close enough his heat punctured her sweater. "But I could rebel and put whatever I want on the shelves—spare violin cases, rosin, extra strings, music paper, pirate gear."

"I'm sure pirates read in their spare time." She had to get back to humor, anything to deflect the Garret whirlpool pulling her ever deeper. *Why does he have to have a library too?* "You know, for when they're not pillaging, playing the violin and forcing bilge-sucking landlubbers to walk the plank."

"This particular violinist's tomes wouldn't even take up a shelf. London took custody of the family books, and with all my traveling, I went mostly digital." He cocked his head, looking puppy-dog hopeful in the window's reflection. "Want to help me fill my library?"

That capricious fluttering, usually dormant beneath the ashes of her heart, went wild. With one sentence he'd painted a fantasy, one she couldn't shut down. A day of Garret, bookstores, lining every shelf in this beautiful library with her favorite stories, more Garret.

Her dry mouth made it hard to respond. "We probably don't read the same kinds of books."

He shrugged. "Doesn't matter."

"Why would you want your house filled with books of my choosing?"

"So every time I'm in here," he said in a quiet, serious voice, "all I have to do is look at a book and remember this minute. If you're not physically near, a shard of you will remain here...with me."

She pivoted to face him full-on and he held her gaze, much longer than polite, her longing a mirrored burn in his dark eyes. Maybe it was the emotional victory of surviving his performance or his mind-numbing kiss or his perfect house, but he painted dreams to life, dreams of all the hazardous things she'd renounced, making them seem safe, manageable. The price for connection and family and life was pain. She didn't have the resources to pay that particular bill. But knowing that didn't curb the wanting.

She drew a deep breath, held it a few seconds then released it slowly. "I like your house."

He raised his eyebrows and watched her warily, as if she might explode into a hundred bubbles. "Thanks?"

"You're a decent violinist."

"So I've been told." His mouth twitched in a poor attempt to hide a smile, his eyes sparkling with restrained laughter.

Pushing through her cowardice, she stepped closer. "Considering your taste in jewelry, I'm skeptical about your potential literary choices. You definitely need my help in selecting good books for your library."

"I would appreciate the assistance." His voice was hardly more than a murmur, and his gaze dipped to her mouth, stayed there. His throat worked.

88888888888888

Everything inside her felt light and molten. Even as she drudged up a last attempt to keep her barriers up, she itched to touch his jaw again, to feel the scrape of stubble beneath her fingertips. "I'm not girlfriend material. I'm pretty sure I'm not even good friend material right now. Whatever you're looking for, you won't find it in me."

There, she'd said it. Now he knew and would let her go back to her safety, her solitude, stop tempting her with his unstoppable smiles and sunshine.

"When I met you, I made a promise to myself." He dropped his chin, deepening the intensity. "And I always keep my promises, no matter the effort or length of time. A few failures along the way won't stop me."

That wasn't at all the direction she'd expected this conversation to go. Whatever his self-promise might be, she needed a time frame, something to reference so she could prepare for the onslaught and weather the storm. "How long did it take for this house to be built?"

After a hesitation, he caressed her cheek with his knuckles, a whispering touch, and she leaned slightly into it. "From dream to completion?" He watched his fingers trail her jawline, as if he dared to touch an artifact that might crumble. "Twenty years, give or take."

A lot could change in twenty years. Lives could turn upside down in even twenty minutes. No way would he spend twenty years working on whatever weird goal he'd made surrounding her. Still, knowing that goal would be helpful. She cleared the knot in her throat. "What did you promise yourself" — her sweater was suddenly so tight she could barely breathe — "when you met me?"

"You're not ready to hear it, *neshama*." His voice was secret soft. "But I'll tell you this—like a house, the material you have is enough for whatever you want it to be."

"What about the holes?" She couldn't look away from his full, sensual, perfect mouth. "The rips, the stains, the frayed ends?"

"They merely tell your unique tale." His jaw clenched and a low snarl thrummed deep in his throat, jolting her straight. "Adara, if this is your idea of vengeance from the tickling throw-down on karaoke night, I surrender. I told you I wouldn't push for anything you didn't want to give tonight, and I stand by that. Tomorrow, though, I can't promise to be so accommodating. Revenge goes both ways."

She blinked as that aberration inside doubled, filling her ribcage, rising to her throat. Their mouths inches away, it would be so easy for him to lower his head and plant one on her. Instead, he left it up to her. The knowledge was somehow freeing.

"I don't want to lead you on." She bit her lip and dropped her gaze to his open collar, his tan throat and the pewter cross nestled there. "I can't promise anything more, physical or emotional." She lifted her face to his again, courtesy of his finger beneath her chin. "Are you okay with that?"

"Like material, a kiss can be anything you want it to be," he murmured.

"Material can be misunderstood."

"Do I seem addle-brained to you?"

"You really want me to answer that?" She grinned.

His eyes flashed. "Are you going to kiss me or not?"

He made things so easy, so simple, as if it were completely natural for a girl to break down at a community college music concert. As if it were completely normal to be disconnected. As if it were completely rational to surround herself in silence. She lifted onto tiptoes and pressed her lips to his, light as rain, a thank you for accepting her as is, for not asking for more than she could give.

He slipped his fingers into her hair and grasped her head, keeping her mouth on his. He curled his other hand around the small of her back and pulled her close, snug against his heat. Soft, seductively, his lips brushed hers and the world around them dimmed.

She leaned into his solid strength and fisted his shirt with both hands, everything inside her awake and alive. So much for keeping things out of emotional range. Right here, with him, there were no memories, no grief, no fear—only a mesmerizing man who banished her resolve and anchored her firmly in the here and now. She didn't want him to let go, didn't want to fade back into the silence.

His fingertips, callused by a lifetime of violin strings, caressed her neck in a slow descent and sent a hot bolt down her back. His warmth seeped through to her skin, sinking deeper until she swore he invaded her bones. The bristle on his face scraped her chin and launched sparks along her nerves. She was on sensation overload, and whether or not the leading-on factor had been addressed, pressed tight against him, she couldn't mistake his body's response to hers. Or hers to his.

Coaxing her lips apart, the silken thrust of his tongue shot straight between her thighs, and her blood caught fire. If this was him not pushing for more than she was willing to give with the promise of all bets off tomorrow, she'd better start running now, sore ankle or not. But her legs refused to cooperate, trembling so hard she couldn't believe they held her upright. As he deepened the kiss, a knot loosened inside her, a knot that had been stuck for so long she'd accepted it as part of existence.

The sudden sense of freedom combined with Garret's low, hungry growl was intoxicating, making it impossible not to respond. Every cell burning, she squirmed against him, unable to get close enough. She released one hand from his shirt and dragged her fingers though his loose hair, the silken texture igniting her imagination, taking her to all the areas on her body it would feel just as fine. A small voice in the depths of her brain warned her to stop touching him but she smothered it. With so many places to explore, she slipped her hand down the hard pillar of his neck, along the muscled ridge of his shoulder.

A tide of sensations rushed over her, drowning out anything unattached to him. A fine tremor ran through every inch of her body, trailed by heat. She couldn't quite catch her breath, yet coming up for air wasn't an option. He was her dock, and floating free into the current was the last thing on her mind.

A muffled trill echoed in the distance, a familiar song snaking into her haze. Adara opened her eyes. Gia's special ring tone, *Girls Just Want to Have Fun*, coming from her phone, which she'd left at the door with her coat.

Garret broke from the kiss long enough to say, "I hear nothing." He reclaimed her mouth as if to reiterate, allowing no response time. He slid a hand beneath her sweater, warm and deliciously abrasive on her back, another assault on her senses.

But Gia never called late. Still gripping Garret's shirt for balance, her knees more than a little weak, she eased back.

"Don't answer it," he murmured at her ear. He grazed her earlobe with his teeth and she shuddered.

"It's Gia. I have to." She rested her forehead on his chest and closed her eyes as he wrapped his arms around her, shackling her close. Staying in this moment forever, like this, with him, would be her idea of heaven.

He rested his chin on top of her head, his breaths as ragged as her own. "Remind me to sic Ian on her later."

She smiled against his shirt. "Then I'd have to kill him *and* you."

"But at least Gia wouldn't interrupt us again."

"Trust me, she'd find a way. It's her superpower."

Adara released her death grip on his shirt and smoothed the material. Focusing on that was better than looking at him, seeing what might or might not be flashing in his midnight eyes, or how she might react. The ring tone returned to the chorus, blaring the last round before voicemail. Without another word, not knowing what to say anyway, she raced for her purse and picked up just in time.

"Gia? What's up?"

Gia's answer was a fast, loud string of shrill curses, and Adara held the phone away from her ear.

Joining her in the foyer, Garret propped his back against the wall, his hands in his pockets, eyebrows high. His golden hair sparkled in the chandelier light, disheveled by her fingers, and with the added bonus of his shirt slightly askew despite her effort to smooth it, he made every inch of her tingle with need. She wanted to pitch her phone out of the door, pretend Gia had never called and go back to kissing until she forgot anything else in the world existed.

Dangerous man, dangerous dream.

"I'm done with men. Done!" Gia screamed, no speaker phone necessary.

Adara's stomach knotted and she brought the phone back to her ear. "What happened?"

Between the angry sobs and creative ways Gia planned to make some guy she'd never heard of pay for ditching her, she got the gist of it. Gia had gone out with an online connection, found him nothing like his profile, and he apparently didn't appreciate being informed of the disparities. He'd left her behind at a seedy countryside bar, where she'd promptly proceeded to drink way more than two margaritas.

"Stay put. I'll be there in a few." Adara dropped the phone in her purse and scrambled into her coat. "I have to go— Crap!" She raked her fingers through her hair and met Garret's gaze. "My car isn't here."

"I'll play chauffer." Probably sensing her hesitation, he hit her with his sunshine smile, knocking all her recently realigned senses askew. "Driving you there will be faster than going to your house, dropping you off then getting Gia. And no self-respecting musician would allow his muse to brave a dodgy bar alone."

She went still. *His muse?*

He stepped close and tucked her hair behind her ear, the move so natural and comforting, the urge to object didn't even rise. "And I'm nowhere near ready to let you escape my clutches."

Which was exactly why she should refuse, but he was right. Going straight to Gia would save time. "Fine. Only if you promise not to drive like a grandma."

"I'll kick it up to grandpa with a walker." He jangled his keys and shrugged into his jacket. Opening the door, he glanced over his shoulder and wriggled his eyebrows. "Or Adara on crutches."

She lunged for him, but he was already out the door, showing off his questionable non-athlete skills again. His frickin' muse.

I'm in so much trouble.

Chapter Nineteen

"Is the date and ditch routine normal for Gia?" Garret's voice drew Adara away from the car window and her thoughts, which were almost as dark as the night beyond.

The dreamscape she'd wandered with Garret during the last few hours frayed at the edges and reality pushed in, stronger with each second. She wasn't ready to wake up. Yet, in focusing on her own issues, she'd completely blown the promise she'd made to her brother, and Gia was paying the price.

"Only once since…" She clenched her jaw and forced herself to finish. "Since Joey's been gone. At her firm's Christmas party last year." She added some venom to her voice. "With Ian, which had nothing to do with dating."

"Ah. One clue in the Ian-Gia mystery."

"Is there something else I don't know about?" She refused to blink in case she missed some telling emotion in his expression. Letting Gia down again wasn't happening.

"You know as much as I do." He kept his gaze on the road. "Gia is an off-limits topic for Ian, and that alone is cause for contemplation. Women are his favorite subject, so when he's tight-lipped about a particular female, my curiosity goes wild. With Gia, he's vaulted tight."

"Good." She glared at Garret, as if she could burn Ian through his friend. "I don't understand how such a jerk won your loyalty, let alone your friendship."

"Ian has his good points. He simply prefers to come across *not* good. He claims it makes everything less complicated." He glanced at her and smirked. "You do realize you just essentially admitted you like me, don't you?"

She rolled her eyes. "Not being in the same category as Ian simply makes you human, not necessarily likeable."

His smirk broke into a high-noon smile. "So you didn't like kissing me?"

She crossed her arms and forced her expression to stay serene. If she gave him any wiggle room, she'd have no hope of escape. "It was tolerable."

"Tolerable?" His smile died, and she had to bite the inside of her cheek not to laugh. "As in not exactly painful, but not something to get excited about? That's like comparing me to a prostate exam."

"The Ambrose dramatic gene runs strong in you, my child." The grin she'd been holding back escaped. "Fine. I'll concede and say kissing you was probably more fun than any medical procedure."

He glanced at her, and his attention dropped to her mouth. "*Ben-zonna*, you have a beautiful smile. Every time I get a real one from you, I start plotting ways to earn the next."

Adara hunched in her coat and let her smile fade. While she flirted with Garret, Gia was stranded with tanked Hoedown Joe and Farmer Fred, probably up to her eyebrows in margaritas. And it was all her fault. Gia was there, in that state of mind, because she'd neglected her promise to Joey. Joey had predicted Gia's reaction to life without him, had assigned her to guard duty and she'd abandoned her post. No matter the excuse, she'd made a vow and broken it.

Again.

"I hate it when you sink into your thoughts and shut me out." Garret brushed his fingers over her wrist, a soft reassurance. "Tell me what you're thinking."

Normally, she'd leave the silence on, keep her secrets close, but he probably already knew about her promise to Joey anyway. "I feel responsible. I promised to look out for Gia, and instead, I was selfish and neglected her."

"You shouldn't and you aren't." He glanced at the electronic map in the dashboard guiding them to their destination. "Eventually, people need to make their own choices, deal with their own mistakes."

She blew out a breath. "I know that. But until Gia has her head on straight again, I promised to be there. And I flopped."

"What if she never figures it out, Adara?" He pulled into the gravel parking lot of the Idle Heifer and they both winced as the tire hit a pothole the size of New York.

The distraction was a relief. Joey hadn't specified a timeline, and guarding his girlfriend for the rest of her life wasn't what she'd been thinking of when she'd agreed to his promise. More than that, the question strangled, her own situation the noose. What if she never figured out a remedy beyond the temporary fix of silence and solitude? She escaped the car before Garret pressed her for an answer.

The neon-green sign flashed like a beacon to the freeway half a mile away, probably what lured enough customers to keep it open, and calling the bar 'seedy' was generous. Even with details dulled by the streetlights, she wouldn't walk in there alone without a gun, a chain and some brass knuckles. If Gia was still alive and in one piece, it would be a miracle.

Garret slid up beside her. "I say we poke our heads in the doorway, and if we don't see Gia, we run," he said in a sober tone. "I don't want to die tonight."

"Scared?" She elbowed him in the hip.

"Sh-h. I'm praying." But he followed on her heels, and before she reached the door, he edged ahead of her and opened it himself, a protective gesture she appreciated. In silence.

Despite the no smoking law, a cloud of sweet smoke emerged, and Adara coughed.

"Oh. Idle Heifer." Garret smirked and shielded his eyes. "Makes sense now. Too much grass made the cows lazy." He coughed. "Get it?"

How could she not. The marijuana fumes made her eyes burn and her head pound. "I changed my mind about feeling bad. If I kill her, don't stop me."

Through the haze and across the room, Gia slouched at the bar counter, a margarita glass in one fist, a ginormous guy in overalls and baseball cap next to her. Adara marched to the counter and shoved into the empty seat beside her. "You're so dead, G."

Gia pivoted in her stool. Her eyes were bloodshot, every golden curl fallen flat and her silk blouse was rumpled, as if she'd been toying with the buttons all night. Blinking slowly, she gave Adara a sloppy smile and threw her arms around her neck. Only Adara's grip kept the other woman in her seat. "Dar!"

"What part of 'dead' did you not understand?" Adara disentangled herself from Gia's embrace, glaring enough to make any glamor-girl cower. "You attended a social engagement without me."

A dismissive wave followed, and Gia's blue eyes widened on something behind Adara. Her mouth dropped open, and it took all of Adara's strength to keep her upright as the smaller woman tried to leap from her stool and stumbled in her stiletto boots instead. Her gaze bounced between Adara and Garret like a pinball machine in slow motion, finally settling on Adara.

"You tricky miss." She clicked her tongue and shook her head. "You were with him when I called, weren't you? After the irate lecture proclaiming the absolute ridiculousness of my theory, the I-want-to-be-alone routine and the how-dare-you silent treatment afterward?"

"What theory?" Garret asked, stepping between them despite her firm request to not interfere while she killed Gia.

Gia was so, *so* dead. "Nothing."

"Yeah-uh." Gia walked her fingers up Garret's arm, pausing to squeeze his bicep. "Jumping on Garret Ambrose is totally a 'something'. I bet that would cure just about anything."

Garret lifted his eyebrows, and his gaze went straight to Adara, probably immediately noticing the flush in her face and misinterpreting it. He clamped his lips together, the only thing that saved him. If he'd smiled, she would have punched him in the throat, plucked the car keys from his fingers and left him to discuss the merits of Gia's theory with the independent counsel of Farmer Ted.

The stool still occupied by Gia's drinking companion squeaked, and the farmer stood. He had to be at least seven feet tall and looked put out at the interference in his two-person party, more specifically that Gia focused her attention on Garret. Maybe he was the bartender slash owner too. Other than a couple of hipsters smoking in one dark corner, no one else occupied the joint. *Joint.* Adara fisted her hands. It was definitely time for takeoff.

She cleared her throat. "Where's your purse, G?"

While Garret silently endured the attention, his expression set on mildly amused, Gia traced small circles over his arm and flung her free hand at the bar. Her leopard-print purse rested on the floor between stools, right beside Monster Farmer.

Perfect. She could either politely ask him to move or crawl in the space between the bar and stools, and she wasn't sure which one would be easier. She lifted her gaze to his rugged face. Sunburned skin, glaring blue eyes, an ax-murderer frown. Yeah, she was better off wriggling along the floor, nabbing the purse and bolting.

"The lady wasn't finished with her drink." Farmer's voice thundered, a warning before the storm hit. He folded his arms over his flannel shirt and overalls. "I paid for it. She's drinking it."

Adara stiffened. This was why Joey had asked her to be Gia's backup. Gia had a tendency to attract attention of all kinds, and despite two years with Joey's positive reinforcement, she hadn't learned she didn't need to absorb or accept it all, that she was worth more than a one-night fling in a back-room office or an online romance scam.

Without breaking the farmer's gaze, she jerked a twenty from her purse and set it on the counter. "Compensation. Thanks for keeping her company until I got here. Good to know chivalry still exists."

Slowly, he dropped his arms and curled his hands into table-cracking fists. "We were having a fine conversation. I don't think she's ready to go."

"Her call to me, asking me to pick her up, says otherwise." Adara trotted out an apologetic smile, leaned over Garret and pushed Gia's hand off his arm.

"Her words to me, five minutes ago," Atlas rumbled, "indicated the only person she was leaving with was me. After her drink." His gaze slid to Gia, who was again exploring Garret's arm.

Adara resisted narrowing her eyes. She really didn't like Gia touching Garret, especially now that she knew how firm his arms were, how she'd liked having her hands on him. Having his hands on her, his lips. Maybe she *should* leave. If Gia wanted Garret, she had every faith in her friend to win him over. Gia could save her from herself because, clearly, she was losing the battle on her own.

Garret brushed her fingers with his, the barest slide of skin on skin, breaking through her thoughts. The heat in his midnight eyes curled through her like winter fire, contained, comforting despite the hint of danger. And he was dangerous, dangerous to her walls, her solitude, her heart.

"I say let the lady speak for herself." Farmer's booming voice regained her focus. "She's an adult."

Garret kept silent, wise considering the farmer's hellfire eyes watched Gia's hand on his arm, each second of contact making the blue burn brighter.

"An adult whose judgment is impaired by marijuana fumes and—" Adara leaned into Gia's personal space, breaking the farmer's line of sight. "How many margaritas did you have, G?"

Gia cocked her head, lifting her gaze to the stained ceiling tiles. She blinked a few times and chewed on her lower lip. Finally, she brightened. "Four!" Her high-octane breath blasted Adara's face. "I think."

Strapping on her no-nonsense teacher expression, Adara straightened to her full height and tipped her head back, giving Farmer Fred the full brunt of her third-grade authority. She launched into a Tatum-sized dose of *Pride and Prejudice*. "I find it reprehensible, good sir, that instead of charitably escorting a member of the fairer sex to safety, as any gentleman of unquestionable dignity and character should, you sought to besmirch an inebriated lady in good standing with society and possibly leave her reputation in ruins. She is most certainly in need of a hot compress, some tonic and a good night's slumber, not additional poisons in her delicate system."

"Besmirch?" Gia whispered to Garret, who shook his head once.

With an offended sniff and praying the farmer's befuddled expression meant he wouldn't pound them all quite yet, she pressed between the bar stools and swiped Gia's purse from the floor. A few quick backward steps took her out of immediate pummel range and beside the reinforcing comfort of Garret's solid frame. While not giant-tall, he didn't have the wimp vibe going on. He'd be some help in a fight, whether or not he claimed to possess any athletic abilities.

Adara shouldered Gia's purse and met the farmer's slitted gaze. With one finger, she scooted the twenty-dollar bill an inch closer to him. "We shall take our leave now, sir, and have no fear of us intruding upon your solicitude again."

Not daring to breathe, she grasped Gia's arm and dragged her to the exit, Garret right behind them. She opened the door and the cool night welcomed her, sweet and fresh. Her pace didn't slow until they reached the car.

"I'm relatively certain we owe our lives to the soothing nature of cannabis." Garret opened the door and helped Gia into a slouching heap on the back seat. He flashed a smile over his shoulder. "And going Miss Lizzy on Dolph Lundgren was a brilliant move. He's still trying to figure out if he would've got lucky by offering Gia his handkerchief—or the grease-stained diesel rag in his back pocket." He shrugged. "Whatever was handy."

Adara grasped his coat sleeve as he shut the back door. "I'm probably going to regret saying this." She blew out a breath. "Thank you for coming with me, for being here."

Something unnerving moved in his dark eyes, strong enough to show up in the streetlamp's glow. His customary smile changed, slipped into a yearning, tender expression that made her ache, like she'd just lost another piece of her soul that she'd never get back. "All you have to do is ask, *neshama*. Wherever you're going, that's where I want to be."

He stepped close, and she was too spellbound by his words to move away. Cupping her face between both his hands, he bent his head toward hers, but instead of taking her lips as she expected, he pressed a soft, lingering, devastating kiss on her forehead.

Her heart squeezed, struggling beneath the web of emotions clamoring for dominance. His kiss seemed to echo inside her and awaken all the emotions she'd been trying so hard to keep buried, not merely because it was meant to comfort rather than entice. It thrummed between them in unspoken communication, deeper than any words, a decision made and unsaid, waiting to be acknowledged. She trembled at the intensity.

A pounding came from in the car, and Gia pressed her face against the window between her flattened palms, distorting her pretty features.

Adara sighed. "You'd better pick up the speed to grandpa on a scooter before she pukes in your beast."

He beat her to the door and opened for her, allowing a gush of mixed intoxicant-laced air.

"Dar and Garret sitting in a tree," Gia sang, hiccupping every other word.

Adara glared at her friend as she climbed in and shut the door. "I haven't yet turned over the death card, G. Don't push me."

On another hiccup, Gia gave her a crooked grin.

Garret opened the driver's side and slid in. He was humming the same tune Gia had started.

"Don't make me kill you too," she muttered to him, glowering at no one in particular.

The humming choked, but she sensed his smirk. She didn't encourage him by acknowledging it, and when the motor crooned to life, she sat back in her seat. Still, she couldn't relax. The heat from his kiss on her forehead remained, seared on her skin like a brand.

"What were you thinking, G?" She directed the words to her right, to the space between her seat and the window, to avoid even chancing a look at Garret. "Why would you let anyone you don't know drive you anywhere, let alone to the countryside and a bar called The Brainless Cow?"

"Idle Heifer," Garret corrected cheerfully as he pulled carefully out of the potholed parking lot and onto smooth pavement.

"We've been talking online for weeks." Gia huffed. "It's not like he was a stranger."

Adara's best response was a strangled noise.

"So he wasn't all that." Gia's voice snapped. "At least I'm not sitting at home avoiding life."

"Online dating isn't what I equate with life." Adara gritted her teeth and faced the windshield. Feeling the weight of Garret's watchful gaze on her, she focused on the darkness beyond. If only she could just drift into it and disappear, no promises, no pain, no memories.

Garret reached across the center console and hooked his pinkie with hers. He squeezed once and let go, an 'I'm here, stay with me'. Annoying tears burned her eyes. She hated his seeming ability to read her mind. Hated it almost as much as she hated how he effortlessly slipped into her solitude. She didn't want to extricate his presence, didn't want to return to life as is, which was becoming a predicament.

The scent of fumes strengthened, and Gia stuck her head between the front bucket seats, clearly not wearing her seatbelt. "I'll tell you a secret, Dar." The slurred words were hushed. "I miss Joey too. All the time."

Adara's throat tightened. She didn't want to discuss Joey, not tonight, not ever. especially with Garret as a helpless eavesdropper.

"He's irrepressible." Gia sighed.

Adara snorted softly. "You mean irreplaceable?"

"Uh-uh. And I figured out how to deal with life minus Joey."

Twisting in her seat, Adara met Gia's droopy, bloodshot gaze. Solitude was her preferred method of warding off the pain, and while it might not be the healthiest coping technique, at least it didn't include drugs or dishonorable dudes. "Losers who take you to pot bars aren't what Joey wanted for you."

Garret wisely focused on the road, obviously trying to be less intrusive while a painful, personal conversation went on right beside him. He just kept adding gold stars to the progress chart in her head.

With an air of dismissal, Gia slumped and rested her temple against the headrest. "Life is too short to stay stuck in misery and too long to hang your heart out to dry. Switch the care burner off and have fun while you can, however and wherever you find it. That, my grim girl Dar, is how you survive losing Joey."

Needles prickled through Adara's limbs. Gia spoke the words with solid determination, a practiced mantra proclaimed so many times that belief outweighed any doubt, yet threaded there, nearly hidden, remained a note of desperation. Adara recognized it because she performed the same act, told herself lies until they sounded true, and she wasn't sure what falsehood she'd turn to when it all crashed in.

Chapter Twenty

During Friday afternoon recess, Garret rapped his knuckles on Adara's desk and waited until she raised her head from the red-pen artwork on some unlucky student's paper. "How's online-dating bachelorette number one feeling today?"

She grimaced, and while the expression was intended to convey displeasure, it merely drew his attention to her lovely mouth and reignited the memories from the previous night. He'd replayed kissing her uncountable times, imagination taking him to what might have progressed if Gia hadn't called. Grieving or not, the woman deserved a vicious hangover.

"The aspirin and water I made her chug after puking and before passing out worked like a charm." Another angry, red line scratched into existence, joining the others on the paper. Someone wasn't getting an A. "She dragged me off the couch before my alarm went off, the witch."

"Nice of you to stay with her last night." He propped his hip on the edge of her desk and crossed his ankles. "I would have preferred to have you all to myself."

Adara sat back in her chair and gave him the look he'd pegged as her third-grader seek and destroy. "Mr. Ambrose, despite the occurrences last night, which I appreciate—"

"And enjoyed." He grinned.

Her eyes narrowed. "We're at work, surrounded by impressionable young minds."

He made a show of looking around the empty classroom. "It's recess, darling. Break time."

In answer, she jerked open a drawer, grabbed a pink pad of paper and scribbled something on it. A quick rip and she handed the top paper to him.

Reading it, he laughed. "Detention in third grade?"

"For calling me 'darling'." One eyebrow quirked up.

Slow and suggestive, he eased his gaze from her eyes to her full mouth and lingered there. "I could conjure many more names I'd like to call you, Miss Dumont— enough to make an impression, no matter the age." He leaned forward and dropped his voice to a murmur, inhaling her coconut shampoo. "I can't stop thinking about you, how sweet your lips were on mine."

"Stop it. Seriously." A hiss entered her whisper, but she couldn't hide the flush in her pale cheeks or the fast beat of her pulse against her collarbone. "Sexual harassment, Ambrose."

"I believe all harassment was utterly under your control last night, *neshama*."

"Tonight." She jabbed a finger in his face. "I'm looking that word up tonight. I'm sure it's synonymous with 'pushover', 'sucker' and 'morons who fall into musician traps'."

He resisted caressing that one lock of glossy raven hair that shadowed her face, tucking it behind her ear so the delicate angles of her bone structure would be on full display. She had no idea the beauty lying in every line, and that unawareness only made her more intriguing. "If you care to postpone your canvassing preparations, it so happens that I'm free tonight, to aid in your word research."

"Now you're implying I'm incompetent." She folded her arms and sniffed, the twinkle in her eyes betraying her.

"Stubborn. There's a difference." He flashed a smile. "Admittedly, I have an agenda for coming over."

"Wow. Shocker."

"Besides our required weekly report, I'd like your input on the ideas I have for the recital."

She dropped her hands into her lap and she studied his face with sharp, gray eyes, as if searching for fraud. She wouldn't find any. While recital ideas might not be the only reason he wanted to be with her tonight, it was one of them. He wanted her approval, and that approval extended beyond his music. Adara had the ability to affect him deeply, and no one had held that power since his mother.

'You can't inspire everyone.' Bob's earlier words at the school carnival chose that inopportune moment to surface in his memories, right when he was feeling middle-school vulnerable. Next time he saw his brother-in-law, he'd ask him to keep his advice to himself so it wouldn't bother him when he was trying to weasel his way into Friday night Adara alone time.

The first bell rang, signaling the end of recess, the end of their discussion. No matter how he tested the rules while alone with her, he'd never sabotage her position as teacher and chief, third-grade mind-warper. He pushed from her desk and stepped back a second before the first student skipped into the room, face flushed with early spring cold and eyes bright. With an audience, he had to play his part as music mentor, not a man who struggled with winning his reluctant, enchanting muse.

"Seven o'clock." Adara bent her head over her paperwork, her red pen scratching again. "If you want to eat, bring food."

He chained down his smile and strolled away before she reconsidered.

* * * *

Five hours later, Garret trotted up the stairs to Adara's house, homemade Chinese in one hand, store-bought ice cream in the other — food bribery at its best. Since both hands were full, he hit the doorbell with his elbow. Beethoven's *Fifth* bellowed from deep in the house and he chuckled softly. It was a true shame he hadn't had the privilege of meeting Joey. He had a feeling that, if they'd banded together, they could have changed the world — or at least set it on fire.

"If you're Garret, just come in!" Adara's muffled voice barely made it past the door. "If you're a serial killer, there's a blonde bimbo at the pink house on the corner."

In other words, she hadn't locked her door again. Plastering on a frown, he tucked the ice cream carton beneath his arm and went inside. He locked the door behind him before hunting down Adara, finding her in the kitchen, flat on her back under the sink.

"You, Miss Dumont, need to lock your doors." He set his treasures on the counter and crouched beside her, ducking to look under the sink. "Runner, teacher and plumber too?"

"My sink keeps clogging up and has proven all department store brand solutions incompetent, so I went to the experts." She handed him a wrench. "YouTube."

"Ah, the new-age oracle, keeper of all truths and wisdom."

"Exactly." Adara clambered out of the cupboard and sat on the kitchen tile. "Look what I found." She held up a ring. Blackened with grime, a wolf's empty eye socket stared out at him, its grin malicious, and a chill prickled down his back. "Next time you invade my kitchen, leave your Gothic jewelry home."

His heart gonging a hollow, uneven beat, Garret plucked the platinum ring from her grip. He wiped it off with a dish towel and angled the inner band beneath the kitchen light, just to be sure. The initials *GAA* shone back at him, inscribed by London years ago.

Feeling sick, he dropped the ring and it clanked heavily on the counter. "I lost that ring six months ago...in Belgium."

Adara's forehead puckered. "So how did it end up in my sink?"

Taking her wet hands, he pulled her to her feet, fighting the urge to drag her into the protection of his arms. Instead, he settled his hands on her shoulders and held her gaze. "Remember my number one fan, Belgian Beauty?" He waited for the expected eye roll before continuing. "I never had solid proof, but I believed she finagled her way into my motel room while I was away. That was just before I applied for the protective order."

Her head cocked, she looked doubtful. "So your Belgian beauty snuck into my house and stuck your pilfered pirate ring down my sink in a dastardly plot to clog my drainpipe?"

She clearly didn't comprehend the potential danger, and he clenched his jaw to control the rising need to sling her over his shoulder and carry her off somewhere safe. He compromised with dragging her to the living room couch.

"I didn't want to rehash this." Pushing the entire scenario from his mind forever would have been preferable and not possible if Bella had truly followed him home. He wiped a hand over his face and braced his forearms on his thighs. "I told you before about the dinner interview with Bella." He waited for her to nod, glad she picked up on his gravity. "I learned later that, during our interview, one of her colleagues was clandestinely taking photos. I thought her behavior was a little odd. Reporters generally don't touch you, but I didn't think much about it until a few days later when we crossed paths at my motel, a hundred miles away."

"I assume you don't keep your tour schedule a secret." Adara clasped her hands together, the only sign of her discomfort. "But the odds of ending up at the same motel are questionable."

"That's how she explained it, that the only tickets still available were at this particular concert, and what a surprise to find we were staying under the same roof. I brushed off her invitation to compare rooms."

He air-quoted the last two words. What she wanted to compare had nothing to do with the room and everything to do with a bottle of vodka and either her bed or his, no preference.

"I mistakenly believed she got the hint." He sighed and dropped his head in his hands. "Everywhere I went, she was there. She didn't always make contact, and those incidents were almost worse. They made my skin crawl, as if she wanted me to wonder why she was only watching." Cold crept into his veins at the memories, the tingling sense of being watched followed by the startled discovery of her face in the crowd. "Then the texts started, the pictures, the crazy. She didn't do anything dangerous in Belgium, but I never dismissed the potential, and the fact she followed me here, knows who you are, was in your house..." He nearly choked. *Ben-zonna.* Bella had been inside Adara's house.

Adara curled one leg up and shifted slightly toward him. "I won't second-guess you and question the probability of your weird ring in my sink." She paused, her gray eyes cool, revealing neither worry nor disbelief. "Do you think she meant to leave it as some kind of I-was-here signature to creep me out or did she lose it by mistake? I mean, if she went to the effort of swiping your ring, I can't imagine she'd want to lose her stolen treasure."

"Normally, I'd enjoy your speculation, but the 'why' of it isn't as important as the fact that it actually happened." He sprang to his feet, that unnerving feeling of unseen eyes too much to bear. "*Chara.* You never lock your door. She could still be here." Holding his hand out to her, he wriggled his fingers impatiently. "I've watched too many horror movies to leave you alone while I search your house."

"And looking for the murderer always works out well." Adara arched an eyebrow, but she obliged his paranoia and took his hand. "Shouldn't we get a knife from the kitchen or something?"

"I trust your sharp words to protect us." Pulling her to the hallway, he went for flippant to hide the clenching in his gut. While Bella had never threatened him or done anything violent, mentally off-kilter meant unpredictable.

The bathroom shower curtain hid nothing beyond soap and shampoo, the hallway closet was free of watchful eyes, no monsters under the bed. With Adara at his elbow, he opened the door to the den...nothing but a desk, papers and bookshelves.

"You haven't noticed anything misplaced or moved?" He shut the door.

"Nope." She shrugged. "And I wouldn't call my pantry adequate for two. I'd notice if my hummus went missing."

"I'll remember not to mess with your hummus. Do you recall hearing anything suspicious?"

"No, I—" Her face paled and her gaze skittered to the closed door of Joey's room.

The knot in his neck ratcheted tight. Opening that wound for her wasn't what he wanted, but he wouldn't risk her safety. He kept his voice to a soothing murmur. "We need to check."

She released a long breath and nodded.

Before opening the door, he took her hand and lifted it to his lips, pressing a soft kiss to her knuckles. Her throat worked, and while she didn't smile, she didn't pull away, either. Not breaking their connection, he opened the door.

Adara sucked in a breath as he endured another bout of chills. The room he'd seen once, by accident, remained largely the same. Dust-covered piano, violins and sheet music…the broken guitar. But the bed was unmade, as if someone had slept in it. Several fast-food bags littered the floor, and the abandoned stale air now held a flowery hint. *Bella's perfume.*

He leaned against the doorframe to steady himself, the walls collapsing in. Bella had not only been in Adara's house, she'd stayed, maybe for days.

"*Ben-zonna,*" Adara murmured and latched onto his arm. He would have laughed at her use of his favorite curse if he had it in him.

Forcing his feet forward, he entered Joey's room, Adara clinging firmly to him. Apparently, potential danger was an avenue to closer contact, information to ponder later when his heart was pounding hard for different reasons. They both crouched and peered under the bed. The dust bunnies had built an army, but they weren't hiding Bella. A quick inspection of Joey's closet revealed only clothes and personal effects. Adara still kept a pair of ratty Converse the Salvation Army would reject and a computer from the dark ages. What he wouldn't pay for her to love *him* that way — deeply, freely, ferociously, unwilling to let him go.

"I should call the police." Adara's voice was smooth, a testament to her strength. She released his arm suddenly, as if realizing she still held onto him.

He smoothly took her hand and tucked it back in the crook of his arm. "Bob's best beer buddy is on the force. I'll call him, but don't expect much. Based on my own experience, any investigation will amount to a cursory examination and life will go on. You're not staying here."

When she didn't offer the expected argument, he turned his gaze from Bella's discarded trash to Adara's face. She stared at the violin case leaning in the corner.

"I haven't been in here since his funeral." The strength in her voice only seconds ago fractured into vulnerable shards. "I buried every part of him that day—his body in the ground, what he left behind in this room. The memories refuse to be buried," she said, so soft they barely counted as words.

Garret lightly squeezed her limp fingers. He could tell her that embracing memories was like having Joey always close, that the heart never forgets. Or that while the pain might sometimes feel like razor blades slicing her soul, that softer, fonder flashes of moments would counterbalance the agony. Or that she controlled the way loss carved her future, that life without Joey would be different but it didn't have to be bleak or empty. Instead, he kept his words trapped tight and wrapped Adara in his arms, allowing her the courtesy of silence. And when the stiffness in her shoulders relaxed and she leaned into him, nestling her cheek against his shoulder with a shaky sigh, he was completely and endlessly lost in her.

Chapter Twenty-One

Adara forced herself out of Garret's arms, away from his strength and warmth, and the loss nearly staggered her, almost as much as how she'd unthinkingly revealed her grief to him. She sped into the hallway and to her bedroom, leaving him alone to reseal Joey's tomb.

"You don't have to hang around," she called over her shoulder, dragging her duffel bag free from the stack of dusty photo albums in the closet. One album fell and thumped to the carpet. It flipped opened, and she slammed it shut without looking. "I'll grab some things and find a hotel room. Tomorrow, I'll add security system research to my agenda."

She spun toward her dresser and almost smacked into Garret. He blocked her path, his eyes glittering like onyx, a straight, white line replacing his usual smile. Every inch of him nearly vibrated with tension. He looked positively ruthless.

"Don't you remember what I said?" His fierce, tight voice held an unmistakable threat. "Bella broke into my hotel room without any problem. You're coming home with *me*."

A strange thrill spiraled deep into her soul. His bossiness inspired an urge to argue, dig in her heels and tell him to kiss off, yet the savage protectiveness called up an irresistible warmth. She felt like a moth caught in a lantern, craving the light as much as she knew it would burn her. And after discovering a stranger had been hanging out in her house without her knowing, she really didn't want to be home tonight — or alone, even if it meant spending more time with Garret. "Okay."

"No arguments." He paused and his eyes narrowed. "No trickery, either."

"All trickery has been postponed to a later date." Her gentle push to access her dresser only gained a few inches. He barricaded the door as if she might make a run for it. "Ambrose, I said I'd go to your place. You don't need to be privy to my underwear drawer too."

His features softened and his shoulders visibly relaxed. "Oh, I don't know about that." He wriggled his eyebrows, sense of humor safely regained. "Go ahead, darling. Grab your things. I'm keeping watch."

"I'm not your 'darling', and I'm pretty sure Bella isn't folded up among my socks." Ignoring him as best as she could, Adara opened her top drawer and stuffed a pair of socks and underwear in her bag.

"Black and lacy." A tease entered his voice. "Good choice."

"Hope you got a good look, pervert." She swiped a shirt and sweatshirt from another drawer. The heat in her face better be gone before she had to face him full on. "That's all you're going to see."

"Just making an observation."

"So was I."

"The difference between you and me, *neshama*, is that I'd gladly show you my underwear drawer and take your opinion to heart." He leaned a hip against her dresser, a long, lean line of jeans and black T-shirt. "I'd only keep what you like."

And now she was thinking about his underwear. *Briefs or boxers?* She straightened and gave him her best unimpressed look. "The difference between you and me, violin boy, is that I actually *have* an underwear drawer. You don't have any furniture."

His smile worked free. Not even a stalker could keep it down long. "I ordered some, but until it arrives, my suitcases are free for your inspection."

"I'll pass." But still — *boxers or briefs?* She tried her best to keep her focus on his broad shoulders as they left her room, but it wasn't her fault he stopped and bent to tuck a loose shoelace into his boot. She bit her cheek. Definitely boxers. Definitely. And she'd rather think about his underwear than what Bella had been doing in her house instead of Garret's.

* * * *

The drive to Garret's home was short, and Adara let him fill the void with idle conversation. She trailed him up the steps and waited in silence while he disabled the alarm. If he noticed the humble vibe, he didn't say. Any need to heckle him about his overdone locks and security system had vanished at the sight of Joey's desecrated bedroom. He led her past the gorgeous staircase and the library to the farthest room, only glancing back once to confirm she followed.

She paused beneath the curved archway marking the entrance and waited for the inevitable convulsing of her heart. So this was his live-in room, the one she'd missed on the previous tour, thanks to Gia's call for rescue. Like the rest of his house, carved woodwork warmed every surface of the oblong room. Three windows in one wall opened to the night, frosted as if to let light in while not distract with the view, a baby grand centered between them. An assortment of stringed instruments in their stands, from cello to violin to fiddle, lined another wall like trained dogs awaiting their master's order. A black, silver-veined marble hearth cozied up in the opposite wall, waiting to glow for whoever sat in the couch facing it.

Garret set her bag beside the couch and studied her cautiously, clearly waiting for her to change her mind and bolt. She *should* bolt, but if she ran now, it would raise uncomfortable questions she wasn't ready to answer.

Adara forced her seemingly fifty-pound feet to move until instruments flanked her and the couch was close enough to catch her if she collapsed.

"Now I deeply regret not ordering a bed sooner." His voice reverberated, as if it rose from a well.

"You mean beds," she said absently. A sense of déjà vu made her lightheaded, all the instruments an echo from an hour ago and the expected gut-punch still hadn't come. Maybe after airing out the Joey closet today, her emotions had flat-lined, incapable of absorbing any more blows.

"No one has ever spent the night with me before." He plucked the bags of food from her and stooped in her face, forcing her to focus on him. His smile was slow and completely playful. "And if we're sleeping under the same roof, *neshama,* I prefer one bed." He darted out with the food before she could think up a snarky response.

She dug her fingers into the back of the couch and resumed digesting her shelter for the night. While the rest of the house waited for Garret's final touch, this room had his fingerprints everywhere—his running shoes in the corner, a pair of jeans and a graphic T slung over one couch arm, a black beanie on the piano bench, music paper spread above the keys and notes penciled in his loopy handwriting. Despite the fact he'd been in her bedroom several times and she was more than familiar with him, being here felt extremely, awkwardly personal.

As if tugged by a gentle tractor beam, she wandered to the piano and sank onto the wooden bench. She ran a finger over the smooth rows of black and white keys, not pressing hard enough to make any noise. Once upon a time, Joey would pound the keys and she'd sing. His enthusiasm would drag her in so fast and hard that she wouldn't realize she was neck-deep in his music until it was too late. He had been so much like Garret.

But what Garret awakened in her definitely wasn't brotherly.

"Do you play?" Garret's voice preceded the aroma of warmed up Chinese food only by a second. He swung a leg over the piano bench, straddling it, facing her. Each hand carried a paper plate holding enough rice to feed China.

"Of course." On a whim, she lifted her chin and positioned her hands on the keys. "I'll show you the meaning of prodigy." She plinked out a stilted version of *Chopsticks*. A year of avoiding music couldn't erase her first memorized piano tune.

"Bravo!" Laughing, Garret balanced a plate on each thigh and applauded. At his piercing whistle, she couldn't completely hide her grin. "You shouldn't have done that, darling. Now I'll have to keep you locked up here. Once people hear your surely divine-inspired talent, I won't have any fans left to support me."

"What was your backup career?" Abandoning the piano, she angled his way and took a plate. "If you didn't make it as a musician?"

His smile faded, and he handed her a fork from his shirt pocket. "I didn't even comprehend until my teenage years that I could defy my mother's wishes and pursue a different occupation if I truly wanted to." He shrugged. "I was born with music in my veins, and my mother recognized that. Despite how she relentlessly drove me, even in days I wanted to punch my violin until it was only strings and slivers, I never second-guessed music as my life."

Must be nice. She hadn't figured out she wanted to be a teacher until she was almost done with her accounting degree. She slowly chewed rice that tasted like it came straight from a restaurant. Switching majors had added another two years of school.

"But," he added, jabbing his fork at her, "if I couldn't be a musician, I'd go for paranormal investigator."

Adara swallowed before she spluttered. "Seriously?"

"Oh yeah." His dark eyes sparkled, as if considering his glorious life as a ghostbuster. He was so full of crap. "Being paid to enter morbid places and try to communicate with the otherworld would be phenomenal. Plus, I'd be helping both people and restless spirits by sending them on to the light." He wriggled his eyebrows. "I'd let you be my camera girl. Want to hear the song I've been writing?"

It took her a second to catch up with the subject change, and by that time, he'd exchanged his plate for the violin innocently hiding on the piano. The rice in her mouth lost all its flavor. "Nuh-uh. Nope. No way."

He gave her a long-suffering look. "You're my muse. It's your song. As a duty of muse-dom, you're required to listen."

"I never signed up to be your muse." She set her plate down and stood, ready to run into the night. "We're working on the school concert tonight, nothing else."

Dropping the bow and violin to his sides, he lowered his chin and peered at her beneath his dark lashes. "Please?"

A lightning bolt forked through her, pulsing electricity into every secret place. That look could coax the Pope into organizing a slavery ring. "I'll think about it." *Not really.* "That's my best offer."

"You thinking about me for an indeterminable amount of time is good enough for now." His husky voice sent aftershocks along the still-smoking lightning trail.

She squeezed her thighs together. "Focus, Ambrose."

"I am." His gaze never left her face.

"Third-grade children." She spoke slowly, so he'd understand. "Upcoming music recital. Weekly report."

He thankfully replaced his violin on the piano and perched on the edge of the couch, just like Joey used to. "I'm still formulating a master plan and a concert theme, but a few things are figured out. Some are no-brainers, like separating the three terrorists in training. They can't focus on anything beyond scaring any boy within range, if they're together." He looked a little terrified himself. "I want Haley on finger cymbals. She thinks they're cute. Ava has shown a surprising knack for the xylophone and Dalaynee has kazoo written all over her. She particularly likes making noise."

Back in the safety zone of school subjects, Adara sank onto the piano bench again and picked up her plate. Most people wouldn't notice such intricacies in her students or decipher how to make the most of them. She shouldn't be surprised, not after seeing how he so easily interpreted her. Even if he hadn't learned how to rule kids with an iron fist, he was a practiced people reader.

He nabbed a magazine and blank page of sheet music and set them on the piano bench beside her. Kneeling on the floor, his head bent over the paper, he penciled a rough sketch of a stage and marked each student's place with their first initial and abbreviated instrument as he went down the list. His hand was fascinating, tendons shifting subtly beneath his skin, a dusting of golden hair at his strong wrist, long fingers. The rousing scrape of his callused fingertips still echoed on her skin.

School. Recital. Students… Right.

She stopped him after Sammy. "Even if you want them both on a drum, don't put Sammy and Adam together. They'll destroy each other before the first song."

"Percussion needs to be together." Garret rubbed his bottom lip, studying his chart, and she tried to breathe normally. His mouth and hand in unison, in one spot, was an unfair play on her focus. "And no one else has a particular leaning for drums."

It took her a moment to replay his words, another to respond. "Give one of the girls a crow sounder. Put her between them, but Adam needs to be on the outside, as far as possible from other kids. He can't keep his hands to himself."

Smirking, Garret glanced up. "When you're around, I have that problem too."

"Har." She rolled her eyes. It was better than everything else other body parts suggested. "Plus, Adam's a tripper. He never ties his shoes and has a perpetual scab on at least one elbow or knee the entire year."

"I planned to give Sammy the bongo and Adam bass. Bass needs extra room, so it doesn't make sense to place it in the middle." He sat back on his heels. "While it goes against all my musical sensibilities, I'll acquiesce to your judgment this once, Miss Dumont."

"Good call, Ambrose. For once."

He grinned, and it took every ounce of willpower not to grin back like an idiot.

"What about Ashton?" The perfect subject to get her unruly thoughts back on track. Ashton was skittish, hardly spoke and coaxing her to make eye contact took a sticker, sometimes two. "I'm worried about getting her on stage, let alone keeping her there for a few songs without crying."

"I've got it covered." He flicked his fingers in the air, grabbed his plate and shoveled rice into his mouth like a starving vagabond. If she didn't know how much he loved to blab, she might accuse him of avoiding the subject.

"Are you sure?" Maybe his certainty included whatever he'd been doing with Ashton and her brother when she'd run into them at the school after hours. If he flubbed up, she was ultimately responsible, and with Ashton's timidity, she felt extra protective. "She's super shy, you know."

He paused, fork halfway to his mouth, and gave her an offended royalty look. "I'm not a blind buffoon. Ashton is—" His phone rang, and he frowned at the screen. "It's Roman, Bob's police buddy...with Bella info."

Chapter Twenty-Two

At the footsteps drawing closer, Adara turned from the library window she'd stared through for the last half-hour while Garret had been on the phone with Roman. The night offered a blank canvas for her thoughts and no answers, its silence made bearable only by his muffled voice from the kitchen. There were a lot of trees out there, so many places a stalker could be hiding, close and watching.

Garret's expression was untroubled, a good sign. "Roman will check out the perimeter in the morning, and he'll swing by here to chat afterward. Nothing's going to happen tonight. Ready for ice cream?"

How he blazed from stalkers to dairy products with such ease, she'd never know. She swiped a hand over her forehead, weariness a sudden weight, as if Garret's presence had finally made it okay to relax. She shook her head and yawned.

"Raincheck." His smile was knowing. "Teacher's tired."

"So we know Bella isn't at my house, but what about yours?" She shuffled past him, and he fell into step beside her, tagging along to the music room. Since it was his house, she didn't complain. "What if she's spying on you from the Ambrose Forest?"

"Unlike others I know, I always double lock my doors and windows. Spiders can't even get through my security system, and while my fortress is impenetrable, dispatch is sending an officer to keep an eye on the grounds here too. You can sleep safe and sound." He paused as she stooped for her duffel bag beside the couch. "Did you bring those adorable sheep pajamas?"

"What else?" She shouldered her bag and ignored how his dark eyes sparkled. Only a weirdo would be turned on by flannel pajamas decorated in fluffy white farm animals. It didn't help that she happened to appreciate weirdness in all its forms. "Which way to the bathroom?"

Fifteen minutes later, face washed, breath minty fresh and sheep pajamas on, Adara ambled back to Garret's music slash living room, the hardwood floor smooth and cool beneath her bare feet. The magnitude of the situation finally smacked her in the face. She was in his house, spending the night. *With him.* Her heart seemed to be out of sync, going from sledgehammer to finger taps to a death metal drum solo. She should've gone to a motel or Gia's. *What am I thinking?*

The problem was she hadn't been thinking, and if she backed out now, he'd know why. He'd know he was getting under her skin. Then, he'd never leave her alone and she could kiss her safety net goodbye.

As she entered the music room, the main source of her brain malfunction smiled, pulled the blanket off the back of the couch and patted the cushion. "Get comfy, darling."

"Where are you sleeping?" The no-horseplay teacher tone she attempted fell flat, her throat strangling the words. She seriously hadn't considered the potential consequences. Worse, she knew she should have when she made the decision to go with him, but she'd chosen not to. It was all completely Garret's fault. He made her forget.

"It's a big couch." He looked hopeful.

"Not big enough for the both of us." A lie. It was plush and oversized, clearly made for lounging more than sitting.

"I don't mind snuggling." One corner of his mouth lifted, and his voice lowered an octave. "I'll keep you toasty."

"Not a chance." Staying toasty was at the bottom of her concern list. It was the rest of her stays that worried her. Whenever Garret was around, they loosened without permission, and imagining him keeping her toasty was far too easy. Far too tempting.

"I had an inkling you might say that." He grinned all the way, letting her off the hook. "I'm patient. Tomorrow's a new day." He dropped his head, forlorn. "I'll cozy up on the floor like an abandoned dog, shaking in the cold, longing for the warmth of his mistress."

"The Ambrose dramatics are alarming." She snatched the blanket from him.

"It's a gift."

"Or a genetic defect." Adara plopped onto the couch, sinking into the cushions. His couch was made for Sunday afternoon naps, definitely made for snuggling. A combination of this couch and Garret would be hazardous to her health.

Watching her, he pressed his lips together, as if reconsidering his decision to sleep on the floor. "I'll be back."

"Thanks for the warning." Since his back was turned and he couldn't see her, she smiled at his chuckle and curled up into the cushions. The forest-green blanket was clearly handmade, crocheted by the softest yarn, and as she pulled it up to her chin, she drew in a lungful of ode de Garret. Sparks sizzled through her, gathering in her belly. This was where he slept every night, probably the same blanket he draped over his strong, lean, sexy body.

Closing her eyes, she struggled to push away the image of him on the couch with her, in his arms, their legs entangled, his mouth on hers. No matter how tempting, it was the right decision. Even if she was ready for a deeper relationship, he hadn't mentioned his plans after his mentorship ended, and she hadn't asked. He was like a tidal wave, and the only way to survive was to tread water and hope she didn't drown while he passed through.

"Roman assured me your neighborhood would be heavily patrolled tonight. Maybe they'll find her." Garret strolled toward her, a blanket slung over his shoulder, a pillow tucked beneath one arm. His golden hair was completely free, low-slung, black pajama bottoms replaced his jeans and showed nothing else but skin and coiled, graceful strength.

Her mouth went dry. Fully dressed, he made her pulse jump. Shirtless was prone to cause heart attacks.

Apparently oblivious to her ogling, he dropped the blanket and pillow beside the couch and looked at her. The dark, burning sweep he gave her body under his blanket didn't help her failing functions. "Need anything before I kill the light?"

You.

Gah.

It was not a thought she could entertain. Since her tongue had lost its ability to move, she shook her head.

He walked back to the light switch by the door, every step a supple roll of muscles beneath honeyed skin. Non-athlete, her bony patootie. The man was hard, lean and long, from the ridges of his shoulders to his narrow waist. The rest of him might not be bare, but her imagination made up for it.

The light clicked off, darkness disrupting her view, and the soft slap of his bare feet on the floor marked his approach. Material rustled, and his sigh drifted, soft in the gloom. "Comfortable, *neshama*?"

As comfortable as she could be with the sudden, scalding need squirming in her veins to surrender to the irrational sensations he inspired in her otherwise-reasonable being and pounce on him. "Peachy. I'll try not to step on your sensitive parts when I sleepwalk."

"Any sleepwalking secrets you want to share?" Interest colored his voice. She wouldn't put it past him to follow her around while she zombied out, taking pictures to blackmail her into a date later.

"Kidding. I sleep like a corpse. Sorry to ruin your demented musician plans."

"And I was having so many fantasies." He tapped the couch, sending a vibration through the cushions. "Still canvassing tomorrow?"

Another problem she didn't want to think about. The next board meeting was coming up fast and she had a long way to go before her job was secure. Then she'd have to whip up a renewed budget of her own. Cutting her salary would hurt, but it was better than being in the unemployment line. "Yep. If I run into Bella, maybe I can recruit her to my cause."

His voice darkened. "That's not funny. I'll go with you."

"That would be great for your reputation. The local golden violinist boy supporting the death of music in schools."

"I don't support that," he said quietly. "I support Adara Dumont. Big difference."

Her throat tightened. Her world would be so much easier if he was a selfish, unlikeable jerk.

"Good night, *neshama*."

"I'm so looking up that word tomorrow."

"Let me know when you do."

Tired as she was, the minutes still passed a slow march toward dawn. Garret was a simple reach away, and somewhere in the night, a stalker with unknown intentions. She couldn't understand what drove a person to hunt another like prey, to hide inside a stranger's house. Didn't Bella have a job, a family, a life? It didn't make sense to travel half a world away simply to spy on Garret. There had to be another reason. Despite the warm, Garret-scented blanket pulled up to her chin, she shivered. Tomorrow, she'd carve out some time to study up on stalkers.

"Adara," Garret whispered, "are you asleep?"

She stared into the shadows. He had the hard floor to blame for not snoozing, and if she didn't answer or move, she could go back to the useless wheel of her thoughts. Go back to listening hard to the subtle noises of an unfamiliar house at night. Go back to pretending.

"Not really." With a sense of resignation, she rolled onto her side and scooched until her back pressed tight against the back cushions. "It's nice of you to let me crash here, but this is your house, and you shouldn't have to sleep on the floor. I made room for you up here."

A hissing noise followed, as if he'd released a breath between his teeth. "That, darling, is not a good idea."

She wriggled to the couch edge, only able to make out his dim silhouette. "It's a big couch."

"The woman I'm insanely attracted to is on my couch, under my blanket a mere sit-up away. In case you haven't noticed, I'm a man." His chuckle held no humor whatsoever. "I have my limits. If I join you, I'll make you mine in every way, and with you, *neshama*, there will be no refunds or returns. I don't believe you're prepared for that, so I deem it wisest to remain on the floor and suffer alone with my imagination and the side effects."

Oh. Her breath caught and her temperature shot up several degrees. *Oh...*

"Unless you've finally realized the truth?" It wasn't hard to picture his hopeful expression. "That fate has drawn us together and there's no escaping destiny?"

She snorted.

"I thought as much." He sighed, but his words held a tolerant smile. "In an attempt to counter the visions my mind continues to replay of you, me and all the fun and life-altering activities we could be doing on that soft, pliable couch, I've been considering the Bella situation."

Answering wasn't possible, not with where her mind took her. Garret leaning over her, his skin pale in the gloom, golden glints in his hair as he brought his mouth to hers, pressed his weight into her, hitting all the right girly spots. She pulled her arms free of the blanket and hoped he couldn't hear the allegro pace of her pulse.

"I sometimes wonder," he said, "if it would've been better to stay unknown, less accomplished."

The quiet sincerity in his tone jarred all thoughts out of the Garret gutter. Adara rolled onto her side again, close to the couch edge, to hear him better. Keeping his talent contained, the affect he had on people dimmed, would be a civic injustice. Not that she'd tell him that. "Why?"

"Before I started getting noticed, I never questioned a person's motives. Friends and enemies weren't difficult to distinguish—people either liked me, ignored me or didn't like me." He shifted, sliding a hand beneath his head, and the gloom couldn't hide the fact the blanket had slipped to his waist.

She tried not to think about how easy it would be to reach down and stroke his firm, smooth, deliciously bare chest. In case her hands decided to act of their own volition, she clasped them to her thrumming heart.

"I've since discovered," he continued, "that people are skilled at hiding their motives and honesty is a rare characteristic. I've been befriended for all manners of reasons, but those reasons generally relate in one way or another to my music, not me."

Surrounded by admirers of all ages, an extended family who adored him and he still walked the edge of loneliness. Something uncomfortable wedged beneath her heart. In their own ways, they'd both chosen solitude. He traded a settled life to share his passion with the world. His path contained elements of sacrifice, a noble sacrifice. Hers, not so much.

He swallowed audibly, regaining her full attention. "I was, undeniably, a late bloomer, and at first, the attention from the female population was flattering, beyond any fantasy of a pudgy, middle school nerd who couldn't get a date."

Even as she smiled at the memory of his growing-pangs story, a wire coiled inside, barbed with jealousy. Picturing him, pudgy or not, with someone else wrenched that wire tight. Slowly, she forced her jaw to relax. She was the one who'd set the limits. He wasn't hers, so she had no right to feel anything. If only reconciling her brain with her heart was so easy.

"Did you fall asleep on me?" he asked.

She cleared her head, along with her throat. "Nope. I'm waiting on the edge of the couch for the exciting conclusion of the female conquest chapter in your biography."

"I'd call it more a series of sad mysteries than a conquest." His soft laugh curled low in her belly, warm and intoxicating. "I might not be the sharpest tack in the box, but I caught on fast. Take away the spotlight, the prestige, the money, the shampoo-commercial-worthy hair and my irresistibly sexy bod —"

She flicked her fingers in his general vicinity, and he shifted out of reach, chuckling.

"My point is I'm exhausted of being wanted for everything besides the person I am." The unexpected vulnerability in his voice destroyed her. "And I appreciate, deeply, that you're real with me, Adara. When you finally swoon at my feet, I know it'll be sincere."

Her forehead burned, as if branded by the word 'fraud'. Biting her tongue was the only way she kept from blurting her thoughts — that he was the best man she knew, despite being a musician, that she loved how he inspired the shyest kid in her class to respond, that she didn't really mind it when he interrupted her space because he made her forget why she'd chosen solitude, that every smile she wore since his unrelenting intrusion on her life was his fault.

There'd be no going back from saying those words aloud, and he was right. She wasn't ready for the repercussions of voicing that truth, didn't know if she'd ever be ready, so she went with a different truth.

"I don't really hate music," she whispered, her voice hoarse and halting. "So much of it reminds me of Joey." Under night's cloak, speaking fragments of her heart was somehow manageable.

"I know." Garret's whisper matched hers, as if speaking louder would break the spell between them. The pale line of his arm shifted, and he found her hand in the darkness. He hooked their pinkies and squeezed.

"Losing him... I can't take another hit like that." Admitting her weakness cracked something inside, and the words tumbled out, freed from their cage. "The only way to function is to keep people out of my personal life. No problem, right? Wear only black, don't smile, be somewhat threatening, should be easy. Only it wasn't. It isn't." She took a shaky breath. "I can't stop caring. The best I can do is distance myself and care from afar, out of the danger zone."

Silence stretched between them, long enough that she suspected she'd stumped him.

"Life is pain, *neshama*," he said at last. "There's no getting around that, but you're doing yourself a disservice by shutting out the joy."

If only everything was as easy as he made it sound. "The pain isn't worth it."

"I respectfully disagree. Pain is an inevitable byproduct of the world we live in, and there's no escaping it. Life is about finding the joy amid the pain, not letting pain rule your life." He paused and huffed. "Funny... I never took you for a dropout, Dumont."

Dropout? Her face heated. Dealing with life after Joey in the only way she knew how didn't make her a dropout. She shouldn't have told him anything. She struggled to disentangle her pinkie from his, but he held onto her wrist, his large hands callused and unrelenting.

"Don't get mad." He chained her hand to his chest, pulling her halfway off the couch.

"I'm not mad." Her voice betrayed her, tight and reedy.

"I understand the need to protect your heart, Adara. It's not easy to open up, knowing there will be pain." His breath brushed her tense forearm, warm and steady. "Thank you for sharing your thoughts with me instead of shutting me out with the rest of the world." Without warning, he sucked her pinkie into his mouth.

Lightning shot from her breasts to her core, and before she could recover, he bit her finger, hard enough to sting. He immediately licked the spot he'd bitten and replaced her hand on his chest.

She drew a sharp breath, her entire body throbbing hard enough to hit the Richter scale. "You're so...*bad*."

His low laugh flowed over her like honey heated by the sun, smooth and rich. "Pursuing the woman I want, doing whatever it takes to inspire her to think about me, doesn't make me bad. On a scale from Hodor to Ramsey Bolton, I'm a Jon Snow."

"A nerd too." Her arm was tired — the only reason she surrendered to his shackle — and when he relaxed his grip slightly, her palm landed right above his heart. His pulse vibrated in a counterpoint to hers.

"Once a nerd, always a nerd." He caressed her hand with his thumb in slow, sensual strokes. "I don't suppose you were a pudgy nerd in middle school?"

"Not even." She smiled against the couch cushion, one leg slung over the side. "Joey called me 'chicken legs' all the way into college. I lived vicariously through books, had zero interest in boys, and Joey commandeered the majority of my free time, dragging me into his musical whirlwind." Her smile died and another confession slipped free before she could leash it. "When I lost my brother, I lost my best friend too."

"You don't have to be alone, *neshama*." His voice was gentle with understanding, and for the first time since Joey's death, she didn't really mind not being alone.

Chapter Twenty-Three

A far-off ringing pulled Garret into awareness, and he opened his eyes. Every muscle ached. Morning light drifted through the windows, gray and brittle, highlighting the slender fingers limp on his bare chest.

Adara.

Electricity sparked to life in his veins, throbbing in all the right places, but he kept still, unwilling to disrupt her. One arm and leg hung over the edge of the couch as if undecided whether to escape or join him on the floor. Her other arm curled over her dark head. He sucked in a breath. *Chara,* her full, perfect mouth was parted slightly in invitation, and he fisted his hands to resist tracing her lower lip and following up with a kiss. Hazy with sleep, she might not resist, and he wasn't willing to test his own mettle when it came to seducing Adara, especially when one appendage in particular was eager, hard and ready. He wouldn't stop, not until she surrendered and admitted she belonged to him, and despite the substantial progress he'd made the previous night, she wasn't ready.

But she would be. Her resistance couldn't match his perseverance.

A heavy thumping on his front door erased his musings. *The doorbell.* That was what had interrupted his sleep. He sat up and Adara stirred. She lifted her head and squinted at him through a curtain of fuzzed raven locks.

"Coffee." The word was hardly more than a growl, and she promptly tugged the blanket over her head, shutting him out.

"Wish granted." Since she'd tucked everything in besides her foot, he kissed her ankle, receiving no protest. Either she was too tired to care or had already fallen back asleep.

A duet of doorbell and pounding rattled through the hallway, and Garret shuffled barefoot to the front door, scratching his stomach. Roman wasn't due to report on Bella until later, and the long driveway tended to keep most people away. Bob and London were taking the kids to see Bob's parents today, so it wasn't them.

At the door, he put his eye to the peephole. Ian stood on the porch, lawyer-polished even in jeans, boots and fisherman sweater, his short hair gelled to perfection. Garret snorted softly. And people accused *him* of being vain. Next to Ian, he was dime-store shabby.

A few finger jabs and a beep disengaged the security system. He flicked the deadbolt and opened the door. A blast of cold air hit him square in the bare chest, and Ian shoved past him.

"A little early, isn't it?" Garret shut the door fast, goose bumps on his arms.

"Roman called me." Ian pivoted, his blue eyes flashing. "What part of 'press charges' didn't you get, dude? If you're not going to take my legal advice, the next time you ask for it, I'm charging you my full rate."

"No interrogations before coffee, counselor. I didn't get much sleep last night." Rubbing his eyes, Garret shuffled into the kitchen and flicked on the light. "I know you stopped by the coffee stand on your way here to flirt with the high school girls. You could've brought me one."

When Ian didn't answer, he pivoted. No Ian behind him. Empty hallway. His chest constricted. Ian finding Adara would be disastrous. Suddenly and ferociously awake, he raced back to the music room and entered just as Ian lifted the blanket off Adara's head.

"What have we here?" Gleeful venom dripped with each word.

Adara opened her eyes, focused on Ian and sat up fast. Her glare made the temperature drop a degree. "Ian." She said his name like a curse and made the sign of a cross in the air between them. "I thought you couldn't be in the sunlight without combusting."

"And I believed you'd freeze the testicles off any man who got too close." He smirked over his shoulder at Garret. "Bravo, my friend. You truly are a virtuoso, no matter what instrument you use."

Ben-zonna. Garret swiped a hand down his face. "It's not what you think."

Throwing off the blanket, Adara leaped up and pointed a long finger in Ian's face. Even in flannel sheep pajamas, she was magnificently formidable. "If I hear even the hint of a rumor surrounding this, I'll use that ice you love to associate with me and frickin' frostbite your miniscule testicles."

Ian's smirk didn't waver in the slightest. He turned to Garret, courtroom challenge glittering in his eyes. "You're my witness. She threatened me."

"Fair warning. I'm not an impartial witness." Garret smoothly stepped between them before Adara unleashed the fist at her side and Ian added assault to his list of charges. He pivoted, his back to her, keeping Ian's cage-rattling gaze mostly blocked. Hopefully, she'd resist tearing through him to get to Ian. "Again, it's not what you're implying, and since you spoke to Roman, you know why I insisted that Adara stay with me last night."

"I didn't imply anything." Ian flashed his shark smile, predatory and vicious. "I didn't need to. Reactions are very telling."

Garret pinched the bridge of his nose as Adara's growl vibrated along his spine. "Let it go, Ian. She slept unmolested on the couch while I snoozed on the floor, as evidenced by the pillow and blanket at your feet and the aches in my bones."

Ian's gaze dipped south and his smirk widened. "You shouldn't have said 'ache' and 'bone' in the same sentence."

He grabbed the pillow off the couch and held it over his groin, joining Adara's glare for his oldest friend. "Further proof in our defense."

"Is it? I mean, I know I'm always up for another round in the morning — "

Garret slammed the pillow in Ian's face, shutting him up, but the muffled, unrepentant laugh didn't defuse anything. He fisted Ian's sweater and dragged him beyond Adara's reach, out into the hall. She'd returned to perching stiffly on the couch, but he wasn't taking any chances. "Why did Roman call you, anyway? I didn't realize you even knew each other."

"We have an arrangement." Ian wrested free of Garret's hold and smoothed his stretched-out sweater. "That's all you need to know."

He agreed. When it came to Ian's work, ignorance and bliss were an inseparable pair. "What did Roman tell you?"

"That you should have followed my advice in the first place and pressed criminal charges on that psycho instead of a protective order hand slap. Paperwork can't stop crazy."

He sighed. "I counted on the ocean to be enough of a barrier."

Ian raised his eyebrows, his way of calling him an imbecile without saying a word. "The 'woman scorned' adage is absolutely true. All she needed was a passport and a cheap flight. When you land in one place, you're not that hard to find, and she had no problem finding you when you *weren't* staying put."

Garret leaned against the wall, needing the support. He didn't understand stalking. Tracking him like an animal wouldn't change his feelings, and hiding in Adara's house? It was beyond unsettling. If Bella paid attention at all in her spying, she knew how he felt about Adara, and if her obsession turned rabid, his favorite teacher would be the most likely target. He shifted toward the music room. His muse sat ramrod straight on the couch, looking quite rabid herself. Then again, Bella might be the one who'd regret taking that particular turn.

"Serving her with a stalking order on home soil will be problematic, since her location is unknown." Ian recaptured his attention, going into full lawyer mode. "Unless she threatens you in some way, a restraining order is out. Your best hope is to slap her with a burglary charge for entering the Princess of the North's house. But I wouldn't count on that. There's not enough proof."

"What about fingerprints?"

Ian quirked an eyebrow, a superiority look picked up in law school. "You watch too much *CSI*. Roman is a meticulous investigator, but getting a good fingerprint off fast food wrappers isn't going to happen. Even if he does manage to get a good print, unless your Bella has been in the legal system here, it won't show up in the database. Your only chance to get her off your back is if she gets caught, which is why you should hire a bodyguard."

"While you play *Hardy Boys*, I'm getting coffee." Chin high, Adara marched past them. Her usually smooth and sleek hair was tousled in a way that made Garret want to kick Ian out, renege on last night's gallant, self-sacrificing decision and drag her back to the couch, onto his lap and into his forever. He should've hung on to that pillow. It took every ounce of willpower not to trail her into the kitchen, cage her against the counter and kiss her until she surrendered. He wasn't above using coffee as blackmail.

"Sweet pajamas," Ian drawled, his tone appreciative, his gaze glued to Adara's perfect, slender rump.

"Stop leering at my girl." Garret punched his friend in the shoulder. His own leering wasn't up for discussion.

Ian rubbed his shoulder, grinning. "I thought that wasn't how it is."

"That's not how *that* was, but it's unconditionally how *it is*. Got it?" Garret narrowed his eyes in his menacing, no-more-crap look. He'd picked up that particular look in middle school, no lessons required. "Be respectful."

Ian's grin slipped to half-done. "Possessive is a side of you I've never seen."

Adara probably couldn't hear their conversation from the kitchen, but he lowered his voice anyway. "It didn't exist until I met the one woman I don't want to live without." He blew out a breath. Discussing his feelings for Adara with Ian wasn't on the itinerary. "I'm with you on the bodyguard, but it won't be for me. It'll be for her, something she doesn't need to know. And he'll be a back-up because I have every intention of staying with her whenever possible."

All traces of humor in Ian vanished. "If you push me, I'll provide statistics of others who didn't take their stalker seriously and wound up dead. These admirers didn't target a loved one. They went straight for the throat of their number one idol."

A chill spiraled through Garret, making his scalp crawl. Violence couldn't always be predicted or prevented, he knew that, even though it had never touched him personally. He preferred to keep the status quo in that regard.

"I'm not disagreeing with assigning a musclebound, hardcore SWAT member to watch Miss Crabapple." Ian leaned near and looked him square in the eyes. "A fan's admiration isn't always rational. You need protection too."

Since the day Ian had jumped into a schoolyard fight that wasn't his own, knocked a fourth-grader off Garret's first-grade back and proceeded to break the bully's nose, Garret had recognized what drove Ian O'Connor. He had a soft spot for the underdog, a ferocious need to protect those he loved and, no matter the shiny exterior, he'd fight fang and claw for whoever made it into that secret space inside the shark suit. Once earned, his loyalty was irreversible. Bromance eternal.

The last of his annoyance drained away, and he nodded. "Fine."

"Good." Ian clapped him once on the shoulder, both in approval and reassurance. "Roman knows some guys, very discreet. You won't even know they're there."

Garret raked his fingers through his hair. What a quandary. "Is this a nonnegotiable part of expanding my musical horizons—looking over my shoulder, hiring bodyguards, worrying that someone I love might get hurt because of me?"

"Look on the bright side, dude." Smirk back in place, Ian headed for the door. "If you were ugly and untalented, you wouldn't have to worry about it."

Chapter Twenty-Four

The unnatural silence in Adara's classroom itched beneath her skin. She dropped her red pen on the desk and the *plink* echoed between the graveyard of empty seats. The clock ticked a loud, dismal beat she'd never noticed before. Garret had taken the kids to the auditorium to begin realistic concert practice. *Alone.* He'd insisted she stay behind so when the performance actually happened, she'd enjoy the full surprise. Secretly, she loved the idea. Publicly, she'd protested.

They'd been gone ten minutes. He was probably already duct-taped to the flagpole.

She drummed her fingers on the desk, anything to fill the quiet. She'd survived a night on his couch, midnight confessions and an unfortunate early morning Ian encounter. Then, a Saturday spent overseeing an emergency home security system installation and collecting far too few signatures while her house was molded into an impenetrable fortress. Keeping Garret from playing guard dog on her porch had taken several threats, a poke in the butt with her umbrella and a broom aimed at his perfect hair.

If only she could push him out of her thoughts and reclaim every piece of her heart as easily. One by one, he'd picked up the broken fragments while she wasn't looking and tucked them away, out of her reach. She wasn't sure who held the majority now. He might win the vote.

She slouched in her chair. Sunday had been even worse. He'd shown up at dawn with a peppermint mocha bearing her name and proceeded to ruin her untouched kitchen with cooking and other sordid activities best reserved for restaurants. Food fumes still lingered, reminding her with each breath. He'd completely neglected the microwave, and it had been hard to protest his presence with her mouth constantly full of irresistible culinary feats. While she'd never admit it, his noise had been a relief to the foundation-deep stillness of her house. The silence had lost its solace, and she wasn't sure if the blame belonged to Bella or Garret.

And she was still short on signatures, with the next board meeting barely two weeks away.

The clock tolled a few more seconds, slow and somber. Twelve minutes since he'd left with her kids, long enough for sufficient torture, long enough for her sense of responsibility to kick in. She'd better check on them. If one of her kids was injured while taking down the music mentor, she'd feel terrible.

Adara opened and shut the auditorium door without a sound and proceeded to lurk. She bit the inside of her cheek to hold back a laugh. Kids swarmed Garret like starved piranhas on a hunk of meat. His overwhelmed expression reminded her of the night Tatum had dragged her through the carnival, straight to him, while he searched for his lost niece in a crowd of sugar-crazed children and frazzled parents. Her humor softened into something warm and gooey.

Kids, always in tune with the weaknesses of their warden, took advantage of Garret's distraction. The ones who'd already lost interest in haranguing him went for the instruments on stage. The Triple Terror huddled around the piano, banging keys, while Sammy experimentally twirled a pair of drumsticks. Tatum, her sights on Zachary, crept behind the piano, hunting her prey. Hell was about to be unleashed, and Garret hadn't a clue. Someone had to save him, and since she was the only other adult present, the cape went to her.

Taking her time, Adara strolled toward the stage. The closer she got, the easier it was to decipher bits of the chaos surrounding Garret.

"I wanted to play cymbals!" A girl, she couldn't pinpoint which one.

"Yes, well—" Garret's unsuccessful attempt to explain.

"How come she—?" Adam, tugging on Garret's sleeve.

"I—" Garret.

"Not fair!" Zachary, when he wanted to, could match Tatum in dramatics.

"Okay, let's—" Another Garret fail.

Tatum leaped from behind the piano with a yell. Zachary and another girl squealed, and the chase was on, but they made the tactical error of running straight at Adara. She latched onto their arms as they sped by.

"Listen up, class!" Her yell thundered across auditorium, and every student snapped into still silence, aware of the consequences of disobedience.

Garret gave her a look of such utter adoration and relief that she almost lost control of her stern teacher mask. "For the next hour, Mr. Ambrose is in charge. Obey him and you'll prosper. Misbehave and you'll go back to the classroom with me for a pop quiz and be eliminated from concert participation."

Twenty-five pairs of eyes went wide. *Make that twenty-six.* Garret looked just as scared as the kids.

"If you behave," she added on a whim, "I may find the key to the treasure trove."

There was a collective gasp from the kids, and their eyes went wider, brighter. The treasure chest she kept in the classroom corner held all sorts of cheap toys, plastic gadgets and stickers the kind children everywhere eyed longingly in quarter machines. Despite many requests, both innocent and whiny, she hadn't offered to open the chest this school year. She hadn't felt like it.

Confident Garret could handle students who'd perform for prizes, Adara came back at the end of practice. Everyone had survived. The kids even lined up in single file behind Tatum without being asked. Whispering excitedly among themselves, they made a jittering train through the hallways to her classroom, Garret and Adara making up the caboose.

"You're equally terrifying and adorable," Garret said, low enough the kid caravan couldn't hear. "No matter what sinister trade you made to acquire them, I'm once again in awe of your freakish control skills. What are you doing after school?"

"I have papers to grade, musician messes to clean up. You know, teacher stuff."

"And after that?"

She lifted her eyebrows. "Nosy much?"

"When it comes to you, *neshama*?" He grinned, sly. "Always."

Since he possessed a natural immunity against her unfriendliness, she sighed a surrender. "If you must know —"

"I must." He bumped her shoulder with his, bringing a whiff of his cologne, which didn't help her failing protective walls.

"I still have to convince at least thirty-seven parents to kill the music program and I only have two weeks to do it, so I'm plotting a final push." Her stomach twisted a bit. She didn't want to tell him that more than half the parents had resisted so far. If that ratio stayed true, she'd be unemployed at the end of school. "I can't petition on school time, and I've been avoiding evenings. Interrupting dinner makes people grumpy, and grumpy people don't sign petitions, but I might have to risk it. I'll figure that out tonight. First, though, I'm going for a long, slow run."

His grin vanished. "What about your ankle?"

"It's fine. Ache's gone, doctor gave the okay and I need to get back into my routine. You fed me too much. I might get pudgy."

"What about" — he dropped his voice to a whisper — "my misguided fan on the loose?"

A few goosebumps sprouted on her arms. She refused to fumble through each day looking over her shoulder. Having one foot in the past slowed her down enough already. While she hadn't installed the electrical barbed wire fence and booby traps Garret had recommended, she wasn't worried about unwanted visitors. Plus, everyone agreed Roman was a super-sleuth. If Bella was still sneaking around, he'd find her.

Stopping outside the classroom, she kept her cool and collected face on. "I'm wiry and my brother liked to tussle. No Belgian beauty can take me down."

"It's not her fists or hair-pulling techniques that worry me." Lines bracketed his mouth, exactly what she didn't want. His concern threatened her battlements in a bone-deep way, digging beneath the surface to erode her roots.

"Hair-pulling?" She added a small smile to her tone. "That's unsportsmanlike."

His jaw clenched. "Not the time to test my humor level, Adara. I'm more concerned about what she may or may not be carrying."

Like a weapon. She hid a shiver. Outrunning a bullet wasn't happening.

"I'm waiting for you after school." He narrowed his eyes in a menacing look and his voice held a growl. "And I'm following you home, making sure your house is secure. If you insist on running, I'll take you to the health club and stand guard while you sweat it out on the treadmill, but you're on a time limit. Bob and London invited us to dinner and you're going. I want all the people most important to me in one spot, where I can see them."

"I can't sit at the same table with Ian and pretend to be polite." She folded her arms. It was a valid excuse.

"Ian has unchangeable plans." His smile still hadn't returned. "Nice try."

His pushiness didn't suffocate her like she wanted it to. Instead, that troublesome fluttering awakened, making her warm and fuzzy. She paused outside her classroom door and faced him. "I'm on bus duty this week."

"I'll wait." He folded his arms and stared at her in challenge.

A thrill raced down her spine. If he used that threatening expression on the kids, he'd control them as easily as he unknowingly controlled her. "Fine. Until Bella's accounted for, I'll forego my trails. I don't do treadmills, so I guess I'll have to find something else to do."

A gleam entered his dark eyes, and his stony expression softened. His gaze dropped to her mouth. "Finding alternatives to running until dinnertime won't be a problem."

His low, honeyed voice brought to life a hundred different steamy possibilities and her mind flat-lined.

"Miss Dumont." Zachary tugged on her sleeve, his brown eyes woeful. "Tatum pinched me and she won't get out of my seat."

When she lifted her head, Garret was halfway down the hall. Unfortunately, the sizzling inside, restless and needy, didn't leave with him.

* * * *

After school, Garret followed Adara home, inspected every inch of her house then promptly dragged her into his car. He didn't release his shackle on her arm until he had her deep inside the pet shelter, where fur, tails and whiskers could work their magic.

She leaned down to look at four squirming kittens behind glass, hooked—as he'd hoped. "This isn't what I was expecting to do after school."

He'd considered keeping her occupied in other ways, with his mouth and hands, which she'd probably suspected, but once he started that route, he wouldn't want to break for dinner...or ever. The weekend with her had ratcheted everything to a breaking point—his body, his head, his need for her, even in sleep. A hint of coconut lingered on his couch, blanket and pillow, infusing his dreams with Adara, and he wasn't ashamed to play the teenage crush card. Until she was with him permanently, he had no intention of washing her scent from his blanket.

Adding the unseen stalker threat to the mix only made him more protective, more aware of their deepening bond. He wanted her in a way that transcended rationality, and if he revealed that, she'd sprint to some uncharted island, beyond his reach. So he'd restrained his urges and kept all body parts and romantic proclamations to himself. Mostly.

Ben-zonna, it was torture. But he'd endure as long as it took for her to admit the truth on her own. He could only hope she was close to cracking.

"Pining for your pirate ship?" From Adara's cocked eyebrow, she'd been looking at him for some time, waiting for an answer to some question he hadn't heard.

"You agreed to help me pick out a cat. An increased likelihood of visitation, remember?" He hovered near her elbow, in case the feline spell broke. And because he liked being close enough to sense her warmth, smell her sweetness, maybe touch her accidentally on purpose. "I need help."

"That's an understatement." Her words didn't hold any edge. "I agreed to help you choose books, not pets." She tapped on the glass, her gray eyes sparkling as one calico kitten tackled another and pranced away. "Aww. I forgot how cute they are."

So she remembered the joy of cuteness. A good sign. He straightened and stuffed his hands in his pockets, content to watch Adara coo over the kittens, if not him. He regretted not tape recording her painkiller-induced question on their first date, when she'd asked if he purred. He would, if she ever decided to touch him again. She seemed to have forgotten the heat they'd shared the night of his college performance. He still hadn't forgiven Gia for the untimely interruption.

"What sort of temperament are you looking for?" Strolling on, Adara kept her gaze on the confined cats. "Frisky or calm, sweet or independent—or more of an attack cat that hates people?"

"Saucy with a side of sweet, independent with a need only for me, and if she wants to attack those who deserve it, I'll be supportive."

She glanced at him and her mouth twitched. "So you're looking for an older cat? One whose pace you can keep up with?"

He nodded solemnly. "One that will let me catch it every so often for a cuddle."

Adara met his gaze then looked away. *Oh yeah.* She understood the subject perfectly.

Barking filtered through the walls from another section, muffled and distant. He'd briefly considered a dog too, an idea quickly killed by London. She'd approved a cat-sitting job for Tatum, should the need arise, but no dogs allowed. Cats were independent. Dogs, not so much. She didn't need another needy creature to take care of, not that he intended to adopt a pet then abandon it, but his plans were momentarily liquid. He knew the future he wanted, every minute with Adara, a future he'd prefer to solidify sooner rather than later. The Bella incident had merely reinforced what he already knew. With a kitten's fate involved too, maybe he should step up his game.

She stopped so suddenly that he bumped into her. "Garret," she said, low and breathless. "Look."

Whatever had made her say his name in that sexy voice was a must have. He followed her gaze. The blackest, fuzziest kitten sat alone in the very center of one cubicle. It watched them with eyes the color of smoke, serious and cautious, as if while they might mean danger, they also might mean freedom.

Garret read the tag on the outside of the glass aloud. "Angel. Four months old. Found abandoned beneath a church. Guarded, but sweet once he gets used to you, which will take time and patience for the right owner." He smiled slowly. Perfect. "Want to hold him?"

Adara folded her arms. "Nope."

He opened the cage door. "Why not?" The kitten cringed as he reached for it but didn't struggle once he had it close to his heart. The fur was irresistible, and he rubbed between its ears. "It's so soft, so fuzzy. Are you sure?"

She shook her head, even as she bit her lip.

He wanted to force her to take the kitten, to pet it and admit she wanted it, to admit life contained moments of joy as well as pain, to admit he could give her even more moments of happiness and that he was worth those potential moments of pain. Instead, he let it go and stayed in their strange comfort zone of teasing and resisting, catching and releasing. He wanted her admission freely, open and willing.

"You aren't allergic, are you?" He rubbed his cheek on the cat's head, who didn't seem to mind. Maybe the warning label was fixed to the wrong cage. "This isn't a diabolical teacher plan to have a ready excuse to avoid me?"

"Rats." She snapped her fingers. "I wish I'd thought of that."

A quiet rumble rose from the kitten, and Garret gave Adara his sunniest smile. "I think he likes me."

"Of course he does. Everyone likes you." She looked disgruntled by that. "You're some kind of snake charmer."

"Charmer of scaly creatures, unruly children and aloof teachers. It's a gift." He wriggled his eyebrows.

She rolled her eyes, and he knew he had his kitten. Soon enough, he'd have his girl too. No warning label would stop him.

Chapter Twenty-Five

After comfortably situating Garret's new adoptee —
which Adara nicknamed Hellion instead of Angel — in
his laundry room, they drove to Bob and London's
house at a pace faster than grandma on a scooter. She
wouldn't have minded if he'd kept to a speed of corpse
on crutches.

She trailed Garret up the steps to the Sullivan
residence, swiping her clammy palms on her jeans. She
shouldn't be nervous. Bob wasn't exactly a friend, but
in all the times she'd interacted with him at school
events, he'd been nice. Tatum definitely wasn't the
cause of her racing heart and she got along with Bryan.
Even Baby G seemed to like her. But she'd never met
London.

It shouldn't matter. London was just another parent,
another person she'd keep at a distance upon meeting.
But for reasons she didn't want to dissect, she wanted
London to at least approve of her.

Without knocking, Garret opened the door and swung it wide for her, releasing a warm draft tinged with home-cooked fare. She recognized the smell because the same aroma still lingered in her kitchen from Garret's cooking. Muffled giggling and the clanking of cookware drifted from somewhere inside, life happening out of sight.

Adara hesitated on the threshold. She didn't want to do this. A step backward and she could be on her evening run, where she belonged, alone and safe, beyond the dangerous reach of interacting.

Garret grabbed her hand and tugged her close, pulling her inside, beyond the point of no return. "I know it's scary." His whisper stirred the hair close to her ear, carrying a tease. "But, with any luck, Tatum hasn't consumed any sugar, Bryan isn't sulking and the spawn still slumbers in his shadowed cave. Any trials will be worth it. London makes the best lasagna and Bob whips up a mean salad, straight from the bag."

Bespelled by his magic, her traitorous mouth curved.

"*Chara*, I love it when you smile," he said in a choked voice. He suddenly stopped and crowded her back a step, against the foyer wall beside a family collage. Caging her, his palms pressed on either side of her head, he studied her, the intensity in his dark eyes paralyzing. "I've spent the last three days trying not to think about all the terrible things that could happen to you, what *could've* happened while you were alone, oblivious to the unstable intruder hiding in your house." His forehead bunched. "I'm not usually a worrier. I entrust my life and those I love to God because the alternative is to go insane, but the reality is I can't stop harm from happening. I can't even control a classroom of children, let alone what the future holds."

The way his tone rasped stirred a nervous whirling in the pit of her stomach. Drowning in him, Adara couldn't look away, couldn't speak, even knowing this conversation headed toward her list of taboo topics.

His gaze raked her face, hot and possessive. "I can't and I won't apologize for being protective. The thought of you hurt or gone freezes me. I can't keep this inside any longer without imploding." His voice was hardly more than a snarl. "I've fallen madly, irreversibly in love with you, Adara, and I won't apologize for that, either."

The fluttering inside went wild, and before she could recover, his mouth was on hers. He kissed her with savage hunger, as if he starved for her. A challenge pulsed underneath, an insistence that she acknowledge the flames raging between them, and he growled, low and deep, a sound of pure, masculine arousal.

A thrill glided down her back. She couldn't move even if she'd wanted to. Desire burned a quick cadence in her heart, tingling through her bloodstream. Piece by piece, he took her apart and reshaped her until she drowned in longing. Resistance thinned to a sheer, fragile veil. Her sudden ache for him was fierce in its magnitude, terrible in its futility, and she latched onto his shoulders, needing to be closer, even while she knew she should push away. He was like a drug, and each moment with him, each laugh, each kiss, brought her closer to addiction.

He slipped his tongue into her mouth and she moaned, not meaning to. Crushed into the wall, his hips pressing into hers, not a shred of shy band geek remained. He'd switched to sexual coercion, a down and dirty tactic, shameless and unshakable. Every sense hummed into a building storm of want, strong enough to ride into an alternate world, an alternate life where pain and memories held no power.

"Uncle G!"

The kiss ended as unexpectedly as it had begun.

Tatum stood in the hallway, her hands on her hips, glowering. Donning a yellow princess costume and antennae headband, she looked like a demented fairy ready to cast a curse. "Stop kissing Miss Dumont. *Gross.*"

Adara's cheeks burned as Garret rested his forehead on hers, both of them breathing hard. This was so bad. By tomorrow, the entire class would hear about this, and by first recess, every staff member would know too. She was hanging onto a cliff by her fingernails while a dark wind ripped at her tenuous hold. It was only a matter of time before she fell, and the drop might never end.

"I was simply communicating to Miss Dumont how much I admire her." Garret straightened, gently smoothed Adara's hair behind her ear, and smiled at his niece. "Without words."

"Mom sent me to tell you dinner's ready." Tatum still looked like she'd stepped on a slug. She crossed her arms and waited, a self-appointed chaperone.

"How did they even know we were here?" Like the relationship coward she was, Adara steered away from the extreme subject a few seconds before. *Love.* He frickin' *loved* her. How was she supposed to balance his confession with the solitude she needed to survive? She couldn't even consider the full impact, what it meant for her. For him. For them.

There shouldn't even be a *them.*

"Porch camera." Garret looped her arm through his and held it tightly, probably suspecting she'd try to escape. "Monitor's in the kitchen."

At least London wouldn't be privy to their make-out session in the foyer. If Gia had done that with Joey, she would've placed Gia in the skank category, no questions. Then again, after Garret's impulsive delivery of the L word, London's opinion fell a dozen spots on her concern list.

"Hurry *up-uh*." Tatum stomped a foot and her scowl morphed to impatient. "I'm hungry."

"Me too." Garret patted his stomach, not releasing his hold on Adara's arm. "Lead the way, princess."

With a final glare at her favorite uncle, Tatum spun and marched away.

Adara dragged her feet, tugged relentlessly forward by Garret's shackle. She didn't want to be a piece of his family dynamics, even for a night. She didn't want to care about earning London's approval, didn't want to complicate her already-tangled connection to this man who refused to leave her in solitude and had slipped seamlessly beneath her defenses. This man who claimed to love her.

Love. She should break his hold now, run fast and hard until only darkness and silence surrounded her.

Too late. The hallway opened into a family dining room. Six cushioned chairs surrounded a walnut-wood table, a highchair in the corner. Plates, silverware and glasses set slightly off-center of the chairs, proof that little hands had helped. It was a room well-loved and lived in. She swallowed hard.

Tatum squeezed into the chair on the end, closest to the single window frosted by night and a hint of moonlight. "This is usually my spot, so I can do this."

She pulled her mouth into a monster face and wriggled her eyebrows, staring into the cabinet mirror behind the opposite chair. "It makes mom mad sometimes, but dad tries not to laugh." She slid out and offered Adara the seat. "You get to sit here, since you're our guest."

Adara forced herself to breathe carefully, her seams stretched and fraying. She couldn't freak out and fall apart, not with an audience, this one in particular. "Thanks. I'll try to refrain from upsetting anyone by making faces in the mirror."

The little girl grinned, her blue eyes sparkling. "You could, you know. Mom doesn't get mad at guests."

"I'm sure Miss Dumont will be too busy making faces at me to spare any." Garret ruffled Tatum's hair, dislodging her antennae headband.

She latched onto the subject with something dangerously close to desperation, keeping her focus on Tatum. If she looked at Garret right now, she might unravel completely. "So true. Your uncle's insufferable."

"Lies." Garret sniffed. "I'm utterly sufferable. Just ask my favorite niece."

Tatum rolled her eyes and squished herself between her chair and the table, which was apparently easier than pulling the chair out. "I'm still mad at you. You know I wanted cymbals." She huffed and crossed her arms, an almost violent move. "Cowbell is *not* cymbals."

"Cowbell requires more play-time and more technique, which I knew you could handle." By the smile in Garret's voice, she'd bet his dimple was showing. She refused a confirmation look. "If Billy misses his cymbals cue, it won't matter much, but the cowbell? Disastrous. I needed someone I could count on."

Dang, the guy was good at smoothing feathers, no matter who wore them. The exchange loosened a knot in her neck, feeling so much like her familiar, safe classroom. Maybe she could pretend this was just another day at work and squeak by unscathed, unaffected.

The aroma of roasted garlic preceded London's entrance by a heartbeat, and the rock in Adara's stomach shifted. London paused in the doorway between the kitchen and dining room, her dark eyes sharp and aware, delving the soul with one glance. *Must be in the Ambrose genes.* That's where the sibling similarities ended. Where Garret was fair, tall and sturdy, London was dark and barely made five feet, her delicate appearance saved by a gymnast's lean muscles, made all the more apparent from the heavy lasagna load in her hands.

As if done with gauging Adara's past and future, intentions and fears, London hit the play button and bustled forward. She laid the pan on awaiting potholders and wiped her smooth brow with the back of her oven-mitted hand. She zeroed in on Adara again and smiled. No teeth. "Since my brother's too busy slobbering over the lasagna to introduce us, I'm London."

Garret straightened from his lasagna-looming pose. "I was being polite and waiting for you to set the food down."

"Sure you were." London's smirk was so much like Garret's that it was impossible not to like her. "So that fork in your paw is merely coincidence?"

He stuck the fork behind his back. "Adara, this amazing creature is London, the best sister in the galaxy. She's beautiful and I'm not. She's talented and I'm not—"

"He's a suckup and I'm not." London reached across the table for Adara, her oven mitt still on. "You endure Monday through Friday with my brother's ego and twenty-five other kids and you still agree to join us for dinner. I can't decide if you're a masochist or some sort of superhero."

"My code name is Ultramoron." Adara shook London's mitt with a grin, the rock in her stomach shrinking from a mountain to a boulder. "Tatum talks about you all the time."

Tatum bounced up and down in her chair. "And I told Miss Dumont all about our girls-only *Pride and Prejudice* nights."

"Which is so cool, by the way." Garret was right beside her, but Adara used the table for support instead. "Tatum's the first eight-year-old I've met who uses the word 'indeed' on a regular basis."

London's smile widened to brilliant, and her adoring gaze fell on her daughter. "I try to bring her up right."

Bryan slouched into the doorway. "If we're going into *Pride and Prejudice*-land again tonight, I'll eat in my room." He lifted his chin at Adara. "Hey, Miss Dumont."

The addition of another Adara supporter eroded the rock in her gut a little more, and when Bob entered with bread tucked in one hand, a salad bowl in the other, his familiar smile on, the weight shrank to barely there. If she played her part right, kept her teacher mask on and ignored Garret as much as possible, maybe she'd survive the night.

Garret shifted and casually hooked her free pinkie with his. The quick squeeze sent a trembling warmth through her.

Who am I kidding? She was going down in flames.

Chapter Twenty-Six

"Told you dinner would be fine." Garret stuffed a last bite of peach cobbler into his cakehole.

While tempting, Adara resisted a pudgy kid joke. The moment was too serene, too fragile to ruin. "I'm impressed. Only one pea and carrot fight."

"Bryan should know better than to insult Tatum's sacred cowbell skills." He looked at his plate as if he might lick it clean. "But I think it might've been Tatum's creative way of not eating her vegetables."

Even with the other chairs vacant, the room felt full, the lingering effect of an overabundance of food, family and life. Tatum and Garret had prattled enough for everyone during dinner, sparing Adara the awkward hell of small talk. Dinners with Joey had never been like this, maybe because neither of them had Ambrose cooking skills.

"I need an excuse to move." She nabbed the plate from Garret and dodged his reach, barely. "I don't know how you people eat so much and still function."

"It's a gift." Garret patted his flat stomach. "Hurry back, *neshama*." His dark eyes flashed with a hunger that definitely wasn't aimed at food. "Bob and London will be cleaning up, the kids are banished for the unfortunate vegetation smack down and I intend to use the alone time with you wisely."

Heat curled down her back and she retreated to the kitchen before she surrendered to the urge to leap over the table and onto him, no matter the emotional danger. Typical. Whenever Garret was around, all her rules and rationality bent.

She paused at the kitchen doorway. Bob and London faced the sink, working at clean-up, the clank of dishes and running water a noisy backdrop to their voices.

"It worries me. That's all." London rinsed a plate and passed it to Bob. "He doesn't need another person like Mother in his lifetime, someone who makes him feel like he isn't enough."

Adara's stomach dropped and tumbled. Over the last year, she'd had a lot of practice catching conversations that magically stopped and switched topics when she showed her face. She didn't need a flashcard to tell her that she was the subject now.

"He knows what he's up against." Bob stacked the plate in the dishwasher and flung a dishtowel over one shoulder. "I warned him she might be unreachable, even for him."

Closing her eyes, she released a shaky breath. Bob had warned Garret about her, and as much as that hurt, she understood. It was the right thing to do. She opened her eyes and cleared her throat.

Both London and Bob jumped and spun, their expressions identical masks of guilt.

She handed Garret's pie plate to Bob. "You're absolutely right. Garret deserves someone who will make him feel incredible. I hope he finds that person." She nodded once, abrupt and final. "Thanks for dinner."

Bob lifted a hand, as if to stop her. "Adara —"

Placating words inspired by guilt wouldn't change anything. She headed for the door. Never slowing, she snagged her coat on the way and shrugged into it once she'd made it outside. The evening air snaked over her hot face as she took off down the sidewalk, the bitter chill a welcome balm. Between scudding clouds, the moon lit her escape route well enough. Her hands shook, and she jammed them in her coat pockets. Overhearing that conversation had been the best possible thing for her, a necessary reminder of the disaster she'd been carelessly skirting since the second Garret crashed her life. He'd made her forget the inevitable pain of relationships, and she hadn't fought hard enough to remember.

Her boots clomped on the pavement, a pulsing staccato in the darkness. Her house wasn't more than a few miles away, and a speed walk session wasn't as good as a brisk run, but maybe it would be enough to burn everything away. If Garret's Belgian beauty tagged along, so be it. She'd welcome a scuffle.

A few blocks farther, her emotions dropping from a boil to a steam, she slowed, a sudden wariness tinging the night. The darkness closed in and the neighborhood held its breath, suffocating. No car headlights or humming motors disturbed the gloom. The windows on each side of the street were black, and the lone streetlamp at the intersection flickered, buzzing.

Adara slowed even more to muffle her boots, goosebumps prickling her skin. She trespassed in a sleeping boneyard, not a family neighborhood. Shadows slithered behind fences and shrubs, midnight wisps that vanished with a direct look. A wind kicked up and rustled through grass and dead leaves, whispering secrets. As it died, a different noise rose up, a pounding. The unmistakable beat of running, coming closer.

A shiver crackled through her. The night screened everything more than a block away, hiding whoever followed her, but that meant she couldn't be seen, either. Yet. She darted to a parked pickup and crouched behind it. The cold tailgate bit into her fingers as she waited, every muscle poised to flee.

The footsteps continued at a fast pace, filling the silence with a steady drum. Adara held her breath. The vibrations echoed through the pavement into her soles. Any second now...

Garret sped by.

Her heart convulsed, and she blew out a shaky breath. She almost preferred Bella. Why did he have to unsettle everything? Straightening, she watched him sprint to the cross street. A nicer person would stop him, but best-case scenario he'd keep on running and leave her alone.

At the corner, Garret skidded to a halt and looked every direction, even behind him. It was too late to duck back into her hiding spot. Sighing, she waited as he barreled back to her.

He slammed into her, scooping her off her feet before she toppled backward. He pressed his face into her neck, his breath hot on her skin. "Don't *ever* do that to me again."

"Do you mind?" Feet dangling, she loosened her arms from around his neck. *Blast*. Grabbing onto him like a lifeline had been a natural impulse. Even her body was in cahoots against her. "You're slowing my trek home."

"London told me what happened." He set her down, keeping her chained in his arms. He wore his menacing look, the one that said she was in trouble.

A tiny thrill rolled through her, which she countered with a scowl. She tried to wriggle free of his hold, but he merely tightened his arms. "So you understand why it's best that I go home."

"Notice anything different about me?" He narrowed his eyes, expectant.

What a weird, off-the-subject question, and so like Garret. She eased back as much as she could, considering his unrelenting grip. Obsidian eyes glaring, nothing new. Golden hair gorgeous as always, even flyaway as it was from an impromptu pursuit. Same stubble that drove her crazy with the need to touch. His mouth, even while set in a grim line, made her lips tingle at the memory of his kiss. She shrugged. "You plucked your eyebrows?"

His mouth tightened. "Check out my breathing. Not a single gasp, even after sprinting seven blocks. I've kept up with my running."

"Thanks for rubbing it in."

His expression went from intimidating to the edge of scary. Pirate—and not a friendly one. "I've been running because I knew at some point in our relationship I'd be required to chase after you." Even his voice was menacing, low and dark. "I won't let you get away that easily."

That tiny thrill turned into a rollercoaster. "Not stalkerish at all."

He snarled, deep and dangerous. "Another subject for discussion after we hash out this one."

"Hash out what, Garret?" She forced her gaze to his, her stomach knotting in a cold ball. "Everything London and Bob said is true. I told you straight out. I'm not girlfriend material."

"You're right. You're not girlfriend material." His expression softened, which was equally bloodcurdling. "You're Garret Ambrose material."

"Gah!" She wrestled free enough to flail. "What does that even mean?"

A dog in the yard beside them barked, and Garret pulled her into a brisk walk. Since he aimed in the direction of her house instead of Bob and London's, she offered no resistance. Once across the street, he slowed his pace. An arborvitae hedge screened the houses, a semblance of privacy, and only their steps and breath interrupted the silence. He glanced at her.

She pretended not to notice, her heart running too hard, too fast. Whatever he was about to say, she wasn't ready to hear it.

He squeezed her hand, a silent signal to prepare for inevitable doom, Garret-style. "I wasn't planning to tell you my secrets tonight." He blew out a breath. "Don't think I'm weird."

"Too late."

He grimaced. "I walked right into that."

"Easy victim."

His smile was tight. "From the moment I saw you on the sidelines, watching life happen around you from the shadows, I understood getting to know you wouldn't be a cakewalk." He lifted her hand and pressed a kiss to her knuckles, as if to lessen the sting in his words, not that it was necessary. She wasn't a pastry in any form. "That night, for a heartbeat, you made my world stand still. That's when I made my vow."

Chills danced over her skin, everywhere, and not the kind that went with the heebie-jeebies. Life poised on the brink of an unstoppable shift. She'd felt it at Joey's diagnosis too, but this didn't carry the same dreadful weight. This felt like an enchantment in a world void of magic. It stole her breath. She opened her mouth to slow the hurricane rushing her way, but he pulled her to a sudden stop and kissed her hard, knowing exactly how to stall her protest. When he released her, her head spun.

"My first vow was to break through your defenses, because I sensed what slept beneath was deeply important." He captured her face with both hands and caressed her jaw with his thumb, his expression gravely serious. "My second vow, later, was to make you mine."

Stunned, trapped in his gravity, all she could do was stare, trembling as he ripped out her seams.

"How long that takes, how much patience and dedication, sweat and tears I have to spend make no difference. I've waited years to find you. I've been looking for you without knowing it was *you* I looked for. I only knew that something wasn't exactly right, a restlessness that wouldn't leave. Then I found you and everything settled into place. I won't stop fighting for you. *Ever.* Do you understand me?"

Nodding, she fisted her hands, her last line of resistance against the storm erupting inside her, a clash of fire and ice. "My comprehension is excellent,

Ambrose, but your listening skills stink. I thought you were awake when I told you I don't want to care. I don't want substantial relationships." Her voice cracked. "I don't want to — I can't — love you the way you deserve."

He blinked. Slowly, he smiled. "You love me."

She shook her head, struggling not to shatter. How could he pick that shard out of everything else? "You're like summer and happiness in a sippy cup. You bring everyone around you to life. That's just who you are, and you need to be with someone who can give you that in return, someone who can be completely invested." Her chest ached, each word driving a new nail into her heart. "That someone isn't me."

"I don't have to surround myself with symphonies and sunshine to be happy." Wearing his dreamy smile, he used the low, honeyed voice that melted her bones and disabled her resistance — a double whammy on her defenses. "All I need is the music of your heart beneath my ear." He slid his warm hand beneath her coat to her back and pulled her unresisting body against him. "The soft sigh of your breath. That little purr you make when I kiss you right here." He pressed his lips to the ultrasensitive spot right beneath her ear.

Tingles spun a web down her neck, into every nerve. He was right. She made that noise without even thinking. He awakened things in her without permission, things she couldn't leash, things she needed to keep caged.

"Don't pretend with me, Adara. You can't hide in solitude and silence forever. You're too bright for that, which is why you can't stop caring, why certain people refuse to leave you alone. They see you clearly through all those walls you lurk behind, waiting to be found."

"Aren't you listening?" Her voice scraped in her throat, strangled and desperate. "I don't want to be found."

"Nevertheless, *neshama*, you've been found, and I won't let you burn out. I won't let you simply exist." He cocked his head and gave her his soul-searching look, the one that saw everything. "I didn't have to personally know Joey to understand that solitude and silence isn't the life he wanted for you. What about the promise you made to him?"

The cold knot in her stomach expanded, unstoppable, a writhing, crawling beast she couldn't control anymore. It dragged up all the deep, dark feelings she'd kept locked down and exploded, breaking every chain. She pushed out of Garret's grasp and words she'd refused footholds even in her thoughts shot free, sharp as glass.

"Screw Joey. Screw my promise. It's not like he's here to make me keep it, is he?" She flung her arms, her voice echoing into the empty sky. "He used his sickness to coerce me into making a promise he knew I didn't want to keep. He got the easy part of the deal. He got to die, while I'm still here. He left me to deal with everything alone." As fast as the explosion came, the flames died, leaving her cold and empty. She sobbed, her chest too tight to breathe, making her next words nothing more than ragged gasps. "He left me."

She couldn't bear to look at him, to determine whatever emotion his expression held. Her own shame, anger and betrayal choked her enough already. As he opened his arms to her, she turned away, which only resulted in her back firm against him, his arms wrapped around her and his stubbly cheek on her temple.

"Joey was like you, too full to contain." Adara closed her eyes, trembling. "People loved him and he loved them. He made the world richer." Her voice rasped, barely a whisper. "It should've been me."

"Never." He squeezed her even closer, enclosing her in a sure, steady warmth. "Call me selfish, but I'm relatively certain your brother wouldn't have passed as my muse. He probably would've fought me for attention. It would've been tragic on so many levels."

She smiled through her tears, unable to stop an image of Joey and Garret battling it out on stage, two unconventional violinists. She would've sold her body to science to see them together. A wobbly gasp slipped out. "It would've been epic."

"That too." His sigh skated over her cheek. "I don't have any sage wisdom to offer. I only know, fair or not, that we're still here while others aren't, and I refuse to believe there isn't joy among the tears. We weren't left here to only suffer." He gently turned her to face him and thumbed her tears away. "I can't guarantee the number of minutes I have left on this earth, but I promise that whatever are left to me, they're yours."

Leaning her forehead against his T-shirt, she shook her head, defeated and drained. "I just confessed I'm furious at my deceased brother, betrayed my deathbed promise to him, admitted my deepest flaw and you twist it all to your own diabolical musician agenda. You're incorrigible."

"Honest." He sounded insulted. "There's a difference. And it's not my fault if the truth happens to align with my intentions, which are honorable, by the way. Some might even go so far as to call them gallant."

She snorted, and the laughter in his chest hummed through her, surprisingly soothing. It would be so easy to surrender to this, to stay surrounded by his warmth, leaning against his sturdy frame, taking comfort in his voice, his laugh, his words.

His love.

Moisture splattered the back of her neck, and she lifted her face to the night sky. Slate gray clouds hid the moon, and rain fell in fat, slow drops. Thunder rumbled in the distance, warning of the approaching storm.

"I'd say we have ten minutes before we're soaked." Without releasing her hands, Garret glanced down at her Doc Martens. "Can you run in those?"

She lifted her chin. "I perfected sprinting in stilettos. I teach third-graders, remember? Boots are a breeze."

A sly smile brightened his face. "Race you to my house."

By the time she'd stomped onto Garret's front porch, Adara's hair was plastered to her skull, her sweater and coat stuck to her with a mixture of sweat and freezing rain, and her feet ached from running almost a mile in shoes better made for kicking in doors. She felt amazing.

Breathless, she spun as Garret joined her, only a few steps behind. Her ankle injury and non-workouts against his regular running made them a close match. Close, but not quite equal. "I'm impressed," she gasp-laughed, dragging in breaths. "You've completely lost your gimp, and the death-warmed-over pallor didn't make a comeback. Of course, I could be wrong. It's a little dark out here."

"Violin aerobics." He gulped for air, bracing his hands on his knees. "I'm starting a new fad." Steam rose from his wet back, ghostly fingers in the porchlight. "Maybe then I can keep up with you."

"Doubtful, but I won't stop you from trying. Watching you flounder is too much fun."

"Whatever it takes to make you smile, *neshama*."

She bared her teeth at him, but a lightness had eased over her with the run in the rain, leaving her surprisingly buoyant. There were so many things she could account it to. It was her first run since hurting her ankle, and it felt good to stretch her legs again. Competition always gave her a shot of adrenaline, no matter the lack of worthy contestants. She'd confessed a darkness she'd harbored since Joey's death, setting it free, and Garret hadn't ditched her. Maybe it was a combination of all those things.

Garret straightened, flipped his wet hair out of his face and grinned.

A ribbon curled around her heart, tentative. *Holy whoa, he's dazzling. Irresistible.* She stepped into his personal space and fisted his wet shirt. Ignoring his suspicious expression, she dragged his mouth down to hers.

His lips were cold, wet with rain and sweat-salty— and the best thing she'd ever tasted. The responsive groan of approval he made spiraled low in her belly, an edgy, pooling heat. She didn't protest when he grasped her head with both hands and angled his face, deepening the kiss. He crowded her back a step and pushed her against the front door, his solid body crushing, taking command of her mouth with his tongue.

Her legs trembled, possibly from the run, more likely from the sudden flames tumbling through her veins. She couldn't process him at all once and instead focused on one piece at a time. The seductive scrape of stubble. Long fingers tangled in her hair. The subtle neroli scent. Callused fingertips trailing her neck. The deep hum rising from his chest. The muscles flattening her breasts and stomach and thighs in delicious conflict, every part of him hard and male, except his lips and tongue. Soft and silken, those he used with relentless, coaxing assault, destroying her defenses. She was running out of ways to fight him off.

He broke the kiss, breathing just as fast as when he'd arrived in second place. The house alarm system beeped, barely audible above her pounding heart. She kept her eyes closed. Thankfully, he didn't move. Without his support, she would've melted on the porch, her legs unable to hold her up.

"We should go inside," he murmured at her ear. "It's cold out here."

Is it? She hadn't noticed, not with the inferno he'd forged inside her.

"And we're wet." He still hadn't moved, his cheek resting on hers. "You getting sick isn't on my diabolical musician agenda."

"Right." She bit her lip and opened her eyes. "We should definitely get out of these clothes."

Chapter Twenty-Seven

Shivering, Garret hung his dripping coat beside Adara's in the shower and grabbed a towel on his way out. He should be steaming, not only from her unexpected kiss but her flirtatious words right after. *Chara*, if she was trying to kill him slowly, it was working.

Adara huddled in the foyer, her teeth chattering. Already relieved of boots, socks and sweater, she had an uncanny way of looking both miserable and beautiful at the same time. Her drenched jeans and black T-shirt clung to each slim curve.

Every muscle stretched until his entire body vibrated, a plucked steel string ready to snap. With any luck, she liked beasts. By the time she accepted him, he'd be hardly human. But right now, she needed basic care more than pawing and licking. He wrapped the towel around her shoulders and herded her into the music room aka living room. Eventually, he'd expand, but his bed still hadn't arrived, and until he convinced Adara she was his as much as he was hers, he was content with one room.

"R-running in the r-rain." She clung to the towel with shaking hands. He clearly needed to cook for her more. The woman didn't have enough natural insulation. "G-great id-dea."

"Too late to protest now, darling." He dug through his clothes, still folded neatly in his suitcases in one corner. Dressers should arrive with the bed. "Especially since you're the victor." His favorite thermal shirt in one hand and sweats she'd need to cinch to keep on in the other, he guided her to the bathroom. "Change, then we can argue over the merits and drawbacks of running in the rain."

He shut the bathroom door and forced his cold feet to the kitchen before he changed his mind and turned to other ways to warm Adara from head to toe. He ached for her, and every time she tried to push him away, the need only intensified, ingraining her deeper in his soul. She thought she couldn't love him the way he deserved, and that little slip-up—that she loved him, whether or not she'd actually confessed it point blank—had sent him soaring. For now, it was enough, and he'd have her full and willing confession before jumping the next hurdle. With Adara, he had to do everything right—no compromise, excuses, rushing or half ways. There'd be no going back, not for either of them.

His fingers numb, he managed to drag two mugs and a bottle of cinnamon whiskey from the cupboard, even poured without making a mess. He wrangled the cups into the microwave with only one splash on his foot.

"Hey, Garret?" Adara's muffled voice drifted from the hallway. "I'm having issues."

He froze. Having grown up with London and her girl issues, a dozen unpleasant possibilities popped into his head, none of which he could help with. He stockpiled food, not feminine products.

Before he could respond, she shuffled in, wearing his shirt. It dropped almost to her knees and swallowed her hands by several inches. His pulse picked up as possessiveness surged, wild and raw. Adara in his shirt was the sexiest thing he'd ever seen.

"My fingers are still too frozen to unbutton my jeans." She raked her wet hair back. "It's a problem."

Ben-zonna. He steadied himself against the counter and gripped it hard. Was this some sort of test of his fortitude? Garret sucked in a silent breath and pasted on a smile. With any luck, it didn't hold a creepy vibe. "My unfeeling fingers barely conquered the microwave, but I'll give it a shot."

Biting her lip, she lifted the hem of her — his — shirt, exposing a strip of pale skin and the top button of her jeans. And he thought his hands trembled before.

He stepped close, and a heady concoction of rain on her skin and coconut slammed his senses. An inch away, he hesitated. "My hands are cold."

She rolled her eyes. "My whole body's frigid, so we're good."

"I won't tell Ian." He grinned at her growl and fumbled with the button, trying his best to ignore a flashback of the scrap of black lace she'd swiped from her underwear drawer the night she'd stayed over. His fingers felt five times their size and a hundred times clumsier, not the most memorable first time of unbuttoning his soulmate's clothes. "For the record, I'm not usually this incompetent in loosening up a woman's buttons."

C.J. Burright

"Your experience or lack thereof doesn't concern me, band geek." The hint of laughter in her tone erased any bite.

He got a halfway decent grip and forced the button through the hole. The steel wire strung through his body flexed, stiff and throbbing. He'd bet anything she wasn't cold lower. All he'd have to do is keep going, slide the zipper down. He lifted his gaze to hers.

Gray as a storm, her eyes shimmered with distant lightning. She was biting her full, beautiful, lower lip. *Chara*, he wanted her to look at him that way every day, not just at unexpected intervals.

"Adara..." His whisper was strained, but he didn't care. "Do you have any idea how intoxicating you are?"

The tiniest of smiles curved her mouth. "Brain overcome by hyperthermia, Ambrose?"

He leaned into her, close enough to rest his cheek against hers. "Overcome is a perfect description."

She slipped her arms around his neck, and he slid one hand beneath the borrowed shirt to her bare back, needing to touch her. Her skin was cool against his fingers, and as much as he wanted to shelter her, wrap her in a dozen blankets to protect her from the cold, the urge to strip everything away and exchange his heat for hers, right there on the kitchen counter, nearly won.

"You're so warm," she whispered, squirming closer, as if she could burrow into him and snuggle there forever, exactly where he wanted her. "How is that, when you're still wearing your wet clothes?"

"Another one of my superpowers," he murmured next to her mouth, and before she could reply, he kissed her.

Adara pressed harder against him and her mouth opened under his, welcoming. His oversized shirt concealed her slender curves but did nothing to reduce the maddening softness of her breasts crushed against him or the gentle flare of hips beneath his hands

He dipped his fingers in her waistband, skimmed cold, damp skin, low enough to brush lace. Fire erupted in his veins, testing his restraint. She was here, in his arms, and with only a quick tug, she could be wearing only his shirt, with nothing beneath but skin. Despite his resolve, he inched his hand down farther, to the slope of her perfect rump, dying to memorize every inch of her, to learn every nuance of her until he could manipulate her responses like a master musician with his favorite instrument. With an effort that made him lightheaded, he broke contact. A lifetime with her included controlling his urges for now, no matter how trying.

"Garret," she said between kisses, "don't stop."

He briefly closed his eyes, his heartbeat clanging in his ears and painfully hard in more southern appendages. If he survived this, he'd tattoo the word 'forbearance' on his butt. "We can't." His voice was hoarse, rough. "Not yet."

She eased back, her hands on his shoulders, her hips still tight to his, tight enough she had to know his refusal had nothing to do with a lack of wanting her.

He drew his thumb over her soft lower lip, the taste of her still on his tongue, the need for her a steady burn in his veins. While igniting faster than he imagined possible, his love for Adara was so powerful, so deeply rooted, that he couldn't imagine a future without her. He held her gaze, the air between them sizzling with all the things he wanted to say and knew he couldn't, not yet. But someday soon.

The microwave beeped, and they jumped apart, as if a trance had been broken.

Adara swallowed hard, her pupils large. She waved vaguely behind her and backpedaled. "Left the sweats in the bathroom. Thanks for the help."

Garret forced himself to breathe as she slipped out of the kitchen, slowly regaining control as the microwave beeped another reminder. Nothing, no one would derail his determination to win Adara forever, not even a few minutes of sexual torture.

* * * *

Wanting to wait until her blush died but too cold to hang out in the bathroom, Adara held on to the waist of the borrowed and way-too-baggy sweats and scampered to where a couch waited with a snuggly, Garret-scented blanket. The music room was empty. She wedged into the couch corner and tucked the blanket around her a second before Garret eased in, carefully balancing two steaming mugs. He was still in his wet clothes, hadn't even taken off his boots. Something warm and fuzzy threaded through her and knotted tight around her heart. He was seeing to her needs first before even changing, even if it meant icing off his man-bits.

"Garret." Her third-grade commander tone stopped him in his tracks and his eyebrows lifted. *Works every time.* "Strip. Now."

He relaxed, his grin sly. "Miss Dumont, I believe you have me confused with that other guy with the bagpipes. I don't play nude for the general public." He resumed his deliberate pace forward and handed her one mug with a wink, setting the other on the end table. "But I'll make an exception for you."

"I actually like the bagpipes, especially when they're played by a Scotsman in the buff." She hid her smile in the mug, the delicious steam warming her chin.

"Sadly, I'm delinquent in both the bagpipe and Scots departments." Rubbing his bottom lip, he studied the neat line of instruments waiting on the wall. "I'll have to do the best I can." In one quick move, without any of the wet clothing struggles she'd experienced, he peeled off his stuck-together shirt layers.

The steam didn't prevent her from freeze-framing. A sharp jolt rearranged the rhythm of her pulse as he obliviously strolled to his suitcase, half-dressed. She'd never spent much time admiring men. Not that she didn't notice or appreciate a good-looking guy who randomly interrupted her line of sight, but it was rarely more than a passing glance and a 'he's handsome' quick-fire thought. But there hadn't been a single instance since Joey's death.

Then there was Garret, reshaping everything.

She couldn't pinpoint one specific detail about him that sabotaged her common sense and made her susceptible to schoolgirl crush syndrome. It wasn't only the tempting ridges of his lean body or his easy charm, not his dark eyes or ridiculously soft hair, not how he personified music or the way he lit up a room with his smile. It was the combination of everything, every nuance of him that formed her kryptonite.

Her gaze still on Garret, she took a swig and nearly spluttered. Liquid fire burned down her throat, toasting everything along the way. "Trying to get me drunk, Ambrose?"

"Darling, if you get drunk on a shot of watered-down cinnamon whiskey with honey, that's all on you." He dragged a shirt over his head, ending her ogling, and slung some sweats over his arm. "Wait until I get back before you dance on the table." He ducked the pillow she threw his way and slipped around the corner, leaving his laughter behind.

She barely had time to hide her lingering smile before he returned, patting his hair with a towel, fully dressed in sweats and a faded thermal shirt sporting the cartoon Schroeder bent over his piano. "Good, you're back. My feet are cold and your stomach looked so toasty."

He paused and met her gaze, his black eyes burning. "You'd better put your mug down."

"I'm not toasty yet." No way was she giving up her hand warmer. "Or drunk."

"Do it." Soft menace laced his voice.

Only because he wasn't smiling, she twisted around and set her drink on the end table.

He dropped the towel, leaped over the coffee table, and tackled her, all before she'd fully righted herself. His sinister, icy hands wormed beneath the blanket and tickled, wriggled under her shirt to her recently-warmed-up back and ribs. His laugh was pure evil.

"Miscreant!" Breathless, she squirmed and flailed and screeched, but Garret merely laughed harder. For his proclaimed zero athleticism, he was strong—and heavy. With her added out-of-practice laughter sessions, she was getting nowhere fast without hurting him, which became more appealing with each second.

He broke from the tickle torment, one hand restraining hers above her head, the other planted firmly on her hip and the dangerously low waist of her overlarge sweats. His body still trapped her, hot and solid. "Warmer now?"

As she tried to suck in enough breath to respond, his playful expression faded into something else, something intense and hungry. Longing washed over her, drowning out her reservations. She didn't want to shatter the spell he wove over her. Tonight, she wanted to stay lost in him and deal with the consequences tomorrow.

"You win," she gasped.

"I wasn't aware this was a competition." His voice was almost as breathless.

"Not a competition." She shook her head, her mouth dry, her heart pounding. Starting this conversation felt like walking a tightrope. Any misstep and she'd fall into a void. "A series of battles. A war."

"No." He leaned in until his lips hovered a few inches above hers. Instead of the kiss she waited for, his dark eyelashes swept down, thoughtful. "It was a cantata with varied tempos and keys. There have been solos, choirs and at times only the music played. But now" — his whisper softened even more, and he met her gaze — "it's a duet."

She cocked an eyebrow, needing to counterbalance his emotional intensity. "Cheesy much?"

"So I've been told." He grinned, meeting her halfway.

"I kinda like it." She exhaled. "I kinda like you. I think I might have a thing for band geeks, chubby version or not."

"Band *geek*, you mean. As in only one. Only me." At her teasing shrug, he assumed his menacing pirate expression. "Don't make me give you a tummy raspberry. My lips are cold."

Adara held his gaze, the sudden need for him so powerful it crushed her. "I can think of a few places on my body you could use to heat them up."

"*Chara*." The word was hardly more than a breath, then he kissed her.

His lips weren't cold at all.

Chapter Twenty-Eight

Lost in the weight of Garret's body on hers, the magic of his mouth, his hands and heat, Adara let her worries float into the night, out of reach. A hint of peach cobbler sweetened his tongue, each luscious stroke a sensual taunt. Unable to get close enough, she arched into him, which earned her a low, hungry groan. He kissed her like he had in London's hallway, greedy and demanding, a challenge still unanswered. Rationality dissolved and her senses took control, demanding he touch her everywhere, fill her empty spaces. And he still hadn't ventured to all the places she wanted.

Disentangling her fingers from his hair, she slid a hand over his ridged shoulder, down his smooth ribs to his waistband.

He shackled her wrist and laced her fingers with his. His breath ragged, he dropped his head to her shoulder. "Adara, I've been thinking."

"Really?" She nibbled the rim of his ear. "I haven't been able to think at all in the last half-hour."

His small laugh was strained. He lifted his head, meeting her gaze. Fire sparked in the depths of his dark eyes. "You said you didn't want to lead me on, and I don't want to give you any false impressions, either. When it comes to you, I intend to do everything right."

She went still, her heart pounding from more than the effects of his coercion tactics. His expression was grave, his smile gone. He shifted, trapping her in the couch cushions, no doubt a calculated move. Whatever he said next, she had a sneaking suspicion she wouldn't like it.

With his thumb, he traced her bottom lip, distractingly gentle. "I won't settle for a shallow relationship with you, friends with benefits, temporary bed buddies, whatever name you want to call it. I want everything from you, *neshama*." He kissed her so possessively her breath snagged, only to release her. "And until you confess you want everything from me too," he continued, his voice rasping, "this is as far as I'll go. Physically, I mean."

She blinked several times, playing catch up to his kiss, sure she'd misheard. He couldn't be playing the chastity card, holding out on her, but she couldn't find a single hint of humor in his expression. "Seriously?"

"Terribly." He didn't smile.

"You big tease." Adara wriggled beneath him, and his mouth—along with the rest of him—tightened. 'Wait until commitment,' said no man *ever*, except the one she actually wanted. But commitment was a line she wouldn't cross unless she was sure, and playing with Garret's heart wasn't something she'd do. "So that's your strategy? Sexual torture?"

"If it's any consolation, I'll suffer with you." He rocked his hips just a bit, enough so she felt exactly how he was already suffering. "You alone have the power to end it, Adara." He kissed the sensitive right beneath her ear, and her eyelids fluttered. "Confess you love me." The hush of his breath hitching prickled through her, calling her to surrender. "Admit you want me in your life." He nibbled her bottom lip. "Commit to forever."

She moaned, melting like wax beneath a flame. "Should've known…a sadist pirate."

"I'm simply using all tools at my disposal in enticing you to accept the truth. Big difference." He took her hand and kissed her fingers one by one. "I don't want whatever scraps you're willing to toss my way in moments of vulnerability. I want all of you, every piece, broken or not. Every day, always. Joy and pain. *Everything.*"

Joy and pain. A rock dropped into her stomach, pushing ripples of panic in every direction, and as if sensing her mood swing, Garret kissed her again. But a kiss couldn't lure her back, not this time. Considering emotions in the recesses of her mind was safe. Confessing them aloud got other people involved, got her heart involved. She'd already stretched her frayed stitches to the snapping point and was nowhere ready to rip out the seam.

When he released her, she exhaled, long and slow. "Garret—"

He kissed her once more, lingering and laced with tenderness, a promise unspoken.

A knot inside her unsnarled partway, a tightness that had been there for so long she'd accepted it as a permanent part of life post-Joey. As it eased, her lungs expanded, finding just enough room to breathe.

"I'll wait for as long as it takes," Garret whispered at her ear. "When you're ready—and you will be, no matter what you think right now — tell me." He lightly bit her earlobe. His bristle chafed as he kissed along her jaw and down her neck, rekindling the fire so suddenly doused.

She sucked in a breath. "You're incorrigible."

His mouth curved against the hollow of her throat. "I'm not above manipulation, coercion or trickery to fulfill my vow, darling. And I'm the patron of patience. I won't think any less of you if you surrender now and save us both the time and misery."

Desire and unease trembled through her bloodstream, a struggle between future and past. It had taken him years to bring his house dream to fruition, even longer to master the violin. He wouldn't blink an eye at devoting the same amount of time to erode her body, mind and soul on a daily basis. She could survive a weeks-long battle on the music mentor front with only a few scars to show for it, but a Garret Ambrose siege? She'd never weather it.

A black ball of fur leaped onto the couch.

"Gah!" Adara would've jumped if Garret hadn't been holding her hostage. Hellion clambered over her shoulder, blinking sleepily. She waited for her heart to settle back into its proper place. "I forgot about the addition to your family."

"How could you forget my ticket to more frequent Adara visitations?" Still trapping both her wrists in one hand, Garret butted the kitten's head. Hellion circled, his tail tickling her nose.

Adara turned her face away. "Remove your butt from my face, fleabag."

A slow, sly smile spread over Garret's face. With his free hand, he guided the kitten's face to hers until soft fur brushed her cheek. A rumbling purr filled her ear.

"Don't bother fighting it. I know you love him. He's irresistible. You don't have to say it aloud. Give in and pet him."

Hellion pressed his wet nose to hers and rubbed his whiskers on her cheekbone, a minion following his master's order. He already smelled like Garret, probably from sleeping in his laundry.

"I thought the chart said he doesn't like most people," she grumbled, relaxing against Garret's hold. It wasn't like she was going anywhere with him still lying on top of her and a happy cat on her neck.

"You're not most people." Garret kissed her nose and rolled off the couch, taking his warmth and weight. "I'll be back." He padded out of the room.

Adara scooched to a sit, holding the kitten to her chest. It still purred and curled in her arms, small and limp and warm. Since Garret wasn't watching, she stroked the cat's head. "You are stinkin' cute," she whispered. "Don't tell *him*. He already knows how to weaken me enough without adding you to the mix."

She sighed and leaned her head on the couch, scratching between Hellion's ears. No matter how much she hated to admit it, how much it scared her, Garret had been tugging her out of her solitude inch by inch until she stood at the center of a minefield crossroads. A step in any direction might destroy her, but she'd eventually have to choose which direction to take—life and pain with Garret or solitude and safety without. Cold slivered through her, working into her marrow. She couldn't have both indefinitely.

Garret returned, wearing jeans instead of sweats, boots on, his hair neatly pulled back beneath a black beanie. "I need to take you home before I stumble and sabotage my plans."

She stopped scratching Hellion's head. "I vote for sabotage and deal with the misfire tomorrow."

Studying her, he rubbed his bottom lip and his throat worked. His grin appeared, an official veto of her suggestion. "And you question my integrity?" He handed her an origami boat made from one of the flowery paper napkins at Bob and London's. "Figured it out yet?"

No, she hadn't. It was annoying. She rolled her eyes to throw him off. "As if I've had time to ponder your weird, ridiculous puzzles."

A knowing gleam brightened his eyes, and before she could take a breath, he scooped her off the couch, Hellion still on her lap. "Your wet clothes are in my car, and since your shoes are still sopped, I get to carry you."

She snuck one arm around his neck, holding Hellion securely with the other. "I'll let you." Leaning close, she licked his ear, and he shuddered. "Sure you aren't up for sabotage?"

Garret hurried toward the door. "The only thing holding me in check is the promise of the end result." He stopped beneath the chandelier and kissed her once, quick and fierce. "You're mine, Adara Dumont, and I'll endure any torment to hear you admit I'm yours too."

Chapter Twenty-Nine

Long after dinner time, Adara slumped back against her front door and let her umbrella slide from her fingers. It *thunked*, limp and damp, into the gathering puddle at her feet. Rain dripped from her slicker, a reflection of the tears she refused to cry. Her job was toast.

Eight signatures short. With the exception of the Sullivans, she'd personally gone to every student's house, talked to each parent in depth, and tonight she'd come very close to pleading. It was a good thing she didn't go to law school. Her persuasion skills apparently sucked.

She shrugged out of her raincoat and left it in a wet heap on the floor. The bond wouldn't pass. She'd gleaned that much in her canvassing. No one wanted to fork out more money for what they believed they'd already paid for.

What a disaster. She sank onto the couch and stared blankly at the papers scattered on her coffee table, evidence that no plan guaranteed success. She'd been so sure she could make it happen, that she could save her job. Some people thought music was more important than people. More important than her.

Her phone buzzed. Garret.

I'm coming over to help you celebrate your victory.

Her heart squeezed, and the tears she'd been controlling pricked her eyes. She didn't want to share her defeat, let him see her weakness, and there wasn't anything he could do to change it. Better to make an excuse and face him tomorrow, when her emotions were more in check.

Too late. We'll talk tomo —

Before she could end the text, an alert came through her phone. A car in the driveway. A few seconds later, Beethoven thundered through her house. *Perfect.* She was too slow to ward him off, and now she couldn't nurse her failure alone in her preferred method, with tissues and chocolate.

Adara trudged to the door, took her time with all the locks and alarms and let him in.

Garret's smile was brilliant, at first. As he studied her, that light faded. "What happened?"

There was no use hiding it. He'd know soon enough. "Music lovers happened." She closed the door behind him and plodded back to the couch. "Thirty-three percent of Graywood Elementary School parents prefer music over a live body teaching, which means a month from now, I'll be..." She gave a strangled laugh. "I don't know where I'll be."

"I do." Garret pulled her against his chest, and she let him, too tired to protest. "You'll be with me."

"Really not in the mood to have that particular argument right now, Ambrose." She pulled out of his loose grasp and flung herself onto the couch. "I don't have magic violin fingers or pirate charm to win me my next gig, and I certainly don't have the financial resources to float around musically harassing people for free until I find something else." At the flash of hurt on his face, she sighed and slouched. "Sorry. Your situation has nothing to do with mine. I know that. I'm sucky company right now."

"Apology accepted." He fingered the papers on her coffee table, keeping his smile contained, considerate of her defeat. She wasn't sure she'd be as accommodating if their roles were reversed. "What can I do?"

She clenched her teeth to contain the tears and managed to keep her voice free of any mushy emotion. "Nothing. I went to every house, talked to every parent. It's a done deal."

He crouched between the coffee table and the couch, close to her knee. "Maybe the school board will find that the signatures you have are enough."

"No, they won't." She closed her eyes and laid her head back. "They were very firm on that. No less than seventy percent."

"You should still go to the meeting tomorrow." His voice was soft, joined by the rustling of papers, the whispered song of her failed plans. "Make a final stand."

"Already on my itinerary." Not that it would make a difference. The board had made both its specifications and its reluctance of her proposal crystal clear. There was no backup plan. Still, if she was going down, she'd go with a boom.

"Good." His big, warm hand rested on her knee for a moment then squeezed gently. "You know I want to stay. I'd do my best to distract you from everything for as long as you want, but I understand if you need some time alone. Just tell me what you need."

Sparks flickered in her belly, not enough to fully respond, and she was too mentally worn out to question why he suddenly had respect for her alone time. As tempting as it was to let him divert her with his sexual coercion tactics, curling up in bed and hiding under the covers until morning tempted her that much more. He'd join her if she asked, another temptation, and one she couldn't entertain. With her emotions so close to the surface, she might break, tell him things she couldn't take back.

Adara faked a yawn. "I need sleep."

He took her hand and pulled her close against his heat and strength. "While you dream, spin a speech that will make the board members second-guess letting you go." He brushed his mouth over hers, a barely-there kiss that made her breath catch. "Whatever you do, don't give up, *neshama*."

* * * *

No brilliant plans or words came to Adara in dreams, and the day passed by in a blur, every minute laced with the knowledge that tonight she'd get the official confirmation. *Job over. Good luck in the unknown future.* Even Garret allowed her the courtesy to mope without harassment, consigning himself to small smiles and a steady presence in the classroom. It was surprisingly comforting, if useless to her cause.

Waiting outside the closed door of the board room, she blew out a breath, unable to hear the discussion going on inside. The file held against her chest, containing the too-few signatures she'd finagled, felt weightless, a mark of its deficiency. It would be nice if they'd just let her in and get the unpleasantness over, so she could go back to...

Her heart convulsed, as if suddenly realizing the enormity of her situation. Without her job, she had nothing to get back to doing. Her life would be as silent as her house, as empty as the solitude she'd sought.

Out of sight, two halls away, the main school door squeaked open and slammed shut, followed by rapid footsteps.

"Miss Dumont?" One board member stuck his head out of the cracked boardroom door. "The board is ready for you."

She nodded and followed him inside. The idea of walking back out, what she'd leave behind, made her want to retch.

"Adara, wait!" Garret's familiar voice pulled her slowly around. He ran toward her, his hair loose and flying behind him. He skidded to a stop, only a little breathless, and shoved a folded paper at her. "You might find this useful for the meeting."

She was too shocked to do anything but unfold the smeared and wrinkled paper. All thoughts drained from her head. Signatures. Nine of them, supporting the elimination of the music program, of parents who had originally rejected the idea. The last two stole her ability to speak. Bob and London Sullivan. She lifted her gaze to his.

Garret was biting his lip, clearly having difficulty reining in his sunshine, so adorable she would've kissed him if not for the waiting school board.

"Why?" she managed to say.

"The best things in life are worth the sacrifice." With a nod at the waiting board member, he stuffed his hands in his jeans' pockets. "Good luck at the board meeting, Miss Dumont." He turned and strolled away, taking another sliver of her heart with him.

Chapter Thirty

Too wired to sleep and bored of counting uncooperative sheep, Adara settled back against her bed headboard and powered up her laptop. One twenty-one a.m. Snoozing should come easy. Whether or not the bond passed now, her job was secure, and the last three weeks had passed like a dream on the edge of waking. Her minutes were spent teaching, along with an hour of unnerving silence while Garret took her kids to their private music practice, and each of those empty minutes reminded her what she had to lose — or what she had to give up. Weekends she pretended to be busy and wound up sucked into Garret's gravity anyway. They found books for his library. He cooked. They argued over the musical capabilities of third-graders. He pressed her to listen to his songs. She refused.

The siege was on full force.

A small, cold chord twisted in her gut. Without realizing it, she'd realigned to his rhythm, and like all dreams, this one drew close to its end. It was barely a week before the recital and Garret's mentorship finale. He hadn't disclosed his plans and she didn't have the guts to ask, not with her indecision. But part of her, a much larger part than she wanted to admit, believed in all things Garret Ambrose. He made everything seem possible.

She gazed out of the window to the darkness beyond. As much as she longed to stay in his world, losing him now would leave a bearable scar. Six months down the road, a year or five? Her blood iced, and she pushed the thought deep down in the pit where it belonged. She was stuck on a bungee jumping bridge, peering over the rail, wanting to take the plunge and unsure if she'd survive the ultimate fall.

The computer switched screen savers, waiting patiently while she procrastinated. On a whim, she searched for 'Belgian Beauty'. If there was proof on her blog that Bella was back in Belgium, everyone would feel better, and maybe Garret would cave on his no-running-outside rule. She missed her trails. A treadmill workout made her want to kill something.

And after she cyber-stalked Bella, she'd finally look up the definition of *neshama*.

The home page of *Belgian Beauty* popped up, boasting a new picture collage. Of Garret. Recent, because he was wearing the same flannel shirt and black beanie he'd worn at her house—her stomach dropped—the previous night. She leaned in closer, and all the blood rushed to her head. One picture was the inside of her house. *Last night.*

Her hands shaking, she called Garret. Each unanswered ring tightened the noose around her throat more. Right when she thought she'd get his voicemail, he picked up.

"I was dreaming of you too, *neshama*."

"Check out *Belgian Beauty*," she whispered, every shadowed bedroom corner seeming to watch her. "Tell me the picture on her home page isn't from last night." She waited while he obeyed, her heart rattling her ribs.

"Ben-zonna." His sexy, just-woke-up voice changed to a snarl. "Stay put. I'm coming to get you. Don't hang up. I'm texting Roman right now. Keep talking so I know you're okay."

"Okay."

He made a strangled noise. "I need more than that, Adara." A rustling came through the phone. "Jeans on, feet in slippers. Got my keys." A jangle joined his voice. "I'm out of the door. Do you hear anything suspicious?"

"Give me a sec." Silence throbbed through her house, nothing more sinister than usual. Then again, Bella must be a skilled stealthtician to hide out in Joey's room without her knowing. "Nope. And zero suspicious activity from the alarm system."

The hum of a motor followed by a screech of wheels filled the phone, and she would've smiled if she'd had it in her. Apparently, Garret could go faster than an old biddy with a cane. She scooted off her bed and gripped Joey's softball bat from beside her dresser. Holding some type of weapon made her feel better.

"Roman's on graveyard, so he'll be there soon. If she happens to be hanging around, he doesn't want to scare her off, so he's cutting lights and siren, but I don't care. I'd rather see you safe now and catch her later."

A tingling swept the back of her neck, and the darkness beneath her bed stared back. Bella wouldn't get past the alarm system, but too many scary movies and *CSI* episodes said otherwise. Her breath sawing in and out, she slowly crouched and flicked her phone to flashlight mode.

Nothing.

She nearly collapsed in relief. If she'd found eyes staring back at her, red, glowing or human, she would've freaked.

"You're too quiet."

"Never been a chatterbox like you." Adara perched on the edge of her bed, stiff and straight. The window burned her back, an unseen presence watching her through the glass, but no way was she going to turn out the light. "Are you almost here?"

"Two minutes tops. Fair warning. I'm keeping you with me from now on. Hellion agrees."

"Appreciate the offer, but I refuse to let a violinist-obsessed blogger dictate my life."

"What about a teacher-obsessed violinist?"

"Is that any better?"

"Depends on the viewpoint." His smile leaked through the phone. "I'd be okay with a particular third-grade teacher obsessing over me, violinist or not."

She refused to mention that she'd been more than a little obsessed, trying to figure out what to do with him. Her phone hummed, showing footage of Garret's Maserati pulling into her drive.

"I'm here."

"I know." She raced down the hall, each doorway dark and ominous. The alarm system was disarmed, all locks undone in record time. She threw herself into Garret's arms — or maybe he threw himself at her. Wrapped in his heat and strength, she didn't care.

A patrol car slid up to the curb at the end of the street, its lights off. An officer in a black uniform, his hair equally black, slipped out and crept toward her neighbor's gated yard.

"Roman," Garret whispered in her hair, his arms still tight around her. "He wants us to stay on the porch like this as a distraction, in case she's still close."

"No problem." She pressed her cheek against his chest, his skin warm and smooth on hers, his citrusy scent reassuring. "You're not wearing a shirt."

"I was in a hurry. I should've brought my violin and went for the new brand of half-naked violinist. Think it would give the nude bagpipe guy some competition?"

She huffed a laugh. "Totally. I'd throw a buck in your violin case."

"Only a buck?" He sounded offended. "I'm worth at least a buck fifty."

"Matter of opinion." She relaxed against him, her arms a loose grip around his waist. Even though Bella was still out there, possibly close, his very presence made her feel safe. "Thank you for coming for me."

"Adara." He said her name as if it pained him and kissed the top of her head. "I'll always come for you." He eased back and cupped her chin, lifting her gaze to his. "I want to be where you are, every minute. We don't need a Bella scare to make that happen."

She bit her lip, wanting to reassure him and unable to. Garret deserved an unswerving decision, all in, no reservations. She wasn't there.

"The premises are clear." Roman clicked off his flashlight and trotted up the stairs.

Adara had met Roman only briefly at Garret's, when he'd taken her statement after the Bella invasion. Under the porchlight, surrounded by gloom, Roman reminded her of a gargoyle, tall, dark and grim. With his death-black hair, pale skin and ebony uniform, he easily fit into creature-of-the-night mold. She wouldn't want to be on his bad side.

His hand always close to his holstered gun, his shadowed gaze pinned her. "I found footprints in your neighbor's yard, behind a boxwood. The grass was still compressed, and I presume she planted herself there, long enough to leave a lasting imprint. I'll talk to your neighbors in the morning, keep patrolling the area. No alerts in your alarm system?"

She disentangled herself from Garret's embrace, at least as much as he allowed. He kept one arm wrapped around her shoulders. "Not until Garret showed up."

Roman nodded and handed her his business card. "Call me right away if you notice anything out of place or suspicious."

Garret pulled her into his side. "I'm taking her home with me."

As tempting as that was, she shook her head. "I need to stay here."

"Adara—"

"I've already rearranged my life for someone I don't even know, and I won't surrender more ground to her." At his worried expression, she added, "Roman can double-check everything before he leaves, make sure it's safe and sound. My alarm system can do the rest, and I promise to call you both if anything weird happens."

Roman shifted past them and slid smoothly inside with only a nod, a predator ready and willing to protect and serve. Adara almost felt sorry for Bella if he found her.

Garret took her face between his hands. "I can stay on your couch. No matter where I am, I won't sleep, especially knowing you're alone." He gave her puppy dog eyes. "I'll cook breakfast."

Since she was ninety-nine percent sure Garret was Bella's target anyway, she didn't argue. Having him close instead of secluded by ten acres of trees would make her feel better, and having him in her house might ease whatever paranoia solitude and silence inspired.

"All clear." Roman stomped onto the porch. "Windows and doors are all secure. You're good to go."

"Thanks, Roman." Garret shook his hand. "Appreciate it."

Roman smiled tightly, jerked his chin at her in his way of goodbye and silently returned to his car.

Adara didn't sleep that night, and for once, it had nothing to do with Garret.

Chapter Thirty-One

The booming song of her doorbell jerked Adara to awareness. She peeled her face off the couch cushion and set aside the personal budget she'd been working on before unintentionally falling asleep. She must have left her phone in the kitchen and missed any alarm signal of unexpected company. After the Bella weirdness the night before, she hadn't slept more than an hour, and despite Garret's power breakfast and an extra shot in her coffee, she could barely function.

She shuffled to the door and dutifully checked through the peephole. *Garret.* Her heart did that now-familiar fluttering thing. Disarming her alarm and all locks, she opened the door and a cold, barbed wire coiled through her. Face-to-face contact revealed what the peephole glass had warped. Garret's face was pale, his smile gone.

He briefly closed his eyes and his throat worked. "Bella has Tatum."

Ten minutes later, they gathered in Roman's tiny corner office of the police station. Adara squeezed onto a bench between Garret and Bryan. London and Bob clung tightly to each other by the door. Nothing felt real or solid, as if time passed underwater, fluid and lawless.

Roman closed the door, muffling the ringing phones, hushed voices and static dispatch radio. The mild scent of leather drifted with his movement, probably from his thick duty belt. "We're still gathering details." He leaned against the desk and barred his arms over his chest, his black eyes knife sharp. "We do know Tatum was on the bus."

Adara nodded. Still the teacher on bus duty, she'd witnessed Tatum poke Zachary with her fairy wand while climbing the bus stairs.

"The bus driver confirmed he dropped Tatum off, and since she didn't make it home, the abduction assumedly happened in the two blocks between the bus stop and your house. We're interviewing everyone on those two blocks right now." His jaw bunched, adding to his take-no-hostages bearing. "The best information we've received is one older lady remembered seeing a pretty woman walking hand in hand with Tatum. She didn't recall any reason to suspect anything. Tatum wasn't struggling. When shown a picture of Isabella, the woman was ninety-five percent sure it was her."

London made a strangled noise. Garret shivered so hard that Adara leaned into him, steadying. She was too numb to tremble. Not once did she imagine Tatum might become a target. She'd have offered Joey's room to Bella permanently and sacrifice her own safety to keep Tatum off the radar.

"Isabella took Tatum to get attention." Roman's gravelly voice softened a smidge. "She'll show up soon enough, I guarantee it. The best thing you can do is stay home so you'll be there when she gets back. I'll keep you updated."

While Adara appreciated his careful phrasing, she knew they were all thinking 'if' instead of 'when'.

Outside the station, she walked with Garret to his car as the Sullivans drove away, headed home. Helplessness prickled through her. She wanted to do something, not go home. Not pretend that a little girl, her favorite student, Garret's niece, wasn't out there somewhere, at the mercy of a stalker. Joey's sickness had left her weaponless. In this situation, she could at least join the search.

"I can't stand the thought of sitting around, waiting. Let's drive around, look for her." She took Garret's cold, clammy hand in hers and squeezed. "It's not your fault."

"I understand that here." He tapped his temple, his never-say-die smile hidden beneath worry and guilt. "But my heart says differently." He scrubbed his fingers through his disheveled hair. "There are so many what ifs, all on me, too many not to take some blame. If Bella hurts her..."

"Wallowing in 'what ifs' is zero help." She grabbed him hard by both forearms and scowled up at him. "Snap out of it, Ambrose. A stalker has your niece." He blinked rapidly, as if she'd slapped him awake. Sometimes, truth made the best smelling salts. Dragging his keys out of his limp fingers, she spun away. "I'm driving."

While driving around like a gangster looking for rivals on her turf was better than sitting around wringing her hands, it was equally productive. They found nothing, not at the mall, any fast food restaurants or playgrounds. They'd talked to everyone, flashing Bella's picture. Nothing. They only quit when it was too dark to see and all the stores and restaurants had closed for the night.

Adara pulled into her driveway, put Garret's car in gear and twisted to face him. He looked ready to either weep or destroy cities. "You should stay with me tonight."

He rubbed a hand down his face, as though needing time to process the easy question. "What if she goes to my house?"

Good point. "Would Tatum even know how to get to your house?"

"Not Tatum." A breath hissed between his teeth. "Bella."

He was right. Bella's focus was Garret. If she knew Tatum's schedule and address, she knew where he lived too. Without saying a word, she backed out onto the street and drove to Garret's house.

"I hired bodyguards for us both," he said, almost absently, gazing out the window into the darkness. "Ian suggested it after Bella broke into your house. You've had an undercover, former SWAT member watching you twenty-four seven." He pinched the bridge of his nose. "I should've done the same for London and the kids."

A man she'd never seen had been watching her closer even than Bella had. *Not creepy at all.* She glanced in the rearview mirror. Sure enough, headlights trailed them at a discreet distance. Two motorcycles. From now on, she'd pay more attention to her surroundings.

Hellion met them at the door with a plaintive meow and Adara picked him up, snuggling him close for a second then handing him to Garret. He needed the comfort more. She hated seeing him this way, stifled by remorse and fear. When he wasn't shining, the world felt wrong.

She shrugged out of her coat, helped him with his and led him by the hand to the couch. He had a bed now, but staying close to the door seemed like a good idea.

As soon as he sat down, he released Hellion and wrapped his arms around her instead, pulling her onto his lap and against his chest. He dropped his forehead on her shoulder and sighed, his breath warm on her collarbone. "Thank you for staying."

Hesitantly, she brushed his hair back. It was almost as soft as Hellion's, and once she started slowly stroking his head, she couldn't stop. His moan was dangerously close to a purr and the way he leaned into her, so trusting, pierced her heart.

Her future felt balanced on a scale, tipping one way and the next. Somehow, without meaning to, she'd become tangled in his life, his family, his fears. She wanted Tatum safe, but she never would've been in this position of intimate family knowledge without Garret undermining her boundaries. She should retreat, go home.

Without saying anything, Garret stretched out on the couch, taking her with him. He tucked her head beneath his chin and tugged her close. Once the soft blanket was dragged over them both, a shudder rolled through his large body.

Everything inside her wrenched into a stony, throbbing knot. The isolation she'd endured while slowly losing Joey was a permanent burn on her soul.

She'd cemented on her positive mask and never let an ounce of despair show, but she would've paid in vital organs to have someone simply hold her tight and refuse to let go through it all, whether she said she didn't want it or not.

Slowly, Adara slipped her arm around Garret. Their future together may be undecided, but she could be a solid, silent presence for him tonight, with no reservations. Settling her head in the crook of his neck, she curled into him and matched her breaths to his.

* * * *

Friday passed at a brain-eating pace, a slow frostbite of the senses, but Adara made her teacher disguise seamless for the kids. Tatum's empty seat and Garret's absence were reminders how easily one person's actions could disrupt routines, families, lives. By the final bell, still no news.

At Roman's suggestion, she went home instead of back to Garret's. A separation might draw Bella out, and they were willing to try anything. Slinging her purse over her shoulder, she trudged up the porch steps. The house across the street was quiet, every low shrub pruned to perfection, no spots for stalkers to hide. The next-door neighbors were away on vacation, and their fence offered a screen for spies, as Bella had already proved. Maybe that's where her bodyguard lurked. She hadn't spotted him today, but she didn't doubt he was there, invisible backup.

Invisible backup. Her pulse hiked. She should go for a run. While she suspected Bella watched Garret, not her, it was worth a shot. Bella might make a move, especially if it appeared she ran alone, and either option was better than sitting home, idle and twitchy. Hopefully her bodyguard wore running shoes.

Adara slipped inside and shut the door. Alarm, deadbolt, conventional lock. Check, check and check. Her phone chirped an alarm notification and she jumped, but the notice indicated movement, not a breach. She blew out a breath, letting her heart slow. Probably some neighborhood cat. Even if a good, long run didn't flush out Bella, it would do wonders for her jitters.

A rap at the back door trickled into the hallway, so light it could be a bird tapping on wood, and the small hairs on the back of her neck stiffened. No one used that door, not even her, and she hadn't mounted cameras in the back. Having the alarm system set up and a driveway camera had felt overboard at the time.

Ready to call Roman, she hesitated. He was busy hunting down Bella, and she'd feel like an idjit if she called him and the noise at the back door turned out to actually be only a bird. Instead, she fired a text to Garret.

Unknown noise at back door. Call back in two.

She snagged her umbrella, the best impromptu weapon at hand, and hooked it on her wrist. Sticking her phone in her pocket, she crept through the kitchen into the laundry room. A scrape came from the back door, and she tensed. Slowly, so slowly, she inched forward past the refrigerator and through the laundry room doorway. Her phone vibrated at her hip, but she didn't take her gaze from the three narrow windowpanes of the door.

There was movement at the windows, and Adara froze. The top of a small head, barely visible at the window's bottom edge, but she'd recognize the unruly blonde hair anywhere.

Tatum.

Adara went into fast forward. She used her phone app to dismantle the alarm and threw open the door.

Tatum looked up, her blue eyes wide in her elfin, tear-streaked face. She wore the same pink polka dot shirt and jeans from yesterday. Adara reached for her and went still, her mouth going paper dry. Standing on the other side of the doorway, out of window view, was a woman she recognized by photo alone.

Bella was even prettier in person, dressed in fancy jeans Gia would approve of and a lightweight jacket over an innocently blue sweater, but the photos failed to capture the 'off' glint in her green eyes. She laid her hands on Tatum's thin shoulders, a silent warning. "May we come in?"

What alternative do I have? Adara opened the door wider and cleared the entryway, making a quick survey of her backyard. No bodyguard there. Her stomach clenched. She was on her own.

Bella's floral perfume invaded the laundry room, unfortunately familiar, as she guided Tatum inside, keeping a vulture hook on her shoulders. No weapons were visible, a small relief, but weapons could be hidden anywhere.

"You okay, Tatum?" Adara kept her voice calm, steady, normal.

Tatum nodded, her eyes glazed with tears, her bottom lip trembling.

"Lock the door and reset the alarm system." Bella's slight accent seemed an elegant contrast to her looney-bin vibe. Her gaze remained fixed on Adara, unblinking. *Unnerving.*

She did, no hesitation. Her phone shook again, and she cleared her throat to cover the noise. The last thing she wanted was Bella thinking she'd called anyone. Not knowing what else to do, she went for *Pride and Prejudice* civility. "How may I be of assistance, ladies?"

Bella's set expression was that of a ceramic doll, empty of emotion. "Tatum wished to tell you goodbye."

Silent tears trekked down Tatum's pale cheeks.

Adara forced a smile, hoping it reflected confidence, not the unease shaking her bones. "Be brave, Miss Lizzy."

"Repeat what I told you." Her gaze still on Adara, Bella squeezed Tatum's shoulder with one hand and slid the other into her pocket, where anything could be hiding.

"We're going to be a family." Her voice cracked and stumbled on each word. "Me, Uncle Garret and Bella."

"Mommy and Daddy," Bella corrected her in a chillingly soft voice. "I already told you that. Say it."

Tatum sucked in a shuddering breath, clearly on the verge of panic. "Mommy and Daddy."

The ice in Adara's veins doubled. The fact Bella stalked Garret was a few points off the mental health chart, kidnapping Tatum a dozen more, but this happily ever after fantasy? There was no reasoning with someone who believed she could create a family unit that way.

As casually as possible, Adara eased closer to the washing machine. A bleach bottle rested on the shelf above, out of reach. The box of fabric softener sheets was useless, no matter the lasting fresh scent. A broom leaned near the laundry room doorway, but she'd have to ease past Bella to nab it. Her only defense was to keep her talking. "Are you certain Garret wants children?"

Bella's eyes gleamed, a snake ready to strike.

Maybe that wasn't the best question to start with. "I don't doubt you know him better than anyone. My point is merely that an eight-year-old child may be an interference and split his focus, when it could be all on you." The umbrella weighed on her wrist, the wimpiest of weapons. "Besides, don't you want your own children? Together?"

Bella's expression softened. Clearly, she was considering all the beautiful babies she'd have with Garret. And they *would* be beautiful, beautiful, mad, musical geniuses. "Once we're together, he'll understand how perfect we are for each other." A heart-tugging vulnerability bled into her voice. "How happy I'll make him. He just needs time away with me to understand, away from everything that distracts him."

Adara couldn't deny a pang of sympathy. What started out as a crush had twisted, inflated and rotted until it had become a demolition. Bella had it bad and there was no happy ending for her. It was tragic. "I'd be glad to return Tatum to her parents," she said carefully, "while you run off with Garret."

As if the suggestion broke a spell, Bella stiffened. She pulled a gun from her pocket and everything inside Adara went prey-still.

"You make valid points." Bella tapped Tatum's ear with the barrel, drawing a whimper from the girl. "And this one whines excessively. There will be no need to return her."

A mistake. She'd made a mistake and they were both going to die for it. Adara casually gripped her umbrella, her mind a blank. She didn't know what to do, could think of no way to get out of this without both her and Tatum dead. Her phone vibrated again, and Bella's gaze dropped to her pocket.

Crap.

Everything seemed to happen in slow motion, all at the same second.

Bella aimed the gun at her.

Adara snapped the umbrella open in her face and lunged low for Tatum.

The back door exploded in glass and wood splinters, and a man clad all in black rolled inside, stuntman style.

A shot blasted and the house alarm wailed.

Time resumed full speed.

Sprawled on the floor with Tatum, Adara's ears rang from the shot, dulling the still-shrieking alarm. Other than the ache in her hip and shoulder from hitting the tile, she had no pain. The bullet hadn't hit her. Her stomach tumbled. Tatum wasn't moving.

Someone seized her arms from behind, and she struggled, grasping for the umbrella lying broken and upside down a few inches away.

"Dumont!" She went limp at the deep, gravelly voice and sobbed. *Roman.* Behind him, an unfamiliar man crouched over Bella's flailing form, handcuffing her.

"Tatum." Her voice sounded strange, raspy and far away as she dropped her gaze to the little girl curled up on the tile, so still and small. Adara couldn't breathe. The walls of the laundry room seemed to push down, crushing her. She wrapped her arms around herself, the cold too fierce to hold back. She'd survived and Tatum had died...just like Joey.

Roman knelt beside Tatum, carefully searching for injuries. For eternal moments, Tatum lay unmoving. Through her tears, Adara couldn't tell if she was even breathing. Each second weighed heavier, dragged her deeper. She should've done something different, attacked Bella right away or had enough sense to drag Tatum inside and shut Bella out. *Somehow, someway.*

"There she is." Roman's voice cut into her thoughts and Adara blinked away the tears.

Slowly, Tatum's eyelids fluttered. She opened her eyes, focused on Roman's face...and broke into hysterical cries — not cries of pain, but of a scared little girl in desperate need of her mother.

Adara still couldn't take a full breath, couldn't stop shaking.

Beethoven's *Fifth* rumbled through the house, adding a musical counterpoint to the piercing alarm. A frantic pounding on her front door acted as drum — an impromptu symphony conducted in her should-be silent world.

"You disable the alarm system, Dumont." Roman stood, cradling Tatum to his chest, close to his badge. "I'll get the door."

Numbly, Adara nodded. Her fingers not working right, she fumbled with her phone and finally managed to access the app to turn off the alarm. The silence ached with her eardrums, a deep, throbbing pulse. The image of Bella's gun and Tatum's terrified face spun in repeating circles through her mind. So easily, Tatum could've been shot. Died. Her young life cut even shorter than Joey's.

Dead like Joey.

Suddenly, strong arms crushed her against a hard chest smelling of citrus and sunshine. Soft, warm lips peppered her neck, her head, her face. Finally, Garret eased back, but he didn't release her. His dark eyes boiled with emotions. "Say something."

Finally, she drew a long breath and released it. "I need a new umbrella."

Chapter Thirty-Two

Numb, Adara sat beside Garret on her couch. Bob and London huddled together on the loveseat, Tatum enveloped by them both. Two silent bodyguards filled the doorway behind Roman as the swarm of officers trickled out, finished with interviews, photos and crime-scene diagrams. A hammering came from her laundry room, the remains of her back door being boarded up. It took every ounce of concentration for her to follow Roman's account.

"Bella trespassed through neighboring backyards and slipped through the fence behind Miss Dumont's house. That was the only reason she wasn't detected immediately. Ethan contacted me the second he spotted her with Tatum." Roman hooked his thumb at Adara's stone-faced bodyguard, his tone casual, as if dealing with gun-toting, niece-stealing stalkers was merely another day at the office. "Stealth was the best option. With a child involved and unknown weapon situation, we had to be cautious."

Unknown. The word slithered through her, cold and knowing. Tatum's stricken face flashed in her mind. The gunshot blared in her memory like tolling funeral bells.

"Ethan hit her with what we call less-lethal munitions. They're meant to take down, not kill. His shot stunned her before she could shoot. The umbrella distraction helped." His mouth twitched, barely perceptible. Garret squeezed her cold hand, barely felt. "She'll have a nasty bruise — nothing to keep her from being deported — and she'll remain in custody until then."

London made a noise of relief and pressed her cheek to Tatum's head. Tatum had yet to let go of London's neck, her face buried in her mother's shoulder. Bob had his arms around them both.

There was some exchange of gratitude, some shaking of hands, people filing out of her living room, all of which skated at the edge of Adara's consciousness. Her mind replayed the scene over and over — Tatum's face, the shot, the fear. That moment of not knowing who lived, who might be dead, gone forever, leaving holes that could never be filled. Tatum had come so close to dying.

Just like Joey.

Memories rushed back, vivid and boiling with emotion. Joey telling her everything would be all right. The brave face he'd worn at every doctor appointment, as if his defiance alone would defeat a disease. His last day, dark circles under his eyes, his skin gray, his hand weak in hers, using her tears to coax unwanted promises...clawing out her heart.

Leaving her behind with the crippling pain.

"*Adara.*" The way Garret said her name indicated he'd already said it more than once. "It's over. Everyone's okay. You're okay."

She focused on his worried face with some effort. "You should go, be with your family."

"Not without you." He gathered her close to his heat and solid strength.

Adara shook her head, pushing free, gently firm. She needed silence, solitude to deflate the vision of Tatum lying on the floor, her eyes lifeless.

Joey's lifeless eyes.

She held back a sob. Barely. "I'm okay. I just…" She stood, putting distance between them, not daring to look at him, not yet. Not until she pushed back the image of Joey's limp hand slipping from hers. "I just need some downtime, to process."

He eased to his feet, careful, as if trying not to startle a wild bird. "If you want to simply think in silence, I'll hold you. If you want to talk, I'll listen. If you want to run until dawn, I'll suffer with you." He stepped closer and stopped when she backpedaled. "Don't shut me out, *neshama*." The hint of a plea colored his voice. "Tell me what you need and I'll make it happen."

She forced herself to lift her gaze to his and hold it. "I need to be alone."

Garret studied her for a long moment, his dark eyes solemn and shadowed. At last, he nodded. "Text me when you're ready?"

"Okay." She let him kiss her on the forehead, followed him to the door and locked it behind him.

* * * *

Saturday passed in silence. Adara had no idea how long she'd stared at her bedroom ceiling. Her eyes burned and sunset cast a last golden gleam through her window. Hours had ticked by, empty and silent. She rolled over and went back to sleep.

Sunday arrived with a house-shaking rendition of Beethoven's *Fifth*. She pulled the pillow over her head and ignored it.

An hour later, Beethoven replayed—and an hour after that and the hour after that. At the tenth time, Adara sighed. She shuffled out of bed and slouched to the door, not bothering to look through the peephole. If she looked, she might not have the strength to open the door.

"You didn't text me." Garret crowded past her, bringing a draft of temperate air laced with honey and summer. He faced her and crossed his arms, hiding the faded lettering on his abstract pub T-shirt. "I've been ringing your doorbell every hour."

"I noticed." She closed the door.

"Did you?" His hell-fire gaze raked her from head to toe, over her bed-mussed hair, the oversized T-shirt, down her skulls-and-crossbones pajama pants to her bare feet. "Funny. I've sat on your front steps since morning, yet this is my first Adara sighting of the day."

She leaned against the wall and slid down until she sat, too tired to stand, too empty to argue or defend her reasoning. "I can't go back."

After a hesitation, he sat cross-legged in front of her. His long fingers curled on his knees, as if restraining himself from touching her. "You don't have to go back, *neshama*." His expression softened, not enough to erase the worry lines on his forehead. "It's over. Bella's in custody. Tatum's safe. You're safe."

"No, that's not what I mean." Her voice sounded dead and distant. She closed her eyes and leaned her head against the wall. "I can't go back to what we were doing."

"Care to clarify?" he asked, wariness underlying his easy tone.

"Seeing Tatum, before I knew she was okay, reminded me of...everything." She forced her voice to be steady. "Of Joey." She opened her eyes. "I can't keep pretending I might be ready someday to forget. It's not fair to you."

"I'm not asking you to forget anything. You *shouldn't* forget." He hooked her pinkie with his and squeezed gently. "You're in shock. Right now isn't the time to make important decisions."

"It will be the same decision tomorrow."

His eyes narrowed. "You don't make my choices, Adara. I'll stay in limbo if that's the closest I can be to you. I won't let you go. The fear stirred up by Bella will fade, and I'll still be here, waiting for you."

She pulled her finger free. "I'm trying to be honest and fair."

"*Ben-zonna.*" He raked his fingers through his loose hair. "By trading what we have for fear of what may or may not come? That's not fair. That's cowardice." He blew out a breath. "You're braver than your brokenness, Adara. I've watched you deal with it on a daily basis, and sometimes it's the day-to-day that's the hardest battle. Don't surrender now. You're not alone. Don't shut me out."

The challenge in his words didn't hit the mark, but the truth sifted dangerously through her detachment. She heaved to her feet before it weakened her. "I need space, Ambrose, not a musician counseling session. I want—" She sucked in a shuddering breath. "I *need* to be alone."

He slowly stood, his gaze never leaving her face. Without another word, he left, shutting the door softly behind him.

Adara couldn't move, her feet frozen to the tile, every inch of her iced over. Silence surrounded her, so keen that she knew he stood on the other side of the door. A long time passed before his boots scraped on the porch.

"*Neshama.*" His voice filtered through wood and metal and bone. "Don't shut me out. *Please.*"

She squeezed her eyes shut and covered her mouth with both hands to keep her sob inside. The desperation in his 'please' was the same tone she'd used to plead with God to save her brother. And her answer to Garret was the same.

Silence.

* * * *

Garret took the beer Ian offered. Instead of drinking, though, he set it on the table and traced abstract designs in the condensation on the bottle. Ian's television in the next room, tuned to some soccer game, added a chaotic backdrop to his melancholy.

'*I need space. I can't go back.*'

Adara's words ricocheted in the newly opened rift in his chest, aching with each hit. While his every minute revolved around her, she needed minutes away—from him in particular—and he had to respect that wish. But what if Bob was right? What if he wasn't enough to inspire her and the space between them kept expanding until it became unbridgeable? Merely thinking it paralyzed him with cold.

Ian flipped a chair and straddled it, folding his arm over its back rail. His long, level stare didn't motivate Garret to respond. He wasn't in a mood to hear the I-told-you-so lecture or a skewed insight into women — what they were and weren't good for.

Exhaling noisily, Ian broke the reign of silence. "I can't believe I'm saying this." He grimaced. "Dude, do you need a hug?"

Garret managed a weak smile. "Not from you, though I appreciate the offer."

"And since that was a one-time only deal, this is all you get now." He lifted his fist, waiting for Garret to bump it.

He tapped Ian's fist with his own. Starting the inevitable conversation himself and getting it out of the way might prevent any argument. "I know what you're, shockingly, not saying. She's not an ice princess. She's lost, finding her way back." He refused to consider the alternative. "If she wants time alone to figure things out, I have to give her that freedom."

"Your mind-reading skills need some work." Ian's responsive smile was vicious. "Some lessons have to be learned the hard way, and if you make the same mistake twice, I'll rip you a new one, friend or not. *That's* what I wasn't saying. You took your shot and missed. Let it go. Move on."

"Sometimes it takes more than one shot to score." He arched an eyebrow.

"Friends don't let their friends be morons." Ian smirked around the bottle as he tipped back his beer.

"Do you know what I'm waiting for?" Garret leaned forward on his elbows and narrowed his eyes. "You, meeting a woman you can't live without. Then, maybe

I'll give some weight to your advice when it comes to those of the female persuasion."

"Never gonna happen." Looking bored, Ian pretended to pick lint off his unholy pink polo.

Garret let an evil smile crawl into his expression. "'Never' is a very long time, especially when there's a blonde assistant at your office who you seem to have difficulties looking at while ogling every other woman on the planet."

"The fact you mention such inane subjects proves you've spent too much time with girls in your lifespan. Since you're freed up from responsibilities and mistaken muses, let's resume our ESPN, poker and pool nights. After three years overseas, surviving a stalker and a close call with commitment, you need a man-up readjustment."

In the other room, the television announcer crowed, "He shoots! He scores!"

Garret's phone buzzed and his pulse jerked. But instead of Adara, it was another text from his manager. He grimaced. "'Free' is a relative term. My violin has been personally requested to replace an injured headliner for the remainder of an Ireland tour. I've been wanting to hit Ireland, but not sure I'm feeling it right now. My manager needs my decision."

Returning to the tour scene so soon felt premature. He hadn't mapped his path forward because all future plans had hinged on Adara. He'd wanted her insight and opinion, what she wanted in their life together, before cementing his next move, and their relationship had been too raw to press such serious subjects. Now he was left with a fast choice to make on his own.

"My two cents?" Ian tapped his bottle. He'd never been able to hold a beat, no matter how much he'd practiced with Garret in their younger years. "You came back to recharge. Instead, you got burned."

"Not exactly." Garret took a swig, the sour beer a perfect match to his mood.

"Dude, accept it. You've been dumped."

He thumped the bottle on the table and didn't bother curbing the growl in his voice. "Adara wanted space. That isn't the same."

"Don't murder the messenger." Ian's cool expression didn't change, but understanding softened his voice. "You say she's lost. I'm saying some people can't be found."

Or don't want to be found. Garret drained his bottle and pushed it aside.

"Your kid gig is done in two days, and your manager chooses this day to call?" He smirked, back to his old self. "Serendipitous."

Garret preferred to apply his favorite word when it coincided with new, exciting and fateful in a good way, not the sense of his universe being remade into ashes.

"Give Miss Stark the space she wanted — a whole ocean's worth — and finish your recharge by taking the unexpected opportunity in a place you've always wanted to go," Ian continued. "Do your usual tour thing and kill all social interaction. Focus everything on your music. Make the break work for you. Maybe that will give you both some clarity."

Garret rubbed his temples. His world had slid off its axis in less than three days and he couldn't blame it completely on Bella. Adara controlled her own reactions. If she didn't want to see him, he wouldn't resort to stalking. "It always worries me when you make a modicum of sense. I begin to question my morals and dignity."

Ian clinked their bottles. "You're welcome."

Chapter Thirty-Three

Monday morning, the budget-cut day, Adara woke well before dawn, her eyes puffy from crying. She pulled her hair into a short ponytail, slipped into running gear, grabbed her water bottle and opened the door.

An origami boat fell onto the threshold. She picked it up, the paper cold on her fingertips. Clearly, it had been there for quite some time. Without opening it, she gently set it on the foyer table and went for her run.

The boat was still there when she returned, breathless, burning and nowhere near serene. She reached for it and hesitated. She'd made the right decision. Garret deserved someone who could love him with zero inhibitions, and hurting him had been awful. She should have run from the start, pushed him away until he gave up.

Still...gently, she opened the paper watermarked with a star and Graywood Police Department. A burst of affection pulsed through her. The man must pilfer paper wherever he went. Inside was a number in Garret's loopy handwriting, as she suspected, but this time he'd written words with it.

30,628 total. Not long enough.

Her breath caught. Holding the boat between her hands like a live moth, she ran to her room and jerked the shoebox from beneath her bed. The origami inside shifted, whispering together, most of them refolded in their original shape. With shaking hands, she lifted one and opened it.

Garret's initials embossed the bottom, the note he'd pulled from his sweatshirt pocket the morning she'd found him puffing along her running trail. The number 47 was penned in the center. She pulled out another, one from the day they'd gone book shopping. 982 was scrawled on the bookstore flyer. The doctor's instructions from her ankle injury on their first 'not-date'. 344. The napkin from the night she'd run into him after the board meeting with the number 7. One after another, she pulled the papers out until the shoebox was empty and scraps of paper scattered her bed like colorful snowflakes. All those numbers.

She sank onto the bed before her legs gave out. They were his way of tracking their minutes together, making her moments count because she didn't have the capacity to do it herself. Her throat clogged with tears she thought she no longer had, but before they could fall, she sprang to her feet and gathered up the notes. She shoved them back into the box by the handful and slammed the lid shut.

But hiding them didn't stop the hairline fracture in her heart from spreading. Trembling, she slid to the floor, drew her legs up and planted her face on her knees. Garret was right, at least partly. In her quest to avoid pain, she had marginalized her life, a life Joey would've celebrated every single minute. What she wouldn't pay to give that back to him.

She sniffed and rubbed her eyes with her palms. But Joey was gone, an unchangeable fact, while her hours still ticked away. She still had time to honor her promise to him — or at least try. Taking a deep breath, she left the origami boats behind and slipped silently into the hall.

Adara paused outside Joey's door. Looking at the space he used to tornado from every morning didn't destroy her like it used to. The ache remained, more a dull throb — a scar rather than the gaping wound from a year ago. She opened the door and paused at the threshold.

Whatever investigation Roman had conducted hadn't left a single sign beyond Bella's trash being gone. The bed was still unmade, the closet full of odds and ends, the instruments and sheet music stacked in the corner by the lonely piano. She clung to the doorframe and drew another shaky, cleansing breath. Bella's invading perfume had faded, barely detectible beneath the dust and stale air, but still there. She clenched her jaw. It had to go.

For the second time since his death, Adara entered her brother's tomb. She marched to the window and opened it wide, allowing brisk air to sweep inside. Loose sheet music flapped and fluttered, as if invisible fingers thumbed through in a search of a particular song. Before it scattered, she gathered the stack and set it on the bed, pausing at the top title. *Glitter Girl.* Joey's nickname for Gia.

Tracing the notes written in her brother's spidery handwriting, she blinked back a film of tears. Gia should have this song as a permanent reminder of the man who loved her wholeheartedly. He'd adored Gia and never let her forget she was a treasure.

She suspected that, in Joey's absence, Gia had forgotten her 'treasure' status.

A chill went through her, a clarifying sense of purpose. It was time. Time to let go of Joey, finally put him to rest—and she didn't want to do it alone. She needed Gia there with her, to share his memories with someone else who had loved him and missed him just as deeply.

* * * *

Twelvish hours, a bottle of wine and an ocean of tears later, Adara sprawled on Joey's bed and lifted his pair of over-loved Converse. "Gross. Remember these things?" She shoved them in Gia's face, which happened to be right beside her. "They still stink."

"Stop!" Gia covered her nose with the neckline of the T-shirt she'd put on during their foray into Joey's things, an ancient ode to U2 from one of Joey's many attended concerts. "Do you know how many times I put those in the garbage? They always came back, like some sort of demon-possessed doll. I should've burned them."

"So you're saying you want them?" Adara grinned.

"I'll think about it." Gia's smile faded and sighed. "I've missed this. Talking about him, remembering... Life with Joey was phenomenal."

"I should've done this sooner." She toyed with the frayed shoelace. "I'm such an idjit."

"No, more of a weird antisocial who takes perverse pleasure in wallowing." Muffling her snicker, Gia elbowed her lightly in the ribs. "But I'm glad you finally did it."

"I was sort of...stuck." Adara didn't bother adding that she was still slightly wedged, but a year, a month, a week ago, she wouldn't have been able to even talk about Joey, and she suspected Garret was to blame.

Blue-diamond tears sparkled in Gia's eyes. "I think I'm going to be stuck for a while longer."

"Without random dudes, right? Because they won't help unstick you, and you deserve better. Settling for anything less than the love you deserve is a betrayal to Joey. If I have to, I'll glue the lyrics to *Glitter Girl* on your forehead."

Gia's pale eyebrows shot up. "Oh, really? Garret didn't unstick you with his stick?"

Her face went insta-fire. "That's a shameless quest for dirty details."

"So he didn't stick you?" She giggled and rolled off the bed as Adara hit her with a pillow. "Violence speaks louder than any words, Dar."

Adara peered over the edge of the bed at Gia, who lay on her back, still smiling. Gia didn't need to know that all sticks had been placed on standby through a lack of commitment on her part. She loosed a long breath. "I love him."

Once the words were out, there was no going back. Maybe that's why she'd blurted them without fully considering the consequences. Maybe she didn't want any excuse to go back, even if she wasn't sure what to do about the confession.

Gia scrambled to a sit, her eyes wide. "And? Does he love you too?"

Adara shrugged one shoulder. "Since day one, I've pushed him away. Yesterday, I shoved hard. I thought it was the right thing to do. Now I'm not so sure."

She nodded slowly. "Because he got to you." Obviously sensing Adara's doubt, she continued. "He knew what he was up against. I made sure of it. I used it to try to discourage him from chasing you, before I was convinced otherwise." A faint flush invaded her cheeks, whether from the wine or something else, Adara couldn't tell.

"I hurt him." Her stomach rolled in affirmation. "I told him I needed space because I did. I *do*. Garret deserves one hundred percent. I don't know if I can give him that."

Gia leaned an elbow on the bed and squarely met her gaze. "I'd trade anything, *anything* for another day with Joey." Her smile wobbled. "There are always a zillion 'what ifs' floating around, and some of them you'll never be prepared for. We both know that. If you love him, that's enough. Don't trade slivers of happiness for slices of fear."

"Wow." Adara smiled crookedly. "You sound like a counselor."

"And that's all the guidance I'll offer without a fee." She grabbed her wine glass from the nightstand and drained it.

Adara gazed out of the window into the night, rain pelting the glass in a gentle, soothing rhythm, and her eyelids drooped. She still wasn't sure what to do about Garret, but with Gia near, wrapped in Joey's presence, the fear felt far away. "I think he's some sort of musical soul guru."

"No way." Gia flopped on her stomach, crosswise at the foot of the bed, making the mattress bounce. "If I'd gotten a hippie vibe, I would've sent him packing."

Adara halfheartedly poked her in the shoulder with a toe. "I thought I was supposed to be the one watching out for you."

"We're supposed to watch out for each other." Gia laid her head on her arms and closed her eyes. "Idjit."

"Can't argue that one. Diva."

"Stark princess."

"I'd totally be okay with that if it hadn't come from Ian." She curled onto her side and nestled into the pillow. "Want to tell me what's going on between you two?"

Gia's eyes popped open. "What? No." The response might've sounded innocent if not for the squeak in her voice. "Nothing. He's off-limits, remember? 'A rotten, scum-sucking lawyer-type', to repeat the precise titles you gave him last year."

"Liar." Adara yawned and closed her eyes. "Staying the night?"

"Is that okay?" Gia's voice sounded small, so hopeful.

"You're the closest thing to Joey I have left," she said softly, repeating the same words Gia had told her weeks ago.

Gia gave a tiny, shuddering sob and squeezed Adara's foot. "I'm so glad you're back."

Chapter Thirty-Four

Tuesday night, wedged between Gia and Principal Austin in the back row of plastic chairs filling the school gym, Adara clasped her hands together and tried not to twitch. Today had been hell. A large part of the day had involved a stern discussion on stranger danger. Tatum had been resilient, showing up to school and having no problem being the center of attention. Definitely a family trait.

Garret had shown up exactly on time, politely taken the kids for a final rehearsal and herded them back after an extra-long practice session. He didn't even set foot in the classroom. She'd asked for space and he'd obliged.

But space didn't fit anymore—too loose in some spots, too tight in others.

"Since you survived the torture of supervising a free music mentor, what are your thoughts on the music program...or lack thereof?" Austin pushed up his glasses and blinked at her. "Or to be more precise, am I going to regret sitting through this next hour and will my eardrums survive?"

Leave it to Austin to kill two fish with one rock and include his own well-being. "I still wouldn't trade my job for the music program, but it's a tragedy we can't have both. Mr. Ambrose figured out how to include even the kids who have zero musical inclination." Her voice scratched, warped by her closing throat. "And even while he gloriously failed in the child control department, he inspired every one of them to be part of the symphony." An ache thrummed in her chest and the air seemed to thin, making it hard to breathe. "He's a musical genius."

"And all this time I thought you didn't think too much of the guy." Austin stroked his mustache, his gaze on the fluttering stage curtain where the random chime of a bell struck too soon and was quickly silenced. "I need to brush up on my body language interpretation skills."

She went still. Had she been that frigid toward Garret in public, enough that the casual observer thought she didn't even respect him, let alone like him? The thought slithered inside, a cold and trembling awareness. Garret surely knew how she felt.

Doesn't he?

"I should have brought a snack." Austin huffed an impatient breath.

She snorted. "What happened to the cupcakes Olivia left in the breakroom?"

He suddenly pretended to find something in the crowd extremely interesting while absently rubbing his paunch.

"Here we go." Gia nudged her arm, facing the stage.

The curtains parted, and there he was. Maybe she should've taken stock of her kids, made sure they were all accounted for, no bloody noses or bruises, but she couldn't tear her attention from Garret. She'd missed him...a lot. She hadn't realized how much until his gravity drew her back in.

"Parents and families, teachers and friends, thank you for coming." His voice washed over her, a soothing lullaby, and she tuned out his introductory speech, content to ogle from afar.

He'd foregone the pirate vibe and gone for clean-cut. She wasn't sure which version she liked more. The stubble she loved was gone, but the absence took nothing away from his handsome face. His soft hair was combed neatly back and secured, and he'd traded his faded jeans for no-holes black ones, a white button-down shirt and black rocker boots. Barely three days had passed since the Bella saga, yet it felt like a chapter from someone else's biography. And it felt like years since she'd looked, really *looked* at Garret. That fluttering in her heart yawned awake.

"To Miss Dumont—"

She jerked straight at the combination of her name and Gia's elbow nudge.

"For loaning me her classroom, students and generous time." His smile seemed forced, less brilliant, and for once, it wasn't aimed at her. He stepped to the side and turned halfway toward the fidgeting students. "There was some disagreement as to themes and songs." He huffed a little laugh. "I learned that 'unanimous' is a term not to be used with third-graders."

Laughter rippled across the crowd, and Adara smiled too. He was finally catching on.

"So, in a celebration of individuality, I now present to you *Chaos Harmonified*."

Austin mumbled what sounded to be a desperate prayer.

Sinking to his knees to be at the third-graders' eye level, Garret played the part of conductor. He nodded at Ava who, for once, looked serious. She hit the xylophone with her mallet and clear notes rang through the air.

By the fifth note, Adara bit her lip to hide a ridiculous smile. *A Whole New World*. Her favorite animated film song, something all her students knew. Riley joined in with the Irish whistle, soft, not overpowering the xylophone, and the two recorders picked up the melody. With only a point from Garret, Zachary on autoharp and Haley's finger cymbals hit their marks perfectly. Finally, the percussion and bells joined in, Dalaynee picking up with the kazoo. Tatum clanged her cowbell, and the xylophone subtly changed tunes. Song melding, Garret Ambrose style. Only Garret would have thought to blend Disney and AC/DC. *Back in Black* had never sounded so cute.

Adara furiously blinked back tears as applause thundered in surround sound. She couldn't be more proud, both of her kids and Garret for getting them there. No matter what Gia said, he was truly a musical guru. He was — she swallowed hard — life-changing.

As the noise died, Ashton separated from the line and sat in the middle of the stage, gripping her Irish whistle. Garret sat beside her, cross-legged, with his violin.

Adara gripped the edge of her seat. This was going to be bad. She could feel it.

The bongo started up and Garret joined with the violin...soft, so soft. Ashton's hands shook, but the simplified melody didn't require steadiness. Poignant and haunting, it held an undeniable Celtic flavor. The finger cymbals and crow sounder added volume, surprisingly not drowning out the Irish whistle, and soon the other instruments joined in.

She clamped her lips together and dug her fingernails into the chair, anything to keep the tears in check. So that's what Garret had been doing when she'd caught him late at school with Ashton and her brother. He'd personally given Ashton a step up in overcoming her shyness.

A rusted lock clicked inside her, sharp and shattering. Without even trying, he'd ripped her apart and patched her up. In the months spent in her classroom, he'd noticed the intricacies in her kids, awakened the beauty most others couldn't see and carefully championed it.

Just as he'd done with her.

Her heart compressed into a hard, throbbing ball, so tight she couldn't breathe, and the intuition that had prevented her from truly pushing Garret away crystallized in desperate recognition. Returning to merely existing would be like pretending *he* didn't exist. Rejecting inspiration he offered the world, specifically to her, would be a complete disregard for something altogether priceless. No matter the potential pain, she didn't want to backtrack or remain shackled to a life safe, empty and illusory. She wanted a life full and real — and definitely with Garret.

Peace washed through her in a cleansing tide, eroding the heaviness in her soul, and she took her first full breath in what felt an eternity.

As if in response to her epiphany, between one beat and the next, Adam tripped, right into his drum. The instrument crashed into Ava in the row ahead, knocking her into her music stand. Almost in slow motion, the stands collapsed into one another, a domino game gone rogue. The music ended in a dissonant screech as children scrambled over each other in a tangle of limbs and instruments, and the crying began. Through it all, Garret froze, his expression utterly lost.

Adara wanted to throw up. This was her fault. She'd insisted that Adam and Sammy be separated, and Garret had caved to her. If the drum had stayed to the side, separate, it would have been a single casualty, not a natural musical disaster.

Someone had the good sense to close the stage curtain. As Principal Austin fumbled with a regretful speech to the crowd on the other side, Adara gently touched the red mark on Haley's finger. "This is what we call a music recital war wound." She met Haley's tear-filled eyes. "Think you'll survive to play finger cymbals another day?"

Haley sniffled, looking thoughtful and finally nodded. "But next time, I want a solo." She skipped off to join the sullen huddle of Ava and Dalaynee. At least one student wasn't scarred by music.

Garret knelt beside Adam, who hadn't stopped crying, and her heart twisted at his haunted expression. He clearly blamed himself and took the recital disaster as a personal failure. Once order was restored, she would assure him it was all on her. Tell him...everything.

Austin poked his face through the curtain slit. "Everything copacetic?"

"The only casualties were a drum, two music stands and a xylophone mallet." Adara ruffled Riley's curls and took the whistle from her little fingers, giving her an encouraging smile. "All small humans survived with only minor scrapes and bruises."

He heaved a sigh of relief. "Parents are waiting, so whenever the kids are ready to go." He vanished behind the curtain.

"Wait here, Riley." Adara headed for the back corner of the stage to Garret and Adam and crouched beside them. Garret flashed her a helpless look. "In a few days, no one else will be thinking about tonight, Adam." She dabbed at his wet cheeks with a tissue. "And the only thing you should remember about tonight is how awesomely you played your drum." She wanted more than anything to grab Garret's hand, to let him know her words were meant for him too.

Adam sucked in a few shaky breaths. "But I d-dropped it."

"True, but until then, you rocked it, and I'm so proud of you." She met Garret's gaze, the shadows in his dark eyes killing her. "Parents are waiting. Would you mind waiting by the curtain and guiding the kids out?"

His throat worked and he nodded. Without a word, he obeyed.

"Third-graders gather." In less than ten seconds, all her students circled her and Adam. She dropped her voice to a whisper. "When I say so, line up single file behind Riley to go find your parents. Before you leave, I want each of you to shake Mr. Ambrose's hand and thank him for sharing the gift of his music." She gave them all a stern look. "Got it?"

Lots of nods, only a few remaining tears.

Adara let her smile fly free. "Move."

One by one, the kids shook Garret's hand with words of appreciation only third-graders could manage, but his expression never changed. If anything, he looked even more miserable by the time Adam slipped past the curtain, leaving them alone at last. Slumping, he shoved his hands in his pockets and briefly closed his eyes.

"I'm sorry." She touched his arm, unable to ignore the tension trembling there. "If I hadn't insisted that you to move Sammy—"

"I'm to blame." He opened his eyes but kept his attention on the curtain, as if he couldn't wait to escape. "This was my project, not yours. I'm responsible for the decisions made." He briefly met her gaze. "Thank you for sharing your students with me."

"Garret, I—"

"I have to go." He cut between the curtains, and he was gone.

Chilled, she stared at the rippling curtains. *I'm sorry for pushing you away. I'm ready now. I love you.* All the things she wanted to tell him remained trapped, unsaid. The curt dismissal was unexpected, and no matter how much it stung, she got it. She'd needed the same privacy when she'd failed to collect enough signatures to save her job.

She'd give him tonight. Tomorrow, she'd tell him everything.

Maybe then the barb suddenly stuck in her throat would be gone.

Chapter Thirty-Five

Screw giving Garret a night to sulk. Adara grabbed her phone. The need to make things right with him burned like coals in her chest.

Have time to talk?

The screen went dark, no response. He might be with the Sullivans—or maybe he'd turned his phone off for the concert and forgot to turn it back on. Maybe his battery had died. Or maybe it was payback. There were a dozen reasons for him not responding, but none of them eased the knot in her neck.

She leaped from the couch and barreled toward the door. Digital communication was overrated anyway. She needed to see him, touch him, put her hand on his heart and memorize his rhythm when she told him she wanted life with him, that she was all in. Midnight might be when the magic ended according to some sources, but sometimes you had to make your own magic.

Half an hour later, Adara pulled up to the Sullivan's two-story residence and ignored her roaring pulse and shaking hands. Rain ricocheted on her roof like dropped bullet casings, blurring the view. Garret hadn't been home, so here she was.

Despite the late hour, lights glared inside, defiantly pushing into the black night. She'd feel better if there was a neon 'Welcome Adara' sign flashing in the window. Since Tatum's kidnapping, she hadn't spoken to Bob or London. Garret wouldn't hide their breakup from his family, proving they were right about her.

One by one, she uncurled her fingers from the steering wheel. *All in.*

Adara lifted her hood and sprinted across the glistening sidewalk to the porch. She hit the doorbell and waited, her heart climbing her throat with each passing second.

Footsteps thumped inside the house, paused long enough for someone to look through the peephole. Paused longer, as if deciding whether or not to allow her entry. At last, the door squeaked open. London filled the doorway in yoga pants and a *Gymnasts Do It Better* T-shirt. A pitbull preparing to attack looked friendlier.

Not promising at all. Adara cleared her throat and tried for a smile. It probably resembled more of a grimace, so she gave it up and went for real. "Sorry to bother you so late. I'm trying to reach Garret. He hasn't answered my texts and he wasn't home. I hoped he was here."

London folded her arms. "He's not."

Adara hunched in her raincoat. *Blast.* He must be with Ian, which meant he'd be lost until Ian allowed him to be found. "Do you know where he might be?"

"Why? So you can rip out another organ along with his heart?" London stepped forward, a predator defending her territory — or brother, as the case may be. "I'll always be grateful for what you did for Tatum, but that gratitude doesn't excuse you for playing games with my brother."

Her throat constricted. "I didn't mean —"

London lunged, so close that their noses almost touched, so close a draft carrying the sour scent of baby spit up mingled with the rain. "I wouldn't give you his location even if he was dying and only your blood type could save him."

So much for the family Welcome Wagon. Adara met London's gaze squarely. "I messed up. I know that. I'd love to rewind and change a step or two — or a few hundred, for that matter — but even if I could, I'm not sure I would."

London's eyes narrowed and glinted, firecrackers ready to explode.

"I'll never regret that Garret invaded my life, and I hate that it took me seeing him at his best then witnessing it collapse to recognize —"

"I'll only say this once." The flames in London's eyes trickled into her voice, making it crackle. "Stay away from him. He doesn't need someone who makes him feel like he's not enough."

"Look… I had a brother too. I understand you want to protect him, and I get that you don't trust me." Adara clenched her jaw, her temperature rising toward boiling. "But you don't know me. I'm going to talk to him, with or without your help."

A sound that sounded strangely like a hissing cat erupted from London and Bob appeared in the doorway. He latched onto London's shaking shoulders with both hands and dragged her inside. After some hushed words, he stepped onto the porch and shut the door behind him.

"You're not going to find Garret any time soon, Adara." The words were harsh, but Bob's voice was gentle. "He's gone."

Gone. Her heart thundered, echoing in her head. "What do you mean 'gone'?"

"He was asked to fill in for a tour. His flight left an hour ago, and once he's on the concert circuit, he's all business. He only carries a private cell connected to his manager. No one will hear from him until the tour's done." He spread his hands...apologetic. "Sorry. Go home and get some rest. It's been a rough day for everyone."

As Adara stood in the rain, paralyzed, he slipped back inside. She still stood there when the lights went out, one by one.

Garret is gone. She'd figured everything out too late. A fine trembling rose up from deep inside, making her legs shake, and she gasped for breath. He hadn't even told her goodbye.

She closed her eyes, ripped off her hood and tipped her face to the sky, letting the rain cleanse away the fear. *No way.* If he believed in serendipity, she did too. She hadn't come back to life only to lose it again.

She texted Gia.

I need help.

Chapter Thirty-Six

The next morning, Adara barely had time to stash her purse before students filed in, bright-eyed and full of energy, except for Tatum. She stomped into the classroom with her glare full-on and deadly. A kidnapping couldn't keep Tatum Sullivan down long.

Tatum stopped right beside her desk and folded her thin arms over her neon pink T-shirt, hiding the sparkly kitten on front. Her London glare sharpened even more. "I'm not talking to you."

The mess simmering in the bottom of her stomach since last night pinched. "May I ask why?"

"Uncle Garret left because you made him sad." She clomped a foot. "He left Angel with us to cat-sit, flew across the ocean to do his music, and now I won't see him until I'm ten and *old*." Her bottom lip trembled. "I'm *not* talking to you, Miss Dumont." She marched across the classroom and flung herself into her seat.

Adara sank into her chair before her legs gave out. Garret was going to be gone two years? While they'd talked into the wee hours, Gia had found his concert location—in Ireland. Of course, it had to be Ireland—and they were meeting tonight to figure out a game plan. *But…two years?* That didn't sound like someone who believed in second chances.

She sucked in a breath. He hadn't given up on her when she didn't want to be found. It was time for payback.

The first bell rang like a warning and the students settled, all attention on her as she stood and circled her desk. Adara stopped dead center and gazed at her kids for a moment. They were all amazing in their own unique ways, from Haley and her ready smile to Zachary's sweet gestures and Tatum's mischievousness. Garret might have been the one who breathed life back into her, but these kids had helped her hang on until then.

"I know last night's concert didn't go as planned, but you all got up on stage, followed Mr. Ambrose's directions and showed off the musical skills you learned. I could not have been more proud of each and every one of you."

"Except for Adam." Ava sniffed. "He ruined the whole thing with his drum."

Adam hunched and stared at his desk.

"That wasn't Adam's fault. It was mine. Mr. Ambrose wanted the drums together and I didn't. I should have listened to him."

They all looked at her with levels of wariness, as if this was some sort of morality test they might be quizzed on later. Adam grinned shyly. Tatum still glared.

"So, in honor of how well you performed last night, I'm opening the treasure chest." Squeals and clapping erupted and she held up her hands, putting her stern teacher mask back on. "I'll open the treasure chest," she said in a raised voice, "*after* the quiz."

A series of awwws and grumbles replaced the rejoicing, and she bit her lip to hold back a smile. "The quiz today is on music. Everyone who finishes gets an A-plus. There are no wrong answers."

Quiet now, students exchanged suspicious looks, clearly waiting for the catch.

"Your quiz is to make something to show Mr. Ambrose how music inspired you. Use whatever craft supplies you want, however you want. Be creative." She let her smile go. "That's it."

No one moved from their seat, looking at her as if she'd sprouted a snoot, whiskers and fangs.

"What are you waiting for, ye barnacle-bottomed landlubbers?" She pointed at the craft supply cabinet. "You've got until morning recess. Go!"

By ten o'clock recess, she had seven poems and letters covered in either glitter, flowers or both, a construction paper drum, a Popsicle stick violin with yarn strings, drawings of notes and birds, rainbows and race cars, several hearts and a pipe cleaner pirate ship. She wasn't sure what the pirate ship had to do with musical inspiration, but it was creative.

During silent reading time, Adara tapped her phone with a pencil eraser, the silence of the classroom choking. She couldn't, wouldn't believe her epiphany had come too late. Other than having her brother back, she'd never wanted anything more than having Garret in her life. Joey and Garret were on equal wish ground, but Garret was still here, still a possibility. She couldn't wait until school broke for summer. She had to find him now, which meant she had to track Principal Austin down at lunch and ask for an indeterminate time of personal leave. And if he said no? Her heart fluttered and she swallowed hard. If he said no, she'd go anyway.

Movement stirred at the back of the classroom. She looked up right as Tatum flicked Zachary's ear.

Adara affected her best teacher scowl. "Tatum, will you come to my desk, please?"

"But, he—"

"Tatum." She made sure her tone held a 'no arguments' warning.

With the sigh of the unjustified, Tatum stood and slogged to the front of the room, every eye on her.

"Back to your reading, class." She hid a smile as students obeyed her crisp command—or at least valiantly pretended to. "Into the hall, Tatum."

The girl's blue eyes widened and a sharper tension strung through the class. *Hall speech. Big Trouble.*

Adara kept her stern teacher façade on until they were both out of the classroom, the door shut. Squatting to Tatum's height, she held her gaze.

"Zachary started it, Miss Dumont." Tatum stuck out her bottom lip. "I was only defending my honor."

"I believe you." She released a smile, which seemed to make Tatum even more uncertain. "I wanted to apologize." Pulling the wildlife sticker sheet from behind her back that she'd grabbed from her drawer, she handed it over. "I made a mistake and it made Garret sad, so I'm going to tell him I'm sorry."

"But he's gone!" Tears gleamed in her eyes. "Across the ocean!"

"I know." She wiped a few stray tears from Tatum's cheek with her thumbs. "That's why I won't be in class tomorrow or the rest of the week." *Maybe never, depending on Austin.* "This particular Jane finally figured out she needs her Mr. Bingley, but unlike Jane Bennet, I'm not waiting around for him to come back. I'm going to get him." Getting London's approval wasn't happening and maybe she was a wimp, but she wanted at least one ally in the Sullivan family. She wasn't above sticker manipulation.

Tatum hugged the stickers to her chest. "Really? You're bringing him back?"

"I'll do my best. The ultimate decision is up to him."

"Rub his head like you would with Angel," she said solemnly. "He likes that."

Yes, he does. "I'll keep that in mind."

Tatum flung her skinny arms around her neck, too fast for Adara to move. School policy forbid hugs, but since she probably wouldn't have a job at the end of the day anyway, she folded the girl close. There was something about a kid hug given freely that stirred up the warm fuzzies.

A sharp pinch on her ear dispelled those dandelion fluffs. Tatum released her and glared. "That's for making Uncle Garret sad."

"I deserved that." Adara arched an eyebrow. "But we're still on my time. No pinching, not even naughty teachers."

Tatum's smile flashed, wide and wicked. "I'm not giving back the stickers."

"Big surprise." She straightened and smoothed Tatum's hair. "And the only reason Zachary keeps tapping his foot and making your desk wiggle is because he likes you."

Her eyes sparkled, blue glitter in full sunlight. Zachary didn't stand a chance. She'd corner him at lunch, no mercy, no surrender. Kids made romance look so easy. If all she had to do was chase Garret down, she'd be golden.

During lunch, Adara did some cornering of her own and caught Austin in his office, stuffing his face with a meatball sub. She planted her palms on his desk and leaned forward. "I need some time off. I don't know for how long, but it has to start tomorrow."

He chewed slowly and his brown eyes gleamed, the thick glasses warping any emotion there. After a swallow, he exchanged sandwich for soft drink and slurped through the straw, his gaze never leaving her, studying and assessing. Deciding.

The rat-a-tat of her heart thrummed at every pulse point, vibrating through her fingertips to drum the desk. Maybe email would've been received better. Austin hated his meals to be interrupted, forget the fact that he ate constantly. But she had no choice. Austin never stayed late on Wednesdays. It was now or never.

He finally set his plastic cup down, daintily dabbed a napkin at his mustache and cleared his throat. "Let me get this straight. You persuaded the school board to consider your plan to eliminate the music program if you collected enough signatures, you managed to get said signatures, kept your teaching position instead of the music program, took a pay cut with it and now you want time off?"

She went for a smile, which he didn't return. "It appears you have a clear understanding of the situation, sir."

His mustache twitched. "Sir?"

"I'm sucking up."

He sighed, settling back in his chair, and gave his sandwich a longing look before focusing on her again. "Miss Dumont, you've worked here not even three years. You're our least experienced and youngest teacher."

There it went, her job flushing down the toilet. She tried to keep her voice steady while ice crept into her veins. "I know."

"Word gets around fast along the grade-school grapevine," he said, toneless. "Parents gossip, kids tell tales, teachers talk."

"I know." Her dry mouth made it hard to talk. "I love working with the kids. I love my job, but—"

"A year or so ago, I asked you to take time off, nearly demanded it." He folded his hands over his belt, which seemed to have shrunk in the last few months. "You were absent one day. *One day.* For the funeral. You never missed another, but your passion faded away, week by week, until the teacher I hired, the person I semi-know and semi-like hardly existed."

Tears scalded her eyes, and she bowed her head to hide them.

"Parents are already requesting their kids to be in your class next year."

"They are?" She blinked, sure she'd misheard.

"You finally snapped out of it." He shrugged. "Everyone noticed. If you need some time off to remain out of your funk, take it. I'll sub for the little monsters until summer if I have to." He picked up his half-eaten sub and paused, his eyebrows lifted. "Is there something else? You're cutting into my meatball moment."

She leaned over the desk and squeezed his forearm. "You're the best principal ever."

He scowled. "I already know that, Miss Dumont. Go, before I change my mind."

* * * *

Adara had just killed her security system and unlocked the door when Gia showed up, armed with wine and rocky road. Gia marched inside, determination in every line, from her stilettos to clingy silk blouse to jeweled headband. "Let's do this."

"I haven't checked out tickets or flights or anything yet," Adara said, following Gia into the living room. She plopped onto the couch and opened her laptop. "I'm still in shock that Austin gave me time off without docking my pay."

Gia slapped the laptop shut, making her jump, and looked her squarely in the eyes. "You're going to have to ditch your comfy little world, face awkward situations with lots of people, deal with the unknown and maybe be rejected. You'll be diving back into life with no prep time. Are you serious about getting him back?"

Her stomach somersaulted and her hands shook. Right. Not only would she have to travel to a place she'd planned to go with Joey—a place she'd never been before—but she'd have to basically stalk Garret if she wanted a chance to speak to him. Even then, there were no guarantees she'd succeed or he'd take her back. It was getting hard to breathe.

"Is he worth it?" Gia asked quietly.

Adara gave the fluttering inside free rein. *All in.* "If I have to storm the stage to get Garret to acknowledge me, I'll do it. He can't run faster than me. Known fact."

Gia's smile lit up like a sunrise. "Let the Adara Overhaul Project begin. No matter what happens, we'll make sure he never forgets you. When was the last time you had a manicure?"

She frowned at her fingernails. "Um..."

"That's what I thought." From Gia's grim tone, one would think she'd committed murder. "Halloween's officially over, girl. Out with the black. You need clothes that say 'I'm here and I give a crap'. Highlights to make your hair pop. Most of all, your eyebrows need tamed. They scare me."

"The direction of this conversation scares me." Adara eased away. If she did it slow enough, maybe Gia wouldn't notice. "I don't think he cares about any of those things."

"He will." Gia lassoed her arm and pulled her toward the door. "We've got to start at the ground up. Then, we'll plot your final destination."

Three hours later, feeling like a coin tumbled, plucked, scrubbed and polished until she sparkled, Adara tossed her shopping bags beside the couch while Gia fetched wine reinforcement.

"After all the suffering I endured tonight, I hope my credit card doesn't get declined when I book a flight." She bounced onto the couch and her hair brushed her cheek, sleek and smooth. The magic of salons even worked on skeptical teachers.

"It's a bad sign when your credit card company calls you while at the salon, concerned about suspicious salon charges," Gia called from the kitchen. "And that red dress isn't going back. You kill in that thing. He won't have any chance of not seeing you."

"Truth," she muttered, opening her laptop and firing it up. The dress was something out of a movie, and wearing it gave new meaning to Miss Scarlet. But the embroidered, sewn-in corset reflected her love for gothic—and made it nearly impossible to breathe. But yeah, she looked good in it. Her students wouldn't even recognize her. Hopefully, Garret would.

"Trade you." Gia handed her a glass of wine while taking the laptop with her free hand, almost sloshing the contents onto the couch. "If your card gets declined, we'll use mine. No going back."

"Wasn't planning on it." She grinned as Gia settled beside her, laptop across her thighs. "If I have to travel halfway across the world, sit through his concert and let myself fall apart just for a chance to talk to him, I'll do it...even in a suffocation bag disguised as a red dress."

"To red dresses." Gia clinked their glasses together and set hers aside. Her fingers flew over the keyboard, and she blinked. Hit another key. Blinked again. "Holy Hades. He's sold out...everywhere."

"How he could be sold out? He just left last night."

"Either he has a wizard manager who sees the future, or he wasn't telling you the whole story." Gia frowned, her face etched in the computer light. "You think he was playing you?"

"He's not like Ian." She arched an eyebrow at her friend.

Other than a mouth twitch, Gia didn't take the bait. "Maybe you should ask Bob for his secret number."

She shook her head, fast. "Even if Bob agreed, this has to be all on me—my doing, my demo. Garret needs to know I'm all in. If I can't get him to believe that, I don't stand a chance."

Blue eyes wide, eyebrows high, Gia nodded slowly.

If she could shock Gia into speechlessness, maybe she could shock Garret enough to give her another shot. "So I can't contact him, can't get into his concert, but there's no way I'm waiting. Are there such things as classical concert ticket scalpers?"

"Brilliant idea." Gia settled back in the couch, getting long-term comfy. "Pack your bags, water your plants, forward your mail…whatever you need to do. I've got this. By tomorrow, you'll be soaring to Ireland."

Adara gave Gia her best smile as a new hole in her soul ached, missing the puzzle piece that was Garret. There wasn't anything more she could do tonight, but tomorrow or the next day she'd find out what path her future would take. With Garret — her stomach knotted — or without.

Chapter Thirty-Seven

Adara didn't relax until the sky had darkened beyond the plane window and the interior lights had blinked off one by one. She quietly pulled her iPod and phone out of her purse. The gruff grandpa next to her had closed his eyes, and from his snore, no amount of escaped blubbering would disturb him.

She stuck the buds in her ears, muffling her neighbor and scrolled through playlists to the one Gia had made for her. *Suck It Up, Girl.* She grinned, even as her heart skipped an uneven beat with the push of Play. The songs on that list could be anything from Irish jigs to Beethoven, but that was the point. She had to let the memories come.

Haunting guitar filled her head, U2's *Bad,* a hard hit right off. Drawing a sharp breath, she fumbled with her phone, needing a distraction as the music pressed in. Research. She'd finally determine the meaning of *neshama*. She'd bet the rest of her savings account it was synonymous with victim. The price of scalped Garret Ambrose tickets had been scandalous.

The definition shone on her screen. *Neshama— Hebrew. The Jewish notion of the soul. May mean spirit or soul.*

All those times Garret had called her *neshama*...his soul.

Tears blurred her vision, and it had nothing to do with Bono crooning in her ear to break away. She folded her fingers around the phone and shifted toward the window. A full moon gleamed on a blanket of stars, close enough to touch. Maybe Garret looked at the same sky and remembered their first not-date, the star-struck heavens he'd arranged for her.

And maybe he wished he could take back the minutes he'd wasted.

Turning back to her phone, she researched some names of her own and let the music play on. *All in, no fear, no going back.*

* * * *

Adara joined the swarm trickling into the auditorium. The hours she'd crashed at her hotel hadn't helped her fuzzy, jetlagged brain. The entire night felt surreal, from the ridiculously red dress she'd squeezed into to the buzzing crowd and lights. But she was in the right place. Garret's name scrolled across the building, a blaze of glowing letters.

Her phone hummed in her fancy clutch, and she ducked into a nook, using a potted plant as a shield from the press of the music-loving masses. Who knew classical fans could be so pushy?

The phone vibrated again, and she popped open her clutch. Two texts from Gia. She shut the phone off without reading them. Whatever was happening at home, she didn't want to know. She didn't need any distractions tonight.

Adara merged back into the crawling mob. Bouncers-turned-doormen guarded all points of entry with sharp suits and sharper eyes. By the time she'd made it to the correct door, her ticket was crinkled and damp in her hand. She handed it to the third floor, entry five doorman with an apologetic smile.

With zero expression, he smoothed the ticket, examined it thoroughly, and took one step back with a sweep to his side. "This row, madam. Your seat is in the middle."

Her heart sank. Back row nose-bleed section, and she had to climb over a dozen people either way to get to her spot. The stage was a mile down and across a sea of bobbing people. She'd paid a fortune for a horrible seat. Worse, the only way she'd ever get Garret's attention was to play Spiderman and swing down from a rope. And the handful of watchdog security guards circling the stage looked like they could run. With her red dress seriously hampering her sneaking and sprinting skills, she wouldn't make it halfway to the stage before being tackled.

"Madam, do you need assistance?" The doorman narrowed his eyes at her, suspicious, blocking the line until she proved her only destination was her assigned seat.

She clearly wasn't stalker material.

"Thanks. I've got it." She held onto her apology smile the entire struggle to her seat, only crushing a couple of toes along the way and earning one muttered curse.

The curse was in a different language, so it didn't count. With a relieved sigh, she plopped down between a grandma in pearls smelling of liquid money and a girl who'd fit into a punk rock band. She got sneers in varying degrees from both. *Awesome.*

She slumped in her seat. None of this was going as she'd imagined. Even in her worst-case scenario packages, Garret had at least acknowledged her before walking away. Here, stuck miles from the stage, there was no chance he'd see her, let alone hear her. She had to acknowledge a kernel of respect for Bella. Getting close to Garret took some serious resourcefulness.

The lights dimmed and the stage went black. The crowd hooted. Adara stiffened, clenching her purse like a lifeline.

As fast as the spotlights died, they flared to life and there he was. Garret with his violin, a handful of other musicians with instruments scattered around the stage. At least, she was relatively certain it was Garret. At this distance, she might be wrong. The golden hair looked right, but he appeared questionably dressed in all black.

Without an introduction speech, he set his bow to strings, and Vivaldi echoed through the hall, wild and untamed. All her identity doubts vanished. He was fast and furious, definitely Garret, every note impeccable and in synch with the other musicians. Years as a devoted band geek had served him well.

At the abrupt end of the song, he bowed curtly to roaring applause. His smile flashed white, and he looked up, as if he could actually see her in the sky-high section. Even if he knew she was here, where she sat, there was no way he could spot her, not with the spotlight blinding him and the distance between them, yet her heart drilled an allegro tempo — too quick, too hard.

He jumped right into *Por Una Cabeza*. The old woman next to Adara clasped her hands beneath her chin, a little girl lost in a favorite memory as the violin sang sweet and slow. The piano joined in, and as the pace increased, the violin strings squeaked, a missed note.

She almost gasped. The only time she'd witnessed Garret mess up was during karaoke Ambrosified, when she'd surprised him with her head banging.

Instead of continuing on as any normal musician would do, he lowered the violin to his side, dropped his head and looked down at the stage. The piano, guitar, cello and drum dwindled out, and the sudden silence ached in a beat of its own. No one in the stunned crowd said a word.

Adara couldn't have used the silence to get his attention, even if she'd wanted to. She sat with the rest of the audience, frozen. She had zero doubt he was reliving the third-grade concert disaster, and it destroyed her.

Finally, Garret pivoted and faced the crowd. "My apologies," he said into the microphone. One brave fan whooped an encouragement, and his usual smile flashed, then faded. "I took time off from touring because my passion for music faltered. Some element went missing, and I felt a break from the concert circuit to smaller, more intimate venues would reignite that passion."

"You can have my passion, Garret!" some woman in the crowd offered.

Adara stiffened. *Good idea.* Maybe she should try yelling too.

But he ignored that one, so maybe not. "My respite worked. I found my passion again, my muse, and yet here I am again, unchanged." He huffed in the microphone, a humorless laugh. "No, not unchanged. *I'm* changed, and yet I'm performing all the songs I'm comfortable with, like they're a favorite sweatpants and slippers. I'm not comfortable. I'm…" He scratched his cheek with his bow. "I'm unsettled."

A few catcalls and hoots went up from the crowd, and he waited until a restless silence resumed. "I'm unsettled, and the songs I had planned for tonight aren't true to my heart." He pivoted toward the other musicians on stage, as if communicating some sort of silent minstrel language only they understood. They all shifted subtly, adjusting, readying. Garret faced the crowd again. "So I hope you'll forgive me for stepping off the expected path, but I have to let this out."

The fans came to life, undeterred by the strange intercession, or maybe even more incensed because of it. Applause thundered to the domed roof, punctuated with whistles, yells and Garret's name, but the second he settled the violin back in place, the noise dwindled.

Adara couldn't relax. She'd come prepared to hear the classics, not whatever he now planned. As usual, Garret kicked through boundaries when she least expected it, breaking rules and spinning her in circles. She blew out a breath and forced her shoulders back into the seat. Nothing would ever be as usual with Garret. If she could handle whatever he threw out tonight, she could deal with anything.

The guitar and cymbals started up together, and Adara unleashed a full, true smile. *Enter Sandman*. How could she not love him? As the heavy cello bass thrummed through her veins, she cut the chain on her emotions, slipped into her memories and went into head-bang mode. The older lady beside her sniffed, but the punk rock girl on the other side joined in with a whooping fist pump. The violin started the melody, and she couldn't stop singing along. When the chorus came, the rocker chick belted it out with her. By the second verse, most of the nosebleed section sang too. More than half the auditorium chanted the last chorus.

It was freedom, and she was high on it — or maybe it was the lack of oxygen due to the location of her seat. Either way, she let it flow through her blood, hot and raw.

Garret played more than a few songs from their not-date *Name That Tune* contest in the planetarium. *I Knew I Loved You* finally uncorked her tears. He moved through some songs he'd performed at the community college concert while keeping her on the edge of collapse. She didn't know if he chose these songs to purge him of her or to torture himself. She didn't dare believe he played them to canonize their time together. It could as easily be a memorial.

When he kicked seamlessly into *Think of Me*, she sucked in a breath. Mrs. Pearls and Cashmere reached over and squeezed her hand gently. She gave the woman a watery, grateful smile. No matter the differences, music connected people, something Garret had tried to remind her. With every note he'd torn her apart and remade her…and he didn't even know.

Garret lowered his violin and paused at the microphone. "The next song is new. Mine. I wrote it in one day." He shrugged at a few whistles. "Well, mostly in one day. It was inspired when I needed inspiration most, by someone who, ironically, refuses to be inspired."

Adara's heart flatlined. This was it, the song he'd harassed her daily to hear.

He closed his eyes, but the dreamy smile he usually wore was absent, and she didn't need to be close to recognize that same lost, forlorn expression he'd worn at the school recital, as if his world had collapsed around him. The melody needled through her, poignant as only a violin could be, ripping the last of her seams out stitch by stitch. It was their relationship in song, a push and pull dance of opposites. Him, vibrant, open, and alive melding with her, haunted, small, lonely. For a few sweet beats, the two opposing threads blended, only to separate again. Yet even while reflecting her chronic grief, his hope and happiness never surrendered.

She released her grip on her ribs, letting her arms fall by her sides, freely unraveling. He'd found beauty in her misery, and even though it spiked his joy with pain, he shared it with the world. Not letting it in, letting it affect her, melt her down and reshape her would be tragic.

Trembling, her tears flowed in silent streams, dripped from her chin, rolled down her neck to dampen her dress. She didn't look away from the stage, from Garret, didn't try to escape the pain bulldozing through her and crushing the last of her broken pieces. She no longer belonged to the solitude and silence.

Whether or not he chose her, she belonged to Garret.

Chapter Thirty-Eight

Still in her auditorium seat, Adara relaxed in the cushions, drained. The stage was dark and empty, and beyond a few stragglers, the other concert goers were all but gone. Her tears had dried but her eyes still burned, undoubtedly a psycho red. Surviving felt like rebirth.

And Garret still didn't know.

Her scheme had failed gloriously, and she had no idea what to do next. But Gia would. She pulled her cell phone from the sparkling clutch in her lap. After gripping it so hard for so long, it remained in one piece, quality made. She'd never scoff at Gia's purse selection skills again. Her phone blinked with the message she'd ignored earlier.

In case of emergency, G's secret phone number.

Her heart, only recently rebooted, stumbled. Garret's super-secret, emergency only, barely-checked-it number. If Gia had it, that meant she'd gotten it from Bob or London. Her face heated. Had Bob or London told Garret her plans?

Too beaten for another meltdown tonight, she slumped in her seat. Garret probably didn't have his phone with him now, while he did whatever violinists did after a show. Joey had been simple. He'd be dancing with Gia, pumped up from his performance. Garret was more complicated. He could be sitting on a rooftop somewhere watching the stars just as easily as yucking it up with strangers in some obnoxious karaoke bar. It was part of what she loved about him. Figuring out what he might to do next was impossible—and unhelpful to her current predicament.

She hesitated, his number taunting her on the screen. If he knew she was here and wanted to talk, he would've texted her by now. But whether or not he wanted to see her again, he needed to know that if not for him, she never would've come back to life.

Unsure whether to go with serious or blasé or apologetic, she settled on a combo.

Your rendition of Enter Sandman sent me into head-banging mode. Pretty sure everyone near me thought I was a crazed fan who couldn't contain herself. Oh, wait. I am. Fully converted. Lovely concert.

Sighing, she leaned her head back and closed her eyes, gathering the strength to move. The phone buzzed in her hand and she almost jumped.

You're here? In Dublin?

Gah. The worst thing about text messaging was the impossibility of gauging emotions with the words. *Is he happy? Horrified?* Maybe he thought she'd totally lost it and quit her job to stalk him across the country. Which she had, but whatever... There could be so many meanings to that message.

Yep. Recovering in the concert hall.

She held on to her phone, expecting another quick response.

It didn't come.

She couldn't blame him. She'd been horrible. Selfish. Blinded by fear. And now that she was here, ready to take him on, he didn't want to retry. Her revelation had come too little, too late. She released a long breath and gazed up at the lights. Going back to the shadows wasn't happening and neither was surrender. If nothing else, she'd try a round of Garret harassment. He'd taught her by example. Gia could score another bank-account-killing ticket, a seat hopefully closer to the stage. She'd show him she was willing to invest in them. Him. Life. She swallowed hard, her hands shaking. Even if he rejected her.

Adara heaved to her feet and her phone buzzed.

Leaving so soon?

Her heart flipped all the way to her stomach. She scanned the stage and empty seats on the ground floor, but other than an older couple probably waiting for traffic to clear before leaving, no one else lingered. Only darkness filled the upper level exits on either side. She pivoted to doorway number five and froze.

Garret leaned against the wall, watching her. Close up, he absolutely embodied the pirate she always teased him about. He still wore the black boots, jeans and untucked shirt beneath an ebony blazer. His blond hair was loose, a smooth, shining frame around his face. He'd let his stubble grow back, and apparently, some rogue violinists wore makeup before performing. Kohl darkened his eyes in an almost sinister vibe, and the fact his usual smile wasn't showing didn't help her confidence.

"Hey." Her throat was so dry that the word came out like a croak.

As she faced him fully, his gaze slid down her dress in an appreciative sweep and his throat worked. Gia was right. He noticed. His eyes burned with obsidian fire. But he remained at the door, his expression serious. "Why are you here, Adara?"

She swallowed. Adara. Not darling. Not *neshama*. "Several reasons, actually. But mostly for you."

His eyebrows twitched, but he merely watched her. She hated the distance between them, the caution in his every line.

"You were right." She didn't miss his mouth quirk. "I was afraid, so I shut out everything, which not only hurt myself, but the people I care about most, the people who cared enough about me to put up with my crap and not give up on me. I was selfish. A coward."

She wanted to move closer to him, but didn't dare, unable to gauge his emotions. His silence was horrible, so she did his duty and filled it.

"I hurt you, and I wish I could change that. I wish I could rewind." She tried for a shaky smile. "I promised Tatum I'd apologize to you."

He folded his arms, adding to his intimidating vibe. "You came all this way to apologize?"

"Not completely." She clutched her purse, needing something solid to hang onto. "There were rumors that the hottest violinist ever was playing in Ireland, so I thought it might be worth checking out. By the way, securing a ticket took a bidding war, an act of God and half my savings account."

One side of his mouth twitched up, a half-smile, there and gone. A glimmer of hope. "You could've asked me. I have connections."

"You were hard to track down. Stalking you is harder than I imagined. But I needed to take this journey on my own, and you're the one who inspired me to take that first step." As if to prove her words, she took a halting step toward him. "So...thank you."

"I'm glad you broke free, Adara. Truly." He remained planted by the door.

Adara. Again, not darling or *neshama*. Cold cut her in tiny slices. When she'd told him to leave, he'd slammed the emotional door on her. *Too late.* She'd come to her senses a few days too late.

Half the lights shut off, leaving her mostly in shadow, but the hallway glow silhouetted Garret in gold.

"You apologized. You endured my concert. You thanked me." He tilted his head, just enough to highlight his features in the hallway light. His voice dropped to a hoarse whisper. "Is there anything else?"

A fine trembling set in. She wouldn't go back. If he shattered her, she'd hold on to the pieces until the grief passed. She'd tuck the memories of him away until she could look at them with fondness, the ache dull, not debilitating. She'd survive. She knew that now.

But she didn't want her new life to be without him.

She exhaled, long and slow. "You inspired me, changed me. Brought me back to life and gave me the courage to let everything go. Can you—" She gasped for breath, the air suddenly gone from the room. She pressed the words out through her strangled throat. "Will you love me still?"

"*Adara*." Her name was hardly more than a tortured whisper.

Before she could process what that might mean, Garret cut the final space between them and wrapped his arms around her, squeezing her so tight she couldn't get the breath she so badly needed. His breath heated the rim of her ear. "*Chara*. Love you still? Are you serious?"

She gulped a breath when he released her, her whole body shaking. "Seriously serious."

He eased back and the typical Garret smile returned for a moment before fading back into solemnity, all humor draining again from his features. He grabbed her hand and tugged her out the exit and into the auditorium corridor.

A few fans still lingered in the hallway, but whatever they saw in Garret's expression must have made asking for an autograph seem too risky. Quite right. A pirate on a secret mission was not one to interfere with, especially when he didn't have his violin. Less than two minutes later, she was floundering in the back seat of a limo with Garret, his violin case between them.

The car pulled smoothly away from the curb, and she wriggled to a somewhat comfortable position. The red straight jacket dress didn't make it easy. She smoothed her hair from her face. "I wasn't expecting you to text me back tonight."

Garret rubbed his bottom lip, still pensive, still absent of smiles. "I picked up my case to put my violin away and the lid popped open. My phone flipped out. I habitually lock the case, even when it's empty, so I never forget when it matters." He met her gaze. "And I always leave my phone at the hotel."

"Serendipitous." She dragged her fingers down the violin case's smooth surface, petting it in appreciation. If it hadn't flipped open at the right moment, he wouldn't have noticed his phone and she'd be wandering back to her room, alone, clueless as to her next move.

His gaze followed her trailing fingers and his hand paused at his mouth. He growled low in his throat, so soft she wasn't sure she misheard.

She went still. "Where are we going again?"

He lifted his finger to his lips in a sign for quiet and turned his attention out of the window. His knee jiggled a restless beat, as if whatever he held in check refused to be completely contained. She'd had enough silence for a lifetime.

Digging through her purse, she pulled out a pen and a lunch receipt. She wrote down the number that she'd committed to memory. Since her origami skills didn't match his, she folded the receipt into a miniature paper airplane, aimed at Garret, and flung it across the limo seat. Its pointy tip stuck in his hair. She wasn't above trying out third-grade flirting tactics.

He lifted his eyebrows at her and disentangled the scrap. Slowly, he unfolded the paper and his mouth twitched. He made a writing motion and held out his hand expectantly. She handed him her pen and waited as he checked his watch, scribbled something beneath her number, carefully folded the receipt into the tiniest origami boat ever, and set it on the end of the violin case. Leaning back in the seat, he crossed his arms and stared her down, his dark eyes deep and unreadable.

As if she'd resist his dare. She quirked an eyebrow and plucked the boat free. Her hands trembling only slightly, she opened the note.

8,064

She made a quick calculation, counting the minutes. Five full days plus a few hours. A rock lodged in her throat. Almost five days apart since she chased him away. Funny how so much could change in so short a time — lives remade, dreams created.

Relationships ruined.

The limo stopped and her door opened. The doorman held out a hand to her. She turned back to Garret, but he'd escaped out the other side, his violin with him.

She slid out onto the covered sidewalk. Glass doors led to a hotel lobby far fancier than the chain hotel room Gia had kindly booked for her. Several crystal chandeliers hung from the vaulted ceiling, flanked by white marble pillars. A flowerpot taller than her displayed an armload of flowers, settled between split staircases. No wonder Garret Ambrose tickets were so expensive.

Another doorman opened the glass doors and smiled at Garret. "Welcome back, Mr. Ambrose."

Garret spared the man a nod and small return smile, latched onto her hand once again and tugged her inside, relentless as Gia. Still silent, still serious, he led her up the curving stairwell, all the way to the fourth floor, down the hall to the very end. He glanced at her once while pulling the room card from his blazer pocket, as if making sure she was still there, that she hadn't run. Maybe she *should* run. It didn't matter how well she thought she knew him, trusted him. With his hair down, the eyeliner and silence, the unreadable gleam in those dark eyes, all traces of band geek had vanished into unpredictably dangerous.

All in. She forced her shoulders to relax. She was all in, no matter what.

The lock clicked, and he opened the door wide. The room was almost as big as her house. Kitchen, separate bedroom, living room, big screen—no wonder he didn't mind being on tour for years at a time. At least a dozen bouquets scattered around the room, most of them red roses. With tags. *Fan gifts.* She should've thought of that.

The door snicked shut and she pivoted. Garret lovingly laid the violin case in the corner. His gaze locked on her, he slowly shrugged out of his blazer and tossed it on a chair. Without looking away, he stalked toward her.

Adara willed her feet to stay cemented and ignored the itch to dodge him and run. Her heart beat so hard it vibrated in the corseted bodice and bounced through her fingertips.

He stopped so close that his toes bumped hers. For an eternity, he simply looked into her eyes in that way he always did, as if he could read every nuance of her soul.

Unable to take the silence another second, she delicately cleared her throat. "You left."

"You wanted space." His voice was low, soft.

"Since when does what I want you to do ever apply?"

A sparkle entered his eyes and he pursed his mouth, curbing a smile. "But I know when to stop, take a break, what lines not to cross. My stalker sensitivities are sharp." The humor faded again. "You shut me out and I didn't know how many nails you'd put in your door, how many locks I'd have to break or brick layers I'd have to demolish. I didn't give up on you. I never give up. I thought you knew that about me."

"But Tatum said you weren't coming back until she was old and ten."

His eyes widened. Chuckling, he pinched the bridge of his nose.

She let her death glare fly. "She's eight, ten in two years. *Two years*, Garret. I thought you weren't coming back."

"Two weeks." He cocked his head, and his gaze swept over her face, hot and hungry. "I was giving you two weeks of respite, to reconsider, to reconnoiter before doing battle again."

She shivered, chilled in a good way. "Reconnoiter?"

He tucked her hair behind her ear, his callused fingers gentle. "Exactly. I wasn't through with you, Adara." His attention landed on her mouth. "I'll never be through. However, that doesn't mean I'll allow you to intrude on my business. There are consequences for crossing me."

"You want me to leave?" Hard words to say, but she needed to know.

"Leave is not what I had in mind, darling."

Darling. One knot in her neck loosened.

His eyes darkened and he curved his mouth into a slow, wicked smile worthy of any pirate. "I try to be a nice guy, but sometimes nice doesn't measure up. Sometimes" — he pressed a soft, scorching kiss on her shoulder — "the only way to get your point across is through a more primal method."

A rope of ice and heat coiled through her, warming her blood even as prickles danced over her skin. Every nerve thrummed to life, a hungry ache. She closed her eyes as he moved his mouth over her collarbone. "Not sure what you mean."

"Well, then." He slowly licked the hollow of her throat. "Allow me to demonstrate."

He grasped her hip with one hand, tunneled the other in her hair and kissed her...hard. Possessive. He swept her mouth with hot laps of his tongue, demanding a response.

Joy burgeoned inside, followed by a searing jolt of desire. Helpless to deny it, she fisted his shirt as the kiss went on, growing more frantic, almost desperate. Heat darted through her veins, an electric charge that hummed and tingled everywhere. A rising tide of pleasure weakened her knees. Her moan was lost in his mouth, and when his fingers trailed along her bare shoulder and down her side, raising goosebumps, she pressed even closer, but not close enough.

Adara tangled her tongue with his, tasting a hint of coffee. Despite her heels, she didn't match his height. She stood on tiptoes, trying to get closer.

Seeming to know what she wanted, he dragged her against him, off her feet, and carried her a few steps to a chair, couch, coffee table. She didn't know, didn't care. Never breaking the kiss, he settled her on his lap, one arm latched around her waist.

Heat pulsed in every sensitive place of her body. She couldn't breathe, needed out of her restrictive dress, needed... He abruptly ended the kiss, and she sucked in a ragged breath. "Something wrong?"

His smile was grim. "Testing my limits."

No way. He was not doing this to her, not after everything. Knotting her fingers in his hair in case he tried to escape, she held his gaze. "Don't throw your

C.J. Burright

vow in my face, Ambrose. No more teasing. I'm here. Isn't that enough?"

He gave her a lofty look, as if he hadn't just knocked her socks off with a single kiss. "Your decision might be different tomorrow. You might run, and we both know I can't catch you unless you want to be caught."

"Not even, *yakiri*." She glared through his silence even as a satisfied thrill coiled through her. She'd surprised him. Goal accomplished.

He cocked his head. "Is *yakiri* synonymous with devastatingly charming?"

"Look it up yourself," she snarled. "I'm all in...no refunds, no returns."

His entire face lit up and his dark eyes glinted, sly. "Prove it. Full commitment, Adara. Marry me."

Chapter Thirty-Nine

Garret wrapped his arms around Adara's slender waist, holding her captive. The sparks in her eyes screamed escape, but he wouldn't let her run, not this time. If she wasn't warm and solid and squirming in his arms, he might believe her presence was a dream, fragmented from his miserable minutes since giving her space.

Serendipitous, indeed. More like a miracle fallen into his lap.

Adara was always captivating, but tonight she annihilated quiet beauty and had gone for his throat. He slid a hand up her ribs, the embroidered design on her corset soft ridges beneath his fingers. Red and black and Gothic—almost as sexy as her wearing his shirt. Her hair gleamed, ebony silk, and the sweet, lingering coconut smelled like heaven. He breathed her in, every part of him awake and alive to her. Merely showing up with that sinful scarlet on her lips would've had him on his knees.

Each nuance of her was a hit to his senses and restraint. Despite the hunger coursing in a hot rhythm through his veins, he refused to lose control and surrender this auspicious advantage. He needed Adara's full and complete commitment—right here, right now. Nothing less would do, no matter how his body ached in protest.

If persistence was easy, everyone would practice it.

She opened her mouth, closed it. Clearly, she hadn't expected a proposal.

Neither had he. But his tongue and lips merely repeated what his heart whispered. "So it's not the romantic gesture I envisioned making to you. I wasn't prepared. I'll do it right tomorrow."

"Marry?" she finally managed.

"I didn't stutter, darling." He grinned at her annoyed look.

"There are a zillion details we've never discussed." She leaned back and studied him, as if unsure he made husband material. After all his cooking demonstrations? Insulting. "I only want to take the matrimonial plunge once in my lifetime."

"Me too." He lifted his chin in challenge. Whatever she threw at him, he'd deflect. No more walls, no more excuses, no more life without him. "Only with you."

"London hates me."

"She doesn't. She's just stuck in protective older sister mode. Big difference." He kissed her neck, and the way her breath caught made his entire body throb. "She only wants me to be happy."

"You aren't the problem. It's me she doesn't—"

He hushed her protest with another kiss, her delectable mouth soft and pliant and driving him insane. If he didn't coax a yes from her soon, he wasn't sure he could keep from crumbling. Adara, here, asking him to love her in that dress. It was enough to sabotage any lifetime goal. But he couldn't cave now, not with all his desires so close to actualization.

Garret lightly bit her bottom lip, licked it and smiled as she shuddered. *Progress.* "London is off the excuse table. You tracked me down despite her disapproval, didn't you?"

"Hold up." She narrowed her eyes. "I thought you hadn't talked to her."

"I haven't." He went for an angelic expression and tightened his hold. Dress or not, she might still outrun him if he let go. "But after I discovered you were here, I called Bob. He told me everything." He pressed on through her growl. "You defied London for me. She might be ticked about it but she'll respect the fact you did it, anyway. Secretly, of course. I, on the other hand, am openly admiring. Next insufficient excuse?"

She blew out a breath, which did nothing to ease the tension vibrating beneath his hands. Until she relaxed, he had to stay alert, battle onward. "We haven't even talked about, you know, important issues."

He cocked his head. "Such as?"

"I don't know what people discuss before getting married!" She flung her hands. "Kids? The future? Houses? Jobs?"

"Flimsy, *neshama*." Garret pulled her closer, needing her next to his heart. "I want two, three, maybe seven kids. Maybe none. Adoption's always great. I want my future to be with you. You're my home, and while I prefer my house to yours, I'm flexible with habitation site. Whatever you want to do, you do. I'll be right behind you."

She sagged against him and rested her forehead in the crook of his neck, shooting a triumphant thrill straight to his gut. "You always make everything sound so simple."

"It *is* simple." He lifted her chin with a finger. "I want my life to be with you. Everything else is workable details."

Her eyes darkened, a sign she vacillated, a sign the battle raged on. Forget niceties. If she wanted a full-on war, he'd gird up to win her. He added a snarl to his voice. "Adara, I—"

"Yes."

He paused, blinked.

"One kid, and we'll see how it goes." She nodded, as if finally figuring out how amazing life would be together. "Your house...because I love it. My minutes are yours, but I adore my job, so you'll have to share."

Joy rushed through him, making his heart pound so fast and hard that he had trouble drawing enough breath to speak. "Done, done and done." He swung her into the air and spun, only to set her on her feet just as fast. Done, but not yet official. He wanted something solid, tangible proof to remind her of this moment should she ever need it, more than an origami boat. Grabbing her hand, he dragged her toward the door. "Let's go."

"Where to now?" She wobbled and clung to his hand for balance.

Garret paused at the door and kissed her so fiercely she wobbled again. "We can't legally get married tonight, so we're doing the next best thing while in Ireland. We're handfasting."

* * * *

Outside Garret's hotel once again, Adara looped her arm through his, hyperaware of the silk braid kissing her wrist. The handfasting had been both simple and lovely, and the reverend's wife had kindly created bracelets with the colors they'd chosen for the ceremony. Garret had chosen red for love and courage. She'd chosen silver for creativity and inspiration. He'd also insisted on black for the simple reason that it reminded him of her.

As if she'd protest.

"I wasn't going to renege, just so you know." Informally married in less than an hour. When it came to Garret Ambrose, everything seemed to click into place with only his smile.

"With your history of running, I wasn't taking any chances." He squeezed her closer. "Especially since you run faster than me."

"Not in this dress."

His gaze trailed over her red prison disguised as clothing again, more leisurely than the quick acknowledgment he'd made in the auditorium. Gia had been right. He'd noticed, although he hadn't mentioned her painfully plucked eyebrows. Next time at the salon, she'd leave her eyebrows as is.

"You," he finally said, his black eyes burning, "should wear red more often." Bursting into a speed-walk, he towed her inside, through the lobby and up the stairs.

"Violin-boy," she protested on a laugh. She pulled on his hand, forcing him to slow. "Limited leg space here. I'm at full speed already."

He paused, she suspected only because his room door blocked the way and he had to unlock it. in the next heartbeat, she was dragged into the room, the door shut, Garret pressing her back against it.

"You do realize that despite your apology, I reserve the right to exact revenge." He chained her hands above her head. "I found you then had to consider what life would be without you, knowing you existed alone, away from me." His gaze locked on hers, all smiles gone. "I didn't like it."

She swallowed hard, hating that she'd hurt him. "If it makes you feel any better, Tatum pinched me to avenge you."

"Sweet, but not punishment enough for me." He ducked and pressed his lips to the spot right beneath her ear, the place that made her moan without meaning to. "Your dress makes me think of all manners of fiendish acts." He spun her around to face the door, her back pressed against his hard heat instead. "Did you wear it for me?" he murmured, his breath warm on her earlobe.

Melting inch by inch, she angled her neck, allowing him access to her throat. If this was his idea of punishment, she might be bad more often. "Only you could inspire me to squeeze into this monstrosity."

"So you won't mind if I take it off." Before he'd finished the first word, he unlaced the last hold of her corset. With his spellbinding lips on her skin, she hadn't even noticed what his nimble fingers had been up to. Those hands possessed more skills than playing the violin.

"Wait a second," she said, breathless. "You need to know something."

He went still. Slowly, he turned her to face him. His smile was uncertain.

Her heart fluttered, but Garret had rescued her each time she'd sunk into her own darkness, and each of those times she'd been too scared to take that next step. Now, this time, she wasn't scared. She didn't doubt this — him, them.

She took his face between her hands and held his gaze, adding every ounce of sincerity she could muster. "I love you. My heart knew it before my head. I don't know when it happened exactly, probably between the personal invasion and musician harassment."

"Say it again." His words barely made a whisper, vulnerable with longing.

Adara wasn't sure when the tears started. She'd never said those words to anyone besides Joey, and since his death, she didn't believe she'd ever say them again. The realization was so powerful, so sudden, that she shook with the force of it. "I love you." Her laugh was watery, thick with her tears and the emotions she'd fought for so long. "And I'm now an undying Garret Ambrose enthusiast."

He sucked in a breath and kissed her so suddenly that she squeaked. By the kiss' end, she was weak and trembling, the bed beneath her, his weight hard and hot on her. But instead of kissing her more, touching or tasting or quenching the liquid fire he'd ignited, he lifted on his elbows and looked down at her, as if memorializing the moment.

"If you're teasing me now, Ambrose," she said softly as she stroked the stubble she loved, "I'll have revenge."

The change in his expression, from yearning to raw and ravenous, sent a thrill through her. "I *will* tease you." A challenge roughened his voice, and she gasped as his callused fingertips slid up beneath her dress.

"You can decide whether you want revenge or not in the morning."

Her only possible reply was a moan, and her eyes fluttered shut as he brought her completely, irreversibly back to life.

Epilogue

Adara snuck into the classroom and shut the door, careful not to make any noise. Leaning against the bookcase at the back of the room, she waited for Garret to finish his lesson, using the distraction to ogle him. The windows behind him gave a glow to his pulled back golden hair and chills — the good kind — swept through her. His music teacher disguise held a suspiciously music mentor edge — jeans with strategic rips, untucked, button-down shirt, black rocker's boots, enough silver rings to please any pirate.

Happy sigh.

The two-week tour had been nothing short of magical. Minutes inhaling Ireland and Garret, making up for lost time. Granted, she'd had to share him from late afternoon to evening, a small price to pay. They'd come home and he'd immediately opened up a music school, just in time for summer break, which had been, she'd learned, part of the reason why he'd managed to collect those reluctant signatures to save her job. But tonight, he'd be all hers.

Officially.

Her blood heated, and she resisted tugging at her collar. The feelings he'd awakened in her were so strong and deep that sometimes the ache in her heart stole her breath. A year and a half ago, that ache had been debilitating. Now, it made her want more.

"Everybody know what they're doing?" Garret asked, his dark gaze pinning each of the ten tweens and teenagers with a weak impression of her no-nonsense teacher glare.

"Practice, practice, practice," they sang in unison, not looking scared at all.

He grinned, ruining any chance of a menacing vibe. "Remember... No lessons next week." His gaze met hers, and the sudden intensity there shot fire to her toes, hitting all the best places in between. "If you show up, I won't be here."

The kids scrambled out of their seats and out of the door, waving to her on the way. Bryan was the last to go. He gave Garret a fist-bump in passing and hustled by, swinging his fiddle case like a weapon. His smile was conspiratorial. "See you tonight. Auntie."

The door shut behind him, leaving a comfortable stillness. "I was wondering..." Garret strolled toward her, his thumbs hooked in his pockets. "Will your students still call you Miss Dumont? Or Mrs. Ambrose?"

When he got close enough, she pulled his hand free and twined her fingers with his. Their handfasting bracelets whispered together as she dragged him closer. "I've decided to forego formal names and upgrade to Supreme Ruler."

"I like Ambrose better." He pressed her hand against his heart and lowered his head. His breath blew warm on her collarbone, followed by a soft, lingering kiss that sent a shiver through her. "Should I persuade you?"

"I thought that's what you've been doing." She closed her eyes and leaned into him. Too bad they had somewhere to go and a timeframe. Otherwise, she'd lock the door and make good use of his brand-new desk.

"You haven't seen me in persuasion mode yet, *neshama*." He buried his hands in her hair, tilted her head back and kissed her, slow and intoxicating, not stopping until her knees wobbled and she clutched his shirt to stay upright. When he released her, her vision was a little blurry, but not enough to miss his smug smile.

It took her a few blinks to catch her breath. "Ready to get hitched all proper like?"

"Tatum hasn't stopped talking about being a flower girl." He tucked her hair behind her ear and caressed her jaw with callused fingertips, drawing another small shiver. "Once we're traditionally official, London will soften. She'll start believing you won't run off and leave me with a broken heart."

"In five years or so...maybe." She smoothed his shirt as they ambled toward the door. "I can't blame her. I hardly believe it myself sometimes. Then you show up and I remember."

"What do you remember?" He linked their pinkies and squeezed.

"Love is worth whatever life might throw my way."

"Even an annoying violinist who steals your solitude?" He wriggled his eyebrows.

Happiness surged, so intense her seams stretched, expanding to make room for more. She smiled, needing to share it, unable to hold it all in. "Worth every miserable minute."

Want to see more from this author?
Here's a taster for you to enjoy!

Music, Love and Other Miseries: Every Breath
C.J. Burright

Excerpt

Weddings suck. Gia Hellman trailed her finger around the rim of her second-round wine glass and tried not to feel jealous or sorry for herself.

Endless strings of twinkling white lights peppered the country club's vaulted ceiling with imitation starlight. Soft, sublime, romantic music performed by professional musicians, all friends of the groom, blended perfectly with the sweet scent of roses lacing the summer air. The food made her wish she had an appetite instead of the twisting pit in her stomach.

In the center of the dance floor, her best friend Adara melted into her new husband. She'd never seen Dar so happy. The fact that anti-romance Dar had followed through with a formal wedding ceremony and until-death vows should've made Gia all weepy in a good way.

It should be me.

She slouched in the cushioned chair and rested her chin in her hand. It wasn't that she wanted Dar's husband, Garret. It was the 'happily ever after' fantasy she wanted, would have had by now if fate hadn't been an unfeeling witch. But her 'happily ever after' had vanished a little over two years before, when the love of her life had been ripped from the world too soon.

Joey. He was irreplaceable.

"Dance with me, Ms. Hellman." The smooth, low voice brushed her ear and sent tendrils of warmth through her, more intoxicating than the wine in her bloodstream.

Gia twisted in her seat and lifted her gaze to the ridiculously sexy man standing behind her, his hand out, waiting with annoying confidence. He knew she wouldn't say no, even though she absolutely should. Ian O'Connor was her co-worker and the off-limits man of her darkest fantasies—breaker of hearts, hater of love, lawyer for the right price. And the groom's oldest friend. Avoiding him was impossible, resisting him a full-time pursuit.

"Have you already made your way through the throngs of willing women?" She batted her eyelashes. "Must be a new record."

"I strive for perfection." Ian's cool, blue eyes gleamed, his hand still out, expectant. The lights danced in his dark hair and gave his every line a magical edge. He always looked good, but in a tuxedo, the tie loosened at a rakish angle? *Devastating.* "You can't blame me, Princess. I had to do something to make the time pass while you made your own, more elegant way through the ranks of men slavering on your heels, waiting their turn to cop a feel."

"Classy." She set her glass on the table and stood, facing him. "All my dance partners tonight have been nothing but respectful." Gia planted a hand on her cocked hip and lifted an eyebrow. "Not all guys are like you, Sugarpop."

His smile was pure wolf. "No wonder you look bored out of your mind."

She sighed and slipped her hand into his, ignoring the tingles that ran up her arm at the contact. Dwelling on them would only bring trouble, and she'd had enough man trouble for a lifetime. "One dance. That's it."

"One is perfect," he murmured, pulling her close to his side as he led her onto the dance floor.

One. She repeated the word in her head instead of dragging in a full breath of Ian's spicy cologne. One was his rule. One night, no more. One night of fun, then on to the next woman who wanted nothing more than casual. There seemed to be an endless supply of women who'd settle for a single hookup with Ian O'Connor.

But she wasn't fling material, not anymore. Still, as he slid his arms around her and pulled her tight against his solid heat, it was hard to remember why.

"Nice dress." His breath caressed her earlobe as he skimmed his fingers over her bare shoulders, drifting all the way to the base of her spine. "At least Adara and I agree on one thing—this dress, on *you*. Off would be even better."

The responsive shiver was impossible to hide, so she narrowed her eyes at him. "Careful, O'Connor. She hasn't officially lifted the ban on you."

Nearly a year and a half before, Gia had drunk one too many margaritas at the annual law firm Christmas party, and in her state of missing-Joey inebriation, she'd been too weak to resist Ian's charms. Adara had come to her rescue, ripped Ian a new one, reminded Gia why she should stop at two margaritas and the Ian Threat Act had been established.

"It's a risk I'm willing to take." His focus flicked to where Adara slow-danced with Garret, oblivious to the outside world.

Gia kept her gaze on the dancing couple, the pit in her stomach expanding. The last thing she'd expected was Adara dealing with Joey's death before her, let alone finding her true love and getting hitched. When Joey had fallen sick, he'd made Gia promise to drag Adara out of solitude—a brother's desperate way of looking out for his introverted older sister when he would no longer be around to do it. Now her vow to Joey and her obligation to Adara were finished, and instead of being happy, a longing for what used to be rose from the deep, unstoppable.

That was why she couldn't keep up the fling routine. She wanted what she'd had with Joey again—more than a mere physical connection, to be someone else's favorite person. She wanted to find someone who made her sun shine brighter, even in the rain, to give her heart to the man who deserved it, a man who had enough sense to notice her excellent taste in shoes.

Basically, the full-price fairy tale, with no discounts.

She slid her hand from Ian's sculpted shoulder to the hard curve of his biceps, a last, torturous hurrah. She was tired of falling for halfway. She wanted it all, and no matter how he made her neurons sing, surrendering to Ian's charms was another dead-end. She had to escape before his melody became an orchestra her body couldn't deny.

"Thanks for the dance." She tried to twirl free of his hold, but he tightened his arms around her. Planting her palms on his firm chest, her push was weak, ineffective. "Gotta go."

"That was only an eighth of a dance, at best." His fingers were spread over her bare back, warm skin on skin, holding her gently captive. "Don't short-change me, Princess."

"Oh look, it's Karen from accounting." She pointed over his shoulder at some random wedding guest who definitely wasn't Karen. "She's asking for you."

"Karen can wait." Not falling for it, he brought his mouth closer, close enough that his breath mingled with hers. "You pressed against me is all that matters for the next two minutes."

She couldn't resist a smile. "Two minutes? That's it?"

"Two minutes is all I need to convince you that the next twenty-four hours should be spent with me…in bed. On the couch, the stairs, the counter…" He brought his lips dangerously close to her jaw. "I promise my hands are slow, my tongue enchanting and, as for the rest of me" — he brushed her earlobe with his nose — "the best things are only definable through experience."

She let her eyelids droop as tingles swirled in the emptiness inside. It would be so easy to surrender just for one night, let Ian work his magic, make her forget. Her gaze drifted to the happily married couple. Adara smiled at something Garret whispered in her ear, her smile so much like Joey's that Gia's throat closed. She ripped from Ian's hold.

"Have to pee." Without looking at him, she escaped the wedding party before she exploded, nabbing her wine glass along the way. She swept through the open double doors and into the hallway, her sparkly silver stilettos clicking a quick cadence on the tile, the raven skirts of her taffeta dress swishing against her legs, while the corseted bodice made it hard for her to breathe. *Leave it to Dar to choose black as one of her wedding colors — Gothic matrimony at its finest.*

She smiled politely at a wedding guest coming the other way and propelled her feet into the banquet room, where vows had been said and lives forever joined. Red rose petals still flanked the black runner leading to the podium, sweetly infusing the air. She flounced onto a front-row chair and drained her wine.

Joey's picture stared back at her from where it still sat on the stand from the ceremony, Adara's way of including her absent brother in her wedding.

"Don't look at me like that." She waved her empty glass at him. "It's only my second." But if someone happened to overhear her talking to the picture of her dead boyfriend, she'd totally blame it on the wine.

His fierce gray eyes stared back at her, holding a secret smile.

"I know, right? Adara…married. It's a miracle." Tears blurred the lines of his handsome face. "I think miracles maybe only happen once in a lifetime. The one we had together turned out to be a complete bust." Aching emotions clogged her throat. "I miss you, Joey…so much."

As if a small part of him were there with her, a sense of comfort curled around her and she smiled through the tears. "Don't worry. Adara reminded me who I am, so you can cross haunting her off your 'unfinished business' list. You were right that I'd forget, but when you're not here to remind me every day how loved I am, it's hard." She released a shaky sigh and pointed at his picture. "So, I'm waiting for another you. I get that he won't be you—no one ever could be—but you promised me he was out there. And I know love slams into you when you're not looking for it, because that's what you did to me. So I'm checking out of the dating game. While I'm waiting for my fairy tale, I'll figure out how to make an impact on the world, like you would have."

She blew out a long breath, feeling like she'd made a sacred vow of her own. And if she was making vows, she might as well get back up. She lifted her gaze to the rafters. "If I'm on the right track, give me a sign — a clap of thunder or flickering lights. *Something.* Throw me a bone or even a fingernail. I'm not picky."

Joey's picture clattered to the floor, so fast that she didn't see it, landing face-up.

"Get. Out." Gia pressed her palm to her hammering heart. "Joey?" She searched for a shimmering phantom or fluttering orb, maybe a ghostly whisper, but only the distant strains of *Death of a Bachelor* softened the silence. If Joey was there, he didn't reveal himself.

On wobbling legs, she climbed the two steps to the podium and picked up his picture. "I can take a hint. Let the quest begin."

* * * *

Ian took another swig of beer and attempted not to look surly. He propped an elbow against the improvised bar counter and pasted on a bored expression instead.

"Another one bites the dust." Roman slid up beside him and clinked Ian's bottle with his. The tuxedo couldn't completely disguise his cop edge. Even without the weapons and badge, he exuded watchfulness, his gaze always alert and cutting, his relaxed pose a ruse. At the first sign of danger, he'd go off like a gun. "At least Garret picked a woman who can defend herself. Ethan's still talking about her unconventional usage of an umbrella against Garret's stalker. He's tossing around the idea of a women's self-defense class focused on making a weapon out of whatever happens to be lying around."

Ian curled his lip rather than respond verbally and focused on the delusional duo still clinging to each other, even after the music had ended, as if no one else in the world existed. He didn't care that Adara had been grieving for her brother, that Garret had forgiven her for pushing him away or that she'd apparently made it up to him by committing the rest of her life to their mutual happiness. She'd bruised his best friend's heart, and that, he'd never forget.

Even if she basically thought he'd done the same to *her* best friend.

But his situation with Gia was completely different. Speaking of, Gia hadn't returned to the reception. An uncomfortable twist sparked against his steel heart, trying to get in. So she'd ditched him on the dance floor. That was nothing his ego couldn't bounce back from.

"Hey, guys." Barak, the guitarist Garret had befriended overseas and who Ian had instantly filed into the 'don't-like' category, joined them at the bar. He ordered a beer and mimicked Ian, elbows on the counter, gazing out at the crowd. "Have you seen Gia? She promised me a dance and I wheedled my way out of playing guitar in the next song." He grinned, all musician suave, charismatic in his black tux. His English was clipped and perfect and the exotic accent had already won him a few hearts at the wedding rehearsal. Gia was undoubtedly too keen to join the ranks of his initial victims — just another reason Ian found her so captivating. "I am surely not allowing her to avoid her vow."

Ian turned a dismissive look on him. "Take a tip from someone who knows her. You're not her type."

Barak's black eyes glinted a challenge. "From what I saw, neither are you. But she danced with you anyway, and I am not one to surrender." He took a casual sip of beer. "I heard she's into musicians."

"Not since Joey died," Ian drawled. That corkscrew against his heart became a drill, a reminder of every non-musical bone in his body. *Joey.* Magical violinist, Gia's lost love and the main obstruction to his unfinished business with the one woman he couldn't get out of his head. He'd tried to exorcise her by dedicating himself to other women, sports and work, but no matter the attempted distraction, the failure had been complete. One night with Gia was all he needed. One night to get her out of his system and move on.

One night.

"I sense a wager opportunity." Roman's teeth flashed, a small smile that was all sorts of evil. "Guitar or not, bet a Ben that she lets Barak down easy and slides away so smoothly that he doesn't even realize he's been dismissed until she's gone."

Ian's approval of Roman rose another peg. Maybe it was the wedding indignities he'd endured, the buzz of dark beer or the bruised dance-floor ego, but he added, "Bet you two she goes home with me instead."

Roman arched his death-black eyebrows and widened his smile. "Easiest two hundred I've ever made, Boy Wonder."

"Your lack of faith wounds me, Baconbits."

Barak glanced between them, his drink halfway to his mouth, clearly wondering what he'd missed. Maybe men didn't happily disparage each other across the sea. Garret should have brought him up better before extending an invitation to his wedding.

Ian plopped his bottle down and pushed away from the counter. "Later, Roman."

Roman jerked his chin in farewell and tipped his beer back as Ian turned to leave.

"Was it something I said?" Drifting on the heels of Ian's impending departure, Barak's tone hinted at humor, a reflection of Garret's effortless charm. Ian liked him even less for it.

"Probably," Roman said, a shrug in his voice. "Are you in on the bet or not?"

Ian smirked and entered the empty hallway. Roman always had his back. Straightening his tie, he strolled away from all the things that reflected exactly what he didn't want—long-term commitment, sharing life and scars with someone else, love and devotion and soulmates. For Garret, believer in all things fanciful and serendipitous, he had no doubt it would work. For him? Never.

As he passed the doors leading to the banquet room, a gleam of gold caught his eye and he backtracked. Her back to him, Gia sat among the abandoned decorations like a lost queen, black-and-silver ribbons lining the aisle, surrounded by red roses. Stuffing his hands into his pockets, he leaned a shoulder against the doorjamb and waited for her to notice him.

Glitter Girl. He'd overheard one of their coworkers call Gia that and it fit. No matter the day, whether it was at the office, social gatherings or her best friend's wedding, Gia always looked the part. Today, though, she was dressed in shimmering black, her blonde hair up to expose the lickable length of her delicate neck, and he was sharply reminded of their delicious backroom encounter at the holiday party going on two years now. Pleasure interrupted.

He'd intended to scorch Gia out of his system that night. Instead, she'd left a permanent burn in his lungs. His smirk faded. That burn had been there before Joey's demise, when she'd been out of his reach. Now, it aggravated him with every breath.

He absently adjusted his straight tie again. There was only one way to alleviate an itch, and now that Adara was occupied with Garret, he had direct access to the cure. Keeping his steps light, he strolled between the decorated chairs and made it all the way to the second row without any sign from Gia that she knew he was there. Ian slipped into the chair behind her and leaned over her shoulder, close enough that her sweet perfume drifted into his lungs, reminding him of blue skies and spring days.

She held Joey's picture in her lap.

That annoying twist in his chest reappeared. Joey, always blocking him, even from the grave. He narrowed his eyes on the image of his constant competition. Joey had been an unconventional violinist like Garret, adored by everyone. Musicians always got the girls.

Not this time.

He scanned Gia's bare shoulders and had a strong urge to follow up with his finger. Until Adara had barged in on them, Gia hadn't protested his touch. A year or so surely wouldn't change her that much, no matter that they'd hardly talked since. According to Garret, she wasn't dating anyone seriously, and despite the dance and ditch, there was no reason he could fathom that she wouldn't want to pick up where they'd left off.

Lightly, he caressed her shoulder blade.

Gia yelped, jumped and spun in her seat. Her eyes wide and wild, she clutched Joey's picture tight, hiding her lovely breasts. *A shame.* "Ian" — she sucked in a breath — "you jerk."

Smirking again, he relaxed in the chair and spread his arms along the backrests. "Sorry."

"Liar." She plopped back down and pushed a loose wave of hair from her face. "Is the 'true love' and 'forever' mush too much for you?"

"Something like that." He angled his chin at Joey's picture still clutched to her chest. "Pining over lost love?"

She bit her delectable, pink-glossed lower lip. "Something like that."

Damn. He *was* a jerk. Ian scrambled for the perfect words to smooth her feathers. "Garret makes it all look easy, doesn't he?"

A tiny smile intruded on her sadness, and the knot in his gut eased. "Garret and Adara remind me that love happens when you least expect it."

"I see they got to you too." Ian unleashed his shark smile. "Weddings are a virus, Gia. They infect suckers with the promise of happily ever after, but no one ever celebrates when the infection spreads and cripples the dream with real life."

"Ian O'Connor" — she said his name like a curse — "do *not* speak that poison to the universe on Garret and Adara's wedding day. It's like wishing them bad luck or something."

He rolled his eyes. "Have you met Garret Ambrose? The universe conspires to fulfill his every happiness. He's immune to bad luck."

Her gaze sharp and knowing, she studied him long enough to make him want to squirm, but he never buckled under pressure — not anymore. "Jealous, Mr. O'Connor?"

"Hardly." He hated it when she called him 'Mr. O'Connor'. It reminded him too much of his father, and he could do without thinking of that bastard ever again. "Garret can have Miss Crabapple, if that's what he wants. Only he has the power to pry the princess of the north from her tower. I would've been content to leave her there."

Gia twisted in the chair and laid her elbow on the backrest, watching him even closer. "You can't stand it, can you? That fate and serendipity and true love actually exist, that love can overcome anyone's secrets or darkness... Garret and Adara are in-your-face proof of it, and you can't deal."

"I don't have to deal." He put on his bored face. "If people want to delude themselves into believing marriage is the key to happiness, that's their choice. No one's going to force me to drink the Kool-Aid."

Lifting her empty wine glass, Gia grinned. "I prefer wine, anyway."

"I thought it was margaritas." Blood pumped hard to all of his best places. Her lips had tasted of tequila and lime that night, and he'd had far too many fantasies about them. That was a drink he'd savor, always.

She shrugged her slender shoulders. "People change."

"No, they don't." He leaned forward, holding her gaze. "They pretend to change, hope to change, but true nature only bends before bouncing back."

"You're such a cynic," she said softly, not moving as he inched ever closer to the mouth that had haunted him for years, the mouth he had to get out of his head, one way or another. "People evolve all the time. If we didn't, we'd never survive."

"I've survived just fine." He trailed a fingertip along her bare arm, reveling in the softness of her skin, the tremor that rolled through her. He hadn't forgotten how she'd responded the same way to his touch before. He was even less likely to forget now.

"Not all of us are as stuck in their ways as you." She dipped her eyelashes, hiding her summer-sky eyes.

A few inches from her mouth, he paused. "Adara will be gone on her honeymoon in a few hours." His voice was husky with growing need, the memories of his brief and not nearly long enough encounter with Gia an urgent tug. "She won't be around to interrupt." On a whim, he turned her hand over and pressed a lingering kiss to the inside of her wrist. The rapid thrum of her pulse danced against his lips. "I haven't forgotten that night."

Her eyes closed, Gia exhaled, but before he swooped in for contact with her lush, pink mouth, she pulled her arm gently free of his grasp and leaned back. "Tempting as that is, I have to decline."

"Actually, you don't." He made his tone a smooth, coaxing caress. "We'll see them off as the admirable and dutiful maid of honor and best man we are. Then we can pick up where we left off at my place. No declining necessary. No one else has to know, if that's what you want."

"What I want..." She bit her lower lip again, and everything from his scalp to his toes throbbed in anticipation. After a lingering pause, she shook her head. "You were right about the Kool-Aid. I drank it, and it gave me an epiphany." She dropped her gaze to Joey's picture on the seat beside her. "I temporarily forgot who I am, but I'm not going back to that girl who seeks solace with men who believe my purpose lies mainly in the bedroom."

"That's not how I think of you." And, surprisingly, he meant it, for the most part—no matter that his relationships never spanned more than one night. True, he wanted Gia, but unlike the other women he pursued or let pursue him, he didn't mind talking to her, which was why he generally avoided her at the office and chose to admire her from afar. Talking to a woman without ulterior motives would ruin his reputation and might make him want something more.

That was a danger he could never allow.

Enjoyable conversation or not, he still needed to burn Gia out of his system.

"Whatever." She gave him a look that said she didn't believe him, even a little. "I've moved on to the next chapter in Gia's book of trials and errors. No more casual, no more flings, no more online dating, no more margaritas. I'm going to figure out how to impact the world in my own way while waiting for my personal Prince Charming to show up and sweep me off my feet, because me looking for him hasn't turned out so great." She patted his cheek—affectionately, not in the sex-kitten way he preferred. "And I know for a fact that Ian O'Connor ain't him."

"I'll file a formal protest. I have a family suit of armor and various weaponry at my house. I'd be happy to show you all my swords, too." He wriggled his eyebrows so she'd know exactly what sword he wanted to show her most. He dropped his voice to a purr, one women didn't resist. "Invitation still stands—my house, a bottle of wine or two, the rest of the weekend to demonstrate the merits of no armor or clothing of any kind." So it was one more day than he'd agreed. He suspected he'd need it with Gia.

She blinked, and it didn't take his persuasion skills to decipher that she was imagining them together, with or without armor, absolutely with a sword. Her gaze refocused and she shook her head. "Good lord, you're a terror, in and out of the courtroom." She stood and stepped beyond his reach, a golden angel wrapped in sinful black. "Go use your silver tongue on someone else. This princess has downed a sleeping potion and refuses to wake up for anything but the right kiss."

"It's been over a year. Memories fade." A strange sense of urgency rose, as if he were a dying man in need of an organ and the donor had bailed at the last second. He'd been banking on this moment to get her out of his system, out of his thoughts for good. "Maybe you've forgotten how right I am."

Gia laughed.

It was his turn to blink. She *laughed,* as if he'd made a cute joke, not asked her to spend the weekend with him exploring every pleasure they'd missed out on earlier. He hid a scowl behind calm composure. Nothing about him was *cute.*

"I already know how wrong you are for me, Ian, but don't worry. There are at least five lovely ladies at the singles table sighing over you." She winked. "You'll be fine without me."

He'd never claimed he wasn't wrong for her long term, just not wrong for this particular moment, and random wedding guests weren't the ones edging into his thoughts at every inconvenient turn. He crossed his arms and gave her his best cut-throat stare while he slid through possible ways of keeping her close enough to change her mind. He smiled benignly. "Want to help me put lewd and suggestive decorations on Garret's car?"

"You're so far behind the game." She flicked her fingers in a dismissive gesture as she floated by, heading for the door. "I did that over an hour ago."

He smirked at her back, watching the seductive sway of her hips until she slipped out of sight. Laughing softly, he faced the stage again, needing time to cool off before returning to the reception. Scandalizing old ladies wouldn't help him reach his goal of rising to partner at the firm of Hamilton & Associates. His smirk widened. *Rising. Firm.* He was on fire.

"Just passed Gia on her way out. Alone." Roman's smug voice came from the doorway. "Pay up, Boy Wonder."

Digging in his pocket for his wallet, Ian rose and strolled toward his friend. He ignored Roman's self-satisfied smile and slapped two one-hundred-dollar bills into his waiting palm. "The best cases can't be stopped by frivolous motions…only delayed."

Roman scrutinized the money as if checking to make sure it wasn't counterfeit, then stuffed it into his shirt pocket. "Someone has to steer the wheels of justice. It might as well be us." He slung an arm around Ian's shoulders as they walked out together. "I'll buy you a drink when this is over. I'm suddenly feeling generous."

"Someplace they won't spit in our cups, Baconbits." Since the offer Ian wanted had been tabled for now, he might as well get some of his lost winnings back. "And wings."

"Sure." Roman gave him a sly look. "Since the legs are out."

Ian let Roman have his laugh. They both knew that if he didn't want to go home alone tonight, he wouldn't. But no one else could erase the lingering taste Gia had left behind in his mouth.

Maybe it's time to switch trial tactics.

Home of Erotic Romance

Sign up for our newsletter and find out about all our romance book releases, eBook sales and promotions, sneak peeks and FREE romance books!

About the Author

C.J Burright is a native Oregonian and refuses to leave. A member of Romance Writers of America and the Fantasy, Futuristic & Paranormal special interest chapter, while she has worked for years in a law office, she chooses to avoid writing legal thrillers (for now) and instead invades the world of paranormal romance, fantasy, and contemporary romance. C.J. also has her 4th Dan Black Belt in Tae Kwon Do and believes a story isn't complete without at least one fight scene. Her meager spare time is spent working out, refueling with mochas, gardening, gorging on Assassin's Creed, and rooting on the Seattle Mariners…always with music. She shares life with her husband, daughter, and a devoted cat herd.

C.J. loves to hear from readers. You can find her contact information, website details and author profile page at https://www.totallybound.com

www.ingramcontent.com/pod-product-compliance
Lightning Source LLC
Chambersburg PA
CBHW020636020726
47494CB00001B/210